SACRED • WOMAN

SACRED • DANCE

Awakening Spirituality Through Movement & Ritual

IRIS J. STEWART

Inner Traditions
Rochester, Vermont

Inner Traditions International
One Park Street
Rochester, Vermont 05767
www.InnerTraditions.com

Library of Congress Cataloging-in-Publication Data

Stewart, Iris J.
Sacred woman, sacred dance : awakening spirituality through movement and ritual / Iris J. Stewart.
p. cm.
Includes bibliographical references and index.
ISBN 0-89281-605-8 (pbk. : alk. paper)
1. Dance—Religious aspects. 2. Women—Religious life. I. Title.
BL605.S74 1998 98-22613
291.3'7—dc21 CIP

Printed in Hong Kong

10 9 8 7 6 5 4 3 2 1

Text design by Virginia L. Scott
Layout by Kristin Camp
This book was typeset in Sabon with Phaistos as the display typeface

Credits: Frontispiece, "Celebration," by G. E. Mullen, ceramic tile. Page vi, Betsey Beckman, Sacred Guild Dance member, performing *Rite of Sprinkling*. Page 121, Bharata Natyam dancers in southern India. Photograph by Payson Stevens.

To Minnie Leigh Evans Stewart
the girl who dared to dance!

and to Drew Stewart and Phoebe and Henry Washer
dancers all!

Contents

Acknowledgments

I would like to express my gratitude and appreciation to all those who helped in transforming a new vision of women's spiritual heritage from the ancient past into a format applicable to our lives today. To my publisher, Ehud Sperling, for being open to a view of women's history not found in the traditional linear written records and for his support of the project throughout its various phases; to my editors at Inner Traditions, Robin Dutcher and Jeanie Levitan, for helping to focus the many diverse but intricately related aspects that coalesce to form a coherent study of women's way of expressing the Divine. Many thanks to Hal Zina Bennett, my agent, for his encouragement and support. Special appreciation to Elizabeth Fisher, whose background as a writer, editor, and producer, as well as her strong dedication to the goal of making this unique and vital information available to women, helped to keep me focused and on track throughout the process.

I am grateful to those who helped bring the still existent record of the accomplishments of women in the ancient past into a visual reality for me on-site where it actually happened throughout the world; especially to Carol Christ, Melissa Miller, Resit Ergener, and others. I also want to thank the many individuals who contributed photos, artwork and graphics, computer help, and help and advice on the formidable job of tracking down photos and other resources, including Drew Stewart Washer, Gayla Meredyth Yates, David Washer, Elizabeth Artemis Mourat, Leslie Cabarga, and Jody Lyman.

Author Iris Stewart. Photograph by Arnold Snyder.

INTRODUCTION

SEARCHING FOR WOMAN'S SACRED DANCE

There was a period when art and religion stood so close to each other that they could almost be equated. Song was prayer, drama was divine performance, dance was cult (magical—holy—powerful). Dance accompanies and stimulates all the processes of life. It enables, in turn, other arts to come into being: music, song, drama. Its motifs have remained the same since antiquity, as the round dance, the spinning dance, the forest ring. All have their origin in the fertility magic of the most ancient times.

Gerardus van der Lewiv, Sacred and Profane Beauty—The Holy in Art[1]

This book is about my journey into the sacred feminine and the secret truths I discovered about women's spirituality on the way. It is also about ways to help you better understand the power, validity, and beauty of women's ways, with direct access to our great-, great-, great- (ad infinitum) grandmothers' spiritual wisdom.

My inspiration to write this book began, oddly enough, several years ago when I accompanied my friend Azar to a belly dance class. Although Azar was ambivalent about going because of the dance's reputation, she

Sacred dance is incorporated into rituals that honor life passages. Here members of the Leaven Dance Company add their blessings to a young couple's wedding. Photograph by John "Pete" Mihelick.

loved doing the dance. She told me she felt she should learn the dance because she was from the Middle East. Her statement seemed rather curious to me at the time, but later I understood it when I began unearthing the many rituals and spiritual practices of our female ancestors.

I had never been athletic or very coordinated, and as I finally began to master the complicated belly dance movements, I became hooked on the intricate Oriental rhythms so foreign to my Western-trained ears but so close to my intuitive soul. I began to notice the psychological as well as physical health benefits of dance because dancing helped rid me of the recurring depression I had experienced for several years.

At that time I asked myself, "What's a nice feminist like you doing with a dance like this?" How did this dance, which moved women's bodies so powerfully and sensually, come from a part of the world where women have so long been under public repression and segregation? Although at that time I had no idea how ancient the dance was, I knew that the version I was studying was an amalgam of several traditional dances. I wondered where the mesmerizing serpentine arm movements—and that snake bracelet the dancer wears—came from. What did they mean? As I went deeper into the dance and began to recognize its mystical power, other questions came from within. Why did the slow undulations, moving in synchrony with the ancient *taxim* of flute and oud, communicate the Grandmother's spirit so strongly to me? It was the serpent that led me to the Goddess, and the Goddess led me back to the dance.

During this same time I was researching, writing, and giving lectures on the history of women in religion and the effects of the transition to patriarchy in the church. I had turned away from organized religion years before because of the negative attitude displayed toward me as a woman. Only after a period of great trial—I lost my health for a time, and my mother died—did I realize I had let my resentment of the church keep me from seeking my own spiritual path. I yearned for something more in my life to sustain me.

It was dance that showed me on a very personal, soul level that there were other planes, other existences I needed to explore. During one of my dance performances, I suddenly found myself outside my body and floating up to the ceiling. I didn't know what was happening; I just knew I wanted to stay with the sensation I was experiencing. Of course, that was impossible, but I began to be able to call on that sense of peace more and more often on my journey to healing. I came to see that I had shut down the intuitive part

Anna Halprin Dancers perform the Vortex Dance from the Circle of the Earth. Photograph by Paul Fusco.

of my mind so much that the spiritual could speak to me only through my body—through dance. As I began to understand what had happened to me I was able to see the powerful spiritual influence of dance and to bring about an integration of my spiritual self and my physical body, which eventually was my path toward healing.

From my own spiritual reawakening it became clear to me that the two subjects, dance and spirituality, shared an important connection. I wanted to know more. My research showed me that dance was the first form taken by worship. It is the oldest, most elemental form of religious expression, repetitive rhythmical movements being essential to the process of union with the deity and the cosmic flow. All art forms began as ritualistic and reverential expression, and because dance was primary in rituals of worship, dance was the mother of all arts.* Teachings

*In Turkish, the word *oyun* stood for the shaman and the rites performed by the shaman. Today the same word is used in Turkey for dance, drama, and poetry.

were composed in verses repeated as incantations while people walked or moved in specific ways. The dancing body called forth the rhythms of music; the rhythms of poetry echoed the rhythms of music and dance; the body in motion inspired great paintings and sculptures.*

The Expression of Dance

Dancing is an elemental, eternal form of human expression. To dance, at its simplest, is to let the body express itself rhythmically. Movement, our first language, touches centers of our being beyond the reach of vocabularies of reason or coercion. It communicates from the innermost soul that which cannot truly be expressed through words. When asked the meaning of the dance she had just performed, the famous Russian ballerina Anna Pavlova replied, "If I could have said it, I shouldn't have had to dance it!" Dance molds feeling into physical form, inviting escape from the purely rational and from earthly tasks and mortal burdens, providing both a physical and an emotional form of release. It awakens us to a deeper awareness of both the sacred and the profane, bringing us into synchrony with one another and with the natural rhythms of our lives.

Dance is divinity, a natural state of grace in which we all reside. In its sacred form, dance is a language that reunites the body, soul, and mind. Working through the body, we integrate energetic information directly at the cellular level. Through dance the mind entrains with the body, and both grow increasingly more receptive to the creation songs of the greater universe.

Dance becomes sacred as the beauty of movement communicates the divine ideal. In sacred dance, one is found and used by the soul of nature, the energies of which are perceived rhythmically as the continuous dance of life and form. Dance invites a state of exhilaration that the Mevlevi Sufi call *hadrah*, or "the presence," each step moving us upward toward a new freedom of the spirit, toward ecstasy. The great Spanish poet Federico García Lorca spoke of this special place or state as *El Duende*, the ability to be filled with spirit that is more than one's own spirit. "The *duende* works over the body of the dancer just as a gust of wind hits and blows over the sand."

Dance and ritual create community, drawing people together both emotionally and physically in a special sense of intimacy and shared abandon. As the community participates, no one is a stranger any longer. We become companions on the same journey.

And dance is history. The truest history of any people is told by its folk dance and its folk music. "These are the foot prints, the earth castings," Agnes DeMille said. "No dancing lies; no body lies."[3] A view of history through the window of dance tells us things about humanity not found in records of conquered countries, generals, and wars. Dance becomes our road map to the history of women's spirituality.

LEFT: DANCING OUT THE SPIRIT OF YEMAYÁ. PHOTOGRAPH BY DAVID GARTEN.

*The early Greek playwrights Thespis, Pratinas, and Phrynichus were actually called dancers.[2] Lucian, Euripides, Socrates, Plato, and Virgil all recognized the deep-rooted sources of dancing and discussed its aesthetic and ethic principles.

Finding Women's Dance in History: A Different Way

DETAIL, LATE PALEOLITHIC, OF MESOLITHIC ROCK PAINTING FOUND IN SPAIN.

I began my search for women's sacred dance for my own personal healing. As my fascination grew, I began to feel the need to share with other women the truth about our wondrous heritage. Very early in my research, I discovered that information about women's spiritual or sacred dance practices was not available in the traditional sense of chronological historical accounts. The study of dance as sacred movement has been divorced from the study of history, cultural anthropology, and religion. Historian Walter Sorell said, "It has always puzzled me that none of the

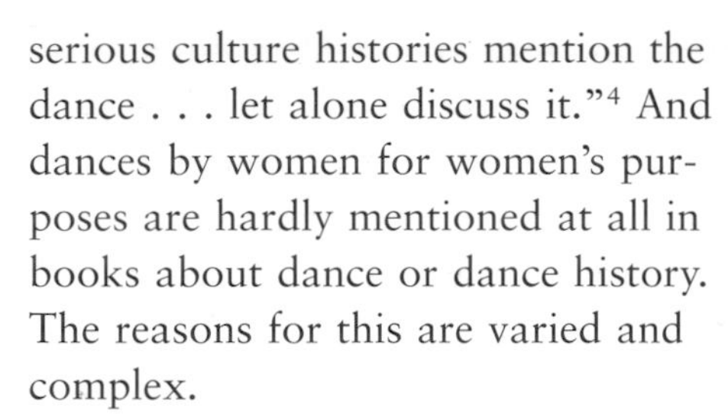

serious culture histories mention the dance . . . let alone discuss it."[4] And dances by women for women's purposes are hardly mentioned at all in books about dance or dance history. The reasons for this are varied and complex.

History has always been selective storytelling, an opinionated interpretation of events. Wrapped up in projecting their own religion, biblical writers recorded history as a moral tale and therefore revised information on existent cultural practices of the people surrounding them that did not conform to the Judeo-Christian worldview. This has enormous implications in regard to the study of sacred dance and women's history, where women's voice has so

SANDSTONE IMAGE FROM THE SHREE MENAKSHI TEMPLE, AN EARLY REPRESENTATION OF SACRED DANCE IN INDIA. PHOTOGRAPH BY PAYSON STEVENS.

often been absent. Herodotus and other ancient historians' "facts" were tempered by their goal: to present a particular theme. Plutarch, who wrote about Greek tragedy plays in the first century C.E., is a good example. He was writing several centuries after the classical period of Greek dance, had never seen the dances of which he wrote, and was writing as a philosopher, not as a student or historian of the dance.

In many archaeological texts, female-prominent religions are frequently referred to in fertility-cult terms, suggesting that these religions contained no depth or sublimity. As Riane Eisler has pointed out, this interpretation is akin to stating that Christianity is a death cult, based on the fact that its central image is one of a crucified man on a cross. Such one-dimensional interpretations suggest an inability on the part of the researcher to extrapolate information at any level but the most superficial. In the case of writings regarding the civilizations that preceded recorded history, they reveal the researchers' assumptions that women were simply vessels for fecundity, conveniences for pleasure, or—worse still—cauldrons of destructive seduction.

The following quotation is illustrative: "For women, mating and fertility dances are important for increasing the population of the tribe and by extension, the crops and flocks."[5] When we move beyond the casual assumption that women in ancient times were concerned only about having all the babies they possibly could, we will discover more about how things really were.

Another complication in my search for women's sacred dance origins and traditions concerned the use of language describing dance. We know that specific words have a powerful influence on any interpretation of the past. In translations and transliterations of ancient stories and texts, it is not easy to determine when words for dance were used literally or metaphorically ("the mountains will dance before the Lord"; "dance of the universe"; "dance

A DANCING GODDESS AT THE SHREE MENAKSHI TEMPLE IN MADURAI, INDIA. PHOTOGRAPH BY PAYSON STEVENS.

The word *history* itself came from dance. *Histor,* from ancient Rome, meaning a dancer, was also the root for many derivatives: from *history* to *minister* (Min-Istria), and later *minstrel.*

Dancers with Goddess (arms aloft) adorn this predynastic Egyptian vase. Metropolitan Museum of Art collection.

of life"). Also, words for dance often became generalized to denote the musical instrument used, the name of the rhythm used, the name of the ceremony or festival itself, or even the name of a group of people. The use of the word *man* as generic for humankind also evokes great confusion in finding women's dance in history. Words like *man's dance, dance of man, his dance* all serve to frustrate our quest for women's history, herstory. Information about the rituals of our ancestors is also clouded by superficial, slanted words such as *frenzied*, *lascivious*, *fertility rites*. The use of words such as *girl, maid,* and *virgin* to describe dancers when the drawings and statues even into late Greek culture and the Pharonic period in Egypt clearly show mature women dancing, obscures vital information.

I also found that few researchers of dance have themselves been dancers. Since those who actually dance have very different views than those who observe, historians who are not dancers cannot have an intimate knowledge of the meaning of the dancer's dance. They can only chronicle the appearance and effect they perceive. This adds another layer of complication to descriptions of women's dance, where our only informants have been men. Because women are less likely to speak freely to men about the world of which they are a part, the feminine voice is lost, and their ways are subject to judgment and misapplication when filtered through the male view. Therefore, even the information we have uncovered about women here should be read, as in Elisabeth Schussler Fiorenza's words, "as the tip of an iceberg indicating how much historical information we have lost."[6]

Nevertheless, if we know what to look for, we can glean information from the angels' circle dance in a medieval painting or from the ancient rituals still intact in a few isolated places. Sometimes we have to glean information from a negative situation and examine it more carefully. For example, Sorell says, "We know from Aristophanes' *Thesmophoriazusae* that dancing was a major part of the rites of Demeter and Persephone because, while poking fun at them, he describes circular formations moving at first lightly and quickly, then in measured rhythms invoking the Goddesses, then rapidly again, rising into a joyous finale."[7]

Sometimes dance is presented in positive forms. The second-century Roman poet Lucian put it simply but succinctly: "They dance out their religion."[8] He described dance as "a thing of utter harmony, putting a fine edge on the soul, disciplining the body."

While I searched for scraps of infor-

What's in a Name?

Hussy is an archaic word to describe a lewd woman. However, this is the way W. G. Raffe's *Dictionary of the Dance* describes it: In Britain were the "huzza" dancers—hussies for women, huzzars for men. They carried *Bezbeh*, a figure derived from Bez-Beza, God-Goddess of Nature, whose annual dances are probably the oldest known dances in the world. Brought to Rome when Egypt was conquered, the dance migrated to Britain with the Roman agricultural festivals of Mamurius. We don't know what happened to the huzzars, but hussies are still with us.

Lewd is a word that is often used to describe women and women's dance. In Old English, until about the 16th century *lewd* referred to "lay" or nonclerical men, those who were not priests or members of a religious order. Perhaps *lewd* is a ghost from the time when women were spiritual practitioners who were not accepted as part of the religious order, and thus they were lewd. And if they danced as part of their spiritual expression, they were very lewd indeed.

Whore is from the Old English *hore*, akin to Old Norse *hora*, or the Latin *carus* meaning dear. The Egyptian goddess Hathor was also referred to as **Hor**, and women of Aphrodite were **Horae**. The word for a Hebrew dance, the **Hora,** means "circle," which might indicate that the word "whore" originally referred to a dancer, similar to the word "hussy." Whore also means "idolatrous practices or pursuits," which could easily refer to worshippers of the Queen of Heaven. Yahweh complained that the people were always "whoring" after other gods. Maybe that really meant Hathor-ing after another goddess. Or maybe it referred to Ishtar, "the great whore of Babylon," according to John in Revelation.

Obscene (*obscenus, obscaneus*), as in "obscene dances," may not be "obscene" at all. In Greek, "ob" means "in the way of, toward," and "scene" (Greek *skene*—a temporary shelter) makes the combined word, ob-scene, "a place of occurrence or action." We can see how it is used in this context as "scenery" in theatrical productions. It tells us that women went to hilltops and sacred groves, or even to crossroads; that there they made their altars and danced their dances for the duration of the festal ceremonial.

mation in books that devoted less than a chapter or a page to women's spirituality or women's dance, I kept drawing on a lesson I learned early in life: that things are not always as they seem. I began to look through "acrostic eyes"—a slightly skewed vision that reveals underlying mind-sets and

Many children's games come from old rituals adapted and simplified: "Ashes, ashes (Asta, Asta), all fall down" was a ritual circle dance for the Goddess Astarte brought to England by ancient Phoenician visitors. Maypole dancing, shown here, comes from a similar Goddess spring ritual. Hopscotch hints at the labyrinth dance and at many versions of the Old Bone Woman "all skin and bones, who goes around picking up bones—Whoo!"

motives. There may have been a hidden motive or a changed story. Perhaps there was another way, another story. I began to pick up clues wherever I could find them. I looked for secrets hidden in legends and fairy tales, in biblical symbols, and in traditional songs and dances. I discovered, for example, the meaning of women's ways by tracing subjects like women's love of jewelry and the use of gemstones for healing and for symbolizing enlightenment within the material world. I also explored the eternal connection between women and the primal power of fire by tracing the history of candelabra dancers. I found a wealth of information in word derivations and in words whose meanings had been changed, like *harlot*, *virgin*, and many others. I realized that if there is a strong reaction to something, it must have power, so I looked for things hidden by taboo. It was like looking through the facets of a crystal. There were always some unexpected insights, and some surprises.

Fortunately, modern archaeological chronology and the ability of forensic dating developed in the past fifty years have provided a wide-angle lens, enabling us to see more of the whole history and quality of life of the people in earlier centuries. Archaeological digs in recent times have unearthed evidence contrary to the formerly accepted historical versions of many events and the previous interpretations of their meanings. While still-existing, "living" evidence may leave much unsaid and may still be open to interpretation from a modern viewpoint, it lets a more truthful picture emerge.

Re-membering—Dance as Woman's Art

Clarissa Pinkola Estes, in her book *Women Who Run with the Wolves,* said that all we might need to uncover the past still whispers to us from the bones of stories.[9] The more story bones you have the more likely you will be able to find the whole story. This is one method I have used to find out much about women's dance.

Dancers grace the edge of this Balkan carpet. Courtesy of Melissa Miller.

In searching out the real history of women's dance as an expression of spirituality, we seek to learn our heritage: How did it shape us? How does it continue to affect our lives today? Building on the knowledge already gathered, and rethinking the ways things might have been for women, from a woman's viewpoint, we get closer to the voices of our Grandmothers and hear them more clearly.

To actually reconstruct the kinetic reality of ancient dance practices, though, we have to call on our imagination, experience, and intuition. One modern writer, Ann Cain McGinnis, described it this way:

> The first dancing, I imagine, was movement which surrendered conscious intention to felt rhythms, the larger rhythms which we are all part of. The first music, I imagine, was the voices of women, incantations for the birth and nurturing of new life, for death and mourning, and for rebirth. Early sounds and movements gave form to a cycle of birth, death, and rebirth—human form expressing felt life rhythms connecting the world around and within us. The early myths rose from this collective expression, the Great Mother, and a way of living organized around the earth and active human participation in the cyclical processes of the earth.[10]

With the upsurge of interest in the body's relationship to mind and spirit, sacred dance has made a phenomenal revival worldwide in recent years. Anna Halprin, one of this century's primary innovators in dance form, and author of several books, advances a practice that she calls the Life/Art Process.[11] In the introduction to her Dance of Power class, she set forth the tenet that I have adopted for this work:

Dancing Apsara of Asia. Eighteenth century Sri Lanka.

> The larger theme, as I see it, is once again renewing our faith in what our bodies have to teach us. I feel that in this culture and over all too long a period in our history, we have been totally alienated from the true wisdom of our bodies, as well as from the wisdom of the larger body which is nature itself. My interest in dance is to reconnect with the innate intelligence within our bodies and with what our bodies have to say to us. Our bodies contain all the wisdom of the ages, wisdom that goes back before we were even

born. That wisdom is in our cellular system, in our nervous system, in our circulatory system, in each breath that we breathe. We are not an event; we are a long evolutionary process.*

In this book we shall learn about "becoming the dance," becoming WomanDance—giving ourselves up to the music and experiencing our own emotional depths. Dance will be the very link to connect us to that life force and to our heritage. As women, let us try to imagine what it must have been like to have our own sense of spirituality. Imagining can help us regain spirituality through the power of dance, connecting us with the life force. The past is not to be discarded but understood and eventually transcended, providing us with an even better opportunity to apprehend and evoke our soul work. The search is really the quest for continuity—knowing where we have been to create a sense of where we are going. So, we shall call on Old Bone Woman, called *La Trapera* (The Gatherer), to help us dig up the bits and pieces of dance history that may be lying around under layers and layers of changed history, distortions, and just plain neglect.

We take this journey together as wanderers through strange lands, playing guide to our many selves and investigating our bountiful opportunities while discovering the wonders of distant worlds and distant times, all coming alive together. As we gain ever more understanding of the connection between dance and women's ways, we can begin our journey toward regaining both our own spiritual dance and our own spiritual power.

*Introductory remarks to a workshop I attended in August 1992.

PART ONE

In the Beginning Was the Dance

The fourth gospel of the New Testament commences with the statement "In the beginning was the word . . . ," but before the written word—before the codification of language and the use of clay tablets to record stories, the messages of prophets, and laws—was dance ritual. Located in and originating from the body, strong emotions of reverence were expressed in groups and individually through body movement: circling, whirling, dipping, jumping, stamping, shaking, arching, and contracting.

In our time we are so accustomed to dance as a form of entertainment that we may find it difficult to visualize its ritual origins. For most people, except for professional dancers, their students, and folk dance enthusiasts, dance is mainly a spectator sport. Yet, there was a time when dance was an integral part of religious ritual and ceremonial expression; it was not just for spectacle, exercise, or socializing. It was indeed the highest expression of spirituality in humanity's search for communion with the deity.[1] Dance is the essence of mystery. Through dance we experience a dimension that the linear mind is not structured to perceive. It may have been dance that enabled us to first conceive of existences beyond our immediate physical experience, thereby creating the concept of spirituality, of "God."

We shall now explore the ritual origins of sacred dance by looking at the influence and role of the Goddess and her priestesses, the clothing and symbols related to sacred dance traditions, the Judeo-Christian influence on sacred dance, and what may have been the very first women's dance ritual: the birth dance/belly dance, which I have renamed WomanDance.

1

The Goddess Danced

The Goddess leads us into the spiral dance of life. She sends forth the winds, the whirling energies that bind existence in eternal motion. Through dance, She teaches her children movement and change.
Merlin Stone, Ancient Mirrors of Womanhood[1]

The Goddess holds the key to the most ancient forms of sacred dance—she is inextricably linked to dance. Dance was the principal form of worship of the Goddess. In some cases, in addition to her role as creator, giver, and protector of all life, the Goddess herself was a dancer, celebrating through dance the cycles of the seasons and the cycles of life. It is here then—with the Goddess—that we begin our journey into the world of sacred dance.

My first contact with the Goddess and her connection to dance was quite unexpected. At the Metropolitan Museum in New York City, I stood in front of a small bronze sculpture of an elegant woman seated in a chariot pulled by four lions with no reins. I was in awe of her elegance and majesty, and yet her sweet face reminded me of my mother. I very much wanted to know who she was. She appeared to be a figure of great importance, perhaps a queen. She carried a cymbal in one hand and a drum in the other. This seemed rather curious to me. Why would instruments of entertainment be significant enough to be included in the symbolism that

CYBELE ENTHRONED ON A CART DRAWN BY TWO LIONS, ROMAN SCULPTURE. BRONZE. 2ND CENTURY C.E. THE METROPOLITAN MUSEUM OF ART COLLECTION.

spoke of who she was? The little placard on the pedestal gave no hint.

For some reason, the image stayed with me. Years later I came across a picture of her in a book: she was the Magnificent Cybele (Kybele), mother of the gods and friend of humankind, who taught dancing to her attendants and priestesses as a gift to be passed along to her mortal children. It was Cybele who opened the door for me to discovery of the Goddess and her important role in sacred dance.

THE OLDEST OF THE OLD. AMRATION (PRE-EGYPTIAN) GODDESS WITH ARMS RAISED PERHAPS IN DANCE, PERHAPS IN PRAYER, 4,000 B.C.E.

As I focused my search on rituals of the Goddess, it quickly became apparent to me that wherever the Mother Goddess* of the Old Religion reigned—in the Middle East, the Indus Valley, China, Japan, Europe, Africa, Greece, Crete, Indonesia, Asia—no matter where she was found, music and dance were integral components of spiritual expression in her rites. Here, then, are some of the images and mythological and historical accounts I found from cultures around the world that together form a beautiful picture of the sanctity of dance in relation to the Goddess.

*When I use the term *Goddess*, I am speaking of the symbol that designates the deity enjoined with the universe where all things—plants, animals, planets, humans—are imbued with the sacred life force. The phrase *cosmic mother energy* is a more all-encompassing term to describe the creative powers permeating and animating the earth. The need arose for symbols, for a tangible token or visible sign of the presence of a deity, but the female figure was just one of those symbols.

Dancing Goddesses of the World

My search to uncover the dancing goddess and the rites of worship to her led me to Crete: the place that Greek classical tradition associates with the origin of dance. In addition, Crete is credited with the origin of several of the most important musical instruments—the triangular harp, the seven-stringed lyre, and the double pipe—which were played there a thousand years before the times of the Minoan palace era. I also felt myself being drawn to Crete as it became more and more apparent to me that Crete is a place where feminine culture lasted the longest.

The lyrical art of these peaceful egalitarian people had fascinated me for years. Their open conception of life, of the sea and sky, of the animals and flowers is represented with a lively naturalism expressed in a fable-like atmosphere and a colorful pictorial language that has no equivalent in the ancient world. I visited Crete with Carol Christ, Director of the Ariadne Institute for the Study of Myth and Ritual,* and was stunned by the

*Carol P. Christ holds a Ph.D. in Religious Studies from Yale. She is the author of several books, including *Rebirth of the Goddess*, *Diving Deep and Surfacing*, and *Laughter of Aphrodite*. For information about the Ariadne Institute for the Study of Myth and Ritual, see Resources.

Altar at Eileithyia caves. Photograph by Iris Stewart.

dramatic contrasts of the place where the Minoans lived. The rugged mountainsides, covered with volcanic rocks, towered over sparse valleys. The mystery of these people deepened when I learned how they had invariably chosen mountain peaks and caves for sanctuary—places extremely difficult to get to, even today. As we made the pilgrimage to those peaks, however, the majestic views took my breath away, and I began to understand. When we visited the Ida and Eileithyia caves, I immediately felt the encompassing comfort and protection of these places, caverns that are large enough to hold a giant cathedral. They provided a holy place for women seeking the protection of Eileithyia, goddess of childbirth and motherhood. Inside the caves, I saw stalagmite-formed sculptures of a pregnant woman and a mother with children. Natural altars dripped with wax from candles of more recent pilgrims' expressions of respect and hope. There we danced, looking back at the long, long line of the ancient Minoan sisterhood and linking them with the sisters now returning to sacred dance. We lit candles, poured libations of honey and herbs, and quietly reclaimed those sacred places through our dance.

At the Herakleion Museum in Crete, I saw votive images from sanctuaries and shrines, and statuettes recovered from graves and tombs that show various postures of a sacred dance, including the gesture of benediction familiar in portrayals of the Mother Goddess. I also saw the earliest representation of the goddess Persephone found to date (Middle Minoan period, about 2,000 B.C.E.), excavated in 1955. It is a small ritual bowl, the inner surface of which shows two women (possibly Athena and Artemis, but they could also be two priestesses) dancing in lively attitudes around Persephone. The figures are drawn in the exquisite lyrical style of the ancient Minoan (or pre-Minoan) culture. They wear flowing long dresses, and their tiny faces are almost birdlike, with hair curling away from the head in suggestion of energy or plants growing. The downward spiraling design on either side of Persephone's gown is representative of her as the Snake Goddess.[2]

DANCERS WITH PERSEPHONE AS THE SNAKE GODDESS. CRETE C. 2000 B.C.E.

BIRD GODDESS, CRETE. 1600 B.C.E. PHOTOGRAPH BY IRIS STEWART.

The annual dances in honor of Persephone and her mother, Demeter, were the most sacred and revered of all the ritual dance celebrations in ancient Greece. These rituals were part of the Mystery School at Eleusis, which is believed to have begun on the island of Crete. Euripides (c. 484–406 B.C.E.) wrote about the Mysteries at Eleusis, "the Moon Goddess dances, and with her the fifty daughters of Nereus dance in the sea and in the eddies of the ever flowing streams, so honoring the Daughter [Persephone] with the golden crown and the holy Mother [Demeter]. . . ."[3]

Greek mythology also provides examples of the Goddess herself as dancer. Aurora, Goddess of the Dawn,

The Mysteries

There were several so-called mystery or esoteric schools at various times throughout the Middle East. Some examples are the Thesmophorians in Alexandria, the Dionysian cult of Attica, the Theban cult of Kabeiros, and the mystery cults of Orpheus and Mithra.[4] One of the most fascinating examples of the mystery schools is represented at Eleusis (Saisaria), located next to the town now called Elevsis in Greece on the outskirts of Athens, which appeared before the second millennium B.C.E. The sacred rites at Eleusis were held annually in honor of Demeter and Persephone. Centuries after the final demise of the sanctuary at Eleusis, writers, philosophers, and rulers have pondered the site's power.

Down through the centuries, many artifacts, buildings, and drawings have been unearthed that reveal the variations and alterations Eleusis has undergone. From vases and frescoes we can see representations of many rituals and celebrations. The great frustration for curiosity seekers and researchers alike comes from the fact that while many ceremonies were revealed in these artifacts, they were considered by outside observers to be the "lesser mysteries," or mysteries leading up to the Greater Mystery. It was always concluded that each revelation could not be "the" secret, or else it would not have been depicted.

That the mysteries endured, although altered, down to the 5th century C.E. while other goddess religions had gone into decline or final dissolution, illustrates the tremendous respect and devotion of the participants at Eleusis. It was said the initiates possessed a knowledge that conferred blessedness here on earth, not just in the hereafter; both knowledge and beatitude became possible the moment they beheld the vision. The preparations to attain a state of *epopteia,* "having seen," were said to be active: fasting, drinking the *kykeon* (a mixture of barley groats, water, and mint), moving in a procession, and dancing.

ELEUSINIAN MYSTERIES. DETAIL FROM VOTIVE PAINTING AT ELEUSIS SITE MUSEUM NEAR ATHENS, GREECE.

The ancient Greek writer Lucian commented, "You cannot find a single ancient mystery in which there is not dancing . . . I will not mention the secret acts of worship, on account of the uninitiated. But this much all know, that most people say of those who reveal the mysteries that they 'dance them out.'"[5]

The "secret" of mystical orders may be a misinterpretation or misapplication of that word. The word *mystery* comes from the Latin *ministerium*, from which the word *ministry* also derives, implying more of a meaning of service than of some kind of puzzle.[6] What were condemned as "secrets," and thus as seditious and evil, were not exclusionary. Rather, teachings were presented in the mode in which the student was able to learn. The dance, accompanied by invocations or chanted prayers, was restricted to genuine worshippers; hence the erroneous reputation for "magic."

A Dance to Artemis

The following fantasy description of a sacred dance to Artemis is from a charming book by Charlene Spretnak, *Lost Goddesses of Early Greece*:[11]

The animals were drawn to the tree. They rolled over its roots and encircled the trunk. In a larger ring, the dancers raised their arms, turning slowly, and felt currents of energy rising from the earth through their legs, turning, through their trunks, turning faster, through their arms, turning, out their fingers, turning, turning, to their heads, whirling, racing, flying. Sparks of energy flew from their fingertips, lacing the air with traces of clear blue light. They joined hands, joined arms, merged bodies into a circle of unbroken current that carried them effortlessly. Artemis appeared large before them standing straight against the tree, Her spine its trunk, Her arms its boughs. Her body pulsed with life, its rhythms echoed by the silvered tree, the animals at Her feet, the dancers, the grass, the plants, the grove. Every particle of the forest quivered with Her energy. Artemis the nurturer, protector, Goddess of the swelling moon. Artemis! She began to merge with the sacred tree, while the circle of dancers spun around Her. They threw back their heads and saw the shimmering boughs rush by. When Artemis was one with the moon tree, the circle broke. Dancers went swirling through the grove, falling exhausted on the mossy forest floor. Lying there on the earth, still breathing in rhythm with the earth, they stared up at the constant dancers in the heavens.

GREETING DANCE FOR PERSEPHONE, SPRING RITE. DETAIL FROM A KYLIX. GREECE.

is said to have had her "dancing places," and we are told that Eurynome, the most ancient goddess of the Pelasgians, indigenous people of Greece, rose naked from primordial chaos and instantly began to dance. Eurynome danced a dance that separated light from dark, the sea from the sky.[7] She danced to the south and set the wind in motion behind her, to begin her work of creation. Eurynome's whirling dance caused a great whirlwind.* Catching hold of the north wind, she rolled it into the form of a serpent, and named it Ophion, the wind serpent.[8] Can't you just see the majesty, beauty, and fluidity of that first dance?

Artemis, the goddess of untamed nature, assisted females of all species in childbirth, explaining perhaps the Greek saying, "Where has Artemis not danced?" Central to the worship of Artemis, the most popular goddess among the rustic people of Greece, were ecstatic dances and the sacred bough. Devotees of Artemis danced to lyres and harps, both her inventions.

Sacred dances were performed in honor of Artemis at the festival of Tithenidia in the temple of Artemis Koruthalia in Sparta. The poet Callimachus, who wrote a hymn to Artemis about 300 B.C.E., described the dance and ended with the prompting: "Let not anyone shun the yearly dance"—an apt comment, given that

*Wind, or breath, is the soul. *Ruach Elohim* is Hebrew for "God's breath." The Greek word for nature, *phusis*, is akin to *phusaō*, "to blow." *Phuo*, "to grow or generate," was originally understood as the almost liquid energy that animates all things. *Hagion pneuma* is the Holy Spirit of the New Testament. In Sanskrit the breath is *prana*, the soul.[9]

the festival was attended by worshippers from all over the Aegean Sea. The dancers of Artemis were called *caryae* or *karyatids* (caryatids).[10] They wore beautiful robes and crowns of reeds. The caryatids of Hellas and Laconia, celebrated in the annual Festival of Artemis Caryatis by the ritual dances of Lacedemonian maidens, are known to us from their sculptures in the porch of the Erectheum at Athens.

The Homeric "Hymn to Artemis" (c. 700 B.C.E.) spoke not of dances to Artemis but of Artemis as the dancer herself. "And the sound of the lyre and dancing and joyful cries . . . there she arranges the lovely dance of the Muses and Graces. . . . adorned in elegant raiment, she takes command and leads in the dance."[12]

The Graces—Latin *Graciae* (Greek *Charities*)—were a version of the Triple Goddess who presided over the dance.[13] In Homer's "Hymn to Pythian Apollo" the divine dance of the Graces is revealed:

The lovely haired Graces and
imperturbable Hours,
Harmonia and Hebe
and the daughter of Zeus,
Aphrodite,

Dance all together, their hands
clasping the wrists of the
others,
And among them dances one
neither ill-favored nor puny
But tall and stately to look on and
wondrous in form.

In Egypt, Hathor, Goddess of the Moon for over 3,000 years, was mistress of the dance and also lady of music and wreathing of garlands, as well as mistress of songs. One of the most important celebrations honoring Hathor, enacted yearly during the flood season, is depicted on a bas-relief dating from the reign of Hadrian (76–138 C.E.) at the Museum of Thermes in Rome. It consisted of a ritual dance performed by girls and women, a prayer for fruitfulness entitled "The Opening of Women's Breasts." Hieroglyphs tell us, "The beautiful and gracious singers are drunk as they accelerate the dance movements of their legs."

A hymn to Hathor says:

We rejoice before thy
countenance,
thou art the queen of jubilation,

Calling Forth the Muses

The function of poetry, music, and dance is invocation, or calling forth the muse. The word *music* comes from the Greek *mooseeka* or *mousike*, which literally means "the art of the muse."[14] In classical times, the nine muses were goddesses of creative inspiration in poetry, song, and other arts, as well as history, science, astrology, and metaphysics. Most were musicians and were associated with particular instruments: Terpsichore, muse of dancing and song (viol, lyre, and harp); Erato, muse of lyric and love poetry (tambourine and lyre); Clio, muse of history (trumpet); Euterpe, muse of music and lyric poetry (flute, double pipe); Thalia, muse of comedy and pastoral poetry, who also presided over the dance of all (viol); Melpomene, muse of tragedy (horn); Urania, muse of astronomy (songs); Calliope, "She of the Beautiful Voice," muse of epic poetry (trumpet); Polyhymnia, muse of religious and heroic hymns (portative organ, lute).

Isis, goddess of the Nile.

Sistrum depicting the goddess Hathor.

sovereign of the dance,
Queen of music making,
sovereign of song; queen of leaping . . .
Come ye with jubilation and strike the timbrel day and night. . .
The whole earth makes music for thee, all heaven dances joyfully for thee."[15]

An elaborate ritual dance during the time of the late Ptolemies was performed in the Hathor Temple at Denderah. Some of the dancers' verses excavated there, and now housed at the Louvre in Paris, read as follows:

We sound our drums for her Spirit
We dance by her Grace
We see her lovely form in the Heavens
She is our Lady of Sistrums
Mistress of the sound necklaces.

Hathor is Lady of Delight, Mistress of Dance
Lady of Sistrum and Queen of Song
Our Lady of Dancing, Mistress of Flowery Wreaths
Lady of all Beauty, Mistress of Salutation.

When both her Eyes are open: Sun and Moon
Our hearts rejoice, receiving Light
Hathor is Lady of the Wreathing Dance
Lady of Ecstasy—we dance for none other
We praise None other but her Spirit."[16]

The Tassili rock paintings (6,000 B.C.E.) at Aouanrhet, in what is now Algeria, depict the Dancing or Horned (New Moon) Goddess, deity of the ancient Amazon tribes of that area.

The goddess Isis (Au Set), who is credited as the first to introduce dancing and singing to the Egyptian people, is also credited with the invention of the *sistrum*, a type of rattle.* The sistrum's distinctive voice, full of high frequencies, is the ancient tool said to serve as a focusing device for transcendence in many places throughout the

*The sistrum, above all the musical instruments of ancient Egypt, had sacred associations. On the uppermost part of its handle was the image of Hathor. Other images included the cobra or birds' heads. Small metal cymbals along cross-rods produced metallic jingling sounds. In dynastic times, the carrying of a sistrum was viewed as an act of devotion to Hathor. Later, the sistrum became the scepter in the hands of the secular king.

world. The festival honoring Isis took place in the spring with the annual inundation by the river Nile, upon which the lives of the Egyptians have always depended. An inscription consecrating a temple to Isis reads:

> How beautiful is this dwelling place!
> . . . it will last as long as the heavens;
> it was created for you to dance in every day, eternally; for you to awaken and to sleep, endlessly, on earth, forever.[17]

The goddess Bast (Bastet) represented pleasure, dancing, music, and joy in Egypt. According to the Greek historian Herodotus (fifth century B.C.E.), hundreds of thousands of worshippers journeyed to Bubastis (House of Bast), the center of her worship. Reverence for Bast through music and dance was believed to result in good health, both physical and mental.

In ancient Babylonia there were festivals and hymns to the goddess Ishtar: "The citizens of Kishi, they dance with sistra in their left hands; the center of the town is full of the sound of timbrels; outside, pipes and drums re-echo."[18] And an ancient ritual from Assyria was performed in honor of the goddess Astarte (Eastre, the Hebrew Ashtaroth, Esther) from which the Easter drama-dance derived in later times.[19]

In India, Bharati and Sarasvati were credited with giving their people speech, music, and ritual. In Hindu literature, Sarasvati was the embodiment of all existence, all intelligence, all bliss, and invented the first script, Sanskrit. Goddess of learning and wisdom, she gave poetry and music and arranged music and ritual. She is often depicted holding a *vina*, or lute, and a book, the Vedas.[20]

A RARE DEPICTION OF THE GODDESS PARVATI DANCING. PARVATI, WHO PERSONIFIED MOUNTAINS, IS THE DAUGHTER OF HIMALAYA. ASIAN ART MUSEUM, SAN FRANCISCO. AVERY BRUNDAGE COLLECTION.

Bharati taught the union of dancing with singing and is often called the Mother of the Bards.[21] Bharati (sun) and Sarasvati (sky, water) were summoned in ancient invocations or prayers with Ila (earth), goddess of the rite itself, and were spoken of as a group of three (Triple Goddess, the Trinity).

The venerable goddess Tara, who preceded Buddha by many centuries, is honored in Tibet as the embodiment of enlightened activities of all the buddhas and bodhisattvas. Tara was a woman who, as an enlightened being, vowed to experience the awakened state of mind in the feminine form and to continuously manifest this, thereby inspiring, benefiting, and liberating all beings. She is patron of the arts, music, dance, the written word, and tools of creation. In the Hindu tradition she is the sacred sound of *Om*, out of which all creation emanates. It is said that those who express the enlightened qualities and activities of Tara through dance clarify the obstacles and hindrances in their lives. (See chapter 2 for a dance of the Twenty-One Praises of Tara.)

In Hawaii, dances in honor of Tutu (Grandmother) Pele, the Goddess of Fire and Volcanoes, use only the rhythmic clapping of hands, sticks, and drums. Although Pele herself did not dance, she was a patron of the dance, and her sister, Hi'iaka, was called the spirit of the dance. A series of eight Kauai hulas (dances) and meles (chants) tell the story of the goddess Pele's arrival on the island of Hawaii from Tahiti and how Pele carried her sister, Hi'iaka, in the form of an egg under her armpit on the long ocean voyage, perhaps explaining how dance first came to the island.

Return to the Goddess

Carl G. Jung said, "An archetype is like an old watercourse along which the water of life has flowed for centuries, digging a deep channel for itself. The longer it has flowed in this channel the more likely it is that sooner or later the water will return to its old bed."[22] All truly great art gives form to the archetype, lifting the spirit into the sphere of infinite, psychic kinship. In the art form is the trace of the Spirit; the Spirit cannot be seen save by means of the form. We can certainly see how this would apply to the Goddess symbol.

Women resonate to the image of the Goddess as the feminine aspect of the creation. She is the portrait of ourselves in our many aspects, a mirror of our beauty, purpose, courage, and joy. The cosmic Mother Goddess symbolizes empowerment in harmony with the life force. She is made manifest by our choice to be powerful.

The most basic and most important meaning of the Goddess for us today is the acknowledgment of female energy as a legitimate and independent power, a beneficent power we can trust within ourselves and in other women. I believe it is crucial for us as women to claim spaces and times for ourselves, where we can give free rein to our imaginations and our spiritual longings, in order to discover what it would be like if the feminine principle were paramount, and to lay claim to our power to create rites and rituals—with or without support from others or other traditions. To appreciate the ways of our Grandmother is to respect life and our place in nature. These times may be calling us to make that transformational leap to a new concept of divinity, a balance between the feminine and masculine energies, yin and yang, intellect and intuition. The reawakening of the Great Mother symbol is not a retreat to old ways but rather calls us to seize responsibility for the survival of our planet—to use our inherent gifts, overcome our own fears, and become the authors of our own destinies.

Now Let Us Dance

Danced ritual commemorates that our life begins (activation), is lived (movement), and ends (finale) with the memory of the sacred. The invocation or calling forth of the Divine is also a remembering, a calling to mind. The offering is for our remembrance, commemorating our gratitude for the food—physical and spiritual—by which our life and its gifts are sustained.

How might our lives have been different if we had been encouraged as children to dance our joy, our awe, our reverence? To dance like the Indian goddess Shakti, for the delight of creation? We still can dance. We can now consciously explore beatitude in movement on our own, because we are children of the Spirit.

Dances of Goddess energy can be done by anyone of any faith. They are not pagan ceremonies. These dance ceremonies are not "religious," as we know the word. They are a method of getting in touch with the flow of grace; they are a movement meditation and an opportunity to share in community.

A dance to the Goddess can be done alone or by a group. You may choose to dance the different aspects or names of the Great Mother: Gaia the Bringer Forth; Diana the Huntress, Bringer of Light, Amazon; Aphrodite, Protector of Women and Childbirth. Try on an archetype to see the different movements inspired by the Minoan Bird Goddess, the Cretan Snake Goddess, and the Venus of Laussel, for example. Or try on the three aspects of the Goddess as Maiden, Matron, and Crone. You can wear regal clothes and jewels, or dance completely unadorned.

The wonderful thing about dancing the Goddess is that every dancer is beautiful. Whatever one's size, shape, or age, there is a Goddess figure to model. Why do I suggest the Venus of Laussel—a hefty figure by anyone's measure? We need to see that here was a figure honored for herself. Concentrating on her will help modern-day prejudices about the female body, including your own, drop away.

I have found that another way to dance to the goddess is to emulate the energy patterns associated with her. You might try placing large posters around the room with specific zigzag, spiral, circular, or other patterns from unearthed vases and figurines that depict goddesses throughout Europe from Neolithic times onward. Choose one design and stand in front of it. Concentrate on the visual design, exploring any connection or resonance within your body. For example, the double spiral may inspire undulations or free flowing movements, in standing position or lying on the floor. A swirling design may suddenly make you think of your fingerprint—the part of you that is unique in the world—that may lead you to appreciate your total uniqueness. Books like *The Language of the Goddess* by Marija Gimbutas and *The Woman's Dictionary of Symbols and Sacred Objects* by Barbara G. Walker are full of symbols and energy patterns to inspire you.

Your dance can be lighthearted or more serious, or a combination of both. One such example is famed modern dancer Ruth St. Denis's dance *Radha*. As the goddess Radha, St. Denis rose from deep contemplation to express the sensual joys of human existence. But

Minoan bird goddess.

Neolithic snake goddess from Crete.

Venus of Laussel.

then, after a time, realizing how futile are the delights of the flesh, she returned to her mystic stage of contemplation. Since this is your dance, you may perform it in whatever way you choose.

Here is one suggested solitary dance designed to help you draw strength from the spirit of the goddess within. With veil or shawl covering your head and body, sit in the traditional yoga style, eyes closed and hands below your chin in prayer position. You may want to use this time as a meditation, which makes it a wonderful dance to do as you first awaken in the morning. You will know your meditation is complete when you begin to feel the urge to move. Still focused inward, observe this urge with your mind, just as you did in meditation, but this time follow its command to move the body. As you raise your arms and the veil drops away, gradually become aware of the physical world around you as your meditation takes physical form.

You may begin with an image of yourself as a happy girl, skipping and dancing. Do you remember the sensuous feelings of your childhood—not in your mind as such, but in your body, in the remembered movements? If you get a sense of how those feelings were subtly discouraged or guilt was induced from others' reactions, dance with that child and tell her it is all right, in order to let go of any guilt you still carry.

Try dancing the movements that symbolize everyday, mundane routines. Notice how you feel, not just in your mind, but in different parts of your body. Do your shoulders feel weighted as you think of the millions of things you should be doing even now, while you're "wasting time" dancing?

After you complete all or any part of these suggestions, try bringing the veil back over your head as you sit in quiet repose again. Check your feelings. You may feel, like Radha, that it is all futile and you just want to stay there. However, you may come to feel that life is full of possibilities and that you are ready to forgive all, let go of all, and rise from your dance.

Community Dance Ritual to the Goddess Within

The goddess Kwan Yin is a lovely image for dancing in community. Called Holy Mother of Compassion, Merciful Mother, she is revered in Japan as Kwannon. She came from China, where she was called Nu Kwa in ancient times (*Nu* and *Yin* both mean "woman"—*Kwa, K'uai* means earth or nature). Later Buddhist accounts describe her as having originally been a man who had reached the state of Buddha being but then decided to return to earth as a bodhisattva, a female spiritual teacher. Kwan Yin's androgynous nature can help balance the female/male energy within us individually and within our community.

Without music (a drum is optional), the group forms a circle. Movements and chants are repeated in groups of four, to the beat of four, as participants hold hands and chant "Kwan Yin, Doe Sai." This is an invocation of Kwan Yin's spirit/energy somewhat similar to the invocation, "Hail Mary," and is four syllables.

Starting on the left foot, the group moves counterclockwise (to the left), taking four steps four times in succession

Kwan Yin as goddess of wisdom and compassion; carved wood. Photograph by Iris Stewart.

Left: Rahda and Krishna. Wall hanging. Author's Collection.

Joan Marler, biographer of archaeologist Marija Gimbutas, leads a spiral dance in honor of the Goddess. Language of the Goddess Festival, San Francisco, 1998. Photograph by Karen Preuss.

for a total of sixteen steps. Next, drop hands, face to the right, and take four steps clockwise (to the right), beginning on the left foot, while you bring hands full of "water" from your right side or outside the circle, and pour it into the center. Complete this pattern four times, adding the four chants. Next, fold your arms across your chest, as if you were holding a baby, and make a swinging, or lullaby, movement with your arms as you continue the chant and walk to the right. Last, turn in place four times as you raise your arms high, palms upward. Bring your arms quickly together in front, elbows and forearms touching, hands forming a chalice. Bring the chalice to your mouth, drink, and move the chalice down to your heart chakra in front of your chest. When dropping your hands down to join hands in the circle again, your palms should face downward. Repeat the first movement for the conclusion of the dance, or to continue through another round.

You may want to take a few moments to write in your journal the sensations or feelings you experienced. The idea is to jot them down very quickly before the "thinking" mind begins to stir once again.

1. After you have completed these rituals, how do they change the way you feel about the Goddess, the Goddess within?
2. How do they affect your feelings toward women as community?

2
The Priestess Danced

Will they ever come to me, ever again,
The long, long dances?
On through the dark till the dim stars wane
Shall I feel the dew on my throat and the stream
Of wind in my hair?

Euripides, The Bacchae

The image of the Goddess is an important symbol for women as we seek out our sacred dance heritage. Knowing about the priestess and understanding her unique role, however, is essential because the priestess is a real, historical woman—a woman we can identify with. Through the priestess and her sacred dances, we learn that women were once central to religious and spiritual practices and that women had their own rites—their own symbols and liturgies—separate from those of men.

How, though, do we find the dancing priestess when information about women in the roles of religious leaders and facilitators is so limited? There are almost no written accounts of the priestess's activities. One way is through the incredible art and artifacts that show representations of women in ritual practice or performing sacred dances. We also find clues about the role of the priestess in the mythological accounts of women who no doubt were glorified in these tales because of the leadership roles they played within their communities. From these images and myths, we continue to piece together the ancient sacred rites for and by women, leading us onward in our journey to create meaningful rites and rituals for ourselves as women today.

DANCERS FROM THE MAIN TEMPLE. HERAION SANCTUARY, FOCE DEL SELE, ANCIENT POSEIDONIA (PASTEUM, ITALY), SIXTH CENTURY B.C.E. DETAIL FROM SANDSTONE RELIEF.

The Art and Myth of the Dancing Priestess

In every country of the ancient world, divine symbols represented women in their role as dancers, instrumental players, and singers. In 1934, over 30,000 terra-cotta votive offering figures and over 500 archaic sandstone reliefs dating from the 6th to the late 4th century B.C.E. were found in the ruins of the great temple city at Pasteum, discovered at the mouth of the Foce del Sele (Silaris), a river in northern Italy. This was the shrine of Hera, "mother of the gods," for 500 years.[2] The most impressive reliefs came from the treasury of the main temple, the Heraion, and all, without exception, represented dancers performing a sacred dance—dancers moving with the pure grace, grave delicacy, and intensity representative of sculpture of the Ionic period.[3] One of these reliefs shows the priestess, her long hair flowing free, looking back at the dancers as she leads them. Terra-cotta dance figures from the 4th century B.C.E. were found in the sanctuary of Demeter of Acrocorinth in Corinth, Greece.[4] Also in Greece, one of the oldest examples of the dancing priestess was found in an Ice Age cave painting in which the archaic goddess Boeotia stands in the center of the ring of dancing women performing a dance of energetic regeneration rites. An Upper Paleolithic cave fresco (10,000 B.C.E.) from Cogus in Catalonia, Spain, pictures nine women performing the celestial circle dance, or Dance of the Hours.*

LEADER OF THE DANCE. GRAPHIC AFTER WALL CARVING, TEMPLE AT SELE, FIFTH CENTURY.

We need to call back our memories
of sacral dance.
How did our Grandmother dance?
How did she discover so long ago
what we still seek?
What was it that called to her?
Get up! Join hands! Move!
She wasn't slightly embarrassed to
move her body, as I am today.
She gladly experienced the power
and serenity, opened freely to the
ecstatic divine.
She felt no guilt, as we were later
taught.
Where are those songs our mothers
sang, fitting rhythms to the
whole vast span of life?
What was it again they sang har-
vesting maize, threshing millet,
storing the grain . . . Why don't
we know about the
Grandmother's ways?
Why was it hidden so long!
This is the time we were waiting
for—
Grandmother, here we are, hear us,
help us, lead us again in the
dance!

Iris J. Stewart

Paintings on Sassari Sardinian, Sicilian, and Ukrainian vases and vessels from 4500 to 4000 B.C.E. show figures shaped like hourglasses formed by two triangles, wearing fringed skirts, ritual belts, and earrings. Some dance in a group circle holding hands;

*Buffie Johnson says that this dance was not what is commonly referred to as a fertility dance, and the small male figure with flaccid penis was added at a later date (Buffie Johnson, *Lady of the Beasts*, San Francisco: Harper & Row, 1981).

Dance of the Hours. Detail from Upper Paleolithic (after 10,000 B.C.E.) cave drawing, Cogus, Spain.

others dance singly or in pairs, with one hand at the head and the other at the hip, or holding both hands above the head. Similar figures come from Bulgaria and Mycenean Greece. Dancing hourglass-shaped figures on the wall of a cave in Brittany show the winter sun associated with ritual dances that not only are recorded on the wall but also may have actually been performed there.[5] Tanzanian cliff paintings reported by Mary Leakey, some estimated to be 29,000 years old, show groups of dancing women, some carrying musical instruments. The purpose of their ritual dance was to reveal the mystery behind the deity's forms, names, and symbols through the person of the priestess-dancer. Women participated in the development and performance of these rituals, both elaborate and simple.

From tomb drawings we can clearly discern that women of ancient Egypt performed ceremonial dances and were the official musicians, even into the New Kingdom era. The sacred sistrum, drum, and tambourine, during the thousands of years they were represented in Egyptian history, were always in the hands of women participating in sacred dances and processions or playing in front of the Goddess. From unearthed figurines representing women holding musical instruments, clappers, drums, and flutes, we see that the official funeral mourners and ritual dancers also were most often women.[6]

Egyptian priestess with sistrum.

Early Hindu and Buddhist art features *Yakshis*, usually identified as protective female nature spirits, whose auspicious ancestry traces all the way back to the Indus Valley Mother Goddess, Salabhanjika.[7] And in Southeast Asia, females were generally incorporated into the sculptural program of the temple as dancers or *Apsaras*—heavenly beings of the Rig-Veda.

In India, many aspects of pre-Vedic

BHARATA NATYAM DANCER ANAPAYINI DARI MAYSACK.

religion were absorbed into Hinduism as it was practiced in the villages, in much the same way Judaism and Christianity incorporated many pagan customs. The Kathaks of North India, before medieval times, were temple dancers and musicians who related through dance the vast and rich knowledge of India's Sanskrit sacred texts. *Katha*, or *Kathak*, a Sanskrit word, relates to the Hebrew *Kadesh* (priestess).

In the Indian state of Orissa, the temple dance is Odissi, a tradition with sculptural evidence that it has been practiced for more than 5,000 years. The best-known form of classical dance in India is Bharata Natyam, which arose between 200 B.C.E. and 200 C.E. This dance form is centered in southern India, the Deccan, Madras, and Tanjore. Until as late as 1930, Bharata Natyam was performed by *deva-dasis*, dancers attached to the temple.

The worship of the goddess Shakti in India is conducted through the person of a priestess, who, when possessed by Shakti, is called Matamgi. When a new priestess is to be initiated, a girl is selected and dressed in a white sari; after various ceremonies, she is brought to a place where, if the power comes to her, she begins to dance. The Matamgi participates in all village festivals where the presence of the Goddess is required.

Dancing priestesses or worshippers were also sometimes depicted on the image of the Goddess. The headdress of a Cyprian Goddess sculpture from the 6th century B.C.E. is adorned with images of dancing priestesses or female worshippers. A bell-shaped terra-cotta figure of the goddess Boeotia, from the Archaic period at Tanagra, depicts a chain of dancing worshippers on her dress.[8] And the Three Graces are shown on the abdomen of the great statue of Artemis in Turkey.

Down through the millennia, cultures change, borrow from each other, and overlay dimmed memories with mythology, so there is not always a clearly defined line between real women who were deified and those who were imagined divinities. In Greek mythology, the Curetes were known as semidivinities, dancers who assisted at the birth of gods and goddesses, but they may actually have been real priestesses who became mythological as time went on. Some other examples are the Nine Wild Muses or priestesses of Mount Parnassus, Mount Helicon, and Mount Olympus, who were representa-

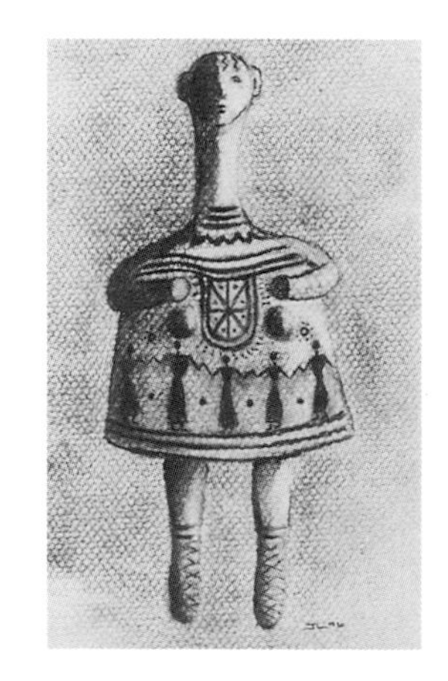

GODDESS BOEOTIA. ARTIST: JODY LYMAN.

ꕤ

The Story of the Maenads

MAENADS ON GREEK VASE.

I'm sure you have seen Maenads—those women painted onto thousands of Greek vases, *hydria*, found in every museum and history or art book. The Maenads are said to be in a frenzy, dancing around in the woods, usually being chased by satyrs. Perhaps you, like I, have been under the impression that the Maenads were mad women. The name has come to literally mean an "unnaturally excited or distraught woman."

The name of the Maenad and the meaning of her dance as we know about them today are the result of interpretations by outsiders. The Maenads were said to have entered ecstatic trances, which gave them great physical strength and a complete indifference to the conventions of their society. Euripides (5th century B.C.E.) seems to have been the major propagandist in his play *The Bacchantes,* or *Bacchae,* but in doing so, he exposed the male fear of ecstasy and women. The Maenads were a figment of his imagination, a literary construct made from elements of myth, reflecting a fear of women escaping Athenian control. The play may have been based on real women doing "mountain dances."

The mythic Maenads are similar to the Korybantes, mythical attendants of Kybele, who were supposed to dance in wild fashion with the Goddess on the mountains. Their historical counterparts were the Thyiads, who were much the same as the female Bacchantes. They were known as the "rushing ones" or "Those who moved direct . . . to the gods."

Madness, frenzy, orgiastic—all these terms were applied to the Maenads of ancient Greece and in Dionysian times also. According to the *Dictionary of the Dance,* the word *orgy* (Greek *orgia*) derived from the ritual process of *orchestrion* (as opposed to exorcism), namely, the deliberate invocation of the *manes* or departed spirits, ancestors, elemental spirits of nature, or the invocation of a higher divine spirit. The author agrees that frequent references to "wild dance" are due "mainly to misunderstanding or mistranslations of the brief descriptions of ancient authors; who perhaps never saw what they describe." The Greek word *exorcheisthai* means "to dance out," rather than "to speak out."[10] Although there is no evidence that the Dionysian orgies actually occurred, or that their origin was Minoan, writers and historians have expended hundreds of pages of imaginative writing bent on making it so.

Entheos-iasmos, or *enthousiasmos,* was another word used to describe the Maenads (*en,* "in"; *theos* "deity"). It means inspiration, belief in special revelations of the Holy Spirit, revelations of *theos* within. It distinguishes "possessed" from *ekphron,* "mad": if you are *ekphron* you are not necessarily *entheos,*[11] which means fiery and passionate in a godlike manner, not in the instinctual sense.

Our word *enthusiasm* derives from this Greek word. Enthusiasm is sharing in an energy that is conceived of as divine, as mana. We all become enthusiastic when we dance, with or without belief in its spirituality, as the mana of shared rhythms carries us along in the waves of the dance. The difference between religious ecstasy and "madness" may be in the eye of the beholder, or rather the onlooker. One has to wonder just how "mad" it all was.

tives of the Omnipotent Goddess who was worshipped on these mountaintops. Pomponius Mela, in the 1st century C.E., describes a community of nine virgins on the island of Sena off the coast of Brittany, to whom he attributed magical prophetic powers, such as arousing the waves of the sea with their singing, changing animals into whatever they wished, curing incurable sicknesses, and predicting the future.[9] And Homer wrote of the Nymphs, who ranked with neither immortals nor mortals: "long do they live, and they eat of ambrosial food, and they glide in the lovely dance among the immortals." Similar accounts can be found of the Maenads, Norns, Nereids, Nikes, Vixens, Furies, Valkyries, Spae-wives, Sibyls, Moerai (Fates who danced with Fortuna) or Graia, Greek Sirens and Spinners, German Lorelei, Fairies, Naiads, and snake-haired Erins. These stories give testimony to the perceived power of woman as priestess and leader of sacred dance ceremonials.

Other examples of the feminine mystic spirit of the dancing priestess include the Oread (*oreos* indicating mountains or *oreios,* rise of mountains and hills) in Greek mythology, who were ring dancers associated with the Oracles. The Horae of pre-Hellenic Greece, daughters of Themis, kept track of the passage of time and the proper season for earthly events through the rhythm of dance. Thallo (Spring) and Carpo (Autumn), celestial beings who performed the Dance of the Hours, acted as spiritual midwives to the gods and inspired earthly horae. Homer described them as divinities of weather and as ministers of Zeus. They are said to be the source of the Hours in Christian devotional practice, as in the *Book of Hours*. The Horae of Hellas were priestesses of Orai,[12] goddess of nature and the seasons, later abstracted to symbolize rule, order, and justice. Their dance was based on the zodiacal circling of "hours." Called "watchers," they were the keepers of lunar/menstrual/seasonal time in ancient cultures.

The *Horo*, or *Khoroi*, were the dancers of the World Mother Kore of the Cretan Mysteries at Knossos. One scene from the palace of Knossos, around the 16th century B.C.E., shows a group of women moving forward in unison but in a rather irregular line, each with one arm raised in front. Beautiful and powerful are these women, with long strands of curly hair flowing from headbands, each with a lock in front of the ear, the rest hanging down the back or flying out to accentuate energetic movement. They are dressed in costumes similar to the ones worn by the representation of the Goddess holding snakes: open-front vest clasping a small waist, above long flounced, pleated, and chevron-design skirts. Minoan seal cuttings also show Cretan priestesses in flounced skirts and elaborate ornamentation dancing before the altar, before the Cosmic Mother, and in the sacred grove.[13]

In Pompeii, during the 1st century C.E., prayers and offerings were made regularly to Vesta (Greek Hestia), goddess of the hearth. From her priestesses, who were keepers of the sacred flame, came the phrase Vestal Virgins. Festivals, with dancing and games, were held in her honor, similar to those for Hera in Greece, predating the

In a small pottery group from Palaikastro, Crete, women hold arms in a ring dance around a woman playing the lyre. A similar piece from a tomb dated 1500 B.C.E. shows four women in a circle, arms linked. Small formal dance groups are pictured in front of the palace of Knossos, whereas other seal cuttings indicate religious dancing that was far more ecstatic in sacred groves and before the Goddess. The drawings on the Hagia Triada sarcophagus tell us that the priestesses had an important presence in ceremonies as late as the 14th century.

Sappho, 600 B.C.E., spoke of how it was:

When the full moon rose
Women took their place around
the altar. . .
(. . . they were dancing) as
Cretan women danced beside
a lovely altar
Their graceful feet treading
down the smooth soft bloom
of the grass.[15]

Olympics.[14] The priestesses in Egypt, on the occasion of the annual festival of Hathor, would stop at each house to bestow Hathor's blessings. This they did by dancing and singing and holding out to the people the emblems of their goddess, the sistrum and manit (necklace).

Persian poetry and ancient miniature paintings depicted the qualities of perfection subscribed to the goddess Aredvi Sura Anahita and a group of female dancers, whether real or imaginary, called the Houris of Paradise.[16] Like the Horae of Greece, the Houris were Arabic-Persian dancing "ladies of the hour" who kept time in heaven and tended the star-souls. They were the symbols of spiritual life, say Sufi poets. Appearing to stand in midair, dancing with frame drum or harp, the Houris awaken the viewer to a higher consciousness beyond the material plane.

Tomb and vase paintings depicting ceremonial movements of pre-Islamic Persia date back as far as 1400 B.C.E. Miniature paintings, although highly stylized, also give clues to what these dances may have been like. Though not as complex as the devotional dance forms of India, with their system of

Were the Amazons Dancing Priestesses?

According to Pausinias and Strabo, Ephesus was founded by the Amazons by at least the 6th century B.C.E., possibly before the Greeks arrived there.[18] Ephesus was the most important center for the followers of Artemis in Ionia in western Anatolia, in what is now Turkey. Around the great statue of Artemis they performed a ritual dance, which was continued in later centuries. Diana's priestesses are said to have used their shields and swords in a circular dance around a sacred oak or beech at Ephesus.[19]

In his hymn to Artemis, the poet Callimachus wrote: "A long time ago, Artemis, the warlike Amazons set up your statue under a beech tree at the place where Queen Hippo made her offerings. Girding their weapons, they performed the dance of shields, and then widening out into a circle, they danced to the accompaniment of a high-pitched flute; their clamorous vibrations shaking the land and the sky."[20]

specific *hasta mudras* (gesture, symbol) and *asanas* (positions), the miniature paintings depict graceful hand movements from side to side, above the head, and about the face while the dancer glides across the floor or sways back and forth, either standing or kneeling.[17]

The Priestess in the Bible

From the Old Testament we can glean some clues regarding the existence of dancing priestesses by looking at the descriptive name "Daughters of Zion" in a new way (Isaiah 3:16–26). Zion was the mystical Mother and Beloved of Israel, and its future bride. Zion was also "the Upper City," the holy place or temple area on Mount Hamoed. "Going up to Zion" is related to ecstatic joy. It equates with the concept of the world paradise of other cultures, situated on the mountaintop: the Indian Himalayas, Greek Mount Olympus, and others. It is here that "God's daughters" dance the Mysteries. "Therefore they shall come and sing in the height of Zion, and shall flow together to the goodness of the Lord." It is on Zion that the "Virgin . . . shall go forth in the dances." (Jeremiah 31:4).

The word *Zion* equates with the Greek *Zona*, which indicates a specific or designated zone, a circle equally divided—usually by the twelve divisions of the Zodiac. The Hebrew word *zonah* is at times defined as "prostitute" and at times as "prophetess."[22] This implies that the priestess at one time was honored. It may also be related to the Egyptian *min-zion* (*min*, "to minister"), which was a circle of ritual dancers moving across the circle in healing rituals, producing a six-point star pattern.[23] As the twelve signs (star patterns), mansions (manzions), or sacred zones, Zion was the feminine spirit or energy of the place. Therefore, the Daughters of Zion in Israel represented the spirit of Jerusalem.* It is interesting that Yahweh came to Zion "as well the singers and the players on instruments shall be there" and declared amid song and dance, "all my springs are in thee." The Daughters of Zion were free women pictured as proud, "walking and *mincing* as they go, and making a tinkling with their feet," mincing steps—dancing steps—much to the dismay of the prophet, Isaiah (Isaiah 3:16).

Another biblical name for priestess is *qadesha* (*kadesh*),[26] or *Qedish'im*, which means "holy woman" or "tabooed woman" and in the original sense was broadly equivalent to the Hindu *devi-dasi* ("servants of the Gods"), according to Tikva Frymer-Kensky, an Assyriologist/Sumerologist and biblicist who has studied the ancient texts from Sumer, Babylon, Assyria, and Israel. Usually feminine, they worked with the Levite priests in daily practice. *Kiddush*,[27] *kedusha*, is Hebrew for "sanctification" and

*Women as "spirits of place" has been a widespread belief demonstrated by the practice of calling a city "she." This is also shown somewhat by the tradition of the Miss America state and city beauty contests, as well as the Statue of Liberty. This spiritual heritage may help explain the insistence that Miss America be a virgin, or at least give testimony to being childless.

ꕥ

Was Mary a Dancing Priestess?

An apocryphal legendary Gospel, *Protevangelium of James,* written around 150 C.E., said that in gratitude to God for giving her a child, Mary's mother Anna, or St. Anne (also Hannah), dedicated Mary to the temple when she was age three. The priest "placed her on the third step of the altar, and the Lord God put grace upon the child, and she danced for joy with her feet, and all the house of Israel loved her." Unfortunately, when she reached puberty at age twelve,* the Levites became concerned that she would "pollute" the temple, and so her ministry ceased. This story was accepted as authentic in Eastern Orthodoxy,[24] was rejected by the West, but reappeared in the West during the Renaissance under the title *Protevangelium.*[25]

I found a rare depiction of this scene on the walls of an ancient Byzantine church of the Virgin of Kera (Panaghia Keras), which I visited at Krista, Crete. Mary and her parents are accompanied by the "Daughters of the Hebrews," whose regal costuming clearly indicates their status among the holy. A manuscript drawing, "Mary and the Hebrew Maidens Dancing," from the Vatican Library reflects the close association of dance and worship in the early Christian period. The word *maiden* here can be seen as a synonym for role of the priestess. In this particular illustration, one priestess beats the cylindrical drum while another plays metal castanets or zaggats.

Mary continued to dance after her ascension to heaven. In medieval Spain, October 1 was celebrated as the feast of roses of the Virgin Mary, in which this hymn was sung:

Virgin, thou dost rise to everlasting triumph
Thou dost rightly share the heavenly ring-dance.

*The number 12 (4 tripled) is significant in that the next number is 13, the number of sudden change or chaos.

MARY AND THE HEBREW MAIDENS DANCING. FROM AN EARLY CHURCH MANUSCRIPT DRAWING, VATICAN LIBRARY.

derives from *kaddesh*, "to sanctify."* *Kadesh* survives in the word *Kaddish*, now meaning prayer, thanksgiving, or mourning.[28] In the Kaddish, or prayer for the dead, benedictions are spoken or read sometimes in a dancelike manner, arms raised three times, hands open, as the supplicant rocks onto the toes. *Qadesh* is usually translated as "holy," but also relates to "a central point, pivot, focus, or motive upon which everything turns."[29]

The term *Qadesh* was one of many epithets given to the Assyrian goddess Astarte (Ashtoreth), the Hittite Kades (Quedesh), and the Cretan Kadesch, who had her ritual and sanctification dance.[30]

From Priestess to Performer: The Transition

The priestess in ancient times was part of the community, the Grandmother. She was a nurse and midwife, a healer, giving advice as needed but without being set above or elevated to "priestly" heights. Accompanying their work with song, our foremothers transformed drudgery into rhythmic dance patterns, neutralizing its potentially adverse effects on the human body and psyche. They marked sacred space and time in words valued for their healing power, associated with breath and movement, with the life force itself. For festival occasions or specific ritual purposes, the priestess wore a special costume, jewelry, and headdress, abandoning her personal identity in order to embody a larger power. Her ceremonial garments were then removed and stored until the next occasion. According to Marija Gimbutas, "Although these sisterhoods or communities of women were endowed with great power, they seem to have functioned as collective entities, not as autocracies."[31]

Over time, priestesses as keepers and leaders of ritual disappeared from the scene with the rise of a priestly caste (the Levites and Brahmans are examples). The altar, which had been centered on the hearth, was moved to the temple. The communal worship/storehouse/living centers were replaced by the church building. Temples were built as separate edifices to house a distinct institution of priests, where ritual came to be the domain of select individuals on behalf of the community, in place of communal participation. Organic rituals became prescribed religion.

Dance as an integral part of women's spiritual practice shared a parallel fate with the priestess. As religions in many parts of the world moved further and further away from communal participation, the priestess-led communal nature dances, dances of

*Kadesh was the name of several places in Erez Israel, Syria, and Canaan to which a sacred character is attributed. Miriam died and was buried at Kadesh-Barnea, a place of a "rich spring which waters a fertile plain." (*Encyclopedia Judaica*, Jerusalem: Peter Publishing House Ltd., 1972).

THE FIRST ALTAR. TWO WOMEN PERFORM A MUSIC AND DANCE RITUAL AROUND THE HOME ALTAR OF SACRED FIRE.

EGYPTIAN MUSICIANS AND DANCERS. METROPOLITAN MUSEUM OF ART COLLECTION.

religious ecstasy, and birth/fertility dances were frowned upon and eventually forbidden. A few religions incorporated the priestess as a sacred dancer into their rites, but these religions made sacred dancers servants of the temple and of its priests.

The momentous split of the artistic form of worship and the devotional setting—a split between the sacred and the profane—was brought about by the social division of priests and worshippers into masters and servants. Devotional dances gradually became commissioned works for the enjoyment of paying or ruling spectators, for provocative entertainment. Dance was transformed from a religious act or ceremonial rite into a work of art intended for observation and subject to judgment by the observer.[32] From these changes arose a culture of dance as theater and entertainment.

By the time of the Roman Empire, the sacred dances of the Etruscans, Greeks, and Macedonians became mere entertainment for the Romans and were performed by paid professionals and imported slaves. Although countless Greek vase decorations during the time of Alexander the Great (3rd century B.C.E.) illustrated girls in positions and poses similar to those in the old fertility rites, they were by then divested of their religious significance and degenerated into exhibitions of bodily charms to suit male desire. As the focus shifted to the extroverted, the

What Was the Temple?

To get a better picture of the loss of women's ways, we need to know the differences between the women's temples and later temples. What is now called a temple was, in the times of the Old Religion, not an empty building that was used once a week on the Sabbath. Quite often, the place of worship and ritual included a sacred ground, a circle of stones, a cave, or a sacred grove of trees. The buildings included the storehouse and the granary, set up to assure a supply of food for all during winters and poor harvests—a very practical idea. They included work rooms and living quarters. Some people even buried their dead beneath the floor.

The Sacred Prostitute

Anthropologists' and historians' habit of labeling the priestess, as well as the Great Mother herself, "prostitute," whether preceded by definers such as "temple," "sacred," or "ritual," entirely distorts the meaning of the ancient customs they are supposedly explaining.

The *Oxford English Dictionary* states that from 1540 to 1677 the word *prostitute* was used in the sense of "to offer with complete devotion or self-negation" or simply as a synonym for "to devote." By the 1700s, *prostitute* denoted "given over or devoted to something evil." It began to be used figuratively to mean "debased" or "debasing, corrupt." By mid-century, *prostitute* was well established in the sexual sense we know today.

The word *prostitute*, meaning "to expose publicly," based on "to set up or decree" and "to devote," developed from female initiatory rites, an important part of many cultures throughout the world. Although there were many variations, in general such rites included a certain period of seclusion during the first menstrual period, a time of education in sexuality and fertility, customs of the people, and religious traditions relevant to the future role of women within it.

After the period of segregation and instruction ended, the rite began. Again, it varied according to time and place, but it usually included dances, songs, sometimes ritual baths, and ochre body painting, tattooing, etc. When this rite was completed, the public rite began. The essence of the public rite was the solemn exhibition of the girl to the community as a ceremonial announcement that the mystery had been accomplished and she was shown to be an adult, now assuming the full responsibilities of womanhood.

Mircea Eliade wrote about the significance of this ceremony:

> To show something ceremonially—a sign, an object, an animal, a human—is to declare a sacred presence, to acclaim the miracle of a hierophany. This rite, which is so simple in itself, denotes a religious behaviour that is archaic. . . . Very probably this ceremonial presentation of the initiated girl represents the earliest stage of the ceremony.[34]

Fundamental to these rites was the essential revelation of the woman's role as a creatrix, which in itself constituted a religious experience exclusive to her gender. This, indeed, may have been the basis of the mystery schools and the Eleusinian Mysteries.

In India, though not in Tibet, Tantric Buddhism and Vajrayana Buddhism viewed goddesses as "lightning conductors" that diverted human energy currents straight to the World Soul. As this belief became entangled in the Tantric sexual route to nirvana, legends evolved of the Goddess who revealed herself through the priestess as the sacred harlot to attract men for the purpose of transformation. It became common in India for *deva-dasis*, temple women who had a special symbolic sanctity, to be imported as partners. These women were known by Buddhists as *dakinis*.

In the Mesopotamian story of Gilgamesh there is a trace of earlier myths and belief systems when the wild man Enkidu is humanized by having sexual intercourse with a priestess of Ishtar, thereby helping him to "become wise, like a god." Eisler says, "There are also strong vestiges of sex as a religious rite in Eastern religious traditions . . . as in the Mesopotamian stories where love-priestesses are reduced to 'prostitutes'—the use of erotic pleasure as a means of raising consciousness (or attaining higher spirituality). . . ."[35]

mimetic, the masked, and the theatrical, the gradual decline and alienation of the sacred, the inward, and the mystic was inevitable. In Egypt, by the early dynastic periods, the functions of the priestesses were diminished. They were allowed to sing and dance only in temple choirs, and in later periods the office was purely honorific, with no duties.[33]

The dances of the sacred mysteries became dance dramas exported through the trade routes, where, out of their original context and in the eyes of foreign audiences, they would be seen as exotic and sensational. The universal feminine principle of spirit-matter connection was transformed into the duality of seduction/virginity, and the priestess/midwife changed from a spiritual channel to a sorcerer holding the keys to magic—black magic. In some cultures, the archetype of woman as the dark side of the personality was projected onto the dancer, the mysterious yet powerful, the primal, the unconscious where erotic and exotic feelings are born. The illusion appears time and again in history and myth: Salome, Delilah, Jezebel, even Mata Hari in this century.

As the transition from mother-religion to father-rule took place, the maternal aspects of ritual diminished. Sexuality and procreativity were split and separated from a concept of belonging to nature or the natural flow, to the concept of belonging to the tribal unit, belonging to the father/king/state. The model of a woman in a state of pregnancy became repulsive; the Earth Mother was replaced by a more youthful, slender model like the later Greco-Roman version of Venus representing romantic love, for example.

In these transitions, the meaning of *virgin* changed from the woman who chose to remain with the temple to the sacred prostitute who was forced to devote time at the temple. As sacred prostitutes the role of these women changed to the exercising of fertility magic through the simulation of sexual intercourse. The firstborn girl of a slave was consecrated to the temple, thus defining her role, while wealthy women paid others to substitute for themselves or their daughters. Dancing as part of sacred rites developed into dancing to please the king. The king ruled by divine appointment, and court dance became a vehicle for control of his subjects. A royal court ballet developed out of the chorus of temple dancers; once women danced for their Goddess, but now they were forced to entertain the prince.

The same shift occurred in India. Ancient Eastern mythology was shaped around the idea that the universe was created through a divine dance and that musical instruments were the tools of the supernatural, which poured forth through the "music of the spheres." These epic dances were prescribed rituals in the Vedic scripts in 550 B.C.E., which continued into the Hindu culture of India, where every gesture became highly stylized. Over the years, the performed epic stories of kings and merchant princes crept into the sacred Hindu texts' pantomime, and the dancer became the entertainer of royalty. Under Mogul rulers of the 11th century, music and dance long sacred to the temples were performed first in the courts of the elite and then among common people.

Author Steven Lonsdale makes a

Male Kathakali dancers dressed as women. Photograph by Payson Stevens.

keen observation about the subject of men taking over women's rituals, especially dance: "In masquerade the coincidence of male dancers disguised as women and animals is frequent enough to make one speculate that both are regarded as the original source of fertility magic, which the males steal and appropriate for their use in exclusive rituals."[40] So while sacred dance was corrupted and secularized, men simultaneously sought to tap into the power of these sacred rites by adopting or emulating the rituals and making them their own.

Nineteenth-century writers such as Gustave Flaubert and Gerard de Nerval wrote extensively about this

Men Doing Women's Dance

In addition to sacred dance becoming a spectacle of entertainment, another major transition occurred when men gradually began emulating and then taking over woman's rituals, wearing her costume, and thereby grossly corrupting her image and increasing the propaganda against her and her rituals.

In 204 B.C.E. the rituals of Cybele were taken over by Phrygian men, who "wore their hair long, dressed in female clothes and celebrated the Goddess in wild orgiastic dances to the point of exhaustion."[36] Although the majority of Dionysus's followers were said to have been women, the men who joined in these rituals often dressed as women when they participated in the rites.[37] Members of the Greek *choreutae* (chorus of singers and dancers) were always men wearing masks, who frequently impersonated women.[38]

Kathakali dancers and actors from the South India state of Kerala are all males, with boys or young men playing the roles of women. In their dance drama they enact Kali as the malevolent aspect of the goddess Devi. Originally the Kathaks were women who preserved and shared the sacred Sanskrit texts through their dance. By the time the males took over these practices, the praise of gods had declined, replaced instead with the praise of kings and heroes, some of whom became "divine" as time went on.

Marija Gimbutas wrote about a custom found in Scotland, where "Around the New Year, men still dress as women with antler headdresses to perform the famous stag dance to promote regeneration and secure happiness for the coming year."[39]

Dr. Curt Sachs, one of the world's foremost authorities in the fields of ethnomusicology and the history of dance, said that there are countless examples of the custom of masked men dancing "in the manner of a woman" in carnivals and festivals: the European Mardi Gras, the Brazilian Pareci'-Cabixi', on the island of Mallorca in the folk dance *els cossiers,* in Portugal in the *foliass,* and in similar festivals in Guatemala, Australia, and old China.

custom in the places of entertainment they visited in the Middle East. In conservative areas of Morocco, Egypt, and elsewhere, where wedding celebrations had traditionally required the presence of the Scheikha, or Almeh (learned women in the arts who were teachers to women), public performances at the time of their visits in the 19th century utilized professional male dancers dressed in drag, or wearing a woman's kaftan and d'fina to acknowledge that they were dancing women's dances.

A noted historian of Arabic music, Henry George Farmer, also wrote about this phenomenon, saying that Arab men, like the men who established other male-dominant religions, knew all too well that music and dance were of women's religion and that in order to establish their own validity, they had to imitate the women at the same time they were suppressing them.[41]

Even through these dramatic changes, women retained particular or very specific religious and social spheres of influence in some areas for a greater length of time. It appears that priestesses retained certain degrees of autonomy in Babylon and other places even into biblical times. In pre-Buddhist days in Burma, formal dancing was done exclusively by priestesses, who held a position of equality with men.[42] Ancient Armenia was also rich in dance-mimes, ballads, and dance rituals led by the Parik priestess-dancer. The Hushka Parik were "mournful dancers."[43] The alma/courtesan was well regarded for her knowledge and art down through the centuries, even as she became a societal outsider. The alma mater, "soul-mother," was a Roman teaching priestess especially empowered to give instruction in the sexual mysteries.[44] The name was based on *Al-Mah*, a Middle Eastern name of the Moon Goddess, also a title of her temple women, *almah*.

The sacred dance of the priestess, as we shall see, also still survives. In the Arabic countries of the Middle East, adherents of the older religions went underground or formed separate castes of dancing tribes and sects, such as the Ghawazi and the Ouled Nail (see chapter 4, WomanDance). Thus, many of the ancient sacred dance customs come down to us in the present day with much of their original form preserved.

TWO EXAMPLES OF MEN DOING WOMEN'S DANCE: MOHAMMED, FROM THE 1893 WORLD'S FAIR, AND MEI LAN-FANG, A FAMOUS PEKING OPERA STAR IN SAN FRANCISCO IN 1930.

The Dance of the Priestess

My first real glimpse of the dance of the priestess came when I saw a performance by a dancer from India when I first moved to the New York City area. She seemed very exotic, of course. But beyond that, her intricate, complex, and controlled movements; her concentration; and her seeming indifference to the audience all intrigued me. The pamphlet I received at the door spoke of communing with divinity. What I soon discovered was that I was viewing part of a very ancient lineage of the dancing priestess.

I learned that in Indian dance, the basic motivation is one of worship, and for this reason the dance embodies a certain austerity. Every movement of a finger or eyebrow is significant and is performed with control. The hands, face, and eyes express the liturgy; the arms trace bold geometric space patterns, and the feet create the intricate rhythms. There are twenty-four head and eye movements, four neck positions, fifty-seven hand positions, and 127 facial expressions.

When part of a religious ceremony, these dances are like prayers offered in the temples of India. They are designed to inspire the worshipper to transcend the sphere of illusion—the mundane world in all its pettiness—and experience a transpersonal sphere, that of Divinity, or the Absolute. Dancing is a catalyst, like a sacred chant or litany.[45] If, to the uninitiated, the gestures, songs, and mimetic passages seem flirtatious at some points, one must remember that the coquetry is directed toward the Godhead and that the interplay is an allegorical one in which

Dance of the priestess. Photograph by Payson Stevens.

the human soul seeks oneness with God, according to dancer and author La Meri.[46]

The priestess is the lens focusing for the others the higher life energies, the sustaining energies that constitute and define earthly existence. She acts as the transmitting agent of divine emanations. Her dance is a system of movements, gestures, prayers, and songs in veneration of the invisible forces of life.

The function of the priestess is to facilitate the group's and the individual's process and to teach all how to be receptive. To be receptive means to be open to receiving and considering. The group is the focus. Her dance is concerned not with the personal but with the transpersonal, or rather with connecting the personal and the transpersonal, the eternal.

The creative forces that pour through the priestess vitalize the lives of those in the group. That ability to transmute divine events into spatial configurations is her power and her service.

Now Let Us Dance

We may be able to once again find the priestess, to reawaken her role as spiritual guide, as we look into each other's eyes and share our stories, meeting in the ancient way of women—

communally —to create our own sacred rituals. As we gather together as women, it is important that we become aware of each others' unique contributions and that we affirm the strength and beauty in each other through our dances so that we can then bring strength to the greater world. Our rituals, whether public or private, group or individual, may be directed to a deity as worship, thanksgiving, and communion aimed at communal integration, or they may be dedicated to personal enlightenment.

Although a leader acting in the role of priestess may introduce a dance, once the dance is raised, the group joins in and the creation becomes collaborative. That is the unique way of the priestess. She may be the initiator, but she shares her leadership role—her responsibility for the dance and ritual—with others. In fact, for the purposes of our dances, the leadership role of the priestess may be passed from one member of the group to another, either within a specific dance itself or by another woman becoming the leader for the next communal dance ritual.

Because sacred movement can serve as an opening into a higher plane of reality, find music that allows the group to explore emotions, instead of suppressing them. It can be music by Pachelbel, Gregorian chants for calming and going inward, or music that is more uplifting to the spirit. There are also numerous audiotapes of songs, poetry, and chants available (see Resources). Participants in the dance should remain open to what will happen in the music and its effect on the movement of the group, working toward a consensus about steps, regardless of how long it takes. The goal here is not a polished presentation; it is the process of creating the dance that is important. Spiritual confirmation, consciousness-raising, and the creation of a sense of community, healing, and love resonate at the heart of these dances, speaking directly to the heart's own mind. By tapping into traditional sacred dance movements (see Part Two), ancestral memory is restored.

Although the dance of the priestess is usually a communal dance, you may choose to dance as a priestess as a solitary act to invoke a particular goddess or to increase your own intuitive powers. Allow your attention to expand as you dance, and you will find that your understanding of yourself will grow through your dance experience. Then, like the priestess, you will be able to teach others how to achieve this same outcome. You may also choose to be a dancing priestess for an audience. In my experience with this type of dance, a dialogue happens with the members of the witnessing audience—an emotional, spiritual, and intellectual call and response—that together with their concentrated support, makes them part of the ritual. However, as a powerful priestess who is as one with the earth; is not ashamed of her hips and her stomach; and has the ability to enjoy fantasy, illusion, and her own sexuality; you should also be aware of your ability to excite tremendously strong emotions and reactions in your audience. A woman moving her body in free and energetic ways can cause a degree of anxiety in the viewer, and it is something you may want to become aware of. With this in mind, your dance for an audience may be different than one done for or with your inner circle of women.

LEFT: PREMA DASARA DANCES AS RADHA AT THE KONARAK SUN TEMPLE, ORISSA, INDIA. PHOTOGRAPH BY ANANDA APFELBAUM.

Twenty-One Praises of Tara

This suggested dance is adapted from the work of Prema Dasara, now living in Maui, Hawaii, and can be done as a solitary dance, as a group ritual, or for a witnessing audience. Prema, an international teacher and performer of sacred dance, was schooled in the traditions of India, Nepal, Tibet, and Bali. Breaking through the male-only sacred dance tradition of Tibetan Buddhism, Prema performed her Tara Mandala Dance of the Twenty-One Praises of Tara to a high lama for the first time in 1985. She has also performed the dance for His Holiness, the Dalai Lama.

In her workshops, Prema tells the story of Tara, the Green Goddess, the most beloved of the female bodhisattvas, to whom temples are dedicated throughout the Buddhist world. Many millennia ago in another world system, it is said that she was an ordinary woman who practiced very diligently and had reached the stage of total enlightenment. The monks of that time told her that now she could assume the form of a man and enter nirvanic bliss. She thought and then laughed, telling them, "There is no difference at all between the body of a woman or a man as far as its capability in obtaining enlightenment. I will remain in the body of a woman until the end of time, a protector, a Buddha, one who is fully awakened, answering swiftly the prayers of those who call out to me. I will help them to cross the ocean of sorrow, to establish them in enlightenment."

Venerable Lama Bokar Rinpoche spoke of Prema's dance presentation: "This is not just a regular common performance. Those of us who are witnessing such activity are thus inspired by the manifold qualities of Tara. We allow our own rampant upheaval of conflicting emotions to subside. There is at least temporary and momentary clarification from confused preoccupations. At the same time there is the possibility of clarifying hindrances, particularly in pursuing the path of spirituality in one's own life . . . giving rise to longevity as well as . . . the unconditioned wisdom inspiration of Tara."[47]

Prema Dasara says, "The Praises of Tara remind us of our potential, that we are worthy of honor, capable of greatness, wise in the ways of heaven and earth. As sacred dancers we train ourselves to open to the energy of our possibilities, to make the connection with the wisdom beings that empower us through their compassion. We see every atom of our bodies vibrating with enlightened energy. And we send this potency out into our communities, praying that all may be blessed with abundance, that all may be free from sorrow, that all may be established in wisdom, in love, in peace."[48]

Here are three sample praises with accompanying colors, qualities, and insights. The essence of this work that makes it so powerful is the mirroring of these enlightened qualities in yourself, to yourself. I have studied with Prema and can say it is one of the most powerful and transforming experiences I have had.

As you study the praises, visualize how you would express them through mime, facial expression, and body movement so that they become part of your expression and so that an audience would be able view them in your living form. Your dance should give

Twenty-One Praises of Tara. Photograph by Katheryn Wilde.

expression to the many faces of the Mother who is ever ready to rescue beings from suffering.

As an example, I suggest the following rather broad moves for interpreting the praises: framing your face and then reaching for the "hundred full autumn moons," whirling as your arms and hands punctuate the air with your fingers unfurling to illustrate the "light of thousands of stars." As you focus your concentration through repetition, you will discover yourself refining and simplifying your movements as the distilled, essential qualities come through. If this dance is done in a group, everyone should move forward together, following a figure-eight form. Each dancer

Dancer with cymbals and veil. Pompeii House of Mysteries.

performs her interpretation of a praise as she reaches the center of the figure.

You may wish to begin with an invocation to Tara, the embodiment of outer, inner, and secret practices of the path to enlightenment. We open toward the Divine, turning to Tara, the embodiment of wisdom and compassion, for refuge. You may also say the following invocation based on the Root Mantra: **Om Tara Tutare Ture Soha.** *Tutare* means that Tara removes all fear and that any anxiety that clouds the mind is based in ignorance. *Ture* indicates that just thinking of Tara brings good fortune and the fulfillment of inner and outer needs. *Soha* (or the Sanskrit SVAHA) is the unity of oneself with the Divine.

> **OM** *I praise the Venerable Exalted Tara*
> *I praise You* **Tare** *Liberator Swift and Courageous*
> *Through* **Tutare** *Remover of All Fear*
> *Through* **Ture** *Bestower of Good Fortune*
> *Through* **Soha** *I bow at Your Feet.*

You may chose your own music to accompany your dances, or order Prema's audiotapes and videotapes (see Resources).

Praise No. 1
Tara, Source of Attainment

Color, copper; quality, radiant health.

> *Praise the One who is radiant with light*
> *Her clear eyes full like the sun and the moon*
> *Chanting Hara Hara Tutare, She removes the fiercest illness.*

As the sun and moon dispel all darkness, Tara dispels ignorance. The sun is hot and wrathful, the moon is cool and peaceful, but both emit a radiance that is capable of overcoming the recurring illness of attachment to the causes of suffering. Hara is a fierce mantra; Tutare a peaceful one. Apply the correct remedy and cure any illness.

You might begin your interpretation of this praise by taking an invocation or praise posture. As you chant the mantra Hara Hara Tutare, move among the audience or other dancers with healing intentions. See what happens.

Praise No. 2
Tara, Accomplisher of Bliss

Color, yellow; quality, triumphant joy.

Praise Her the Swift One arising
from the seed word Hung
She stamps Her foot shaking the
greatest mountain peaks
The three worlds tremble beneath
Her dancing feet.

Tara is swift to assist all who call out to her. She appears from the transformation of the primordial sound of Hung. She is playful with her power: one stamp of her foot, and Mounts Kailash, Meru, and Mandhara all tremble. The three worlds include beings dwelling on earth, underground, and in the heavens. Her dancing produces bliss in all minds.

You might begin your dance by lying prone on the floor, then awaken and rise to a standing position of power where you stamp your foot with "attitude."

Praise No. 3
Tara, All-Conquering Great Joy

Color, red; quality, laughter.

Praise Her whose diadem shines a
garland of light
Her Joyous laughter of Tutare
brings the world under Her
sway.

Her jeweled crown is adorned by the presence of the five wisdom Buddhas. It sparkles, emanating a multicolored garland of light rays about her. With great joy, Tara laughs the mantra of removing fears, "Tutare," and all beings in heaven, earth, and the underworlds are completely captivated. She fulfills all wishes and removes all obstacles.

For this praise you might indicate a diadem (a royal headband or crown) rising from the top of your head with your hands as you pivot. Extend this motion with undulating hands like a snake floating through the air to indicate the garland of light. Laugh out loud as you swoop the air into an imaginary ball.

Once again, you may want to take a few moments to process in writing the sensations or feelings you experienced with this dance. Consider these issues:

1. How does it feel to think of yourself as a priestess? A little frightening? Delightful? A little of both?
2. Do you find dancing with other women in community to be empowering?
3. Have the dances changed your idea of spirituality and the expression of spirituality?

3
Dancing through Theology

Let them praise his name in the dance: let them sing praises unto him with the timbrel and harp. . . . Praise ye the Lord. . . . Praise him with psaltery and harp. Praise him with the timbrel and dance: praise him with stringed instruments and organs. Praise him upon the loud cymbals: praise him upon the high sounding cymbals.

From Psalms 149 and 150

One of my main objectives in researching the history of women's dance was to determine what happened to women's religion and to women in religious expression. I found that much of women's ways and women's power had already been eroded—in different ways and at different times in various places throughout the East and Middle East—by the time of the advent of the Christian era. Still, I wanted to know what happened to the Grandmother as she tried to be a part of the evolving ideas about the sacred and the holy, and to her danced expression of the holy in religions like Judaism and Christianity. This exploration was particularly complicated because the ambivalence developed by religions toward dance has obscured its history, and women, with few exceptions, were not allowed leadership roles or allowed to express the feminine aspect of religion.

RIGHT: SANDRA RIVERA, OF THE OMEGA DANCE COMPANY, IN *EN ESPIRITU: ST. TERESA OF AVILA* AT THE CATHEDRAL OF ST. JOHN THE DIVINE. PHOTOGRAPH BY MARY BLOOM.

O Mío Yemayá! Santeria priestess possessed by Yemayá. Painting by Raul Canizares.

Three things prompted me to see what I could find: an experience my mother had as a young girl, a memory from my own childhood, and a story a woman told me some forty years later. My childhood memory goes back to when I was growing up in Louisiana. We lived close to a United Pentecostal church and an African-American church, both located on the winding country road that led past our house. We would sometimes go to those churches on Saturday night and during their summertime revival meetings. Church members, predominantly women, would pray over the sick, shout, stomp, and dance about with great energy and enthusiasm. I watched with wonder as members left their seats, moving to the altar while praying, shouting, and singing—so different from the reserved Southern Baptist church services to which I was accustomed. A call from the altar brought others up for special prayers and a laying on of hands for healing.

One or more of the congregants would invariably start "talking in tongues," a rush of words that sounded like gibberish to me. Although I was mesmerized by their words, what really fascinated me was the way they began moving and shaking, their arms raised toward the ceiling as their whole bodies were caught up in a staccato response to the music. It was such an exuberant expression of their faith and longing for connection to the holy. I didn't fully understand what was happening, but it seemed to me that those people might be on to something.

During a revival meeting at age twelve, I could see the excitement rising and sense all around me the charged and anticipatory atmosphere. I wanted to have that feeling, too, and so one evening, in that little old weathered wooden country church house lighted only by coal-oil lamps, I responded to the call. Overcoming my shyness, my feeling of being an outsider, and even my parents' conservative presence, I impulsively went to the altar. Neophyte that I was, I knelt there waiting for something to happen, while above me were women swaying, shouting, and praying loudly. Nothing happened. I did not "get the Spirit," as it is called. It would be many years later, in another church and in another situation, that I would begin to "get" it—to sense that there are other planes of existence, that there truly is a spiritual experience and a new spirit. My revelation would come to me through dance and through certain extreme life experiences, both of which I later learned were yet another way for the Spirit to work its wonders.

In the Fiddler's House, Everyone Dances

In the Protestant South, the idea of dance was strictly secular and strictly suspect. My mother, Minnie Leigh Evans, born before the turn of the century, used to say that she always felt happiest when dancing. She never understood why dance was viewed negatively. She said, wistfully, "I never had an evil thought in my life when I was dancing." I was curious about why she made such a statement, and also where my mother, a young girl living in the rural South at that time, would dance—certainly not in bars. When violinist Itzhak Perlman, visiting his Klysmer roots in Europe, quoted an old French proverb—"In the fiddler's house, everyone dances"[1]—I then understood. My mother was part of a large family, almost all of whom were musicians. The story is told that my mother's father played the "fiddle" on Saturday night and the "violin" on Sunday. Minnie Leigh, her mother, her sisters, and her brothers all loved to dance, whether at the Saturday night community square dances or with the family at home.

Years after her death, a cousin told me that Minnie Leigh at age sixteen had been brought before the church elders and told she must not dance. She apologized for breaking the rules of the church, even though she didn't know that the church had such a rule, but that she would not apologize for dancing. As a result she was "turned out of church." She was a deeply spiritual person, so I know it took a great conviction on her part to hold firm to her own truth. While it may be hard for us to imagine such a strong reaction from a church, those were the realities of the times.

I found that those realities at the turn of the century in the South were still evident in the 1970s in cosmopolitan Los Angeles when I had a conversation with a woman remembering her high school days. Her experience echoed my mother's reality and confirmed for me how slowly things change. This woman explained how she was acutely aware of her church's attitude against dancing, but she still wanted very much to learn to dance. She would leave her after-school dance class and go directly to a church youth meeting. There she stuffed her dance shoes into a brown paper bag and hid it in the back of her locker, always fearful she would be found out. It caused a great deal of conflict in her life then and even later, between feelings of guilt and feeling betrayed.

These two stories inspired me to dig deeper into the past to find out why dance was viewed so negatively by the established church and why it has been kept so separate from certain religious traditions today. Frankly, I did not expect to find much about dance in Christianity when I began my search, but as my pursuit of understanding turned into the idea of writing a book on the subject, I was determined to uncover what Christians themselves might have to say about dance. I also wanted to glean whatever information I could that would shed light on the history and meaning of women's dance in particular. In my labyrinthine windings I found myself descending into the subterranean archival sections of the Union Theological Institute Library in Berkeley, California. Feeling somewhat like a spy at the time, I delved into their indexes. Surprisingly, I found journal articles turned yellow with age, unpublished theses, and paperback books written by others who had preceded me in earlier decades, searching and writing about liturgical dance within the context of the church. Following their guidance, I began to delve into ancient writings and am pleased to share with you some of the things I learned.

Any references to dance in the Bible will, of course, be open to a variety of interpretations. I have tried to include research from a wide spectrum of scholars who have shown interest in the subject of dance in order to highlight information that a lay person would not normally be able to access from reading the versions of the Bible available to us today.

The Israelites Were a Dancing People

From the pioneering work of W. O. E. Oesterley, D.D., Vicar of St. Alban's, Examining Chaplain to the Bishop of London, and author of *The Sacred Dance*,[2] and the contemporary research of Mayer I. Gruber (*Ten Dance-Derived Expressions in the Hebrew Bible*)[3] and others, we learn that the Old Testament language contains more than eleven verbs to express the idea of dancing and various types of dance. For example, *Hagg* (*Haji* or *Hajii* in Arabic), the word for pilgrimage festival, has been thought to be a circumambulating dance—also well known in Arabia. Indeed, the name of a festival is sometimes the same as the name of its dance (i.e., *Hagg ha Asiph Sukkot* is the harvest festival dance done as Sukkot).

The Hebrew word *chôlelthî*, usually translated "brought forth," can also mean to turn in a circle, whirl, twist, reel, or be in the labor of childbirth. The Hebrew word for circle dance, *cholla*, is based on this and can also mean to bear a child. Behind this is the root CHL, which refers to any effort to extend the self, to develop, or to stretch. It also stands for hope and expectation.[4]

It is now thought that the mysterious term *Selah* (from *tzala*, which refers to ritual steps) at the end of the Psalms means, "Having sung, now dance."[5] Similarly, the words *al mahalath*, meaning "according to *mahalath*," that appear in the headings of two Psalms are musical directions and suggest that some form of dance, as well as singing, was to be performed.[6] Another word that indicates dance in the Psalms is *mahol* (Akkadian *melultu*), which connotes highly active movements such as turning or whirling. Some other word roots (intensive verbs) that indicate dance are *sabab, raqad, qippes, dilleg, kirker, pizzez, pisseah, sala, siheq,* and *hagag*.

I was surprised to learn that dancing was a common element in worship because when I read the Bible I didn't see passages specifically mentioning dance. Dr. Oesterley illustrates how later revisions and reinterpretations obscured the original meanings of Hebrew texts in his analysis of Psalm 48:11–13: "Let Mount Zion rejoice, let the Daughters of Judah be glad, because of thy judgments. Walk about Zion, and go round about her; tell the towers thereof. Mark ye well her bulwarks, consider her palaces; that ye may tell it to the generation following. For this God is our God for ever and ever: he will be our guide even until death." Oesterley says: "In a Midrash exegetical exercise of a typically Rabbinical type on Psalms 48:13, 14 (14, 15 in Hebrew) we are told that the words 'Mark well her bulwarks' should be rendered 'Direct your heart to the dance'; for instead of *lehelah* [bulwarks] one must read *lehulah* [to the dance]. It is said, further, that in that day the righteous shall point with their fingers and say, 'This is our God, who will lead us,' i.e. in the dance." Oesterley then explains that the last word of the Psalm, *`al-muth* (unto death), should be read *'alamôth* (Maidens), i.e., "God will lead the dance of the righteous in the world to come just as the Maidens lead the dance in this world."[7] This provides us with evidence that the passage was not only about dance, but about women performing ritual dance.

Who were the "Daughters" or "Maidens" alluded to in these passages? Dr. John Stainer, writing in 1879, provided a very strong clue about *Alamoth* as referred to in 1 Chronicles 15, 19–21 and Psalms 68:25: "For *Alamoth*, while meaning maidens or 'those kept apart,' was very probably the title of a school or company of trained female singers and dancers attached to the religious worship of the Jews. In Egypt at the present day the *Al'meh* is a highly cultivated singer and performer—a truly 'learned woman' as the Arabic name now implies—far removed from the common low-caste dancing girls (*ghawazee*)."[8]

"Praise him with the timbrel and dance . . ." The daughters of Zion go forth in dances. Illustration by Gustave Doré.

Dance is also implied in phrases like "let them exult before God; let them be jubilant with joy" (Psalms 68:4). Prophesying by the earlier prophets was quite often the result of whirl dancing—*kirkur*, or KRKR in Biblical Hebrew and in Ugaritic—as in 1 Samuel 10:5 and 1 Chronicles 15:1. This is also seen in 1 Chronicles 25:1: "who should prophesy with harps, with psalteries, and with cymbals."[9]

Doug Adams, professor of Christianity and the Arts at the Pacific School of Religion in Berkeley, California, found in his survey of Hebrew scriptures that group dance was normal in worship, and that although communal dance was not always a dance to God, when it was included in Israelite worship, dance took a communal form. Adams points out that dance was a metaphor for harmonious community. "The Hebrew language suggests that actual dance may lead to a sense of community. The Hebrews recognized the need for the people to dance literally with all their might to achieve this end."[10]

Did Israelite Women Dance?

Writers and interpreters of the Bible do not always make it clear whether women are included in its references to dance. And yet, *The Catholic Encyclopedia*, when describing various situations in the Bible that refer to people dancing—including the dancing around the golden calf (Exodus 22:19), the inhabitants of the cities dancing to appease the army commanded by Holofernes, even people dancing around the Ark—explains that from these various places "it might be inferred that dancing was a manifestation of joy ordinarily exhibited by women,"[11] meaning that dancing was the domain of women. Other biblical passages that reveal the dances of women include Psalms 68:25, which says, "The singers went before, the players on instruments followed after; among them were the damsels playing with timbrels." This passage clearly indicates a procession that would include dancing. A less obvious example is found in 1 Chronicles 25:5, where the three daughters of Heman, with their fourteen brothers, assisted their father, who was a singer in David's reign, with cymbals, psalteries, and harps for the service in the house of the Lord. Although the actual word *dance* does not appear, scholars now agree that these activities were centered on dance rituals. In Canaan, the land where the Israelites settled, cylinder seals used between the time of Abraham and that of Solomon show female temple personnel mediating in rituals that included dance alongside rulers and the deity they address.

There are also enigmatic references to dance as a feminine force by the prophets. Jeremiah 31:4: "Again will I build you, O Virgin of Israel: thou shall again be adorned with thy tabrets and shall go forth in the dances"; and 31:13: "Then shall the Virgin rejoice in the dance." These types of sparse fragments are often the only documentation available.

A 16th-century Kabbalistic story confirms, although in a negative way, the dance of women.[12] It recounts an annual encounter in the desert between Lilith, the first wife of Adam, and Mahalath, the daughter of an Egyptian sorcerer, who was said to have been a "compulsive dancer" because her name means "turning," or "whirlwind."* As

*Since Biblical names often have additional meanings that connote a religious title or story, it may be no coincidence that the granddaughters of both Abraham (Genesis 28:9) and David (2 Chronicles 11:18) were also named Mahalath, for they may have been princess/priestesses or prophetesses who performed the whirling ritual.

found in Genesis 1:15, the word Lilith (*laîlah*), from the Hebrew root LL or LIL, points to all circular movement that magnetically draws toward and away from a center.[13] In the story, Lilith marches into the desert at the head of her bands of destructive angels or demons and "goes into dances and gyrates in ring dances" in an attempt to terrify her enemy—or at least that is the way the writer interpreted it. Knowing how stories are changed over the years to accommodate current idiom, I like to imagine that there was an earlier version that illustrated how these two great goddesses danced *together* to join the two communities of Israel and Egypt. In any case, it must have been a dance of great power.

The Dance of Judith

Judith was another biblical woman who danced. The Book of Judith (which for a while was left out of the books that make up the Bible) tells how Judith was crowned with an olive wreath and "went before all the people in the land, leading all the women," a phrase clearly indicative of ritual dance. Judith is known in the Bible as Jael, a Kenite (a tribe who were descendants of Moses' in-laws). She was an associate of the prophet and judge Deborah, who held court outdoors, on the top of a hill, at a place called "Deborah's Palm Tree."

The Daughters of Shiloh Come Out to Dance in Dances . . .

A story in the Book of Judges, 20 and 21, tells us about women's dance from about 1100 B.C.E. Although the story in its entirety is one of war and mayhem between Israelite tribes, a portion reveals the women dancing the harvest festal, the *Hagg ha Asiph Sukkot*.

We enter the story when, after killing all the women and children of the Benjamites, the men of Israel realized they could not let one of their tribes disappear. So they kidnapped 400 virgins for the Benjamites from another tribe, the Ja'bes-gil'e-ad. When they found that was not enough, the Israelites told the Benjamites they could go capture the Daughters of Shiloh for their use. "Then they said, Behold, there is a feast of the Lord in Shiloh yearly . . . Go and lie in wait in the vineyards; and see, and, behold, if the Daughters of Shiloh come out to dance in dances, then come ye out of the vineyards, and catch you every man his wife of the Daughters of Shiloh, and go to the land of Benjamin."

The place where the Daughters of Shiloh met for their annual harvest ritual was called *Abelmeholah*, "the field of dancing" (1 Kings 19:16) because of the festival dancing that took place there regularly.[14] Shiloh at that time was the chief sanctuary of Israel and was located in Canaan, which indicates these women were probably priestesses.

Shekinah—The Spirit of Divine Dance

References to the Shekinah (the Divine Mother) bring forth other insights into women's dance as spiritual expression and the unique attributes of the Divine Feminine that we will explore. In the Jewish trajectory that developed after the close of the biblical canon, the Spirit of the Divine typically came to be spoken of in the feminine symbol of the Shekinah. The term derived from the Hebrew verb *shakhan*, "to dwell," or "indwelling" a synonym for divine presence among the people (in contrast to male gods who ruled from mountaintops or the high heavens).[15]

MIRIAM, LEADER OF THE DANCE. FROM DETAIL OF ILLUSTRATION BY GUSTAVE DORÉ.

Manifestation of the Shekinah as the source of vitality is often described by expressions of movement: covering the earth like a mist or fire, radiant light that descends, radiance that flashes out in unexpected ways in the midst of a broken world, overshadowing or hovering as a mother bird, descending as a dove. She was before the beginning, she moved throughout the creation. "She reaches mightily from one end of the earth to the other, and she orders all things well" (Proverbs 8:1). The Shekinah was always inviting and leading her people, journeying with them even into exile. She sent her maidens, her priestesses, out to invite the people to come to her, an indication of inviting people to join her in the dance.

In ancient Hebrew scripts, the symbolic stones called the *Urim* and *Thummin* used by priests to answer questions and tell the future (*Urim*, revelation; *Thummin*, means of communication) were also used in a ritual associated with the Shekinah that was composed of chants of praise and prayer with ritual dances and gestures. Always circular in shape, the dance measured the sacred surface; the "count" of steps or degrees gave the days and years. This ritual later became a mechanical Wheel of Sun for telling fortunes by the Levites.

Miriam's Dance of Freedom

While we usually focus on the exodus as the escape of the Israelites from captivity, with pursuing armies and new lands, the story also includes a recounting of an important women's dance ritual. Exodus 15:20 describes how, once Moses led the Jews safely across the Red Sea, "Miriam the prophetess, the sister of Aaron and Moses, took a timbrel in her hand and all the women went out after her with timbrels and with dances." Miriam was also a religious leader, and the dance was a religious or ritual dance, not just a celebration or spontaneous expression. The phrase "the women went out after her" tells us it was a female rite, possibly one they learned from the Egyptian priestesses in the temple of Isis. Rabbi Lynn Gottlieb, in her book *She Who Dwells Within: A Feminist Vision of A Renewed Judaism*, also confirms this was a female rite because the word *maholot* in this story, meaning "round dance," appears only as a women's dance (Exodus 15:20).[16]

Miriam's dance was an essential and indispensable part of the festival commemorating the exodus and became one of the climactic ceremonies of the ancient Hebrew Passover festival, *Pesach* or *Pesah*, called the *Hagg Mazzoth,* sacred dance of the pilgrim.[17] The purpose of the *Pesach* festal or dance was the letting go of and forgetting a troubled past, a ritual also associated with the Midianites or Kenites, who worshipped the Great Mother in the copper mines of Sinai.[18] In Hebrew tradition it is also prophesied that at the great banquet in the time of the Messiah, Miriam will dance before the righteous.[19]

Rejoice and Dance! The Christian Tradition

Throughout the centuries, in countless churches, clergy and people wound sacred dance around the sober core of Christian orthodoxy. In Aramaic, the language spoken by Jesus, *rejoice* and *dance* are the same word. Hence, Jesus is quoted in Luke 6:23: "Rejoice and leap for joy!" The *New English Bible* translates the phrase as "dance for joy."[20]

Many early Christian groups (1–400 C.E.) adapted, incorporated, or brought with them customs from other cultures in the Mediterranean area, including the traditional use of dance as an integral aspect of worship.[21] Philo (about 30 C.E.) wrote of the use of dance by the Therapeutae, Christian Jews ascribed by Augustine to the Priscillian sect, which flourished in Spain. In their services, men and women stood to dance: "they then chant hymns in many metres and melodies, sometimes in chorus, sometimes one hand beating time to the answering chant; now dancing to its music, now in processional hymns . . . turning and returning in the dance. . . ."[22] Dance also often accompanied services in the Eastern churches, continuing this early Christian tradition, as seen in Byzantine art.

Perhaps the most well-known people to make use of dance were the Gnostics in Greece, in Asia Minor, and around Rome, who traveled in missions throughout Europe and even to Britain. In the Gnostic Acts 1, seven handmaidens are described as dancing a ring dance before Sophia, Daughter of Light. The "Hymn of Jesus" described in the Gnostic *Acts of John*

EARLY CHURCH PROCESSIONS INCLUDED DANCE AS AN INTEGRAL PART OF WORSHIP.

SOULS DANCING WITH ANGELS IN PARADISE. DETAIL FROM *THE LAST JUDGMENT* BY FRA ANGELICO, C. 1430.

tells how Jesus, anticipating arrest, gathered his followers into a circle, holding hands, to dance, while he stood in the center, intoning a mystical chant. As late as the fourth century, the "Hymn of Jesus" was still regarded as a ritual of initiation.

To the Universe belongs the
dancer—Amen.
He who does not dance does not
know what happens—Amen.
Now if you follow my dance, see
yourself in Me who am
speaking
You who dance, consider what I
do, for yours is
This passion of Humanity which I
am to suffer.
For you could by no means have
understood what you suffer
Unless to you as Logos I had been
sent by the Father.
Learn how to suffer and you shall
be able not to suffer.[23]

In a vision that same night, Jesus told John that he had transcended the cross, and "even that suffering which I showed to you and to the rest in the dance, I will that it be called a mystery."

Although Pope Leo the Great (c. 447) later condemned the *Acts of John* because of its Gnostic associations, a small part survived in the canonical Bible in the text of Matthew 10:16, where Jesus asks, "but whereunto shall I liken this generation? It is like unto children sitting in the markets, and calling unto their fellows, and saying, We have piped unto you and ye have not danced; we have mourned unto you, and ye have not lamented."

The Chorale, The Carol

The Hymn of Jesus is just one example of the integral role of dance in liturgical chants and songs. Although we think of the word *chorale* as meaning only a "hymn tune" or "sacred melody," sources published in 1524 show that the original form of chorale was a much more impressive rhythmic form of movement, with an irregularity of phrasing and meter.[24] The word *choros*, the Greek term for the choir that sang, spoke, and danced with the purpose of intensifying a mood, reveals the important role of dance in early Christian rituals.

The connection of liturgical dance to the carole, or circle, is illustrated in the paintings of the Middle Ages. In Fra Angelico's (c. 1400–1455) "Dance of the Redeemed," part of *The Last Judgment,* choruses of angels glide along the spheres, while saints, angels, and blessed figures dance through flowery fields upward to heaven.[25] It was the chorale or *Reigen* dance that was always depicted in these pastoral scenes in heaven: a sacred circle dance dating from prehistoric times.

Other manuscripts from before the 13th century also describe the carol in dance form. The Italian *Carolare* was originally a medieval ring dance or round dance that was accompanied by singing. It survived in that form into the Middle Ages[26] and was also performed at the seasonal ceremonies we now know as Easter, May Day, and Christmas. The chorale later became a chorus or group of people singing while standing still.

Church built over Eileithyia cave, the temple of the goddess Eileithyia. Crete. This site is typical of other goddess sites usurped by Christians. Photograph by Iris Stewart.

Dances of the Church

Early church leaders wanted to incorporate the familiar practices of the older Goddess traditions to ease the transition to the new Christian religion for its followers. Many of the Church's observances of holy days were at similar times as the Goddess celebrations. As Christianity spread throughout Europe, the Middle East, and Asia Minor, churches were built over the caves and on the shrines and temple sites of the Goddess. The church also borrowed the use of familiar symbols—the bell, candles, incense—as well as the use of dance from these older traditions. Dance for the ancestors and for the departed was an ancient custom that was readily converted to special festivals for martyrs and saints, usually celebrated outdoors.

In the early church, Christians danced in processions and in the interiors of churches and basilicas. A homily written at the close of the 4th century, on the anniversary of the martyrdom of Polyeucte, talked about "our customary dances." Such dancing was sometimes recommended with zeal and defended with vigor, as testified by the Councils of Auxere (c. 585), Chalonsur-Saône (639–654), Rome (826), and others.[27]

The bishop also led liturgical dance in the gallery above the altar in the early church. Dance as a means of linking the faithful to the angels and souls in Heaven was praised by St. Basil, Bishop of Caesarea in the 4th century: "Could there be anything more blessed than to imitate on earth the ring dance of the angels, and at dawn to raise our voices in prayer and by hymns and songs to glorify the rising Creator."*[28] "In Latin, the prelates (bishops) were called *praesules*, for in the choir, at the divine office, they played the same part as the leader of the dances," wrote Menestrier, a Jesuit in Paris in 1682.[29] It was thought that during Divine Service, especially at Mass, the angels were present in the choir participating with Christ in the performance of the Mystery.

Clearly, there was an ongoing acknowledgment of the transforming power of dance in praise. There was the recognition of a need to fuse the spiritual with the physical and also to transform dance to be symbolic of Christian ideals. During the greater part of the first thousand years, many dance forms were associated with the church. The *ballet d'action* (story ballet) was served in the Mass before the altar, and the "moralities" was a method of spiritual instruction. In fact, one historian has said, "The institution that had conserved choreography through the brutishness of the Dark Ages was the Church."[30]

The Decline of Dance

As time passed, however, the church grew more and more ambivalent about dance.[31] Agnes DeMille, dancer, choreographer, and dance historian, said that theologians, feeling that dancing was distracting and too often suggestive of impious and worldly ideas, began to root it out of holy ritual. Christianity focused more and more on repentance and the subduing of the flesh, which many viewed as opposed to the spirit. St. Augustine's claimed spiritual experience in which he opened the Pauline Epistles and read the words

**Ballo dei angeli*, dance of the angels, was said to be the principal pastime in heaven.

Woodcut of a bridge collapsing under a group of "sacrilegious" dancers while their priest crosses safely. Maastricht, the Netherlands. Private collection: Debra and Madison Sowell.

"But put ye on the Lord Jesus Christ, and make not provision for the flesh, to fulfill the lusts thereof" became the preamble for the Church's condemnation of all dancing.[32]

In the establishment of hierarchy and movement toward the power of the written word, the spoken Mass took prominence. Doug Adams explains that the Roman Catholic objection to popular participation in dance actually reveals a political dimension of dancing "as the hierarchy came to recognize the power of the communal dance. The superior position that Roman Catholic clergy developed over the laity by restricting all forms of lay participation required that dancing be suppressed as too equalizing and revolutionary."[33]

The splitting off of art forms such as dance from spiritual expression also coincided with the developing philosophy that denied mortal connections to, and dependence upon, nature. A gradual transformation occurred from the mystery rites of overt devotional expression to the presentation of specific quest dramas with predictable predetermined outcomes. This was accompanied by an elevation of the intellectual over the intuitive, leading to a compartmentalized collective psyche. The transformation of the image of the Divine as a male god, while denying the feminine Divine, was the outcome.

Organized religion moved more and more into the hierarchical and rational, asceticism and theology, and the spontaneity of movement as ecstasy and rapture was deemphasized or even

DEATH LEADS THE MAIDENS.

suppressed. The remnants of the old sacred ceremonies continued to be performed in the village squares at holidays by the people, but often without an understanding of their significance.[34] Instead, the performance of bawdy dances and slapstick comedy grew and gained popularity as a separate genre in the theater atmosphere; carnivals and circuses arose in place of religious festivals.

The one dancer still officially permitted in the Christian religion, however, was the Devil.[35] In the Middle Ages, owing to injunctions against dancing by the church fathers, the Devil alone was allowed to be portrayed dancing in works of art. As a close cousin to the Roman Stultus or Stupidus, or the cloven-hoofed satyr of Greek plays, Satan and his minions, the Vices, tempted and tripped up the main characters, such as Adam and Eve, in Christian miracle plays. Satan also became the dance partner of the witch's sabbath.

Still, the People Danced

Dr. Curt Sachs, one of the world's foremost authorities on the history of the dance, found that the Church inevitably failed to stop the people from dancing.[36] When people could no longer dance in the church, they still danced in the churchyard and the cemetery for some time. Thus developed the *Danse Macabre*, or dance of the dead.* Whether this dance was linked to the ancient Hebraic or Egyptian funeral dance and dance for the ancestor is hard to say.† In France, the *Danse de Misere* (also called *Danse Triste*) was a popular performance of a Dance of the Dead (a line dance). This dance was often performed in the town church of St. John at Besancon in 1393 and was revived in 1453.

"What is revealed in these dances," says Sachs, "is . . . a piece of ecstatic inner life, which since the Stone Age has been disguised and concealed through innumerable racial influxes but never extinguished, and which must break out through all restraints at the favorable moment."[37]

Christianity, in fact, was not totally united in its antipathy toward dance. A renaissance of sacred dance appeared in the late 14th century in Germany. A sect developed called the *Chorizantes* with a membership in the thousands, including both genders, who danced

*The Arabic word *makabr* or *Magh Arba* was the formal symbol of the "Great Square," a design often found in church, temple, and castle courtyards as the symbol of the World of Humankind, or Earth, with all the multiples of four symbols.

†Ancient Egyptian funerary dances were traditionally performed in honor of the deceased and were a ritual for the enlightenment of the soul on its journey to the other world.

through the streets and in and out of churches. They first appeared during the festival of John the Baptist at Aachen in 1374 and then spread to Cologne, Metz, and other parts of Germany. Boys and girls also danced on the altar for the Christ Child in English church Christmas festivals as late as the reign of King Henry VIII (1509–1547). Mediterranean countries and the Orient also maintained liturgical dance in some form.[38] In the southern part of Italy and in France, dancing in the church could be found well into the 17th century. Religious church dances also continued in places like the Basque provinces of Spain, Seville, the Coptic Christian Church in Abyssina, and to some degree in the Greek Orthodox Church. The dancing procession at one of the medieval pilgrimage centers, the tomb of St. Willibrord at Echternach in Luxembourg, survived into the early 20th century, ceasing only at the time of the First World War.[39]

It was not until after the Protestant Reformation began that the Council of Trent (1545–1563), combined with Luther's opposition or at best ambivalence to dance, became the sounding of the death knell for liturgical dance. Dancing was totally banned from the Roman Catholic Church in the 16th century, followed by the Greek Orthodox Church, Church of England (Episcopalian), Church of Scotland (Presbyterian), and Calvinist, Lutheran, and Quaker religious bodies, although male priests were still allowed to perform dance as part of the Mass for some time. Solemn processionals led by the bishop or pope, with choirs standing in place and singing, became the format that has prevailed to the present day.

In this painting at the cathedral in Pienza, Italy, real women, not angels, circle St. Mary and dance. Photograph by Sara Silver.

And What of the Dance of Christian Women?

After seeing how the Church tried to remove all forms of dance from its religious services and practices, I was not surprised to find that women dancing and worshipping in their own way, whether in the public congregation or in private ceremonies in their homes,

Absorbing the Competition

The Catholic Church absorbed several divinities of indigenous people by transforming them into saints. For example, the Triple Goddess became the "three Marys" associated with Jesus, the goddess Brighde became St. Brigit, and Artemis became Saint Artemidos. Venus of Eryx, the most powerful and loved deity in ancient Sicily, was turned into Saint Venera. She was said to have wiped the face of Jesus with her scarf or veil, and danced before Christ in heaven.[47] "O Santa Venera, si´ bella, si´ tenera, che in Paradiso, Tripa avanti Gesu" (Oh Saint Venera, lovely lady who lives in Paradise and dances in front of Jesus). A statue of St. Veronica in St. Peter's Basilica in Rome shows her turning with her veil.

St. Veronica's veil dance. St. Peter's Basilica, Rome. Photograph by Sara Silver.

was an ongoing conflict for the church hierarchy. One early example of this dates back to the 4th century C.E. with assemblies or associations of women called Collyridians. These women worshipped Mary as a form of the Divine Feminine with dance and a feast that included little round cakes called *colenruada*, or *collyrides*, a ritual derived from far back before Christianity.[40] In fact, worship of Mary in her own right as a form of the Divine Feminine originated with these women. The Collyridian assemblies began in Thrace, located between present-day Greece and Turkey, which is the place where the Maenads are said to have come from. Assemblies similar to the Collyridians were widespread in the lands west and north of the Black Sea, Scythia, and Arabia, although there is no evidence that it was an organized movement of any sort. Theodoretos, a Syrian churchman (393–457 C.E.), wrote in his *On Hereticks* that "In Alexandria . . . they sing hymns to accompaniment of hand-clapping and dancing."[41] They also used mesmeric energy to heal the sick.* Perhaps here was the ancient practice of the Zar or similar healing dances.

These women were a problem for the establishment, and their name eventually became a term of derision.

*These ecstatic or healing dances were later labeled madness or possession.[42]

Ephiphanius, bishop of Salamis in Cyprus about 374 C.E., wrote in his book *Panarion* (Medicine-Chest) that the Collyridians worshipped Mary as Queen of Heaven—as a goddess. He listed eighty heresies in his book; Heresy No. 79 was aimed at these women, saying that, after so many generations, women should not once again be appointed priests. About Mary he said, "[God] gave her no charge to minister baptism or bless disciples, nor did he bid her rule over the earth."

The bishop's concern about worship of the Divine Feminine had long before been similarly expressed by Jeremiah in the Old Testament (Jeremiah 7:18) about those who worshipped in women's ways and made such offerings to the Queen of Heaven: Astarte (also known as Ashtoreth or Ashtaroth), which would have included dance. In Jeremiah 44:15–19, the people were rebuked by the prophet, but the women declared that they intended to continue on the same course, to burn incense to the Queen of Heaven, as their people had previously done, and that they saw no evil in such a practice.

Basil the Great, Bishop of Caesarea in the 4th century, like Augustine and others, while praising dance as religious expression, condemned those dances performed by women as having "frivolous and indecent movements." The church consistently reacted strongly against dances by women, whether they were danced in the church or at the graves of martyrs.[43] The Stone Dance of British folklore was represented by the ancient stone circles such as the Merry Maidens at Boleigh in West Cornwall, which were said to be women turned to stone for dancing on the Sabbath.[44]

There were also condemnations of related arts for women. In the 4th century, Augustine sermonized: "Oh how times and manners change! What once was the business of lute-players and shameless women only, namely to sing and to play, this is now considered an honor among Christian virgins and matrons who even engage masters in the art to teach them."[45]

From earliest times, however, women found a way to dance. Prohibited from dancing in the church, they danced in their homes. They also

The etymology of the word *rant*, from the Latin *orante*, carries with it some interesting information about the perception of women's sacred dance. *Orante (adorante)* was a chant-dance form adopted into early Christian ritual from the Greek *ora*, or hours (hora).[46] Figures of the *orante* are seen in the Roman catacomb paintings, and the dancers were often women. The dance was marked by much gesture and movement.

By the time the word reached England, however, the term *rant*—to talk at excessive length and with excitement—was all that remained. On a positive note, though, the word *oratory* comes from a secular use of this sacred ritual, as the mystery teachings moved into the theater as *oratoria*, a sung mode of drama that eventually developed into the opera.

danced inside the walls of seclusion of convents. The spanish mystic St. Teresa of Avila (1515–1582), who, in spite of intense opposition during the Inquisition, reformed the Carmelite Order and founded seventeen convents throughout Spain, said the nuns "danced with holy joy." On feast days she would hand out castanets and tambourines so that the sisters could rejoice by dancing. Teresa herself played drums and the tambourine. In the 17th century, two other noted Carmelites imitated St. Teresa: Bienheureuse Marie del' Incarnation and Anne de Jesus, who danced before *le Saint Sacrement* at Carmel in Dijon.[48]

The nuns of Villaceaux in France celebrated the feasts of the Holy Innocents and Mary Magdalene with dances. Because the name *Magdalene* is derived from *amygdal* or *almond*, I wonder if they might have danced the Allemand. The Allemand, known so well to square-dancers today, is a spiral formed by two lines of dancers: the first two dancers extend and join right hands as they pass each other and then extend and join their left hands with the next person down the line moving toward them as they spiral their way from the head of the line to the end. This folk dance came from English and/or German salon dance variations, which are also called Allemande, Almond; or Alman, Almaye, or Allemagne in France.[49] The Allemand also descended from the ritual dance for the festival of Al-Monde, celebrated at the Feast of the Assumption on August 15 in conjunction with the *Sacratissima Cintola della Madonna*. The dance was originally the dance of the almond.

The almond is a very significant religious symbol and has some interesting connections to women and their ritual dances. The almond tree was a symbol of new life, or spring, the almond flower being the first flower to appear after winter. The almond shape was a female-genital symbol from very ancient times, again connected with the emergence of new life. Aaron's rod sprouted almond leaves in token of power through fructification (Numbers 17:8), and even the Israelite tabernacle used this fertility symbol (Exodus 37:20). Caryatids form the pillar supports in the Acropolis in Athens in remembrance of the Divine Daughter Car (Kore) as almond tree.

The almond shape was also the *mandorla* known as *vesica piscis*, the Vessel of the Fish, used by Christian artists to frame the figures of saints, the Virgin Mary, and Christ. A European mandala of a three-dimensional carving entitled "Allemande Ritual Dance" by the Gislebertus Guild oversees the West Porch of the 12th-century Autun Cathedral in France. In ovoid form (almandala), it shows four dancing angels moving away and toward the central, large holy figure.

Given that the name *Magdalene* is derived from *almond*, it is perhaps no coincidence that Magdalene was with Jesus for his spring equinox resurrection—his rebirth—which we call Easter. According to the *Dictionary of the Dance*, Mary Magdalene was a ritual dancer, and in the 15th century in France, a ceremonial dance called *Marie Magdaleine* was still performed on Easter Monday, recounting the meeting of Mary with Jesus. In spite of vigorous synodal diocesan decrees of

1585 and 1601, which threatened severe penalties for the continuation of ancient customs, the dance was still in full force at Ste. Marie Magdaleine's Church, performed in the nave in rainy weather, until 1662.[50] Even after the custom ceased in the church, it was performed outside. It eventually turned into a hymn, "Hail, Festal Day," as the choir circled the cloister three times.

Religion and Dance in America

As I delved deeper and deeper into the subject of sacred dance, I soon discovered that I was not the only one puzzled by the opposition of the major Western religions to dance and determined to find out why. Ann Wagner, professor in the Department of Dance and chair of the Fine Arts Division at St. Olaf College in Minnesota, researched more than 350 American primary source books and tracts, in addition to periodical literature, for her book *Adversaries of Dance: From the Puritans to the Present.*[51] Following a trail starting in the mid-1600s with the Puritan cleric Increase Mather into the present century, Wagner's research helped me understand the cultural influences at various times in history and why, for instance, my mother had to choose between the church and dancing.

The period beginning after the Civil War and lasting into the early 1900s witnessed a time of great change in the United States. There was a mass influx of immigrants who brought with them their varying religious convictions, the rise of cities, and shifts in the social order due to greater economic opportunities. The growth and status of older Protestant denominations were threatened by these events. Conservatives feared the growing trend toward liberalism and education within their own congregations. This resulted in the rise of fundamentalism, as the banner of hellfire and brimstone evangelists like Dwight L. Moody (1837–1899) was taken up by Samuel Porter Jones (1847–1906), William A. "Billy" Sunday (1863–1935), and others

AUBREY BEARDSLEY'S *SALOME,* 1894. SALOME WAS OFTEN CITED AS PROOF OF THE UNLAWFUL BEHAVIOR THAT WOULD RESULT FROM DANCING.

in the South. As concern grew about the spread of urbanization, affluence, and the accompanying amusements available to more and more people, social dance became a symbol of the loss of puritanical church control over people's lives. Dance as a part of religious expression was not even a consideration at this time—the ancient tie between religion and dance had long been severed.

The big problem for these fundamentalist adversaries of dance, as Wagner points out, was the control of women:

> Dance opponents, almost without exception for several centuries, were male. This point should be reexamined in light of the fact that opposition concentrated on moral and spiritual arguments. . . . Dance opponents cast women as either pure and pious or fallen and sinful. If the former, they were to be protected from the dance. If the latter, they were associated with dancing, either as victims of its evils or as perpetrators of its evils by their role as temptress, "taxi-dancer," or prostitute. . . . Over the centuries, adversaries' citations of Salome's dancing as proof of the art's unlawfulness further confirmed this fear.

Wagner also said, "Resorting to a strategy of threat and fear in trying to get parishioners to avoid dancing served to reinforce that traditional authoritarianism." Of course my mother, that little sixteen-year-old girl down in Mississippi, had no way of knowing that she was the innocent victim of this phenomenon.

RIGHT: THE PRAYER OF THE DANCE. LEAVEN DANCE COMPANY. PHOTOGRAPH BY RAY BLACK.

Reclaiming the Sacred Dimension

In reclaiming our connection to sacred dance, we reclaim spiritual expression. One of the many examples of this is the description by Jane Litman, feminist writer and Judaic scholar, of her experience during the celebration of Simchat Torah in Mea Shearim (the ultra-Orthodox Jerusalem neighborhood) in 1976.[52] Because of her deep disappointment at being excluded from the Simchat Torah devotional dance, Litman felt a divine insight—a picture provided by God, as she put it. She wrote, "This Rosh Hashana I celebrated with a group of women. . . . We read and sang outdoors, under an arbor of oak trees and danced until midnight the dances our mothers have danced with each other for three millennia. We blew the shofar and listened to its haunting melody fade into the soft darkness. We sang *henaia mah tov u' mah nayim shevot achiot gam yachad,* how good it is when sisters sit together." Their ceremonial included blessing and affirmation. They wove a web of yarn "in and out our fingers, back and forth across the circle, each time reaffirming our pride as women and our connection to the Eternal One, blessed be She."

From this experience, a powerful truth emerged for Litman—the connection between dance and joy. "I suppose," Litman said, "I felt for my [Rosh Hashana] service a similar feeling to that which male Hasidim feel after they dance and pray all night—a feeling of tremendous joy and oneness with the Creator." In creating their own ceremony, she felt they as women

reclaimed their right to define themselves. They also reclaimed a direct knowledge of dance as women's spiritual expression.

We Are Dancing in the Church Today

When I traveled to the Pacific School of Religion in Berkeley, California, to research dance history, I was very excited to discover that Doug Adams, Carla DeSola, Cynthia Winton-Hiller, and others were actually teaching sacred dance and the arts at the college. I also discovered that there was a national Sacred Dance Guild, whose origins I describe in chapter 6, which was having its annual festival at the college in a few weeks. At this festival I learned that dance has returned to the church to some degree, in large part because of the diligent work and educational efforts of organizations like the Sacred Dance Guild, the International Christian Dance Fellowship in Australia, the Sacred Dance Ministries International in England, and others. In fact, a recent survey in *Dance Magazine* found churches in more than twenty-three denominations that now embrace dance in some form as a part of worship: Methodist, Lutheran, Catholic, Unitarian, Mennonite, and Russian Orthodox, as well as some Jewish synagogues.[53] Could it be that the return of dance as religious and spiritual expression coincides with the rise of women in leadership roles in the church?

I also discovered in my search the existence of sacred dance in other parts of the world today. Browsing the Internet brought me into direct contact with sacred circle dancers in England, Bulgaria, Italy, and other countries around the world, and a videotape entitled *The Dancing Church* by Dr. Thomas A. Kane, a Paulist priest, opened my eyes to the rich variety of dance found in many Catholic churches in Africa (Ethiopia, Zaire, Ghana, Malawi, and Cameroon)—dances adapted from traditional forms of worship.[54]

One very memorable segment from this videotape took place in Lilongwe, Malawi, showing the sisters and lay members of the Poor Clare community celebrating the Feast of Our Lady of Africa, *Misa Chimalawi*, with dance and song. The dance is not performed publicly but takes place in the chapel before the Marian statue. The Mass begins with prayers before the participants enter the sacred space. Once they are inside, there are prayers for the saints and ancestors to be present in the celebration. There is a hushed reverence to the a cappella singing. Percussive sounds of sifting grain and grinding mortars accompany movements of unified dance gestures, illustrative of the combining of holy work with holy worship. The danced Eucharistic Acclamation, a patterned step with arms raised and swaying side to side, is a moment of intense adoration and celebration.

Another ceremony in the monastary's sacred grove includes the fire dance as part of the psalm dance, which incorporates the presentation of bread and wine, prayer and song books, farm implements, and the fruits of the harvest. All are placed near the sacred fire. Holding lighted fire poles, turning and

Church embraces dance. Alleluia Dance Ensemble, Baton Rouge, LA. Photograph by Mildred Feldman.

Alleluia Dance Ensemble at First United Methodist Church, Lake Charles, LA. Dancers: Betty Woody, Anne Marks, and Leslie Akin. Photograph by Greg Smith.

moving in a spiral around each other, the dancers reenact the coming of the Word. Singers join in with praise to Mary: "We love you more than the drums of the evening, we the children of Africa want to praise you with great joy."

The Prayer of Dance

It is becoming more and more evident, both here in the United States and around the world, that liturgical dance can help us rediscover the profound human expression that communes with and draws us closer to the power of the Spirit of the Divine. Dance is particularly timely and suitable to worship today as more and more people begin to reaffirm the human body, recovering the body-spirit connections. This is not an abstract theory, as participants can attest who see and feel the power, the majesty, and the prayerfulness of dance in the context of liturgy.

Dance can express a deep sense of reverence, a profound participation in worship, arousing joy and union. Carlynn Reed wrote in her book *And We Have Danced:*

> Movement complements words as the vehicle of prayer expressing praise or confession, supplication or surrender. Spontaneous movement by one who seeks communion with God can flow from violent turbulence to a restful quiet. On the other hand, slow comfortable gestures might become full risk-taking movements as God challenges one to a prophetic ministry. Tears of joy or repentance may follow the prayer as the dancer yields a body willing to be transformed to the God who is willing to reveal. Movement before God is at the same time a tremendously courageous and humbling offering. One becomes vulnerable before a God who seeks such for His Kingdom—people willing to be molded as clay in His hands.[55]

The Sacred Dance Guild, founded in 1958 by Margaret Taylor-Doane, a student of Ruth St. Denis, has been one of the leaders in bringing dance back into worship. The Guild believes that sacred dance is a catalyst for spiritual growth and change through the integration of mind, body, and spirit. Through the Guild's workshops and other events, dancers and nondancers alike share the opportunity to experience movement as worship, prayer, healing, and meditation; as an agent of change; and as a message of peace. The movements in these sacred dances are not geared to any specific dance style or particular body techniques. Instead, they grow out of the dancer's inner motivation, which allows the revelation of the spirit through the body.

The goal of sacred dance is the integration of worship—whether as part of an established or traditional religious practice or as an individual's own private spiritual expression—by bringing forth and recognizing our own inner wisdom. It is tuning in to that "still quiet voice," flowing with the laws of harmony and beauty, honoring the body's wisdom, uniting the physical and the spiritual, the spirit and the mind. The self-generated ritual possible through dance may give fresh expression to prayer and mysticism when it is experienced through the aid of the arts, following the long tradition of worshippers we now know about who have gone before.

Now Let Us Dance

Think about the kind of dance you want to create. Ask yourself, "How would I dance to honor the sacred?" Will it be an expression of Joy? Thanksgiving? Love? What do I want to express about our Creator, the Source or Spirit, that would move me to dance in celebration? Your dance may be directed at an audience, telling them through movement a story or teaching. It may be a processional that others eventually join. It may be a personal expression of faith and incorporation of Spirit. Here are two sample dances that may inspire you to create more of your own.

Dance of Our Foremothers

In this dance we call forth the spirits of our foremothers, women whose lives are symbols of strength for us today. Join hands in a circle and begin with grapevine steps* to the right, while saying: "Lillith, Eve, and Hanna, from the very start; Blessed mother, sister, lover—take us to your heart." With hands still joined and walking forward to the center of the circle, bringing arms up: "Miriam, Rachel, Anna, Mary full of Grace." In place with arms above head: "Deborah of the Palm Tree." Release hands and turn back out to the original circle, with hands cupped before your face like a mirror: "Let us see your face." Stop in place, facing inside the circle, and bring hands to prayer pose: "Teach us your mercy, strength, and compassion." Sweeping hands, palms down, to connect with the hands of others on either side to reform the circle and taking grapevine steps to the right once again, say: "Let our dance anoint this holy place." Repeat the pattern three times.

Amazing Grace Dance

The numbers in parentheses are recommendations for the number of times to repeat the step. You may find the number of steps or counts you need to do will vary according to the style of the music you use, i.e., how many notes the singer uses in a phrase. A gospel singer, for example, may stretch "amazing grace" into five to seven syllables.

---

*The grapevine step is a sidestep used in traditional folk dances of the Middle East and Europe. If you are moving to the right, put your L foot behind the R, step sideways with the R, then step in front of R foot with the L, step to side with R, etc. Continue this pattern as you link hands or shoulders. Reverse to go in the opposite direction.

You may choose to sing your own heartfelt version as you dance.

In a circle, holding hands, dance to the phrases:

Amazing Grace Face to the right, walking counterclockwise, slowly, R, L (5)
How sweet the sound Face center and slide feet R, together, R (4), the circle still moving counter clockwise
That saved a wretch Rock forward into the center of the circle on L, back on R (4)
Like me. Slide clockwise L, together, L (2)
I once was lost (Repeat dance pattern)
But now am found
Was bound
But now am free.

On the next verse, repeat steps:

Twas Grace that taught / my heart to fear, / and Grace my fears / relieved; / How precious did / that Grace appear, / the hour / I first believed.

4

WomanDance

In ancient Egypt, the ab, one of the seven souls, was supposed to come directly from the mother's heart, in the form of holy lunar blood that descended into her womb to take the shape of her child. The hieroglyphic sign for this eminently matriarchal idea was a dancing figure, representing the inner dance of life perceived in the heartbeat. As long as the dance continued, life went on.

Barbara G. Walker, The Woman's Dictionary of Symbols & Sacred Objects[1]

As an aficionada of what in this country is generally known as belly dance, I wanted to perform it but did not like the "patriarchal male gaze"* and the nightclub attitude toward the dancer. I established my own troupe, named it WomanDance, and chose my audience from among women's groups, libraries, and art fairs. I was careful to

*For more information on feminist "gaze theory" and the consequences of male gaze and voyeurism on women's dance, see Ann Daly, "Dance History and Feminist Theory: Reconsidering Isadora Duncan and the Male Gaze," in Laurence Senelick, ed., *Gender in Performance* (Hanover, NH: University Press of New England, 1992) pp. 239–259; Christ Adair, *Women and Dance: Sylphs and Sirens* (New York: New York University Press, 1992); Susan Manning, "Borrowing From Feminist Theory," in *Proceedings* (Riverside, CA: Society of Dance History Scholars, University of California, Riverside); Judith Butler, *Bodies That Matter: On the Discursive Limits of "Sex"* (New York: Methuen, 1984) and *Gender Trouble, Feminism and the Subversion of Identity* (New York: Routledge, 1990).

WomanDance is dance for women, by women, and for women's purposes. Women dance for each other is this woven Persian wall hanging. Author's collection.

explain the history and meaning of the dance for women, both in the cultural context from which it came and as an expressive art form for American women. From this I began my research and accumulation of information about women's dance traditions, which gradually developed into this book. What I found was an intricate, complex synchronicity between women, giving birth, dance, and the Divine.

Searching for Birth Dance Ritual

The traditional and private dance of women that, collectively, I call WomanDance has been referred to in a variety of ways by writers, researchers, and performers. It has been called muscle dance, convulsive dance, and stomach dance. The entertainment version as we see it today may be called *danse orientale*, oriental dance, or Middle Eastern dance.* It was dubbed "belly dance" (from the French *danse du ventre,* "dance of the abdomen") by the entrepreneur Sol Bloom, who brought the dancer he called Little Egypt, along with an exhibit of a "typical" Tunisian village, to the Chicago World's Fair in 1893. There is now a movement among performers of this dance to change the name to Oriental dance in

*Traditional Middle Eastern names for the belly dance are *raks sharki* or *raqs sharqi* (oriental dance), *raqs Masri* (Egyptian dance), *raqs beledi* (regional or folk style), or *raqs Arabi* (Arabian dance). *Raqs* means joy, or celebration, as well as dance, as do the Turkish *raklase* and the Syrian *rakadu*. *Rag* (*raga*) means "color" or "emotion" in Indian dance. The dance is known in Greece as the *cifti telli*, which is also the name of a Turkish rhythm.

order to remove the negative connotations of the name *belly dance*.[2]

I have seen night club performances and folkloric versions of Middle Eastern belly dance presented on the stage in Egypt, Turkey, Greece, and Morocco, as well many videotapes produced by dancers* who have lived, studied, and conducted research in the Middle East. Their challenge, like mine, has been to identify the real women's dance, its purpose, and its origin as opposed to the publicly presented versions.

Whereas nightclub audiences are exposed to a dance emphasizing sex and sensuality, the traditional Middle Eastern dancer performs in family groups to celebrate circumcisions, weddings, harvest festivals, or national holidays, and will instead stress abstract rhythmic intricacies and musical interpretation. The dance often includes a rhythmic dialogue between dancer and drummer, with the dancer displaying the skill of individualized muscular control.

I found that the belly dance came not from the harem, as is casually assumed, but was adapted from a traditional and private dance, a dance in celebration of womanhood, a dance by women and for women's purposes to celebrate the various stages of life. The following are eyewitness accounts of this ancient and enduring custom.

Rabbi Lynn Gottlieb, in her book *She Who Dwells Within: A Feminist Vision of a Renewed Judaism*, said, "Belly dancing has survived thousands of years as a remnant of women's religion . . . Jewish women from Middle Eastern cultures have kept the practice of belly dancing alive to this day. I have witnessed it in ceremonial contexts time and time again."[3]

In 1923, Armen Ohanian, an Armenian dancer from the Caucasus and a defender of Oriental dance, described the belly dance/birth ritual this way: "It was [a dance] of the mystery and pain of motherhood . . . In olden Asia which has kept the dance in its primitive purity, it represents the mysterious conception of life, the suffering and joy with which a new soul is brought into the world."[4]

Ethnic dancer and author La Meri also wrote about this dance form: "The seeker after knowledge in the East will often come upon conflicting opinions regarding the origins and beginnings of an art that has not been documented by the written word. When I studied in Fez in 1929, I was told by my teacher, Fatma, that the *danse du ventre* was of ritualistic origin and was, at that time, still performed at the bedsides of women in childbirth. She also told me that in its ritualistic form, men were not allowed to see the dance."[5]

Carolina Varga Dinicu, a New York City writer and dancer who is known by the name Morocco, was told by a Saudi Arabian dancer, Farab Firdoz, that the slower movements involving the abdominal muscles stem from one of the oldest religious dances, in which the movements imitate the contractions of labor and childbirth.[6] The dance is

BIRTHING, SYMBOLIZING THE UNIVERSAL PHASE OF CREATION. FROM C. 18TH CENTURY WOOD CARVING, SOUTH INDIA.

---

*An incomplete list of researchers, to whom I am most grateful, includes Aisha Ali, Carolina Varga Dinicu, Delilah Flynn, Laurel Victoria Gray, Elizabeth Artemis Mourat, Magda Saleh, Leona Wood, Eva Cernik, Jamila Salimpour, Karol Harding, Andrea Deagon, Edwina Nearing, and *Arabesque* and *Habibi* magazines.

part of a ceremony honoring woman as the continuer of the human species through the act of giving birth. Firdoz said she had been present when the women of her grandmother's tribe gathered around a woman in labor and did these movements. Other dances, as well as a more elaborate repetition of the actual birth dance, were done afterward to celebrate the birth.

Varga Dinicu describes her firsthand observation in 1967 of a traditional birth in a village three and one-half days' travel from Marrakesh. She was able to witness the private moments of this birth ritual by posing as a mute Moroccan servant.

> [The pregnant woman was] dressed in a caftan and *d'fina* and was squatting over the small hollow that had been dug in the center of the tent. . . The other women had formed a series of circles three deep around her. . . . All the women were singing softly and undulating their abdomens, then sharply pulling them in several times. The movement was much slower and stronger than what dancers call the flutter, seen in some Schikhatt dances [an erotic dance in Morocco]. They repeated the movements while slowly moving the circles clockwise. The mother would get up and do the movements in place for a few minutes and then squat for a few minutes and bear down. She didn't seem particularly agitated or in any pain. The only sign of strain was the perspiration that soaked her hair and forehead. We stopped only for midday prayers.
>
> About an hour later, she gave a gasp and we heard a soft thud. She lifted her caftan and there was a baby in the hollow. She held up her hand: it wasn't over yet. Fifteen minutes later, another gasp and another soft thud. It was twin boys. . . . The women kept up the singing and dancing till way past sundown. It was so moving that I couldn't help crying. . . . This was more than sufficient to me to prove the origins of some of the movements of what has become incorporated into oriental dance.

It is easy to see that if the bodily movements associated with the birth ritual were transposed to the king's palace or a nightclub for the entertainment of men, those same movements would be viewed in an entirely different way. The belly dance in the context of the birth ritual, however, was done not to project eroticism or to present the woman as a lure but to display a consciousness of the wonder of birth and the awesome power of motherhood.

Sacred Womb

Long before the building of cavernous temples or the construction of the biblical Ark, humanity recognized that Nature had provided our first sacred space: the womb, the empty space in which life miraculously manifests itself from nothingness and from which life emerges. The Sanskrit word for sanctuary, *garbha-grha*, means "womb-chamber." The ancient Japanese recognized the abdomen as the residence of the soul, rather than believing the soul to live in the chest or head, as in Western culture. In the ancient Chinese healing art of qigong, the *qi* comes from what is described as a ball of energy—life

LEFT: LA MERI DANCES THE MAHGREB. MUSEUM OF MODERN ART COLLECTION.

Egyptian Wall Drawing. Three goddesses disguised as dancers/midwives arrive to assist in the birth of Horus.

force—residing in the abdomen, just below the navel—in other words, at the womb area. In Kundalini yoga, this center is known as *manipura*, the emotional, fire chakra (chakras are centers of energy in the subtle, inner bodies that govern our physical and emotional well-being, according to both Hindu and Buddhist philosophy). In Tama-Do it is called the *hara* center, the figurative and literal center of a person, and is associated with vitality and health.[7] The *hara* receives energy from nature and the cosmos, integrates that energy, and dispatches it in the four directions of the body.

The mystery of birth is the basis of all mysteries. Even in this time of advanced scientific knowledge, when the process of pregnancy and birth can be explained in minute biological and physiological detail, we still view the entrance into this world by a new person, a new soul, with nothing less than awe. It is the seen and the unseen, a phenomenon so apparent, so natural and commonplace, and yet a miracle. We can sense the presence of a new being because we see the mother's abdomen growing larger; by the same token, we have faith that the new being exists because we can't see her or him. Meanwhile, the baby has already gone through innumerable miraculous metamorphoses by the time we meet it.

Pregnancy and childbirth are apt symbols of initiation and transformation for women today, just as they were in the past. Surrender to the very real risk of death involved in bringing forth new life is known and felt by all women who participate in the birth experience. On some level, every pregnant woman acknowledges her personal willingness to answer a possible call to sacrifice in the true sense of the word. This is still true in our modern day, just as it was 25,000 years ago for our nomadic female ancestors. Death and infection were real and present dangers at the time, and despite vast improvements, modern technology has never succeeded in totally eliminating such possibilities even today. It is not difficult to understand why women have from the beginning employed every aid, human and divine, to assist and assure success.

I found, however, as with all of women's ways, that the birth rituals of our ancestor women served not only as practical physical birthing aids but also as important forms of spiritual expression. The birthing process is a very personal spiritual growth experience that is open to women—a very complex experience that brings both happiness and tears. It has a profound influence on women's spiritual lives. A woman surrenders her body to be a vessel during pregnancy, giving over conscious control so that another being can emerge. Birth rituals helped women perform this selfless act without surrendering their own being. It helped them become aware of the awesomeness and privilege of what they were doing.

As our Indo-European ancestors settled into communities, they began to have time to contemplate their lives, death, and life after death. The early birth dance rituals provided an external gesture of a spiritual awakening to the awesome mystery of birth and life's meaning. They emphasized the mother as the giver of life. It seems only natural that reverence grew for the one who could produce another being from her own body.

The role of woman as the vessel for new life was represented by bountiful Paleolithic figures such as the Venus of Laussel, the Venus of Willendorf, and others. One palm placed over the abdomen and the other at the breast, the female figure was seen as the earthly representative of the mysterious force of creation.* Through concentration on the symbol of the pregnant female image, our ancestors hoped to achieve regeneration. Woman, the producer of offspring, thus also became the inspiration for the dance of reincarnation/regeneration (described further in chapter 10), a dance performed in the hope of immortality, for a life after death.

Science Confirms

As with other aspects of women's ways, I wanted to see whether I could find modern scientific verification of the power and effect of the birth dance ritual, and women's intuitively and experientially acquired wisdom. Indeed I did. From over thirty years of research, French physician Alfred A. Tomatis found that the fetus "gathers numerous memories and establishes an outline of psychic life from its sensory experiences of communication within the womb." His research showed that the rhythms and intonations specific to the mother's voice constitute emotional nutrient, a source of vital energy transmission through the ear to the brain and an entrainment of the nervous system. "From this primordial dwelling, this envelope that has enclosed every human being, many archetypal memories find their ultimate origin."[8] In this sense, the mother is priestess to her unborn child, channeling the essence of life to it.

DRAWING OF PREGNANT WOMEN DANCING IN A LINE, HOLDING HANDS. GRAPHIC DETAIL FROM TERRA-COTTA VESSEL FRAGMENT, RAI, IRAQ, C. 3000 B.C.E.

The rhythm of the traditional or primal female dance is the heartbeat, the beat heard by the infant *in utero*. Tantric tradition calls this rhythm the Nada, the sound of power or heartbeat of the Absolute made manifest in the

*Classical Greek art shifted the hands to be in front of the breasts and at the pubic area, creating an enticing modest/seductive image.

human heartbeat.[9] The heartbeat is basic to all rhythms. The fetus lives in an internal syncopated sound world, hearing the pulsation of its own heartbeat of 140 beats per minute and the mother's heart rhythm of 70 beats per minute, as well as the mother's voice, which is heard as a high-frequency rustling and hissing. Researchers note that a six-month-old fetus moves *in utero* to the rhythm of the mother's speech. Slow-motion photography, which catches the subtle emphasis a casual observer might miss, shows that within a day or two after birth a baby moves its arms and legs in rhythmic synchrony with the sound of the mother's voice.[10] The newborn is literally dancing to the music of the human voice long before it can utter a distinctive word.[11]

Furthermore, Tomatis found that the movements of the mother are recorded by the unborn child. As with other sensory stimulation, these movements have an energizing effect on the child's rapidly developing brain and contribute to the future development of motor functions. Paul Madaule, a Tomatis method practitioner and former patient, says in his book *When Listening Comes Alive*, "walking, rocking, swimming and low impact exercises are activities that should be practiced by the mother-to-be. To facilitate the harmonization of both levels of the child's ear—the auditory and the body level—the mother should synchronize these movements with the sound of her own voice. For example, she could rock while telling stories or reciting poetry at the same time, or dancing to the sound of her own singing."[12] Thus, we see from scientific research and clinical application that the birth dance ritual is as beneficial for the baby-to-be as it is for the mother and her community of women.

Great power coalesces around a woman who participates fully and without inhibition as the awesome energy of new life surges through her. Research has shown that a standing position may actually be best in the early stages of labor, and that staying mobile during contractions lessens their pain and speeds up delivery. Staying mobile also provides for good blood flow between the baby and the placenta. Psychologically, being active decreases the feeling of helplessness and dependency fostered by the passive reclining position, promoting a feeling of acting in support of the birthing process rather than being acted upon.

Belly dance and other ancient birth dance rituals prepared the woman's body for the physical act of childbearing. The traditional form of the dance emphasized the abdomen more so than the pelvis. Wendy Buonaventura, in *BellyDancing: The Serpent and the Sphinx*, observes this distinction:

> Abdominal muscles, together with those of the buttocks and thighs, are more important than any others during childbirth. They are controlled by the pelvis which—to take a much used comparison—resembles a basin which we can tilt forwards and backwards and from side to side. . . . Another movement helpful in early pregnancy is the belly roll, which keeps abdominal muscles supple. These muscles crisscross the lower trunk in different directions, just as threads of silk bind themselves round a cocoon. During

labour they exert pressure on the womb to open and allow the baby to exit.[13]

This contraction/release movement is also evident in the hula, the dance of the Maori, and others.

The Lamaze method of natural childbirth includes two exercises similar to the belly dance that prepare uterine muscles for the job. Although Dr. Lamaze may have been given credit for "inventing" such natural childbirth exercises as the roll and rapid breathing, the history of women's dance shows that this French physician was a late interloper in a practice known to women for thousands of years.

Women's fitness expert Karen Andes, author of *A Woman's Book of Strength* and *A Woman's Book of Power*, says that the hip, abdominal, and lower back motions of belly dance are not only excellent for the birthing process but also very beneficial after childbirth in regaining and maintaining muscular elasticity.[14] "During pregnancy and birth the muscles that get most stretched are the pelvic floor muscles (the Kegel muscles) and the transverse abdominals (deep abdominal muscles that act as a torso 'girdle')." She says that during a belly dance, the transverse abdominals get a great workout by pulling in the belly muscles, allowing them to naturally flutter out again as you move your hips and rib cage.

Another contemporary example of the birth dance in practice can be found in Healdsburg, California. There Oriental and Kathak dance teacher TerriAnne Baglien, who is also an emergency medical technician and has been a midwife for over twenty-three years, teaches belly dance movements to her pregnant clients to help them prepare for childbirth. Because Baglien leads a cultural dance program that includes three dance troupes, she is also able to have dancers from her troupes assist in the home birthing process by dancing. She says, "The energy flow and relaxing effects of music and dance are very helpful. But even more important is the 'tribal' feeling that results, the powerful effect of the combined energy of women being together during the birthing process."

Thus we see that the dance was performed not to project eroticism or the woman as a lure but to display a consciousness of the wonder of birth and the awesome power of motherhood. The belly dance puts a pregnant woman deeply in touch with her power and beauty as creator and progenitor and, when practiced throughout the duration of a pregnancy, can go a long way toward helping her stay fully connected to her own inner authority as she joins in the primal ritual of birthing. Birthing is Life taking over, and yet positive participation in the process by the woman is absolutely essential. Thus, it is the priestesshood personified.

Origins—The Ghawazi and the Ouled Nail

In search of the origins of ancient birth ritual mysteries, we now go to the Middle East and explore, as much as we can, the lingering dance traditions in the keep of a few scattered families of hereditary entertainer castes: the Ghawazi and the Ouled Nail. We shall also look at other

Ouled Nail, Algeria, early 1900s. Courtesy of Elizabeth Artemis Mourat private collection.

dances in surrounding areas and ponder the influence of the Gypsies.

Although many believe that the belly dance is Egyptian in origin, other theories suggest that it was brought to Egypt from elsewhere. One reason for the mystery is a group of wandering professional dancers in Egypt called the Ghawazi (also Ghawazee or Ghazye), whose origins are unknown.* The history of this interesting caste of entertainers is uncertain, but an image on the wall of an early Eighteenth Dynasty tomb of Neb Amon attests to their antiquity. Many of their customs, including their attitude toward marriage, predate Islam.

Some say the Ghawazi may be part of the Indo-Persian Gypsies who migrated from northern India up toward Spain and Eastern Europe. The Ghawazi, like the Gypsies,† are of non-Egyptian origin, stay apart from the rest of society, have carefully preserved their own traditions and oral history, and have their own language of obscure derivation that they speak among themselves.[15]

The dance (*raqs sha'abi*) of the Ghawazi still in existence today is characterized by continuous hip shimmies from side to side, which can also be seen in classic belly dance movements. They dance to a rapid 4/4 beat. Their music is derived from the folk instruments such as the mizmar, rebabi, and tabla baladi.

The Ouled Nail of Algeria, another group of people of mysterious origins,

Ghawazi dancing girl. A wood engraving by James Augustus St. John, 1845.

*Perhaps the most famous Ghawazi was Kutchuk Hanum, who was banished to Esne by Mehemet Ali. She was visited and written about in the mid-1800s by French writer Gustave Flaubert and an American popular writer, George William Curtis.

†It is generally accepted that the Gypsies originated in the area of Northern India. Generically known as Gypsies, these unique nomadic people are called by various names in the regions in which they are found: Egypt, Halab, Nawar (Nuri), Ghagar; Persia, Luri; Turkey, Cingana or Cengi; from the Punjab in India, Jats or Zutt. In Europe they are known as Zigeuner, Zingaro, Czigany, Sinte, Romani or Rom, Gitana/Gitano.

Najat, Touha, and Karima Yousef, probably the most famous Ghawazi in Egypt at the present time. Photograph courtesy of Aisha Ali.

have kept themselves apart and thereby maintained their ancient traditions. Their customs provide yet another clue to the origins of belly dance. These unveiled public dancers of the Sahara Djurdjura were famous for their jeweled crown, or *zeriref*, as far back as the 6th century B.C.E. Made of plaques or coins of silver or gold, and decorated with turquoise, coral, and colored enamels, these headdresses are held together with rows of chains and pendants. The pendants are similar to some found on Phoenician funeral stelae and reminiscent of headdresses worn by the women of North Africa in Punic times. Many symbols in their jewelry have been identified as coming from ancient Carthage or Babylon.

Under layers of jeweled belts and caftans, their dance features the *danse du ventre,* a rhythmic "rolling" of the abdominal muscles. Beginning slowly, in a stationary position, the dancer first rolls her belly in a circular movement. As the tempo increases, arms and feet come into action. Hips join in the rhythmic revolving, together with shaking of the shoulders. After women earn their dowries by their dance, which in no way affects their reputation at home, they return to their village to marry and live according to the Muslim society that surrounds them.

Other Belly Dance Traditions

Flamenco, which incorporates some of the serpentine arm patterns and hip rotations seen in various versions of belly dance, has been conjectured to have come from a variety of sources, including Hindu Romany (Gypsies), who settled in the caves of Sacromonte and mixed with the Mozarab, a community of Moors (Arab and Berber), Jews, and Iberians in the eighth and ninth centuries C.E. They brought to Andulasia, Spain, the combination of complex Indian rhythms mixed with Arabic melodic themes, incorporating many traditional characteristics of Spanish dancing and thus preserving them.* The Houara tribe in Morocco today perform a dance that is said to be the mother of Flamenco.

One particular flamenco dance, the Zambra Mora, has a very strong Arabic flavor. It is known for its hip rotations and its portrayal of strong emotion and passion. There is also a dance called *la danza serpiente* (dance of the serpent) that Spanish Gypsy women do at their own private gatherings, which also has hip movements similar to those of belly dance. The name refers to the dance of Arabian women.

In some Middle Eastern countries, wedding celebrations traditionally require the presence of a particular kind of belly dancer—one who possesses knowledge, experience, and wisdom—specifically "carnal" knowledge. In Morocco she is the "scheikha/sheikha"; she is known as the "Hannana" in Egypt. The Hannana oversees the seven days of women's ceremonies and rituals before the wedding and bestows her blessing on the bride.*

In addition to entertaining the all-female guests with ribald improvised verses, the scheikha dances in front of the bride-to-be, singing verses about the pleasures of marital relations that await after the ordeal of the wedding night and the loss of her virginity.[16] Her troupe dances with exaggerated hip, stomach, and other movements that are visible in spite of the large, loose caftans and *d'finas* they wear. Although this is not the Raqs Sharqi Oriental belly dance, the movements are similar in the control and articulation of the torso and hip muscles.

Hajja Noura Durkee, an American university professor, writer, and member of the Shadhdhuli Sufi order, once described to me a wedding she witnessed in the 1970s that incorporated belly dance:

> In Jeddah [Saudi Arabia] the wedding parties take all night. The men were off somewhere else, drinking tea and dancing. Several hundred women were in a huge open courtyard, in the front of which was a raised sort of stage holding two huge throne-like chairs and an open floor, with a canopy over it. For a long time nothing happened except talk and music, and then a young adolescent girl got up on the stage and began to dance. The Saudi

*Flamenco's origins may go back even further to an ancient fire ritual involving the *flaminca*, who once performed priestly duties alongside her husband.

*The name of the Hittite birth goddess Hannahannas is considered to be an adaptation of the Hittite kinship term *hannas*, meaning "grandmother."

dance has very little footwork, a kind of shuffle with a hesitation in it; all the intensity is on the swiveling hips, circling arms, and the eyes. Soon another girl got up and the two of them went around and around, not showing off for the audience but concentrating inside. I could only call it a sexual meditation. Others rose and danced—middle-aged women, little girls. All did the same dance in the same circle on the stage, energizing, charging it.

According to dance historian Curt Sachs' writings in 1937, this type of woman's dance, by whatever name it is called, is universal.[17] The pelvic dance of the Bafioti Loango is ancestor worship, directed toward past and future generations. Pygmies of Uganda have a dance in which the rolling of the pelvis and the abdomen are especially significant as the seat of sexual and childbearing activity. In their culture, when a child is born the mother dances while carrying the baby papoose-style to begin its dance education.[18] Similar dances are seen in the South Seas, in southern and central Australia, in Namoluk and Tuk of the Caroline Islands, on the Sepik River of New Guinea, on the Shortland Islands of the Solomon Archipelago, in East Polynesia, and in Africa from the north coast to Loang in the west and Zanzibar in the east. According to Sachs, there are even records of such a pelvic dance from ancient Hellas. He

ORACION DE LAGRIMAS, A FLAMENCO INTERPRETATION OF THE WOMEN OF THE CROSS. OMEGA DANCE COMPANY, CATHEDRAL OF ST. JOHN THE DIVINE, NEW YORK CITY. DANCERS: MARISSA MADRONE, MELINDA MARQUEZ, ALEXZANDRA DE MESONES, AND SANDRA RIVERA. PHOTOGRAPH BY MARY BLOOM.

explains that women's dances developed from concepts of a matriarchal collector/planter culture, and women were often the only participants. "It is also quite clear that 'belly dance' was the hangover of ancient religious custom and that women have maintained, in spite of all the fading of the original religious significance, the position conceded to them."[19]

The Hawaiians are a very good example of a people attempting to retain their birth dance tradition through a dance known as the Hula. As a result of colonization, most of the Hawaiians' indigenous dances were lost, victims of Victorian missionary misconceptions and ignorance, but in recent years they have been reclaimed and honored for their traditional meaning. The Maoris also have a dance called Ohelo, a lying-down Hula, with movements that are specifically to strengthen the muscles for childbirth.

Another woman's dance related to belly dance that is still in existence is the Dinka Virgins' Dance, found in Southern Sudan. There are four distinct movements, all of which must occur at the same time. The step is a forward shuffle with feet close together; the women move in a small circle, and as they dance around from time to time they sink slowly down on their heels and rise again, working their stomachs in a *danse du ventre*. Shera Khamisi, Director of the Medasi African Dance Theatre in Cincinnati, Ohio, observed this type of woman's dance in Senegal in 1990:

> Often the dances in Africa have dual purposes behind them. For instance, in the Wollof's initiation dance the young girl's dance movement influences the dancers to obey the community's expectations by abstaining from sex before marriage. This same dance demonstrates movements that will, when the time is right, be necessary for love making. The movements actually strengthen the pelvic area and the legs. It prepares the dancers for child bearing. Traditionally in Africa women gave birth standing.

Sachs also said one can see parts of women's birth dance ritual within other dances—in Cambodia, for example:

> [R]ight in the midst of a formal mythological dance, it may happen that the woman pauses, relaxes her leg muscles, and trembles with a slow undulatory motion seeming to start at one of her hands, which are held with the palms upwards. Gently the snakelike movement slides along her arms, passes on to the other shoulder, lifts her breast scarf, goes over to the other arm, and disappears in the fluttering vibration of the other hand. At this moment her hip is arched. Her abdomen recedes beneath the flood of the heavy glistening folds of silk and metal. When she opens her eyelids one can see her eyes roll and turn in her entranced whitened face.

The Loss and Rebirth of WomanDance

Writer Jamila Salimpour explains the changes that occurred to women's ritual birth dance in Middle Eastern countries over the years:

> And so, the change in religion brought about a change in the form of worship and ritual. The adherents of the Goddess religions withdrew from public, although still practicing and believing in the "ancient" way. As the new religions were impressed over the older ones, many of the "harmless" practices were allowed to be absorbed. As time passed, the meanings of the rituals became obscured. Although most of the priestesses were banished, the birth magic ritual persisted as a ceremonial necessity at marriages, birth and circumcisions, and any ceremony pertaining to women in need of the talismanic presence of the priestess.[20]

The emphasis in the dance shifted from birth to dance for sexual enticement or display. In this context, nature's energy inherent in the muscles, the blood, the instinctive pulse of rhythm became too connected with the material end of the spectrum and had to be harnessed to achieve cultural control and redirected for religious ends. Social schizophrenia transformed life-potential menarche into menstrual taboos. Fear of dance as a regression to what is referred to as the Dionysian frenzy resulted in the degeneration of its sacred function inside the temple. Dance became relegated to an entertainment for the outside world. It was a very long and disempowering road from the Paleolithic mother dancing to express gratitude for an easy birth facilitated by the dance of birth, to the dancer of the 1893 Chicago's World Fair and the nightclub.

Yet, through this ancient woman's dance, women are rediscovering not only their own power, true beauty, and

EDWINA NEARNING, HISTORIAN, RESEARCHER, AND DANCER, DANCING WITH THE GHAWAZI. PHOTOGRAPH COURTESY OF EVA CERNIK.

spirituality but also a connection with all women once again. Over the years, I have noticed that although my students may have begun taking belly dance classes to "be more sexy," they invariably forgot their original purpose. Instead, I witnessed many a transformation of students into women who felt confident about their bodies, positing a new definition of what it means to be a woman. Week after week, I watched women perform for each other and for themselves in a safe atmosphere of camaraderie and mutual appreciation.

This picture of women performing an ancient woman's ritual that had been subverted to male voyeurism for so many centuries, but is now being performed once again as a woman's rite of passage, confounds the sense of division between the sensuous and the spiritual. Accessing the mystery of another culture so different from our own allows for a purpose different from the expected. By moving her body in a way that is at once sensual and at the same time very energetic and strong, without coquetry or seductiveness, the dancer and her dance return us to the depth and power of the feminine.

Woman's Body as Vessel, as Temple

From birth, the body and psyche are one. It is the physical body that gives shape, existence, and boundaries to our selves, the carrier of our being in the world that concretizes this life in this world. Only within a body is human psychological and physical growth possible. The body is the womb and birthplace of the ego. It provides the first awareness of the "I"—I am this body, I am finite and separate from all others.

On the other hand, the body is a terribly awkward thing, at times unreliable, embarrassing, messy, and it appears to stifle the ego's flight. For many of us, the body comes, sooner or later, to be a problem. It is prone to addictions, compulsions, eating disorders, injuries, illnesses. This in turn causes psychological problems and impedes the development of higher consciousness. As a result, the ego may at times lose a direct connection to the body as a source of natural wisdom and energy.

However, a woman cannot forget her body—not only because society won't let her, but also because she is ever reminded of its presence by her monthly period and by the dependence of others upon her for nurturing and nourishment. A woman's psyche resides in her body, and her wisdom grows out of an instinctual and acquired knowledge of what to do with her body when she gives birth, when she comforts another through the birthing process, when a warm and comforting body is needed by a distraught child, or friend. Her dance comes out of the womb of her experience when she has had to go deep within and labor to bring forth her own power. A woman gives herself over to the dance because of her need for the creative process that wants to be given form through her. Potential takes shape in the dark and becomes active in the light. Like a birthing, it comes out of her, yet has a life of its own.

LEFT: DANCE TO THE GREAT MOTHER. DELILAH FLYNN CREATES THIS DANCE DURING HER 8TH MONTH OF PREGNANCY. PHOTOGRAPH COURTESY OF VISIONARY DANCE PRODUCTIONS.

Through dance training comes a slow rediscovery of inner consciousness. The mind is always there, eventually listening to and learning to respect the natural instrument. Nature's energy is harnessed to the creative goal, redirected for spiritual ends, reconnecting with the material.

Creating Rites for Today

With today's excessive emphasis on the shape of girls' and women's bodies, there is a need for women to formulate rites that recognize purposes for the female body other than as an expression of sexual enticement and unattainable physical perfection. One reason many women endure rather than enjoy pregnancy is that our society bombards us with the message that a big belly is ugly, no matter what its purpose.

Western women are generally so fearful of having a protruding belly that they often keep their abdomens chronically tightened. Often this contraction is held totally unconsciously. If you try keeping a leg or arm muscle tightened all day, you can imagine how much harm this does to the body.

Things are changing, however. I sense that something in the feminine archetype is struggling for recognition, for expression. Today we find many feminists among belly dancers. It is also not uncommon to find the same women interested in the Goddess, spirituality, and women's ways as well. Dr. Jean Shinoda Bolen says in her book *Crossing to Avalon*, "At this particular time, many women are birthing Goddess consciousness."[21]

This changing consciousness is beautifully expressed by Delilah Flynn, a dancer living in Seattle, in a videotape she produced during the third trimester of her pregnancy entitled *Dance to the Great Mother*, a dance of praise to the mother-to-be:

> I believe that locked inside this dance is a secret language that tells the stories of women's lives, of their history. It speaks of their passions and their spirituality, their intuition and emotions, it speaks of their sacrifices, joys and their life dreams. Because it speaks to them about their lives and the way they've been living their lives for centuries, it doesn't add up the way you might think. . . . The term "belly dance" is, oddly enough, appropriate, as all life is centered around the belly, the archetype of the Great Mother and feminine creative principle is best expressed by this dance.

Let me be clear, however, that the text in this chapter is not meant to add to the societal programming of women to the maternal mode. The wish to become a mother is so saturated by sociocultural conditioning that it is difficult to know whether you are making an individual decision. Many biologists, psychologists, psychiatrists, and sociologists are now of the opinion that maternal instinct has been programmed into the female gender as a social convenience. The priestesshood or creatrix role that I speak of is available to every girl and woman in whatever role she chooses in life—even if it includes her right and option not to have children. As I have shown in this chapter, this dance has power in all aspects of life.

Now Let Us Dance

Belly dance (by whatever name it is called) is poetry of the body expressed in ancient meaningful gestures. It is a symphony of moving pictures and framed poses, a revelation of the human soul, and a sensuous feminine art. It is, as I stated earlier, a celebration of womanhood, a dance by women for women's purposes. It is excellent for any age; it can be practiced in preparation for childbirth, to deepen the connection with the baby inside, through a deep concentration on the miracle of new life. After childbirth, the dance can be practiced as a way to tone the abdominal muscles and to recall the depth of your female sensuality, a sense of self as an individual that is often lost to women postpartum. This dance has also helped many women who have suffered from PMS and menstrual discomfort because the movements bring about better circulation and blood flow in the pelvic area.

Performance of this dance by women in a circle around a girl as an initiation when she begins her menstrual period is an empowering way of welcoming her into adulthood and the community of women. It alters the prevailing attitude of the menstrual period as "the curse" and instead tells the young woman that she is growing into her spiritual power, into the ability to form her own rituals, to look to experiences of everyday life as her initiation ground. What a powerful difference it would make if girls were raised with a consciousness of their future roles as priestesses for the children they may have. Such a ceremony would be just as beneficial for a woman moving

IRIS STEWART IN BIRTH RITUAL DANCE. PHOTOGRAPH BY ARNOLD SNYDER.

through menopause, a positive initiation into the freedom of the postmenopausal Crone phase. From our vantage point today of having scientific research data, as discussed above, and from our ability to compare information carried forward from ancient centers of knowledge, we might conclude that our ancient Grandmothers were practicing an esoteric and holistic approach to health, harmony, and spirituality in this enduring dance, WomanDance.

The Belly Dance

Belly dancing consists of several basic moves: hip shimmies, hip rotations, serpentine arms, snakelike head movements, and abdominal undulations. Each of these moves works in concert with the others and can be used in any combination.

The hip shimmy is the most familiar belly dance movement, but actually it

Rina Roll and Karen Gehrman, members of Fat Chance Belly Dance, San Francisco. Carolena Nericcio, director. Photograph by Marty Sohl.

is the abdominal undulation that is the foundation of belly dance. To learn this abdominal undulation we focus, surprisingly enough, not on moving our muscles but on our breath (see Using Your Breath to Create the Dance, below).

Once you have mastered the basic undulation of your pelvis and abdomen, you can extend this wavelike motion to your chest, ribs, shoulders and arms, and head and neck. A classic belly dance will often include head movements in a straight line from shoulder to shoulder in a snakelike motion, or "doddling"—a shaking motion with index finger to chin in rhythm with the music. It will also include undulating movements of the hands and arms, again snakelike; soft shoulder shakes; and circular movements and raising and lowering of the rib cage to accompany the undulations of the chest and abdomen. Stomach muscles are flexed and contracted with great control or are fluttered rapidly as the pelvis moves forward and backward. Altogether, these movements present an incredible flowing or wavelike motion.

The specialized hip and rib cage undulations and rolls that are done in a belly dance should form a figure eight. Often the extensive shimmying or vibration of the hips is sustained while other parts of the body are moved at a different pace. Sometimes the entire body is caught up in a minutely controlled trembling. Additionally, your head, shoulders, hands, or hips can thrust forward or back with a dramatic accent as the music demands.

Beyond these basic belly dance movements, there may be other movements you'll want to try to complement them, according to your skill or mood and depending on the music. I recommend swirls, turns, backbends, or even dropping to the floor. The belly dance, despite its name, is a full body dance. You will find, however, in belly dancing that the feet and legs are not emphasized. One might say they are simply utilitarian, moving you from one spot to another for variety and to enable all of your audience to see you from several angles and distances. Some have even said that a belly dancer resembles a serpent in being "all torso and no legs."

Using Your Breath to Create the Dance

Probably the most important thing I can teach or emphasize for belly dancing, as well as for your physical well-being and spiritual clarity, is how to breathe. As babies we breathed naturally into our belly. As we grew up and were schooled to hold the belly in, our breathing became shallow. In belly dancing there is great emphasis on the breath, and you will need to reteach your body this "natural" way of breathing—the same breathing technique used by singers and those who play wind instruments.

THE ARCH AND CONTRACTION MOVEMENT.

Stand with your feet flat, about hip width apart, knees flexed, pelvis pushed slightly forward. Head, neck, and shoulders remain relaxed. Because the pelvis is shaped like a bowl, when you push forward, the pelvis actually tilts backward. As you breathe out, pull in the belly, allowing the pelvis to tilt forward and upward, tightening the buttocks, as you drop the rib cage. Now breathe in, allowing the belly to expand, as you begin raising the rib cage; this lengthens the back, giving more room for the belly. Raising the rib cage will give you a lifting feeling through the torso, causing you to straighten your legs. Pause.

Breathing out again, allow the rib cage to relax back into place, as you release the pelvis and the stomach. Give a little extra push of the pelvis forward to complete the arch and contraction movement.* You might hold your hand in front of your stomach and practice pushing the abdomen out to meet the hand.

Repeat these two movements in succession—inhaling: raising rib cage up, belly out; exhaling: rib cage releases, belly relaxes. By swaying slightly back and forward, this arch and contraction becomes the beginning of an undulation—a wave—the motherwave, the movement essential to the belly dance form. As you practice you may want to place your hands on your hips to counterbalance your movement; in the dance, however, the arms are extended. By sliding one foot forward with each undulation, you can begin to move forward or turn in a spiral. Practicing in front of a mirror keeps you coordinated. At first, you may not feel comfortable doing the movement at all, but once you get the different elements synchronized, you will begin to feel a rhythm develop. The head and neck are relaxed, the spine is liquid channeling energy in this undulating serpentine movement, and it becomes one of the most freeing things you can do for yourself.

*Martha Graham's famous and dramatic contraction-and-release dance technique was based on this same pulsation of breath and pelvic thrust movement. (Martha Graham is discussed in chapter 6.)

For the purpose of a Birth Dance ritual, the undulation can be practiced by itself, with attention to opening the first and second chakras, at the perineum and the pelvis, respectively, in order to encourage "stuck" energy to flow freely through these channels. You also can undulate the rib cage itself by swaying slightly forward as you raise it in response to air intake and dropping it again with the out breath. This small movement on its own can be extremely reenergizing and also tremendously effective as a breathing meditation technique. Personally, I have always found that sitting still in meditation or doing breath techniques in a prone position doesn't work for me. My body needs to move, and I dislike the dizzy feeling and numbness of my hands from just pulling lots of air into my lungs. I discovered that if I move in these undulations, either sitting or lying on my side, I can receive much better results and can perform the meditation for a much longer period of time.

When doing the movement as a breathing meditation, breathe with your mouth open, slightly rasping the throat as the air moves in and out. Pull the breath in enthusiastically and just let it go by dropping the rib cage.

5

The Dancer's Costume: Symbolic and Glorious

The Veiled One is brighter than ten thousand suns and yet when she is contemplated she covers herself with ten thousand veils and becomes as pale as the moon to protect you against her brightness. Her strength is in her spirit which is undaunted. She is passive only to the will of God. When a woman discovers the Veiled One within herself, the Veiled One appears as the Mother of the World.

Taj Inayat, The Crystal Chalice: Spiritual Themes for Women[1]

I have always been fascinated by the exotic costumes of traditional dancers like those from India, the Middle East, Bali, and Japan. Whether used in a stage production or for a local folk dance, the costume has a definite impact on the presentation. Some of the grandiosity of costumes represents the riches of the court, of course, but other outfits that are traditional and not attached to royalty are also quite decorative, often utilizing objects from nature such as shells, grasses, and colored stones. While I know the feminine attraction to things of beauty, I wondered whether there might be something more significant behind these adornments. What I discovered was a treasure trove of hidden information about women's ways.

Derivatives of ritual and folk costumes are often seen in theatrical and nightclub performances. Amid a fanfare of music, the belly dancer appears in a flash of brilliant colors and sparkling beads dazzling to the eyes. She moves regally around the dance floor in a flamboyant display of opulence. Watching her dance, whether in an ethnic nightclub in America or any other locale, the audience members will immediately feel they have just been transported to the mysterious Middle East, land of the exotic and the beautiful.

This fantasy is created by the dance itself, and by the dancer who moves in the sensuous ways we have come to associate with belly dance. It is created by the strange, erotic, and boisterous sounds emanating from instruments unfamiliar to many: oud, nay, qanun (canoon), and bouzouki. The illusion is further enhanced by the dancer's costume. Yards of the sheerest chiffon form the voluminous circular skirt extending from below the dancer's hipband to the floor. Sequins sparkle deep within the folds of the skirt or define its hem. Several skirts of different colors glimmer like a rainbow over Gypsy pantaloons. Multicolored, iridescent, gold, or silver embossed panels may accent the skirt and match the enfolding veil that the dancer sweeps about her head and body. Alternately revealing and concealing, the veil floats like a mist behind her as she turns and spins. Covering the bra and hip belt are brocades, velvets, and lamé, which form the base for layers of shiny fake antique coins, bells, small round mirrors, luminous glass beads, refractive jewels or crystals, pearls—almost anything that will glimmer, sparkle, and shine—all designed to glamorize and amplify the dancer's movements. A snake bracelet encircles her upper arm. Elaborate, bejeweled head coverings may form the royal finishing touch.

Tourists visiting nightclubs in Egypt and other countries of the Middle East, seeing a very similar type of costume, some even more elaborate than their American counterparts, easily surmise it is indeed an ethnic, Egyptian costume. The theatrical and nightclub belly dance costume, however, bears no resemblance to the traditional long-sleeved gown and pantaloons worn by Middle Eastern entertainers in the 19th century.* What the audience is seeing is an adaptation of the dress of the *nautchnee* dancers of Northern India, with their divided dress showing a bare torso, hip band, and wide skirt dating from the time of the British colonization of India. When a British protectorate was later established in Egypt, this type of dress was adapted by Egyptian entertainers because that was what the English were accustomed to seeing, and thus the style became the indelible symbol of belly dance.[2] The more glitterized, glamorized, cabaret style of costume—the spangled bra and low-slung skirt with side slits—however, owes its inspiration largely to Hollywood and American night clubs, which subsequently influenced the

*In 1860, Edward William Lane described the Ghawazee dress in *An Account of the Manners and Customs of the Modern Egyptians:* "Some of them wear a gauze top, over another shirt, with the shintiyan, and a creape of muslin tarhah; and in general they deck themselves with a profusion of ornaments, as necklaces, bracelets, anklets, a row of gold coins over the forehead, and sometimes a nose-ring. All of them adorn themselves with kohl and henna.[3]

Egyptian film industry in the 1930s and gradually introduced this more stylized version into Egyptian nightlife.

Despite this glamorized interpretation, I found that the clothing and decorations on figurines and drawings of goddesses are surprisingly similar to the belly dance costumes described above. Clay figurines, statues, and drawings of goddesses found everywhere from the Ukraine and the Indus Valley to China and South America, and spanning many centuries, wear hip belts, fringe, aprons, narrow or flared skirts, stoles, necklaces, bracelets, medallions, and veils. When a skirt is worn, it generally begins below the waist and hugs the hips and often has a decorative texture of white or red encrusted incisions, showing net patterns, zigzags, checkerboards, or dots.[4] Other markings on the figurines include tattoos or incisions in geometric patterns of chevrons, spirals, and parallel meandering lines. Snakes twine around the arms, body, or hair or are borne on staffs, symbolic of healing, initiation and rebirth, and transformation. (For more information about the symbolism of the snake, see chapter 9.)

Marija Gimbutas, in her masterwork *The Language of the Goddess*, amassed nearly 2,000 illustrations of artifacts of goddess figures, revealing a complex iconographic system of mystical thought. The markings on the goddess figures were more than just decorations; they were symbols that transmitted a myriad of messages: reckonings of moon phases, seasons, energy patterns, and powers. Likewise, the pose, clothes, hairstyle, and attributes or symbols surrounding the deity created a pictorial "script." They were a way of signifying something special, set aside, sanctified, sacred, while at the same time providing a very personal identification.[5]

The longevity of these goddess symbols is impressive. Decorations on representations of the Old European Snake Goddesses found on Mycenean terra-cottas of the 14th and 13th centuries B.C.E. are repeated down through the 8th century in Hera's temple and on figures of the goddess Boeotia in the 7th century B.C.E., with little or no observable change in motif.[6] The features include crowns, bands of dotted serpent scales, parallel lines, spirals or coils, and checkerboard and net designs. The triangle, zigzag, net, and spiral found on the goddess figures are all symbols of regenerative powers. These ancient symbols were also carried forward in the weaving and embroidery of women's folk costumes throughout the world. The sacred symbols of the circle, spiral, cross, triangle, and tree of life are also common in the textiles, carpets, and ancient art produced by women.

Old European female votive figurines from the 5th millennium B.C.E. are depicted with nude torso and hipline skirt or girdle, with vertical fringe hanging from the hips. The skirts are often pulled up at the side or in the back, or draped to one side, and caught by a hip belt or girdle. Another feature of the ensembles is the ritualistic apron depicted by punctuating dots and incisions covering the lap area. They invariably have the snake, spiral, V, chevron, or other designs frequently found on goddess figurines.

Just as the symbols on representations of the Goddess were meant to

The Triangle

The triangle is universally a primary symbol and is always associated with the Goddess. The *mons veneris* of the Mother is the triangle of Aphrodite, the "mound of Venus," the mountain connecting man and woman, earth and sky.[7]

The triangle was held to an original form by the ancient Pythagorean initiatic schools not only because of its perfect form and its position as the strongest of architectural structures, but also because it was the archetype of fecundity.[8] In Kundalini philosophy, two overlapped or opposed triangles appear at the Lotus Center of the awakened heart, *anahata,* at the fourth chakra. The upward triangle represents spiritual energy; the downward pointing triangle is physical energy. Thus interlaced, the two represent the physical world informed by the spiritual.

Kali yantra, Nepal.

One or more triangles are not uncommon in the jewelry of the Middle East. Called a *du'a*, the triangle often contains a compartment for prayer papers. As protective amulets, the triangles are also believed, in simple terms, to ward off misfortune, sickness, and death.

The apron on the Goddess's ritual attire often bears a triangle plus a diamond shape, the *tangov*, the Polynesian name for a symbol used in ritual worldwide. In India the *tangov* is analogous to the Great Mother Pattern, *Shri Yantra*, where it was used to supply original points in many ceremonial ritual dances. It reappears in solidified form in the Theatre of Dionysus at Athens in the brick paving of the orchestra space and in the sand patterns used by ritual dancers in Polynesia. The *tangov* appears in the Hebrew Shield of David, formed by a pair of equilateral triangles, one pointing upward (white, symbolizing the spiritual world) and one pointing downward (black, symbolizing the material world).

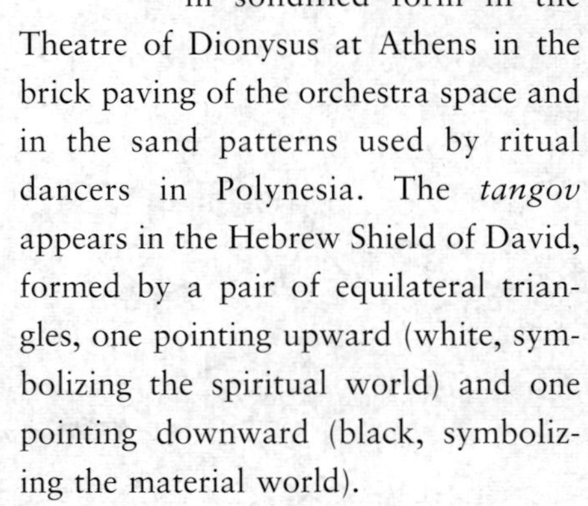

communicate her purpose and power, the priestesses' apparel and jewelry were meant to both reveal and invoke the Divine Goddess. Priestesses and priestess-dancers regularly adapted ceremonial attire similar to that with which they adorned the Goddess. Additionally, tattooing and henna patterns on the skin transformed the devotee's body into the bearer of sacred information.

Mystai, or initiates—followers of Demeter—wore white linen garments, possibly influenced by the Isis Egyptian mysteries. Into the classical period, the garments worn on the occasion of the *myesis* (the first rites to Demeter) were held in high esteem and were even considered holy. The mystai's garments were dedicated to the goddess or kept as swaddling clothes for the new generation.[11]

In Greece, young women and girls in procession carried the jewels and robes of Artemis, with which they draped her statue in ceremonial fashion. Greek girls would make an offering of a dress at the time of their first menarche. After childbirth, the woman's girdle was often dedicated to Artemis as Eileithyia, protector of childbirth. The Ouled Nail, who honor the goddess Tanit or Taurt, patron of childbirth and maternity, wear enormous amounts of jewelry, a large silver belt or girdle, and symbolic talismans, including the Hand of Tanit. They also perform the *danse du ventre* in her honor.

The special markings, symbols, gemstones, and draperies of Goddess attire were later transferred into the architectural splendor and decorations of the temple or cathedral, and then to royalty. Al'mehs (cultivated Arabic performers), courtesans, and then entertainers eventually adapted the ritual ornaments and costumes for their own purposes.[14]

The Ouled Nail's Hand of Tanit is very similar to another familiar symbol worn as jewelry: the Hand of Fatima, as it is called in the Muslim world.[12] On the hand is a large eye of blue ceramic or glass bead outlined with blue-black shadows. In Judaic art, this symbol is called the Hand of God.

We find the handprint in prehistoric rock paintings as a defense against disaster. The hand was a symbolic stimulating force, the energizing touch of the Goddess, and was called the *Mano Pantea*, "Hand of the All-Goddess." It is not unusual for the picture or statue of a holy person or deity to show a hand with the palm held outward, transmitting a blessing. The *khomsa*, Arabic for the number five (five fingers), is a good-luck charm in many parts of North Africa. And in Tunisia, a handprint is commonly painted on the door of a home for blessings and protection.[13]

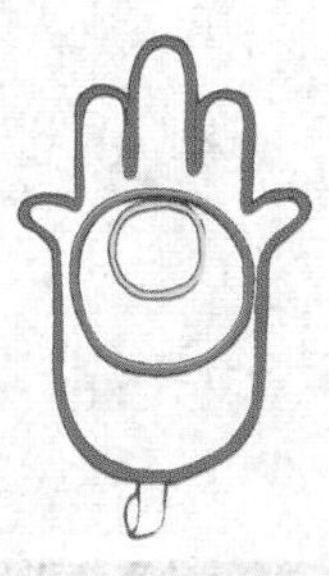

The Power of Women's Clothes

In several special situations, the ritual dress of the Goddess or priestess was itself recognized as powerful. In Crete, the many votive offerings of clay models in long ceremonial dresses speak to us of their special nature. In Kerala,

ST. SARA (SARA-LA-KALI) THE BLACK MADONNA, DRESSED IN SEVEN VEILS. LES SAINTES MARIES DE LA MER FESTIVAL, FRANCE. PHOTOGRAPH BY VALERIE RICHMAN.

India, at a ceremony called *trip-pukharattu,* held eight or ten times a year, a reddened cloth wrapped around the image of the goddess Kali is keenly sought after by pilgrims and prized as a holy relic.[15] An ancient Indian legend also tells that Shiva produced a child out of a piece of Parvati's dress.[16] One of the popular stories about the Resurrection says that Fatima, daughter of Mohammed, will be clad in a garment with a magnificent fringe, and that the women will cling to it and pass over the Bridge with her in the twinkling of an eye.[17]

In a comingling of Christian and traditional beliefs, the *Gitane* (Gypsies) of Arles, in Provence, followers of Sara, the Black Virgin (Sara *la Kali*) or *Gitano* Sara *La Macarena*, touch the ritual garments of their patron saint as part of their yearly pilgrimage to the church at Les Saintes-Maries-de-la-Mer on May 24 and 25. Tradition says that Sara used her dress as a raft to help the Three Marys of the Sea (Mary Salome, Mary Jacobe, and Mary Magdalene), who had been present at the crucifixion of Jesus, safely reach land when the boat they were sailing in threatened to founder.

> Those who arrive devote themselves to Sara in two acts of ritual: the touching and hanging up of garments. The women in particular respectfully stroke the statue or kiss the hem of her many dresses. Then they hook up clothes beside her, clothes they have brought, from a handkerchief to a silk kerchief, a slip or a bust-bodice. Sometimes it is merely a matter of torn pieces of cloth. Finally, they touch the saint with miscellaneous objects representing those absent or the sick.[18]*

The power of the goddess and priestess costumes was also sought after by many male priests who adapted and absconded with them. Ritual transvestitism was a feature of many ancient priesthoods throughout all parts of the world and can still be found today among several traditional peoples. Some examples are the Dayaks of Borneo, the Chukchi of

*A variant of the power of women's garments is reflected in the Gypsies' most dreaded punishment of wrongdoing, excommunication from the group, whose origin is in the Laws of Manu. Says Jean-Paul Clebert in his book *The Gypsies*, "It is sufficient, on the order of the tribe, for a married woman to tear from her dress a piece of cloth and throw it at the head of the *Rom* who has been sentenced." According to Clebert, this rite is also found in some tribes of India: "Among the *Nagos* of Assam, it is a terrible misfortune for a man to find that he has been struck with a skirt of a woman who has been bearing children."

Siberia, and the *hijras* of the Indian subcontinent.[19] Various explanations for the behavior of ritual transvestites have been posited. One theory says they may be striving, consciously or unconsciously, to attain a state of androgyny, unifying the complementary aspects of male and female, thereby attaining a superior, divine or near-divine state. Another suggestion is that at one time all religious and magical knowledge belonged to women. As a result, when men first began to appropriate religious authority they dressed in the symbolic clothing set aside for the priestess so as to make themselves more acceptable to the spirits and forces of Nature.

The word for shaman in Japanese is *miko*, meaning "divine woman." In Korea, where the majority of shamans were historically female,[20] a class of male shamans, the *paksu mudang*, arose who wore female garments during rituals and were believed to be possessed by female deities. In the rituals of the *Sakhibhavas,* which arose sometime during the 16th century in and around Brindaban in northern India, men dress like women and express their devotion by doting on Radha and serving her. Also in northern India, prepubescent Brajbasi Brahman boys cross-dress as they play all the male and female roles in the Rasa Lila of Krishna. Men also cross-dress and dance in temples in the mood of the Gopis, female devotees of Lord Krishna.

Ritual transvestitism for men is also still practiced in Vaishnavism.[21] Men wear the clothes and ornaments of women and even observe a few days' monthly retirement in an imitation of the menstrual period. According to Vaishnavite doctrine, all souls are feminine to the Supreme Reality. It is said that by these ritual techniques, the masculine adept of Shakti worship arouses his own feminine quality and thereby attains the "ideal."

In Greek mythology we learn that Herakles (Hercules) found numerous ways of conquering female mysteries, including spending some years in women's dress, spinning for Queen Omphale. He discarded his lion pelt and instead wore jeweled necklaces, golden bracelets, a woman's turban, a purple shawl, and a Maeonian girdle, apparently without shame.[22] Renaissance paintings show Herakles wearing a yellow petticoat. He even wore women's clothing at his wedding.[23] Priests dressed as women in the Lydian cult of Herakles, and the priest of Herakles at Antimacheia donned women's clothes before beginning a sacrifice.

We shall now explore in greater depth two of the most interesting and powerful garments associated with the Goddess: the girdle and the veil.

Girdle of the Great Mother

The girdle is particularly sacred to women because it inspires and protects the will center, the sacral plexus or womb area, which is the grounding strength of a woman, the source of her bodily creativity in childbearing and menstruation.

Recent historical and archaeological books, bringing us rich pictorial archives, show that many goddesses wore an elaborate belt or girdle; some

wore nothing else. The hip belt of beads or string with fringes is typical of nude figurines from Old Europe, from the 6th to the 4th millennium B.C.E., from the Vinca, Karanovo, and Cucuteni cultures.

The protective function ascribed to the girdle, like the ring, probably derives from the symbolic value of the circle. Because of its circular form and its function of holding something in place, it is a symbol of strength, consecration, and fidelity. In ancient mythology, taking someone's girdle or belt signified robbing that person of connections, strength, and dignity. The ninth labor of Herakles was to capture the girdle of the war god Ares from the Amazonian queen, Hippolyte, founder of the city of Ephesus.[24] Greek men claimed it was theirs, belonging to their women but stolen by the rebellious strong woman. Although Hippolyte actually offered her girdle to Herakles, he killed her anyway, saying he feared some trickery. Herakles massacred the Amazon in order to seize the magic talisman, the insignium of her sex, and thus shear her of all her powers.

By Renaissance times, Juno (Hera), the chief goddess of Olympus, is shown in paintings as wearing a magic belt or girdle, borrowed from Venus in order to charm Jupiter (as in the story where Hera put on her girdle to seduce Zeus), and even borrowed one from Aphrodite to make sure she was irresistible. In this version of the girdle, its power was changed into enticement, with the effect of making its wearer "irresistibly desirable." The girdle of Aphrodite, the Certus, was lovebegetting, as depicted in later poems such as Spenser's *The Faerie Queene*.

The *cintola,* another form of the girdle, is shown tied around the Virgin Mary's robes in European religious art from the 14th century on.[25] In the art of the 17th century, the Virgin Mary was painted as the Woman of the Apocalypse, "robed with the sun, beneath her feet the moon, and on her head a crown of twelve stars" (Revelation 12:l). Round her waist was a girdle with three knots representing the religious vows of poverty, chastity, and obedience. In one story it is said that St. Thomas doubted the Virgin's assumption, so she dropped her girdle as she was ascending to heaven to convince him. St. Francis of Assisi (1182–1226) is shown in paintings with a similar tied belt, which became a standard part of the monk's costume.*

The *cintola* became known as the garland and the garter in England, especially at Windsor. In one of the ancient rituals of knighthood, a material girdle, sash, or riband was granted as proof that the wearer had been admitted to the Ritual of the Almond. This ritual was later incorporated into the Latin church in the 13th century. The cintola is also the Masonic apron that covers the "mystery of the organs that produce God in action."

In Ireland, a party of young people going round on St. Brighid's (goddess

*Among the specifications given in Exodus 28 for the priests' holy apparel was the "girdle of needlework." "And for Aaron's sons thou shalt make coats, and thou shalt make for them girdles, and bonnets shalt thou make for them, for glory and for beauty." Angels were girded as a sign of strength and control over their sexual energy, as were monks and priests serving the Mass.

LEFT: WHEN FAMED MODERN DANCER RUTH ST. DENIS (SEE CHAPTER 6) PERFORMED THE NAUTCH AS PART OF HER REPERTOIRE OF INDIAN DANCES, SHE WORE A COSTUME WITH A BARE MIDRIFF, REVEALING WHAT IS KNOWN IN YOGA AS THE *MANIPURA CHAKRA*—THE CENTER OF POWER. HER INTERPRETATION OF THE TRADITIONAL NAUTCH DANCE WAS BASED ON A FORM OF KATHAK DANCING THAT BEGAN IN THE NORTH INDIAN TEMPLES AND LATER MIGRATED TO THE PALACES AND EVENTUALLY TO THE STREETS. ST. DENIS'S COSTUME AND HER DANCE ARE REMNANTS OF WOMEN'S SACRED DANCES ONCE DONE BY FOLLOWERS OF THE DIVINE MOTHER. NEW YORK PUBLIC LIBRARY FOR THE PERFORMING ARTS.

Brigit or Brigantia) Eve usually carried the *crios Bride* (St. Brighid's Girdle). This was a straw rope, eight or ten feet long, ending in a loop. At each house visited, the occupants were expected to pass through the *crios*, thereby obtaining the protection of the saint and freedom from illness during the coming year. The *cingulam* or cord (red, plaited, and nine feet long) was said to be worn around a witch's waist and was used for symbolic binding rituals. In India, a girdle worn by the goddess, usually called the *katisutra*, provides protection as well as fertility.

The power of the girdle is also shown in many dragon stories and other myths. Legend tells us that the one woman who conquered a dragon, St. Martha, accomplished the feat single-handedly by placing her girdle around its neck. St. George became the first martial saint when he used a girdle to rescue Princess Sadra, who had been left as a sacrifice to a dragon. He put the princess' girdle around the dragon's neck and led it back to the city, where he converted the people to Christianity and finally killed the beast. Perhaps the girdle of Princess Sadra, who no doubt was a priestess, had the magical power that the saintly knight, George, had been seeking. The Gordian Knot, another type of girdle connected with the history of Alexander the Great, also figures in numerous legends.

The Priestess Wore the Veil

The veil behind which the Goddess symbolically remained unseen and free in the pursuit of her purpose was also worn by the virgin priestess. Every five years there was a procession to the temple of Athene Parthenos with the *peplum*, a long veil especially woven and decorated with symbolic designs. The symbolism of the celebration and its dance indicates the investiture of the indwelling deity. A later version of this symbolic veiling and unveiling is found in the Danza Del Duomo Cintola in Florence in the form of a processional dance around and inside the cathedral.[31] The veil was alternatively represented in paintings and sculpture as a robe, as a hanging or temple veil, or as a statue covering.

Iris Stewart, Veil Dance.

The Veil

The veil was originally worn by the Goddess, particularly in her wise Crone aspect, and it represented the future, the unknown, fate. The veil is the vehicle for revelations of the divinity and a safe haven. It establishes a place for meditation and seeking inward wisdom and guidance. The

Left: Bronze statuette of a veiled dancer. Greece, early 2nd century B.C.E. Metropolitan Museum of Art.

name of the Celtic Divine Mother, Caillech, meant "Veiled One."[26]

A temple of the veiled goddess Neith at Sais in Egypt bore the following inscription: "I am all that is and that was and that shall be, and no mortal has lifted my veil." A similar statement was recorded by Plutarch from a carving on an ancient statue of Pallas Athene. Isis as the white goddess Ino-Leucothea was said to have rescued Odysseus from drowning by means of her divine veil. In Greek mythology, Hera draped from her head a glorious veil as white as the sun. The Phrygian Kybele was shown in sculpture from about 700 B.C.E. with polos (crown) and veil. [27]

The center panel of the Greek Ludovisi Throne (c. 470–460 B.C.E.), exhibited in the Museo Nazionale Romano in Rome, depicts the birth of Aphrodite, who was born from the sea. She is being assisted from the water by two Horae, the Seasons, who drape her with a veil. The Greek goddess Harmonia was said to "weave the veil of the universe."

In the story of Demeter (Ceres) searching for her daughter, Persephone (Kore), Demeter descended through seven levels and removed a veil at each gate. [28] When Persephone reunited with Demeter and returned to Earth, she brought with her springtime. In spring, Demeter returns to the world, her veils restored and her secrets concealed once more from mortal eyes. Life springs anew.

In a similar story with a Sumerian flair, Inanna (Ishtar), goddess of Mother Earth, goes to visit her sister, Eresh-kigal, queen of the underworld. At each of the seven gates she must leave a jewel, her crown, her scepter of lapis lazuli, her beads, or a veil.[29] It was at the seventh gate that she relinquished her veil. We find evidence that the action of parting curtains, rending veils, and stripping off diadems, cloaks, or bracelets actually signifies a move toward an *arcanum*, or the penetration of a mystery—certainly a powerful symbol.[30]

The Tradition of Seven Veils

Where did the idea of seven veils come from? And why were there seven? Wisdom is traditionally associated with the number seven. Seven was considered to be the number of perfection and the number of the Great Mother, as represented by her many names throughout the world. Seven veils generally represented the seven planetary spheres (sun, moon, Venus, Jupiter, Mars, Mercury, and Saturn), celestial bodies that in ancient belief had motions of their own among the fixed stars and had profound influence on earthly life.

Maya, the pre-Vedic mistress of the "rainbow veils" of perceptible reality,[32] had a seven-colored rainbow that signified the layers of earthly appearances or illusions falling away from those who approached the central mystery of the deeps. The rainbow is composed of both matter and light, and is at once material and immaterial, a fitting symbol for the Goddess. The rainbow was a bridge uniting heaven and earth, male and female principles, yin and yang. It was sometimes seen as Ishtar of Babylon's seven-colored veils, which figured in the dance of her priestess.

The rainbow with seven colors was also Ishtar's necklace.

The Greek Rainbow Goddess Iris, like the Hindu Maya, personified the many-colored veils of the world's appearances. The many-colored veil of the Egyptian goddess Isis also represented the many material forms of nature in which the creative spirit is clothed, and from which the whole universe was, and is, manifest. The many-colored robe of Isis was obtained by a priestess through initiation and was worn at many religious ceremonials.

The goddess Isis also had seven veils, or stoles;[33] just as Egyptians are said to have had seven souls.[34] The ritual unveiling of the Isis statue was a symbol of the appearance of divine light. Inanna (Nammu), most ancient Creator Goddess of Sumer, also had seven veils.[35]

I have come to see the symbolism of seven veils as possessing several layers of meaning. Perhaps the most eloquent and relevant to me is that the discarding of seven veils conveys the gradual evolvement of the soul from the seven veils of the material plane.

The veil represents the ever-changing form of nature and the material world—the beauty, drama, and tragedy that too often intrigue and distract us, veiling the spirit from our eyes. Because we are both spiritual and animal in our nature, humans exist in duality, belonging to not one but two worlds. The manifest world, our bodies, our emotional reactions, our relations with other humans—all these things seem to have an absolute reality to us. Only in moments of insight, which may be induced by great suffering or moments of great joy, do we suddenly realize that there is a different kind of reality, spiritual and eternal.

The Veiled One

The veil, tunic, or robe often represented the self or the soul. The veil, or cloak, is an expression of the complete self-possession of the sage, isolating her from the instinctive currents that drive general humankind. The veil was seen as protective, just as for the Native American the blanket, sometimes with fetishes (symbols for protective spirits or energies) attached inside, was a shelter.

The veil as worn by the Goddess represented the future, the unknown—something most of us earnestly desire to know about. But we also fear what might be revealed, and so the curiosity and dread have developed in us as ambivalence. The power of the veil became personified in an image known as The Veiled One—the embodiment of all that is precious, all that is valued, and all that is sacred. The Veiled One is the ideal. When the ideal becomes a reality, it is the Veiled One inside your heart. It is not possible to reach the Veiled One unless one comes into a deeply receptive condition, attuning far beyond the created worlds.

Jewelry—Beauty, Power, and Healing

Just as the clothing of the Goddess had power and ritual significance, so too did her jewelry. The important role of jewelry developed from the universal belief that jewelry was endowed with magical and protective religious

The Divine Priestess of Ur

Ancient Ur in southern Iraq, famous in biblical times for gold and silver mined from the Kurdistan hills and worked by local craftspeople, was the home of the *dingir* (divine/holy) priestess and queen Puabi, who lived around 2500 B.C.E. The adornments associated with Puabi represent some of the most elaborate and exquisite jewelry surviving from the ancient world. On her head, Puabi wore a variety of headbands fitted over a wig: a wreath of lapis lazuli beads and carnelian rings with gold ring pendants, and a circlet of beads with gold beech leaves and flowers, topped by a hair comb of gold with three gold flowers inset with lapis lazuli. She wore enormous lunate gold earrings and ten finger rings. She wore a necklace of small gold and lapis beads with the eight-petalled rosette of Innana, Babylonian Queen of Heaven, in the middle. Puabi wore a cloak made of strings of gold, silver, lapis, carnelian, and agate beads. Around her waist was a belt from which hung strings of beads, tubes of gold, carnelian, and lapis, with gold rings suspended from the ends, blue (sky) stones of lapis and sapphire having healing and protective properties.*

Of special interest is another belt fitted about Puabi's hips, made of egg-shaped beads of gold, lapis, and carnelian, of the ceremonial type brought to the shrine at festivals. This girdle not only signified royalty but also was called a birth girdle, as it lay over the womb. Seven stones on the girdle were said to be used by the Goddess to predict the fate of mankind.

*In the Apocalypse, the sapphire is one of the four foundation stones of the Heavenly Jerusalem. It is a symbol of the world when God will dwell among his chosen people.

ARABIC HEGAB, AS DOCUMENTED BY EDWARD WILLIAM LANE IN 1836. CARRYING INSCRIPTIONS SUCH AS "MA' SHAALLA'H" (WHAT GOD WILLS) AND "YA' K'ADI-L-HA'GA'T" (OH DECREER OF THE THINGS THAT ARE NEEDFUL!), IT IS HUNG ON THE RIGHT SIDE ABOVE THE GIRDLE, PASSING OVER THE LEFT SHOULDER. CHILDREN MAY WEAR THEM ATTACHED TO THEIR HEADDRESS.

significance, as is evidenced by the enormous amounts of jewelry found in burial sites, the surviving expressions of ancient beliefs. Beads, rings, spiral arm rings, pendants, and forms of copper artifacts have been found stored in temples or in vases in Old Europe from 6,000 B.C.E. onward.

Jewelry is ritual. In most symbolic traditions, jewels signify spiritual truths inextricably bound up with living and with evolvement. Certain universal, or archetypal, symbols such as fish, birds, snakes, and butterflies are all prevalent images in jewelry. They represent a prehistoric belief that all objects, humans, plants, and even stones are inhabited by the same primal force of nature and therefore have significance for humans.

The gem is symbolic of inner knowledge brought about as the sum of experiences.[36] Gems form the below-ground rainbow, completing the circle with the rainbow in the sky. The ancients believed that gemstones were solidified drops of the divine essence, embedded in rocks when the world was created.[37]

Diamonds "ruled" all other stones by their superior hardness. The word *diamond* (dia-mond) means literally "world goddess."[38] Aquamarine, emerald, turquoise, and beryl are all gems related to the goddess Venus. Certain amethysts were called the "gems of Venus." Quartz, crystal, moonstone, and pearl are related to the moon and the goddesses Diana-Artemis, Hecate, Ishtar, Persephone, and Hathor, among others.

The pearl is seen as the product of the conjunction of fire and water. It has also been identified as the human soul. Hindus believed that pearls sprang from the tears of the Great Mother that fell into the water and, under the first rays of the rising sun, turned into pearls. Eve shed tears of regret that turned into pearls. For Christians, the pearl became the emblem of the Mother of God because Mary gave birth to a "precious pearl."

The Chinese considered jade to be part of paradise fallen to earth and believed it had great healing power, possessing an essential quality of immortality and perfection. Jade is a symbol of the union of the five heavenly virtues (purity, immutability, clarity, euphony, and kindness). It figured in rites and invocations from the 3rd millennium B.C.E. in figures of dragons and tigers intended to represent the cycle of decrease and increase in natural forces.[39]

Silkwood carving, Balinese court dancer.

Jewelry has always been symbolic of power and promise. The necklace symbolized the many in one, the unifying of diversity, binding the Mother Goddess and her people from the beginning of time through endless time, a cosmic and social symbol of ties and bonds.[40] Evidence of perhaps the earliest necklace is the triple chevron worn by the beaked and winged goddess of the Lengyel culture of central Europe in the early 5th millennium B.C.E.

The necklace of the Bronze Age goddess Freyja was the magic rainbow bridge to paradise. Female figures wearing her golden torque neck ring, dating from about 2500 B.C.E., have been unearthed from Scandinavian peat bogs.[41] The goddess Ishtar wore a necklace with the jewels of heaven, its importance illustrated by the promise she made: "By the lapis lazuli round my neck I shall remember these days as I remember the jewels of my throat."[42]

A necklace also serves to identify the deity. The Hindu goddess Kali wears a string of human skulls around her neck, emphasizing the transient nature of all things. Prayer beads (*akshamala*) from seeds, precious stones or pearls strung together (*ratamala*), flowers (*vanamala*), or wood, symbolizing the eternal cycle of time, are a special attribute of protection associated with the goddess Sarasvati. The goddess Lakshmi, it was said, sprang up from the ocean covered with necklaces and pearls, crowned and braceleted.[43]

A crown adorns a person's most noble part and therefore symbolically elevates the wearer. Because of its circular form it also shares the symbolism of the circle: a symbol of heaven, of unity, the absolute, and perfection.

From the 7th millennium B.C.E. the crown was a constant feature in portrayals of the Snake Goddess.[46] Wrested from the White Snake, the crown was a symbol of wisdom and wealth, enabling one to know all, see hidden treasures, and understand the language of animals. The Greek goddess Hera appears crowned with floral ornaments, indicative of her ability to heal through herbs. Among the Minoan goddesses there is a distinct type of cone-shaped headdress that is surrounded by fruits, poppies, and birds, an abstract rendering of earth fertility.[47]

In Buddhism and Hinduism, as in Islam, the crown—sometimes shown as the lotus flower—signifies the elevation of the spirit above the body. In India, the *kiritamukuta* is literally and metaphorically the highest of all crowns. Its shape is rather like a conical cylinder, similar to a mitre, ending in a knot or point.

The Bible speaks of the crown as the symbol of eternal salvation—the crown of life, the crown of immortality. The final inheritance of the saints is figured as a crown of righteousness. The symbol of the crown, however, became divided. On one hand, it was a symbol of power as kings adapted it for public display of their authority; on the other, it changed to a public announcement of virginity for women. Mary's crown was her "virginity." In the Orient as in the Occident, a bride customarily wears a crown, which is considered to be a sign of virginity as well as her "elevation into an esteemed new condition"—at least for that one day.[48]

Navel jewels are another type of adornment with ritual significance. Navel stones worn by dancers in the Middle East are reminiscent of those customarily worn by Hindu temple dancers. These jewels are a reminder of when the navel was accorded much spiritual significance, being the link through which we all first received nourishment from the mother, the

Morrocan women wearing amber necklaces. Photograph courtesy of Morrocan Tourist Board.

place of concentrated life-producing power. In svara yoga, the navel chakra, called *manipura* , the "City of Gems," is a major nerve center of the body that services the transformation of breath. As the golden mean between the upper and lower chakras, the navel is of crucial importance in binding together the Heaven and Earth energies through the breath. In kundalini Yoga this center is known as the emotional, fire chakra. In the ancient Chinese healing art of qigong (chi kung), the *qi*, or life force, is described as a ball of energy residing in the abdomen just below the navel—in other words, at the womb.

The Healing Powers of Gems and Amulets

It may be an unconscious but elementary human need to seek protection in amulets against the unknown and unknowable forces. Faith in amulets (from the Arabic *hamalet*) and gems derives from belief in their iconic ability to acquire help, power, or secret knowledge hidden in Nature.

The Roman historian Pliny wrote that the emerald was believed to assist women in childbirth. A similar belief was held in South America. Lapis was used by Armenian women in preventing miscarriage. The transference of properties from stones is illustrated by the widespread custom of expectant mothers wearing a particular stone

Author and dancer Laurel Gray in Russian Roma costume with gold coin necklace.

called the eagle stone (ferrous aetites), containing iron ore, usually found in streams, as recorded by Greek writers Dioscorides and Plutarch.

Garnet (from *granatum,* the pomegranate, a traditional symbol of the womb) was used in England for women's blood problems. Amber was used chiefly for the throat, head, and womb. The name of Electra, one of the Seven Sisters, means "amber" and may have been applied to a priestess who wore certain amulets of amber as a badge of office.[49] And the crystal, when used as an object of concentration, has been shown to stimulate the purification process because of the perfection of its atomic structure.

The earliest name of the sun is *tsalam* in Assyro-Babylonian and the Sun Goddess, Salambo, meaning image or symbol. This is from the Arabic word *talasim* from which, through Spanish, our word *talisman* comes. While amulets have protective properties, talismans project the wearer's power and bring good luck. Two thousand years ago, they were dispensed by the priestess and later ceremonially used by those who practiced medicine, alchemy, and astrology.

Medical practice among the ancient Jews consisted chiefly of amulets used externally. Lilith is represented among Alsatian Jews on the protective amulets and talismans of women in childbirth (in confinement), and on these talismans are invocations to *Sini* and *Sinsini*. Carnelian was placed inside the mummy in Egypt and was known as the "blood of Isis," a symbol of resurrection.

Indian dancer Indumathy Ganesh lists silver, copper, and/or gold as part of the ceremony for the newborn. "On the 7th day we put bracelets on the baby's legs and hands to ward off negative spirits."[50]

Now Let Us Dance

Now that we know more about the symbolism and power of garments and adornments, we can once again appreciate our aesthetic heritage. Sacred dance is not only an offering to the feminine divine force or spiritual power, it is a way to be Her, to be of

Elizabeth Artemis Mourat uses her veil to accentuate and extend her movements.

Her, a part of the Whole. Therefore, when you come together as a group or when you feel the need to dance and connect on your own, dress your goddess—your goddess within. Putting on special clothes and adorning yourself with jewelry, when done with the proper intent, helps you to experience yourself divinely. It can be as simple as tying a fringed scarf around the hips or wearing a necklace or other items you have set aside for that purpose.

Whatever you wear should reflect the integrity of your dance and enhance its ability to inspire. If your dance is for an audience, you may want to consider whether the performance is for a worship service: Is it formal or casual, ritualistic or charismatic, a regular service or special celebration? If the performance is for a church congregation, is your audience familiar with danced devotion? Each religious community has its own identity, and what is worn must be appropriate for it. Some, for instance, are not comfortable with leotards or bare feet. A good general rule is to dress modestly, taking care to wear adequate undergarments. Some groups prefer special costumes, while others wear regular clothing with a unifying item of stole or sash. Long sleeves with full skirts or loose trousers provide adequate freedom to move and

Dance of the Veils.

are appropriate for a variety of body types and shapes.

Although there are many articles of clothing, costumes, and jewelry that inspire dance, as a dancer I love the movement possible with the beautiful veil most of all. The veil becomes an extension of the dancer, floating like gossamer wings upon the air currents left by her spinning body as she turns and glides. The veil creates an air of mystery, intrigue, and illusion. It is the awakening of the earth to spring, the girl to womanhood; it portrays the unfolding petals of a flower, the mystery of a new love. The dancer is no longer earthbound when she dances with the veil.

The floating veil has a vital life in itself, creating the picture of a rhythmic, moving line of embodied energy and leaving a splash of color behind as you turn. The veil can be an enveloping cloud in which your everyday personality is engulfed and lost. Placing the veil over your head can act like a switch, at the same time forming a protective seclusion and taking you instantly into your inner depths. As in meditation or prayer, your thoughts turn inward, away from the demands of daily existence. There is a mystical feel to slowly dancing and turning under a veil.

Dance of the Veils

To dance with the veil, you need good posture, keeping chin and rib cage elevated. Turns on the balls of the feet give a lighter feeling than turns that are done flat. Practice turns as taught in modern dance or ballet classes, using spotting techniques if you get dizzy. The veil should be held by the index finger and thumb, very lightly. It should always be moved so as to catch the air, to keep it floating. There are many variations, such as holding the right hand close to the body while the left hand holds the veil up and in front, then turning left into the veil to the end under the left arm, then reversing the turn out of the veil. Additionally, you can drop one end of the veil and form figure-eight patterns with one extended arm as you turn in a circle.

You can hold the veil high above the head while running or gliding forward or back, or suddenly drop to a kneeling position, pulling the veil downward with you, and coming to rest with the veil as a covering over your body. The more you play with the veil, the more innovative things you can do with it, but always remember to keep it light and floating.

I recommend dancing to a Strauss waltz, Ravel's *Bolero,* or any of the numerous musical renditions of *Ave Maria.*

PART TWO

Modern Sacred Dance Today

ꙮ

The revival of sacred dance actually began not in the 1990s or 1970s but in the 1920s and 1930s with modern dancers like Isadora Duncan, Martha Graham, and the grande dame of modern dance, Ruth St. Denis, who was the inspiration for two of the major sacred dance organizations today: the Sacred Dance Guild and the Dances of Universal Peace.

We shall look at the influence of each of these women and others, examine some of the styles and practices of sacred dance today, and then explore some of the most enduring and significant themes and symbols from which many sacred dances are derived—the moon, circle, serpent, funerals and other rites of passage, and the four elements of earth, air, fire, and water. Finally, we shall identify important practices and techniques to keep in mind as you branch out to create your own unique styles of dance and ritual.

6

Modern Dance: The Sacred Dance of Eternity

If we seek the real source of the dance, if we go to nature, we find that the dance of the future is the dance of the past, the dance of eternity, and has been and will always be the same. . . . But the dance of the future will have to become again a high religious art as it was with the Greeks. For art which is not religious is not art, is mere merchandise.

Isadora Duncan

Wherever a dancer stands is holy ground.

Martha Graham

For centuries, social convention censured free movement of the female body by eliminating or separating dance from spiritual practices. When dance movement was desired, it was hidden under a layer of cultivated elegance, under decorative but highly artificial forms, with male choreographed postures and moves that were unnatural to the female body. Orthopedist William Hamilton, M.D., has quoted from the writings of a ballet master in 1760: "To dance elegantly . . . it is imperative to reverse the order of things and force the limbs, by means of exercise both long and painful, to take a totally different position from that

which is natural to them."[1] Among the list of "faults of physical construction" were broad hips and wide thighs, and we know breasts were not allowed. In defiance of these preconceptions and restrictions placed upon women, modern dancers such as Isadora Duncan, Ruth St. Denis, Martha Graham, Mary Wigman, and even the great Russian ballerina Anna Pavlova all turned to the past to recapture the original impetus of dance expression and to bring the feminine spirit through. Ruth St. Denis was drawn to the ascetic sense of mysticism found in the ancient dances of India and the Middle East. Anna Pavlova went to Egypt and India to study oriental dance, which led to her performance of the *nataya* (story-dance-scene) of Radha-Krishna choreographed by Uday Shankar. Mary Wigman's work showed a strong leaning to a mystical belief, drawing from archaic symbolism. Her dances dealt with the ultimates of fate, sacrifice, and death within her vision of holism that is life. Her *Witch Dance* reflected the image of one possessed; *The Temple* connected women with worship.[2] Some other dancers were Jean Erdman, who joined mythology with dance at the Theatre of the Open Eye in New York City; Katherine Dunham, who, in the 1940s, performed a theatrical Voudoun exorcism ceremony that had several elements similar to the Egyptian Zar ritual or the Brazilian mambo;[3] Helen Tamiri with her *Negro Spirituals*, and Doris Humphrey and her dance *Shakers*.

It has been said that for each of these dancers, technique was always at the service of a higher purpose: to translate through the art of movement personal emotional experiences, intuitive perceptions, and ethereal truths that elude the intellectual statement of fact. Their work was to raise our consciousness of women's approach to spirituality through the principle of connecting the human body to the Cosmic Body. Doris Humphrey explained her dance as "working from the inside out." She said the body mirrors the impulses within, the unseen reality where creativity resides.[4]

Isadora Duncan: Mother of Modern Dance

Isadora Duncan (1878–1927) at the turn of the century was convinced that movement sprang from the "soul," by which she meant the seat of emotion. Her larger-than-life emancipation, both on the stage and off, was a glorification of woman as a person free from confining garments and social customs, and she celebrated her freedom at center stage for all the world to see. She was inspired by ancient Greek arts and also was deeply impressed by her exposure to Hungarian Gypsy folk music and dance.

In speaking out for freedom and happiness for women in all aspects of life, Isadora Duncan expressed the same things that I feel modern women, although separated by time and space from their ritualistic roots, can still connect with through dance: "It is not only a question of true art, it is a question of race, of the development of the female sex to beauty and health, of the return to the original strength and to natural movements of woman's body."

LEFT: ISADORA DUNCAN AT THE PARTHENON. PHOTOGRAPH BY EDWARD STEICHEN. NEW YORK PUBLIC LIBRARY FOR THE PERFORMING ARTS.

Martha Graham

The political became the personal in the work of Martha Graham (1894–1991). An emancipator in her own way, Graham, too, kept women at the center of the stage in the dances of her early and middle period, often using themes and characters from ancient mythology as the vehicles for showing women in a new and powerful way and using the body to communicate states of the mind and emotions. Her belief that *inner* emotion can be revealed through movement was the basis of her dance creations.

Graham believed that a woman's body in movement is capable of extending the spirituality of nature and connecting it with the fundamental experience of being human. In her *Notebooks of Martha Graham*, she wrote: "Thus the woman is the original seeress, the lady of the wisdom-bringing waters of the depths, of the murmuring springs and fountains, for the 'original utterance of seerdom in the language of water.' But the woman also understands the rustling of the trees and all the signs of nature, with whose life she is so closely bound up."[5] She taught that the language of dance is based on the body's exaggerated, abstract gestures. In dance, a stride across the stage becomes a metaphor, she said.

MARTHA GRAHAM IN *ALCESTIS*. PHOTOGRAPH BY MARTHA SWOPE.

The dance technique Graham invented depended on the principle of contract-and-release: movements that are based on the pulsation of breath, the pulsation of life. The result was a dramatic force and tension in body movement not seen before in Western dance. Martha Graham explained her technique thus: "Every time you breathe life in or expel it, it is a release or a contraction. . . . You are born with these two movements and you keep both until you die. But you begin to use them consciously so that they are beneficial to the dance dramatically." She added, "It bemuses me that my school in New York has been called 'the House of the Pelvic Truth,' because so much of the movement comes from a pelvic thrust, or because I tell a student 'you are simply not moving your vagina.'"[6] Even though Graham's style of dance was innovative for her time, the arch and contraction, or contraction and release, are the very foundation of one of the most ancient and enduring forms of women's dance, belly dance (see chapter 4), linking

Graham to the wisdom and practices of generations of women before her.

Graham was fascinated with the past and said she always felt ancestral footsteps behind her, ancestral gestures flowing through her: ". . . it has always seemed to be that, even as a child, I have been aware of unseen things around me, a certain sense of that movement. I don't know what to call them, sense beings perhaps, or spirits, or a kind of energy that stimulates the globe. I know that something exists there."[7]

As seen in *Primitive Mysteries*, *Judith*, *Herodiade*, *Frescoes*, and *Golden Hall*, there was a recurring theme of woman as heroine and the different aspects of woman as Goddess-Mother-Priestess in Graham's works. In the agonies of *Clytemnestra*, in her *Medea*, and in *Joscasta*, she showed us passions we as women could recognize. In a 1950 note, she related the Indian deity Kali to the release of creative energy that she saw as the theme of her own *Deaths and Entrances* of 1943. She wrote: "Tonight in *Deaths and Entrances* while standing, I suddenly knew what witchcraft is. . . . It is the being within each of us, sometimes the witch, sometimes the real being of good—of creative energy—no matter in what area or direction of activity. . . . It is Kali in her terrible aspect. It is Shiva the Destroyer."

Martha Graham expressed her sense of the spiritual, always. She said, "That driving force of God that lives through me is what I live for." Graham never left the Goddess. At age ninety-six, she wrote her final paragraph and her final tribute: "I have a new ballet to do for the Spanish government, and I have been brooding about pointing it toward the transmigration of the Goddess figure, from Indian to Babylon, Sumer, Egypt, Greece, Rome, Spain (with its Dama del Elche), and the American Southwest. And I am sure it will be a terror and a joy, and I will regret starting it a thousand times, and think it will be my swan song, and my career will end like this, and I will feel that I have failed a hundred times, and try to dodge those inevitable footsteps behind me. But what is there for me but to go on? This is life for me. My life. How does it all begin, I suppose it never begins. It just continues. And one . . . [and two, and . . .]"

At age twelve, Murshida Rabia Ana Perez-Chisti, a Sufi Movement International lineage holder and senior interfaith minister, was a student of Martha Graham. Rabia tells of how Graham introduced her to Buddhism at her studio on 64th Street in New York City, and the positive effects it had on her life. "I began to learn how states of emptiness could become an art to understanding states in spiritual development through the dance. Ms. Graham would talk to me about this, particularly after I pursued her constantly with questions." She, along with Ruth St. Denis, instilled in Rabia "the love of the dance and the view that the dancer was Divine and nothing less was accepted. The moment I perceived this, I felt I was set free."[8]

Mata Hari: Exotic Intrigue

Next to Salome of the Seven Veils, there probably has never been a dancer

Mata Hari. Photo courtesy
Elizabeth Artemis Mourat private collection.

more scandalous than Mata Hari. Mata Hari, born Margaretha Geertruida Zelle, was famous as a World War I spy who died in the shadows of intrigue and double cross. Her infamy in politics, however, obscures her other life as an innovative though sometimes provocative dancer. Like Isadora Duncan, Mata Hari brought her own representation of women's dance to the stage, choosing her own costuming and creating her own interpretations of dance.

Mata Hari captivated Europe with her exotic versions of Hindu *bayadere* dance. She is believed to have studied the sacred dances and native rituals of Java in secret visits to the temples when she lived there with her husband after the mysterious death of her son in 1899. Mata Hari described her dance as "a sacred poem in which each movement is a word and whose every word is underlined by music." She said, "The temple in which I dance can be vague or faithfully reproduced, for I am the temple. All true temple dances are religious in nature and all explain, in gestures and poses, the rules of the sacred texts. One must always translate the three stages which correspond to the divine attributes of Brahma, Vishnu, and Siva—creation, fecundity, destruction. . . . By means of destruction towards creation through incarnation, that is what I am dancing—that is what my dance is about."[9]

Mata Hari presented her dances with great freedom of the body, even though she was living in Victorian times, when movement of the female body was severely judged; no doubt this helped enhance her negative reputation. Whatever her personal reputation may have been, though, she was described as an outstanding dancer and was praised by distinguished Orientalists at the Guimet Museum in Paris for her dance.[10]

Ruth St. Denis: The American Priestess

Ruth St. Denis (1880–1968), fondly known as Miss Ruth, was the grande dame of early modern dance. In her autobiography she described how the experience of seeing a poster of the Egyptian Goddess Isis affected her entire approach to dance and performance:

> I identified in a flash with the figure of Isis. She became the expression of all the somber mystery and beauty of Egypt, and I knew that my destiny as a dancer had sprung alive in that moment. I would become a rhythmic and impersonal instrument of spiritual revelation rather than a personal actress of comedy or tragedy. I had never before known such an inward shock of rapture.[11]

Although she added dramatic qualities to the traditional dance forms she performed, St. Denis's interpretations retained the original ritualistic aspects of the dances, as she searched for her own spiritual essence. Just as Isadora Duncan had done before her, Ruth St. Denis included all parts of the body for spiritual expression—the arms, hands, head, shoulder, neck, face, and eyes. She also used both authentic and creative costuming to augment her choreographed themes.

Miss Ruth called herself a self-appointed prophetess.[12] Her dances of religious and goddess themes included *Radha and the Dance of the Five Senses, Egypta, The Queen of Heaven, A Study of the Madonna, Ishtar of the Seven Gates, Three Apsarases, Kuan Yin, Incense, Dancer at the Court of King Ahasuerus (Esther),* and *White Jade.* She also danced Theodora of Byzantine, the dancer (priestess) who became empress, and the Ouled Nail of Algeria.

In 1906, Ruth St. Denis first introduced her interpretation of a cycle of ancient forms of spiritual expression in an offering she titled "A Program of Hindu Dance."* Ruth St. Denis, along with Anna Pavlova and Uday Shankar, inspired the interest of the Indian people in reviving and preserving their indigenous sacred dance traditions, which had suffered great neglect and disdain during the long period of English colonialization.[13]

In 1918, St. Denis developed the dance *Jephthah's Daughter*, based on an Old Testament story about a warrior named Jephthah, who vowed he would slay as a sacrifice the first person he saw when he returned from battle if Jehovah would grant him victory. As he returned home, his daughter (unnamed in the story) came out dancing for joy to celebrate his triumph. Unlike the story of Abraham and Isaac, wherein the son is rescued by

*On her first tour of the United States, Ruth St. Denis was accompanied by the Khan family, one of India's most famous groups of musicians, including Pir-O Murshid Hazrat Inayat Khan, the great Sufi teacher, master musician, and author.

Jehovah at the last minute, the daughter is sacrificed by her father.*

Ruth St. Denis spent the last thirty years of her life focusing her energies on sacred dance in America, says Kamae Miller in her book *Wisdom Comes Dancing: Selected Writing of Ruth St. Denis on Dance, Spirituality and the Body.*†[14] After visiting a church in the South where she observed "an atmosphere of gloom," "monotonous droning of the minister," and "lugubrious hymns," Miss Ruth said, "A great resentment and a kind of righteous indignation welled up in my heart, and I was jealous for the church. Suddenly I had a vision of a great beautiful edifice with light and motion and harmony as its expression. It was a 'Temple of the living God.'"

Senior interfaith minister Murshida Rabia Ana Perez-Chisti experienced firsthand St. Denis's commitment to this creative endeavor from her studies with Miss Ruth at the Graham Studio in New York:

> Emptying herself, she would disappear and the sacred dance would enter her and all that she conveyed in her movement was the living presence of the One she invoked through her body. What an unforgettable experience to behold. Her effect on my being enraptured me with the desire to learn how to follow this example. She was the one who showed me a way, a path through which one may journey to get to the Divine through the body.[15]

Ruth St. Denis tried to bring dance back to the church. In 1934 she performed one of her Madonna pieces before the altar at St. Mark's Episcopal Church in New York City. That same year she also wrote a manuscript entitled "The Divine Dance," which was never published but which outlined her vision for the integration of dance into church practice—a vision that has become the spirit of the liturgical sacred dance movement today. She wrote:

> For too long have we lived constantly in two worlds, or so we supposed we did, in body and in spirit; but . . . we are not made of one substance and our bodies of another. The whole scheme of things in reality is not two, but One. On this hangs not only the whole law and prophets of the liberating philosophy of the new age but the very starting point and method of approach of the Divine Dance.
>
> My concept of the new forms of worship that would include rhythmic movement in the church services asks for no lessening of the natural dignity and solemn beauty of spiritual realization. But I call for a new, vital expression that will bring humanity into a closer more harmonious relationship with the One who created our bodies as well as our souls.[16]

While the audiences of her day loved Miss Ruth, her exotic images, and her theatrical productions, for the

Right: Ruth St. Denis in *Incense*. New York Public Library for the Performing Arts.

*There is a Greek version of this story, wherein Iphigenia is sacrificed by her father, Agamemnon.

†Miller, an artist and teacher of sacred movement in the Sufi tradition, did a thorough job of searching through over a hundred boxes in the archives of UCLA and the New York Library for the Performing Arts, pulling together a combination of published and unpublished poetry, lectures, manuscripts, and photographs of Ruth St. Denis.

most part they didn't really understand or care about her spiritual message. She passionately wanted the church "in its highest unsectarian sense to embody Christ's gospel of Life and to have the irresistible lure of Beauty with which to heal and inspire the world."[17]

"Looking into the future," she said, "I see thousands of churches pulsing with life and revealing the beauty of holiness; I see thousands of altars where the young Miriams and Davids of today are dancing before the One! I see maturity reborn in grace and strength, and the joyous footsteps of the children dancing down the chancels of the world, bringing to the shrine of God the offerings of praise!"

She summarized her mission beautifully in a poem she wrote that was later engraved on her burial vault:

The Gods have meant
That I should dance
And in some mystic hour
I shall move to unheard rhythms
Of the cosmic orchestra of heaven
And you will know the language
Of my wordless poems
And will come to me
For that is why I dance.[18]

Although I was not fortunate enough to know or study with Ruth St. Denis, I know that I, like so many others, have greatly benefited from her strong belief in divine dance and her pioneering spirit. Ruth St. Denis developed the Society of Spiritual Arts (later called the Church of the Divine Dance) and the Rhythmic Choir in New York City. She was the inspiration for the founding of the Sacred Dance Guild and Samuel L. Lewis, who began the Dances of Universal Peace, was a student of Ruth St. Denis.

The Sacred Dance Guild

One of the legacies of our modern dance forebears was a return to religious themes and the use of dance in church services, and one of the ways this was accomplished was through the formation of the Sacred Dance Guild. The Sacred Dance Guild is an international, interfaith, interdenominational organization that offers various dance forms from a unique blend of religious, cultural, and ethnic backgrounds. Regions and chapters sponsor events and workshops throughout the year, and the guild holds a national festival each summer at various locations throughout the United States. The dance guild brings a full spectrum of activities and information to persons of all ages, backgrounds, and abilities in fulfillment of their belief that sacred dance is a catalyst for spiritual growth and change through the integration of mind, body, and spirit. Dancers and nondancers alike share the opportunity to experience movement as worship, prayer, healing, and meditation; as an agent of change; as a message of peace; and as recreation.

Margaret Taylor-Doane, who was a student of Ruth St. Denis, was one of the founders of the Sacred Dance Guild (1958). She began her work with sacred dance through her role as a minister's wife, creating gestures for the choir. Now the author of several books and articles on how to bring dance into worship, she has taught many liturgical dance choreographies throughout the United States. In the June 1961 newsletter of the Sacred Dance Guild, she wrote:

> The basic requisite of this art is that the participants and leaders are clearly dedicated to use their whole being (body, mind, soul) with integrity as they confront present day issues which become clarified and illumined as the outgrowth of their deepening understanding.
>
> The secondary responsibility of sacred dance is "dance." The movements should grow creatively out of inner motivation, not geared to any specific dance style nor self-consciously involved in body techniques. The dance movements and designs are secondary to the sacred concerns that are being communicated, allowing the clear revelation of the spirit through the body disciplined for this purpose and diffused with the spirit.[19]

There are a variety of approaches to sacred dance within the Guild membership and in the many congregations throughout the world who have brought dance back to worship in their own ways. First, there is the sacred dance choir or soloist rehearsing and performing on a regular basis much like church singing choirs. From this can emerge the "dance spectacular," which is done at a more professional performance level, like a religious drama.

Second, there is congregational sacred dance, which includes audience participation just like congregational singing and Psalm reading. This form of sacred dance can be defined as "the worshipper's physical response to Spirit" in the same manner as movements such as kneeling in prayer and standing for invocation. Basic ethnic-type dance steps may be incorporated, or charismatic movements such as clapping the hands or raising the arms to accompany spiritual songs. These movements may be spontaneous, in which a few or all congregants choose to join in, or may be rehearsed by a group and presented to the others as a gift to be shared.

Other forms of sacred dance include improvisational dance and dance as private prayer. Private prayer dance may be a solitary act or may be done by a small group gathered to dance for its own unified purpose. Several of the recommended dances at the ends of the chapters in this book are prime examples of private prayer dance. Private prayer dance can also be another form and outgrowth of improvisational dance.

Improvisational Sacred Dance

One of the many approaches to sacred dance movement that many people find relevant is improvisational dance. Improvisation in worship gives personal expression to word and prayer. Gail Stepanek, professor of modern dance and founder of Improvisational Inspiration, integrates the use of movement, toning, breath, rhythm, drawing, meditation, and prayer in a spontaneous and intuitive process in order to

Gail Stepanek, founder of Improvisational Inspiration, creates an improvisational sacred dance. Photograph by Nicole Sawyer.

connect herself and others with spirit. She very aptly describes the process and the power of improvisational sacred dance in the introduction to her workshops:

> As we enter into improvisational dancing, we automatically live in the present moment and enter the unknown, moment by moment, as we are creating. As we abandon and surrender ourselves to the dance that unfolds from within, we enter a "thought-free" state where the mind becomes a focused instrument for the song of the heart and we are able to enter deep levels of joy and bliss and a feeling of union with the all-pervading spirit.
>
> In offering ourselves fully to the spirit, to the sacred dance, spirit enters and moves us, transforms us, awakens our soul's passion, enlivens every cell of our body. We become the essence of spirit in motion, the divine cosmic dancer. The sacred dance can take us across from one world to another, from one state of mind to another, from contraction and fear to expansion and love. It is a symbol of life; vibrating, alive and radiant. It can guide us home to our true state of inner freedom.

Doug Adams, professor of Christianity and the Arts at the Pacific School of Religion in Berkeley, California, says, "Theologically, improvisation leaves room for the Holy Spirit who moves in mysterious and not predictable ways."[20]

Dance of Universal Peace. Photograph by Matin Mize.

Dances of Universal Peace

The Dances of Universal Peace, sometimes erroneously called Sufi dancing, are a collection of simple meditative circle dances that incorporate sacred phrases, mantras or chants, music, and movements. This form of circle dancing with awareness of breath, sound, and movement was developed by Murshid Samuel L. Lewis (1892–1971). Lewis (fondly known as "Sufi Sam") felt the dances were a form of sacred movement that could be presented to the public and would create an expanded sense of the self through devotion as well as a form of "world peace through the arts."

The dances are derived from many of the world's spiritual traditions and from a synthesis of spiritual dance techniques from Lewis's study with Ruth St. Denis. They also include training in walking meditation and breathing techniques from Sufi and Zen Buddhist practices. Lewis studied Hinduism and Buddhism, as well as Sufism with several Sufi orders in India, Pakistan, and Egypt, and was authorized as a Sufi teacher by Hazrat Inayat

Khan of India. Lewis first began the Dances of Universal Peace in San Francisco in the 1960s and subsequently taught them throughout the world.

It is said that the song, the chant, is always central and that the dance comes out of that. We learn to bring the breath, heart, mind, and body into harmony as we dance in community. To me, one of the most beneficial aspects of the Universal Peace technique is the opportunity for interaction among the dancers in a structured way, bringing the experience into relationships with strangers or with what the self habitually sees as "outsiders." I once asked a regular participant why she danced, and she replied, "When I let go of my self-consciousness enough to say to another, even a stranger, in the circle, 'Allah/God loves you, I love you,' it makes it easier for me to say that to, or feel that way about, people I come into contact with in my daily life. This is why it is called one of the spiritual paths." Another dancer told me, "I love the dances. Their beauty and the patterned movements have moved me to spiritual experiences I don't believe I would have had otherwise. I give a lot of credit to the fact that the body's being involved allows for the deeper experience."

The Alchemy of Sacred Dance

Joan Dexter Blackmer, a graduate of the C. G. Jung Institute in Zurich who also trained in modern dance, has found there is a sacred power in dance even if that is not the intent of the dancer:

> Anyone who enters the realm of danced theater enters even now, when dance seems so secular, a sacred realm. Behind the effort needed to become a dancer, as I see it, lies a deep urge to be allowed into sacred time and space, to open the earthly body and what it can communicate to an other-worldly energy. The dance itself becomes, for a moment, the vessel into which sacred energies may flow, a vehicle for the manifestation of the gods, those forces which appear in the psyche as archetypal images.[21]

The expression of spirituality and body consciousness that occurs when one dances has led to the development of numerous psychophysical techniques and the burgeoning field of dance therapy. From the physical work of dance comes a process of mental liberation not available from psychological work alone. Carla DeSola, founder of the Omega Liturgical Dance Company at St. John the Divine Cathedral in New York City, reminds us, "Perhaps dance's most important gift to us lies in its ability to unify us and make us whole by uniting our inward life with our outward expression."*[22]

With their interest in ancient dance forms, Isadora Duncan, Ruth St. Denis, Martha Graham, and others created a contemporary link between ethnic spiritual dance and dance therapy. They sought out and learned from expatriate ethnic dancers in this country, and they traveled to other countries, studying and witnessing communal healing and

*Carla DeSola currently teaches dance and Omega Peace Arts at the Pacific School of Religion in Berkeley, California.

Emilie Conrad, founder of the Continuum Dance Movement. Photograph by Ron Peterson.

therapeutic dance in traditional cultures. In doing so, they both directly and indirectly prepared the ground for the development of dance therapy.

Mary Starks Whitehouse, the originator of Movement-in-Depth, studied at the C. G. Jung Institute in Zurich and with Martha Graham and Mary Wigman. Whitehouse's technique, which she called the Tao of the Body, was based on the concept that the psyche and the physical are inseparable and that conscious experience of physical movement produces changes in the psyche. A direct descendant of Whitehouse's work is the Authentic Movement Institute in Oakland, California. The Dance Therapy Association in Columbia, Maryland, grew out of the "movement-as-communication" techniques devised by dance/movement therapy pioneer Marian Chace. Emilie Conrad's Continuum work in Santa Monica, California, was inspired by her study with Katherine Dunham, Pearl Primus, and others. Her approach to the body is based on intrinsic felt movement rather than culturally imposed patterned movement.

Laura Shannon, who lives in Middlesex, England, developed a technique she calls Living Ritual Dance out of her many years of working with folk dances, including dances of the European Sacred Circle Dance Network, and dance/movement therapy theory and methods. In papers published

Turkish harvest dance at a workshop in France led by Laura Shannon.

in the proceedings of the American Dance Therapy Association, Shannon explained, "Living Ritual Dance does not aim to instruct in folk dance technique, or to imitate 'traditional' cultures; its primary intention is to facilitate an experiential rediscovery of the ancient healing dance in which dance therapy has its roots, through the creative exploration of extant folk dances. We seek to relate these ancient dance forms to our modern selves, and to keep them alive in a way that has meaning for us today, by experiencing them in a ritual context."[23]

Dance anthropologists have found that a visible connection exists between the art of the vanished cultures and those still existing. Although the early dance forms themselves have, for the most part, disappeared, their influence is found in the simplest village dances, direct descendants of the more ancient communal healing or therapeutic dance traditions, the ancestor of dance movement therapy.

Shannon says that the dance forms of line, open and closed circle, labyrinth/spiral, and solo formations all contribute in their own way to the provision of a safe and supportive space in which healing can occur. Sharing rhythm and effort creates an atmosphere of mutual holding and support. Simple movements are repeated to evoke the universality of human experience in space and time. This concept is so simple yet so profound; but it can be ascertained only by your own personal experience.

An integral part of Living Ritual Dance is the movement meditation inspired by images of ancient sacred statues and figurines from all over the world. Shannon says, "these strong female images provide a concrete and undeniable historical precedent for the body-oriented empowerment of women." Participants in this women-only workshop, using traditional women's dance movements often centered in powerful yet gentle movement from the pelvis, create a "living ritual" "whereby we can experience the timeless energy of communal dance in a new way."[24]

SHAMAN, PERFORMED BY THE ELINOR COLEMAN DANCE ENSEMBLE, NEW YORK CITY. PHOTOGRAPH BY OTTO M. BERK.

Why We Dance

Dance is a spiritual channel, an opening of metaphysical and sensuous doorways. Every dancer knows her goal: to get to that point where the body no longer stands in the way but becomes the instrument of the soul's expression, the body and psyche working together. Unfortunately, the feelings of joy, hope, and renewal and the spiritual connections that we can experience through sacred dance are not always felt immediately by the beginner. A period of discipline and training precedes these experiences, in much the same way as an initiation into any spiritual or mental training—a type of shaman's journey. Gradually muscles begin to respond; the shoulders, fingers, hips, pelvis, neck, and arms begin to move in coordination. Inner and outer worlds fuse, and the dancer moves beyond conscious concern with the physicality and perfection of form. The dancer knows it has been worth the effort to be able to hear the music through her body, to be ruled by the rhythm, to express that which is inexpressible. When we arrive at this place, we are connecting with the music and the mystical and the ethereal, surrendering to a power that uses us as a willing instrument. We are danced.

Today, the holistic approach to healing by connecting body-mind-spirit as the path to wholeness once again is simply trying to take us back to a very ancient approach. At the same time we will be fulfilling the prophesy by Isadora Duncan when she said, "The dancer of the future will realize the mission of woman's body and the holiness of all its parts. She will dance the changing life of nature, showing how each part is transformed into the other. From all parts of her body shall shine radiant intelligence, bringing to the world the message of the thoughts and aspirations of thousands of women. She shall dance the freedom of women."[25]

7
MOON DANCE

And then,
as the Moon withdrew from sight
the women too withdrew from sight
At the Dark of the Moon
the women descended into Hera's temple
and that close-and-holy dark womb-place
tenderly swallowed them
For their time of wisdom and power was at hand
Their Dragon Time was at hand.

From a poem in Virgin, Mother, Crone: Myths and Mysteries of the Triple Goddess[1]

To understand women's unique connection to the moon, we need to look back to ancient times and ancient ways. The moon has always been associated with the creation cycle in nature, its four phases (new, waxing, full, and waning) reflecting the cycles of life (birth, growth, maturity, and death)—or, in agricultural terms, seeding, growth, harvest, winter rest. The moon's phases also reflect the creation cycle as it moves through a woman's body in the monthly readying, filling, and emptying of the uterus. A woman's menstrual cycle is often referred to as her moon cycle because most women tend to regulate to a monthly lunation cycle of twenty-eight to thirty days, with the days of ovulation and menstruation falling at about the full and new moons.

For many ancient civilizations, the moon symbolized the daughter of

Lady of the Grove: goddess Ashera, c. 1300 B.C.E. Designs on her skirt illustrate the phases of the moon.

creation, daughter of the Mother Earth, or the Goddess of Creation herself. Many believed that the dead lived on the moon. The effects of the cycles of the moon on the body and on nature were recognized in the symbol of the Triple Goddess, the Goddess in Triad: Maiden, Matron, and Crone—new moon, full moon, waning moon.

All the Greek goddesses had some connection with the moon. Euripides, in his tragedy *Ion*,[2] makes the sea and the sky reply to the dance of the Moon Goddess who dances with her fifty daughters, honoring Persephone, the daughter with the golden crown, and Demeter, the holy mother. The oracle at Delphi was connected with an oracle in the moon and was delivered monthly.[3] Hecate is the Moon Goddess as well as the special patroness of witches.

The Hittites of Asia Minor in the 2nd millennium B.C.E. left evidence of women's connection to the moon. Mythological texts as well as birth rituals count the months of a woman's pregnancy based on the appearances of the moon, with birthing expected in the tenth month from the last moon rising before the cessation of the menses. The derivation of "to be pregnant" and "month" from the Hittite root *arma* is identical in form to the name for the Anatolian Moon Goddess Armas.

The story of the Maenads gives us the clue that they were probably dancing outdoor full moon rituals, open-air exposure to the moon being the most efficient way to be in synchrony with the moon's phases. In Euripides' day, and indeed down into the 2nd century C.E., ritual mountain dances performed at night by women could be seen in Delphi and elsewhere. The Roman writer Ovid spoke of the members of Cybele's chorus's "bacchanal strains under the dark of the Moon."

In the Kabbalistic tradition, the Shekhina (the spirit of the divine or Divine Mother) is addressed in prayer, especially during the holidays of Sukkot and the arrival of the new moon. The sage Rabbi Yohanan said, "Whoever blesses the New Moon at the proper time is considered as having welcomed the presence of the Shekhina."[4]

High in the Andes mountains of Peru, dancers of the Quillacingas tribe, wearing golden crescents as nose ornaments, danced for Mama Quilla, the Inca name for the moon. They danced to restore a caring attitude to a hardened world estranged from feminine values.

Menstrual Power

Healthy women of childbearing age have always bled once a month with no harm to the body. In innumerable cultures and across time, women withdrew from everyday life during their "moon" or menstrual cycle, ceasing all social and other intercourse with men, meditating, and performing various rites. In their seclusion, freed from immediate worries, creative psychic energy would flow inward again. The myths of many cultures tell how the moon herself withdraws for the same reason women do: to have her period and renew herself. The menstrual period would often lead to increased consciousness and was the purpose of rites and ceremonies of devotion and possession. It was women's vast moon-based wisdom and understanding of life's cycles that provided the foundation for agriculture, astronomy, and even mathematics.

The earliest known offering of blood was the freely given menstrual blood of women, a symbol of regeneration or rebirth, like the red ochre used in innumerable Paleolithic and Neolithic burials. Over time, however, women's blood gradually became redefined as contaminating rather than sacred, and the self-imposed seclusion of sanctification turned into forced exclusion from the community. For men, who did not experience birth or the non-reproductive blood flow of menstruation, blood was connected with death: in order for blood to flow, a living creature had to die. Thus, in the patriarchal model, menstruation and even birth came to be seen as a consequence of death; menstruating women became taboo, as unclean as if they had touched a corpse. Prohibitory laws were developed that dehumanized and isolated women.

"THE MOON," BY ALEXANDRA GENETTI. ILLUSTRATION FROM *THE WHEEL OF CHANGE TAROT.*

Some researchers, such as Vicki Noble and Barbara Walker, argue that the practice of bloodletting, the obtaining of "sacred blood" by human or animal sacrifice, and the act of circumcision became a necessity only when woman's menstrual power was no longer regarded as sacred and when women were no longer a part of religious rites. Lucy Goodison, author of *Death, Women and the Sun*, points out that "there is not one seal celebrating the actual act of animal sacrifice from the early period."[5]

In ancient times, menstrual flow was

Triple spiral from temple at New Grange, Ireland. The spiral is the basic pattern for the Moon Dance.

seen as a harmonic of natural rhythms, like the seasons, birthing and rebirthing, and was gathered and stored in a menstrual cup. The cup or chalice is often a symbol of overflowing abundance, a vessel providing nourishment. It is also a representation of the womb. The sacred menstrual cup, however, was transformed into a seething cauldron when it was replaced by the chalice of sacrificial blood, which later became a symbol in the Eucharist—the cup containing Christ's blood.

Clearly, men sensed a kind of power derived from the occurrence of the monthly bleeding cycle, given that they sought to emulate this practice through ritual sacrifice, but they misunderstood what this power is all about. The power is the flow—the flow of grace, of energy, for the woman and through the woman. Its very nature precludes manipulation or the use of it for any outward purpose or power by anyone, even by the woman. Nor can it be induced or captured, just as grace cannot be induced or captured. In order to heal the separation of women from sacred rites, we need to return to the feminine symbolism associated with menstrual blood.

Aligning with the Moon

The natural events that cause alterations in a woman's body irreversibly affect her life, her views and values of that life, her personal relationships, and her social identity. First menstruation, first sexual intercourse, childbirth, and menopause all constitute woman's fundamental and powerful participation in the inscrutable mystery of life. It is because these changes and events are so definite and definitive that women have recognized the need for ritual to help them incorporate these experiences into their lives.

Tuning in to the harmonics of the moon is one way women can bring ancient wisdom and rituals into their modern lives. Women who are continuously giving to family and career in this age of the "superwoman" can feel depleted and yet guilty for taking any time for themselves. Entraining with the moon teaches us how to recognize that there are times for doing and times for replenishing.

We as women can use our special connection with the moon to allow for a time of taking care of ourselves—time needed for the formation of ideas and insights, connecting our psychic nature to the moon's. Women who spend extended periods of time sleeping outdoors find their menstrual cycles quickly aligning with the cycles of the moon, just as women living and working together tend to find their menstrual periods synchronizing. The rhythms that make up our bodies are the same rhythms that make up the dance of the Universe; when we feel the two as one, we know we are a part of Nature.

Now Let Us Dance

We all have the moon within us. Sometimes we are full, sometimes we are empty; we are always expanding and contracting, we are unpredictable and changeable. The Moon Dance is a wonderful way to incorporate this part of ourselves into our physical and spiritual expressions.

The basic pattern for the Moon Dance is the double spiral, the symbol of the Moon Goddess. Evidence of this pattern can be found in the ancient monuments and temples of England, Ireland, and Malta; in the vessel designs of Crete; and in Native American petroglyphs. Powerful microscopes now show us the double spiral as the helix of DNA, the very essence of human life.

The spiral symbolizes the way the moon appears to orbit the earth counterclockwise until it becomes full at its zenith, and then turns to orbit clockwise until it disappears near the sun as the new moon. In the past, the moon was referred to as wandering or meandering because it followed a complicated path unknown at the time. Spiral dancing imitates the mystery of death and rebirth by weaving in and out of the labyrinth. The dancer moves counterclockwise from the outside to the center of the circle, then clockwise from the center to the outside.

Since the fluctuations of ocean tides are governed by the moon, in order to more fully tune into the electromagnetic power of the moon's rhythms, you might want to dance by the ocean—if there's one near you. Try dancing to just the rhythm of the pulsating waves against the shore. Experiment with your dance during various phases of the moon, taking note of the differences in the rhythm, strength, and height of the tide and its effect on your dance. You will find, though, that clear moonlit nights are magical no matter where you are—on a riverbank, in a field, or even congregating in a backyard—because dancing to the moon reawakens us to the power and beauty of nature and our part in nature; it reminds us of what we are doing here.

Menstrual Dance

The Menstrual Dance is one of the many possible variations of the Moon Dance. When you create your Menstrual Dance, be sure to include flowers, since flowers are a well-known representation of menstruation in that they also are the result of a seed that has not become the fruit of the womb. Also, the serpentine undulations of the Birth Dance should be included in a Menstrual Dance. The contraction-release movements of the Birth Dance bring increased circulation to the pelvic area and greatly reduce cramping. These movements also bring your consciousness to the pelvic area, not something many women feel comfortable doing. For too many of us, the pelvic area is taboo even to ourselves.

Girls' Rites of Passage

When done as a group ritual, the Moon Dance provides a beautiful way to welcome a girl into the community of adult women. In this ceremony, a mother and daughter stand a few yards apart. The group is in single file formation, holding hands. The leader takes the group into a circular form, then proceeds inside the circle to make another, smaller circular form, creating a spiral around the daughter. At the apex, the leader turns the line back upon itself, leading the line outward along the same path, to eventually

form a spiral around the mother. On the second set of spirals around the daughter, the daughter joins the chain behind the leader. The spiral chain then once again moves to encompass the mother, who now joins the daughter and the group chain for the third spiral.

Through this dance women acknowledge and sanctify the growth and maturation of the child, allowing her to first stand alone and feel the power of herself as an independent adult, and then inviting her to become a link in the chain of her extended family of womankind.

This dance can also be a powerful tool in soothing dysfunctional relationships and strained communication between female family members, especially mothers and daughters. The dance creates a physical bridge between the two separated worlds and invites each person to join hands and embrace the support and strength of her fellow women. Self-empowerment, a sense of cohesion, continuity, and wisdom emerge organically from this ritual dance.

LEFT: DANCING BY THE OCEAN IS ONE WAY TO TUNE INTO THE POWER OF THE MOON'S RHYTHMS. JAMIE PARNUM, DIRECTOR OF SOARING SPIRIT DANCE MINISTRY, DANCING AT APTOS BEACH, CALIFORNIA. PHOTOGRAPH BY KELLY RICHARDS.

8

THE SACRED CIRCLE

We come spinning out of nothingness, scattering stars. . . the stars form a circle, and in the center we dance.

Rumi, 13th century

The circle is perhaps the most ancient of mystical symbols and the most universal of all dances. It is the earth and the sun in eternal movement, an unbroken, unbent line symbolizing continuity and eternity. The circle dance represents the wholeness of things, the roundness of pregnancy, the breasts, vessels, house and temple. The dance brings life full circle.

The circle creates solidarity. Because it takes more than two people to complete a circle, the circle creates community. It is the perfect democracy; there is equality. The circle provides a protected, consecrated, all-inclusive space. It is nonlinear, multidirectional, and endless.

Before the town square became square, it was circular. For example, several villages in the Catalonia region of the eastern French Pyrenees still have a circle in the center, some laid in beautiful mosaic or ornate tiles, specially built for the local circle dance. How wonderful to build a village around the dance floor!

The circle is charmed because it encloses emptiness—an emptiness constructed by, and charged with, the concentrated energy of our moving, connected bodies. When we leave the center empty and direct our dancing toward this unmoved stillness, we create within ourselves the quiet of the unmoved center. Dancing as one person within a group, we feel the rise of this invisible energy in response to our bodily and musical invocations, as in an orchestra when a single instrument merges into the musical sound while remaining an individual part of the organic whole. Like birds flying in formation, a new body is created, linked together as though by invisible elastic threads, and receiving from the unified vibrational wavelengths the energy necessary for each individual's propulsion. In the process, a higher being is discovered, namely, the group soul.

Encircling is the incorporating, the giving and receiving of power. While it encloses and possesses, the circle also empowers through a concentration of energy that is ever-flowing and ever-changing. The circle leads back into itself and so is a symbol of unity, the Absolute, perfection.

But does the circle have any real power? According to Marija Gimbutas, "The circle—be it fairy dance or ring of standing stones—transmits the energy increased by the combination of the powers of stone, water, mound and circle motion."[1] Starhawk says, "Witches conceive of psychic energy as having form and substance that can be perceived and directed by those with a trained awareness. The power generated within the circle is built into a cone form, and at its peak is released—to the Goddess, to reenergize the members of the coven, or to do a specific work such as healing."[2] The natural electromagnetism of the human body is strengthened and enhanced by clockwise and counterclockwise movements. The dance ring literally operates like the winding of an electrical motor, the

ZUNI BASKET DANCE. BASKETS SYMBOLIZING FOOD, WHICH PRESERVES THE LIFE OF THE TRIBE, MAKE AN EVOCATIVE CENTERPIECE FOR THIS CIRCLE DANCE OF THANKSGIVING. FROM A PAINTING BY AWA TSIREH, COURTESY OF UNITED EDUCATORS, INC.

Mevlevi sema turners, Istanbul, Turkey. Photograph by Regina Phelps.

rhythmic movement of the circle inducing the local collection of energy in the cells of the body as precisely as does a metal turbogenerator, albeit on a more subtle level.

Evidence shows that the circle dance was practiced as far back as the Upper Paleolithic era and was carried into the Neolithic era and down through history. Vase supports from the classical Cucuteni culture, dating back to the second half of the 5th millennium B.C.E., are shaped like women in a ring with joined arms, illustrating women performing a circle ritual. These vases, called hora vases, depict ring dances still done today.[3]

In his book *World History of the Dance,* Curt Sachs describes the round dances of devout and solemn character sedately performed in honor of the deity:

> No wonder, then, that the *emmeleia* ["the sacred concept" in Greek] devolved mainly upon the women—it is the old distinction of close and expanded movement. Festive processions to the shrine and fluctuating circles around the altar are the forms these dances take. They have come down to us most beautifully in the marvelously preserved partheniads, in which the Virgins, hand in hand like Graces, worship the Goddess to the sound of hymn-like songs. Here we

have magic elevated completely to worship, to devout celebration. . . . The whirl dance must be acknowledged as the most thrilling expression of the feminine power of conception.

Imitation of astral movements led to the circle dance; the foundation map for astronomy and its companion, astrology, was laid out in large-scale pattern on the temple pavement. Rotating stars, the revolving sun and moon, and celestial turnings synchronized to seasons and cycles were a deeply meaningful mystery to the ancients, and the sky an open classroom. Priestesses, the first astronomers, opened the door to time keeping, mathematics, and science through their dance of stars, a very intricate dance in which, moving in synchrony with the Divine Order, the priestesses danced from east to west around a sun or moon altar, making the signs of the zodiac. The ritual dance, which varied with each month, was performed with appropriate movement and in the correct costume, with chants that affirmed instructions, praises, and prayers for the period.* The Mevlana dervishes (*derv* means "to rotate") move in a circle as one body around the room, with each dancer simultaneously pivoting around her or his own axis, symbolizing many cosmological realities.

Every religious system reveals a system of twelve units of power. There were twelve patriarchs and twelve prophets in the Hebraic tradition. The celestial Jerusalem had twelve gates on which were written the names of the twelve tribes of Israel. Jesus had twelve Apostles; twelve legions of angels could be summoned by him. The Tree of Life bore twelve kinds of fruit, yielding one for each month. There are twelve people in the Circular Council of the Dalai Lama. In Greek mythology there were twelve Titans and twelve Olympian deities. Hercules is given twelve labors, twelve representing the solar number, the cycle of the solar hero, whereas the moon cycle is thirteen. Hermas of Hellas visited the twelve virgins on the sacred mountain, clad in white raiment, who performed a round dance. They symbolize twelve powers that emanate from the hidden secret source. The Etruscan state was itself divided into twelve states. There were historically twelve peers of France. Knights came in sets of twelve, often with a dark or "black" prince as the thirteenth. Henry VIII had twenty-four knights. Even Robin Hood had twelve knights and twelve Merry Men.

THE GRAPEVINE STEP OF THE HORA, A CLASSIC CIRCLE DANCE. DANCES OF UNIVERSAL PEACE, CALIFORNIA. PHOTOGRAPH BY MATIN MIZE.

*The art of the zodiac began as ritual dance, a series of twelve symbols ostensibly attributed to the starry system, against which earth and sun move. It became the primary basis of calendrical and astronomical reckoning and prediction.

Peter Deunov's sacred circle dance. Seven Lakes region, Bulgaria, 1994. Photograph by Barnaby Brown.

Now Let Us Dance

Simple as the circle-dance pattern is, it has a great power and significance. Dancing the circle symbolizes uniting ourselves into one body. An altar, an object of significance, or a person in need of healing or care may be enclosed by encircling dancers, setting that person or thing apart from the mundane by the living wall of the dancers' bodies and thereby symbolically consecrating, protecting, and revering it. We also may choose to dance to the empty circle, evoking the same sense of emptiness inside.

It is important to avoid making the circle dance into an endless repetition. Because circle dancing both reflects and inverts the dynamics of motion and relationship, the potential for reaching a liminal state is inherent in circle dancing. The liminal state (from the Latin *limen*, meaning "threshold") is a condition of being in which boundaries of time and space are left behind without being wholly abandoned. Through the simple process of joining hands or following each other in a circle or spiral, there is a reordering of our normal experience of relationship as we move from the perception of "self" and "other" to the perception of self as part of the continuum of all life.

The choreographic dynamic of a circle dance makes the liminal departure very potent. The pattern of a circle dance provides a clearly marked pathway of experience for the dancer. Starting at the "beginning" position, the dancers progress through the pattern of a designated dance to a new position. This beginning and returning is repeated many times, each repetition familiar and yet unfamiliar, home and yet not home, as the completion of the pattern also marks its inception.

The hora is one example of a classic circle dance that is still done around the globe. There have been more than 1,600 varieties of the hora; the most familiar circle dance form uses the grapevine step as its foundation.

There are now many circle dance groups throughout the British Isles and Europe bringing this ancient dance form into our contemporary lives. Each of these groups, in its own way, aims to illustrate a conscious relationship and exchange of energy between human beings and nature. The most

SACRED CIRCLE DANCE AT FINDHORN, SCOTLAND. PHOTOGRAPH BY PETER VALLANCE.

well known include Deunov's Paneurhythmy (pan-eu-rhythmy), Steiner's Eurhythmy, and the dance practices at Findhorn. Paneurhythmy was developed by Bulgarian spiritual master teacher Beinsa Douno (Peter Deunov, 1864–1944). It is a dance-yoga that is matched to sacred sounds, which, by regulating the physical and nervous systems, draws participants into harmonious attunement with subtle energies of the natural and spiritual worlds. The founder of Scotland's Findhorn Community, Bernard Woisen, brought together over 300 circle dances from throughout Europe. Many are taught in their workshops throughout the world. Dr. Rudolph Steiner of Germany, early in this century, developed the Anthroposophical Society Eurhythmy system, which is taught in the United States and other countries. It incorporates verbal form accompanied by its own appropriate movement form or visual gesture. There are videos and books of instruction available on these and other approaches.

While these dances can link us to ancient practices and to other dancers and cultures around the world, don't feel you are limited to a preexisting form in order to dance a sacred circle. Creating your own circle dance as a rite of passage, as a prayer, or in celebration of an event or season (the arrival of spring, an abundant harvest)

The circular labyrinth at Grace Cathedral in San Francisco, an exact replica of the labyrinth at 12th-century Chartres Cathedral in France. Photograph by Cindy A. Pavlinac.

Labyrinth design, Chartres Cathedral, France.

can be as simple as choosing an evocative centerpiece to symbolize your theme and perhaps some music or sound to accompany your movements.

The Labyrinth Dance

While the Labyrinth Dance is not what we normally think of when we speak of circle dancing, it affords a unique type of circle dancing because, unlike other circle dance forms, it can be done by oneself. A labyrinth shape can often be circular, and by dancing the labyrinth—weaving in an out of the circular pattern, spiraling in and out—we create circular patterns on the ground. To traverse the labyrinth to its in-turning center is a circuitous and timeless path, not a direct, swift, or open one.

The floor of the great Chartres Cathedral in France is one example of a labyrinth in circular form.* It is said that this labyrinth originally came from Crete, but this is not the maze that became part of the Greek myth of the Minotaur. The labyrinth served as a symbol of the spiritual pilgrimage, the progression from the outer veils of matter to the inner light and revelation of Divine Light. There are two exact duplicates of the Chartres labyrinth at Grace Cathedral in San Francisco.

Dr. Lauren Artress, Canon Pastor at

*The Chartres labyrinth was built on the site of the Druids' Sanctuary of Sanctuaries. The ancient ones came to receive the gift of earth. Spiritual faculties were awakened by what the Gauls called the *Wouivre*, magnetic currents that snake through the ground, and were represented by the serpent.

Grace Cathedral, who can be credited for helping to revive the use of the labyrinth, says the labyrinth is an incredible spiritual tool:

> The labyrinth is a large, complex spiral circle which is an ancient symbol for the Divine Mother, the God within, the Goddess, the Holy in all of creation. . . The labyrinth is an archetype of wholeness, a sacred place that helps us rediscover the depths of our souls. . . . When walking the labyrinth, you can feel that powerful energies have been set in motion. The labyrinth functions like a spiral, creating a vortex in its center. The path into the center of the labyrinth winds in a clockwise pattern, and the path back unwinds counterclockwise. The circular path inward cleanses and quiets us as it leads us in. The unwinding path integrates and empowers us on our walk back out. . . . The cusps or points of the lunations serve as conduits for the energy to circulate and radiate outward.
>
> The unicursal path of the labyrinth is what differentiates it and sets it apart as a spiritual tool. The labyrinth does not engage our thinking minds. It invites our intuitive, pattern-seeking, symbolic mind to come forth. It presents us with only one, but proud, choice. To enter a labyrinth is to choose to walk a spiritual path.[4]

CRETAN LABYRINTH.

I have walked the labyrinth inside Grace Cathedral and danced the outside labyrinth there. It is always a profound and illuminating experience that brings immediate joy to my heart. Labyrinths are now being built in communities around the country—in churchyards, parks, and places like teen centers and convalescent homes. Full-size canvas labyrinths are also available for indoor and outdoor use (see "Veriditas" under Resources).

HOPI TAPU'AT LABYRINTH.

9
Serpent Dance

The Galactic Serpent is the wind, breath, the Milky Way, comet trails. Mystical Waters Serpent's rhythmic movements are the falling rain, the undulations of streams, the rolling ocean. The Earth Serpent is terrestrial energy flow and underground magnetic currents; the Cosmic Serpent shows us seasonal cycles, menstruation and moon cycles, life, death, and rebirth, the eternal process. The Astral Serpent is the psychic world of supersensual perception. The ascending Kundalini spiral turns matter into creativity and movement: the Snake Dance.

The poor snake is probably the most maligned and vilified creature that ever lived. And the most fascinating. It is alien to us in so many ways—it moves along in a curiously disturbing manner, seemingly as much at home underground and in water as on land. It is silent, swift, and terrifying.

The serpent has slithered through centuries of the most amazing variety of baseless human fantasies, superstitions, and projections. It probably has as much significance in Christianity, albeit negative, as it had in "animist" religions. Its association with Eve didn't help its reputation, nor did Freud's idea that it was a phallic symbol.

The first time I saw an ethnic nightclub Oriental dance (belly dance) show and heard the audience actually hissing at the dancer, I was shocked until it was explained this was a show of appreciation, unlike in our culture where it is considered a sign of disapproval. I became quite curious about how the snake could have been seen in a different way by other cultures in other times. I wondered about the snake bracelets worn by Oriental dancers—why? What did the snake have to do with belly dancing? Knowing that American performers adapt freely from other cultures, I decided to look further. The serpentine movements of the Far East, Bali, and the South Seas, Flamenco and Indian dancers' arms and hands, the torso, the sliding head and neck, so mysterious, so sensuous and powerful, and so feminine—what did they mean?

The image of the serpent spiraling around the tree of life is associated with life-giving processes, dancing new life. In many early cultures, the word *snake* or *dragon* indicated the womb.[1] The snake also represented the rhythmic, undulating movements of the womb during birthing, that miraculous technique provided by Nature so that two bodies can separate without injury to either.

Throughout the world and down through the ages, the spirit of the serpent has been a symbol of healing, initiation, rebirth, transformation, and secret knowledge—knowledge that only the body knows. The snake sheds its skin and reappears in a brilliant and youthful form, being perpetually renewed. This strange ability was seen as symbolic of the higher mystery of both physical and spiritual birth and rebirth. The snake is also life energy, instinct, and the felt body experience—the facilitator of creative healing.

On another level, the Primordial Serpent became the self-renewing symbol of the Goddess. It was not the body of the snake that was sacred but rather the energy exuded by this spiraling, coiling phenomenon that transcended its boundaries and influenced the surrounding world. It emerged from the depths and the waters and did not need feet to travel. What better symbol could there be for explaining and exploring energy—creative power—the flow that moves matter into vital form?

World Serpent

Labyrinth and snake dances occurred everywhere, from pre-Columbian Mexico to India to Crete. The winding twists and turns in Cretan art follow

The serpent decorates an ancient column at the entrance to Asklepoi, a famed place of natural healing near Pergamon, Turkey. Photograph by Iris Stewart.

MINOAN SNAKE GODDESS, HERAKLION MUSEUM, CRETE.

the trail of the labyrinth serpent from Paleolithic and Neolithic times in the House of the Double Ax to the temple of the Goddess. The original temple was, among other things, a storehouse to provide survival for the community through the winter, and the snake protected the grain.* The principal Minoan religious ritual on the island of Crete was the dance of the Snake Goddess, a symbol of eternity and immortality.[2] Statuettes recovered from the underground repository of the Second Palace of Knossos (1400 to 1200 B.C.E.) portray the Snake Goddess or her priestesses. In ritual dress, arms outstretched, one statuette brandishes a serpent in each hand, personifying power and protection. The other figure is enveloped by a serpentine embrace; she holds the head of a snake in one open palm while its body twines around her wrist, up one arm, across her shoulders, and down the other arm. Two snakes encircle her waist and intertwine to form an apron, while a third peers from her elegant headdress. She is the sacred energy incarnate. Her serene face reflects her ability to harness the snake's sacred secret power. Other archaeological evidence from Palaikastro, Crete (c. 1400 B.C.E.), reveals a group of little clay figures dancing in a circle. One dancer wears two necklaces and carries a live serpent as they move in a sacred dance.

It was in the double spiral that the rites of the Snake Goddess were danced or walked, as evidenced by numerous Cretan pottery designs featuring a double coil with a sprouting end. The movements traced the meandering moon, the soul's wanderings, the pathway to enlightenment, and back again. Each coil is an initiation, a

MORE EARLY EVIDENCE OF THE SNAKE'S INFLUENCE ON DANCE. A SNAKE IS HELD BY ONE OF THESE CIRCLE DANCERS, CIRCA 1400 B.C.E. CRETE.

*In many places, caves (also associated with the abode of the serpent) were often used as natural sanctuaries. Many of them are claimed to be places of divine as well as human births and are associated with the maternal aspects of the Goddess.

rite of passage, a gradually learned dance in the spiral of eternity. The sprouting end represents the second half of life, the growing into wisdom, release, and acceptance.

Later, Homer would reverse earlier myths and archetypes, change Ariadne (which meant "holy")[3] of the Great Goddess into Ariadne "of the lovely locks" in the *Iliad*, and turn the spiral dance into a lover's dance with acrobats and minstrels for large audiences to watch as entertainment. The end result would be to reverse the concept of enlightenment, turning it into a Saturday night movie with beastly minotaurs demanding constant human sacrifice and battling heroes in a maze of trickery and dead ends.

Athena, with her sacred snake on the Acropolis, is, in a way, the successor of the Minoan Snake Goddess, the snake expressing her great antiquity. In the snake mysteries on the Acropolis, devotees of Athena handled live snakes and danced with them long before the classical portrayal of Athena born from Zeus' head. Even in the classical version in which she is depicted in statues with helmet and shield as defender of the city-state named after her, there in the shadow of her shield hides the python.[4] Her aegis, which means "a power that protects or shields," was a goat skin with a fringe of serpents.

Snake dances were performed by the Hopi, the Navaho, and the Pawnee in worship of Mother Earth, a religion of the Great Spirit whose dance attributes great potency on the serpent. Snake dances often reenact cosmic processes. To the ancient Hopi Indians, the snake symbolized closeness to the earth, endurance, and influence on the clouds.[5]

MINOAN SNAKE GODDESS. AUTHOR'S COLLECTION.

To the ancient Mexicans, the earth was the five-fold serpent-skirted goddess Coatlique, the Aztec "Lady of the Serpent Skirt." She was the moon deity, creator preeminent and preexistent. She appeared as a woman with four sisters, who gathered on Coatepec snake hill to dance. Xochiquetzal, her daughter, was Goddess of All Women.[6] Tlazolteotl, an Aztec goddess, rides on a serpent. An ancient Mexican dance

Léema Kathleen Graham, finding the inner serpent through dance.

in honor of the Corn Goddess was called the Seven Snakes. The movements of this dance, lasting all night, were quiet, slow and deliberate, the dancers forming one long single line.[7]

In Australia, the traditional Myall secret cycles are told in dance episodes of the dreamtime, in which dance-mime is more important than words. In these episodes, the divine snake dreams the world and humans into existence. It is clear that these dances are the remains of a most ancient religious scheme.[8] The aboriginal goddess Una, who established the earth, was pictured with the rainbow snake held up in her arms.[9] Similarly, the Haitians have a dance known as Yanvalou wherein people move like snakes, the link between human beings and the earth.

Legends of ancient Ireland describe a circular serpentine dance, bequeathed by former generations, around a tree or bonfire, moving in curves from right to left. Another serpentine dance was called Rinke Teampuill, or Dance of the Temple. The Celtic goddess Verbeia in Yorkshire is usually shown in reliefs holding serpents. This image is also related to the Irish Saint Brigit, as the symbol was adapted into Catholicism.[10] It is also quite likely that the myth of St. Patrick driving all the snakes from Ireland is really the telling of the overthrow of the Snake Goddess.

Léema Kathleen Graham conducts retreats for women in northern California for women on "Finding the Inner Serpent." In the introduction to her workshop, she says:

> Gazing up at an alabaster statue of the Virgin Mary as a young Catholic schoolgirl was how my training with the Goddess began. Fascinated with the serpent at Her feet, it seemed friendly, rather than the foe the Church said it represented. The Virgin was supposed to be stamping out evil, but the serpent was alive and looked happy. I never developed the fear of snakes or their association with evil that the Church and my parents tried to instill. Instead, I became intrigued with this much-maligned creature of the reptile kingdom.
>
> Several years into a career as a classical dancer, snakes began to permeate my consciousness again. I became a snake keeper and a snake dancer with my spiritual focus on the Great Mother Goddess.

Today I still have that same mysterious inner prompting, and have choreographed several dances with my two royal pythons. Each dance becomes a shamanic journey for me, and indeed snake is my totem animal, as it is the universal totem creature for all women.

RUSSIAN DANCER VERA MOROVA WHO FORSOOK CLASSICAL BALLET IN FAVOR OF INSPIRATION FROM ANCIENT ORIENTAL DANCE. A POSE FROM HER *SNAKE DANCE*. NEW YORK PUBLIC LIBRARY FOR THE PERFORMING ARTS.

Now Let Us Dance

Serpentine images of power occur naturally in a woman's spiritual quest as forces or currents of energy that operate in all natural and social processes. These energies are obvious in nature, where life and death forces do their spiral dance. They also operate in the social and spiritual spheres of being, nonbeing, and transformation, moving hope up, out, and around in something larger than the individual. In the categorization of symbols into good versus evil, black versus white, male versus female, the flow is stunted. When we are going through very difficult times, the dark night of the soul, we may see the cave as the mausoleum of death, but it may actually be that dark side of the moon, the resting time, and the cave becomes the womb for germination and gestation of a new growth.

The ritual created with the Snake Dance celebrates the shedding of our outgrown selves—shedding, purifying, and cleansing in preparation for passage to a new self. The coiled snake is actually a symbol for the process of self-discovery. The movements of a serpentine dance are also very similar to and are especially suited for the Birth Dance ritual (see chapter 4), our first transformation.

Individual serpentine dance movements start with the arms and hands while you stand in a posed position. The movements are very isolated yet connected. Begin by raising the right shoulder, bringing the arm up, elbow slightly bent, wrist bent. At shoulder height, the hand follows through until the fingertips rise above the arm. At this point, repeat this movement with the left arm while simultaneously dropping the right shoulder, elbow, wrist, and fingertips, as you roll the shoulder blade toward the spine. Sliding the rib cage to the right and left in conjunction with the arm pattern while your hips hold firm makes a larger, serpentine pattern. You can stand still, glide forward and backward, or turn in a slow circle.

To practice the head movement, look in the mirror. Place your hands on either side of your chin, and try to slide your chin to one hand without tilting your head. During a dance, you can give yourself some leverage and stability by placing your hands, palms together in prayer style, in front of your chest.

The snake dance is a very mesmerizing dance when done slowly and smoothly. The entire body can become involved by lifting the left hip up from a bent knee position, pushing the hip to the left while swaying the rib cage to the right. As the left hip makes a downward circle and comes to rest, the right hip pushes to the right and upward and the rib cage sways to the left. All the while, the arms are extended softly to the side, raised above the head, or performing the undulating arm patterns described above. If you do this dance to Indian music, the Middle Eastern *taxim* (a slow solo piece played on flute or ney, clarinet, or canoon), or a Turkish Chifte Tele rhythm, you may find yourself quite mesmerized, also.

Needless to say, this dance takes great concentration and practice. Studying with a teacher is recommended. The results will be greater flexibility of the spine, neck, and hips. It is better than weight lifting for arm toning.

As you dance, get into the feeling of the serpent—the wind, the rain, moving around wherever you choose on the planet, in the air, on the ground, underground, moving with wisdom, moving with ease and grace. Snake dancing can also be very joyful. If the dance is done in a group, the leader can take the dancers on a spiral journey, in and out, and all around like a chain, which is especially fun for children. Snake dancing can be done as fast or slow as desired and can be combined with folk steps—repetitive and moving in a sideward manner—as it moves forward. In these group snake dances, the individual undulations of the various parts of the body are extended into a larger group movement. There is a special feeling one gets when everyone is moving in unison. It is a feeling you will understand as your group dances together as one. It feels as if a new energy is being born.

A traditional Bulgarian Snake Horo dance provides a good model.[11] The open Horo dance is led at one end, called the "forehead" or "head of the Horo," and its end is the "tail." This chain is thought of as a living body—"the Horo dances itself." Similarly, the popular folk dance Karaguna, from Greece, is another traditional snake dance wherein the line is open so that the leader may "snake" the followers wherever he or she chooses to go. A special feature of this dance is the hissing sound made by the dancers to accompany the circular arm movements and brushed leg lifts done in the first section of the dance.

10

Lamentation Dance

I wear a long tube of material to indicate the tragedy that obsesses the body, the ability to stretch inside your own skin, to witness and test the perimeters and boundaries of grief, which is honorable and universal.

Martha Graham writing about her dance Lamentation *in* Blood Memory[1]

Nursing the ill and the dying, preparing the body of the newly deceased, burying the dead, praying for their souls, and dancing for their spirits have always been part of women's holy work.* While the thought of dancing at a funeral may be a foreign idea to most modern Western minds, lamentation dancing as a very special and potent ritual has been found in many cultures down through the centuries.

The union between the living and the dead in dance ritual arose in civilizations in which the religion expressed a hope for renewal and rebirth—where stars, gods, spirits, and the departed loved ones all dance together on a higher plane. There is evidence suggesting that ecstatic dancing by priestesses was part of Neolithic and early Bronze Age Aegean burial customs, where burial in round tombs symbolized the

*Three women, Mary Magdalene, Mary Salome, and Mary Jacobe (mother of James), brought oil and spices to anoint Jesus when he was taken down from the cross.

dead's return to the bountiful all-giving, all-receiving Great Mother's womb.

Funerary dance is often a chain dance performed with arms interlinked in a protective manner, showing support and comfort for the community and from the community, and symbolizing the unity of life and death, thus sustaining the connection between the departed and the living. Strong emotions, wailing, heavy rhythms, and the loud musical accompaniment that is often part of a funeral ritual all serve to emphasize the drama of the occasion and to relieve fear and grief. The ritual speaks to the belief that death is ultimately another aspect of life, and it therefore becomes the duty of the living to assist the deceased in his or her resurrection.

Agnes DeMille explained the purpose of dancing in funerary rites: "By putting in direct contrast the most vital expressions of life, the moving body and lifeless clay [the dead body], the celebrants thought to guarantee for the deceased a rebirth or resurrection."[2]

Places for the dead, such as the Norse Valhalla of ancient Scandinavia and the Elysian Fields of Eleusis in Greece, were often regarded as places of "happy arrival."* In Greek, the name *Elysion* meant "realm of the

Three lamentation dancers from an archaic Greek vase.

blessed." Iris, the Greek Goddess of the Rainbow, depicted as "a radiant maiden borne in swift flight on golden wings," led the souls of women to the Elysian Fields when they died. As a token of that faith, the Greeks planted purple iris flowers on the graves of women. In writing about the Mystery rituals at Eleusis, Aristophanes said that the leader of the dance on earth was mirrored in the underworld and in the abode of the blessed who in their lifetime had been initiated at Eleusis and now continued to dance in the Elysian Fields. Thus heaven, earth, and the underworld are drawn into the dance.

In another part of the Eleusinian stories, it is said that Demeter has her temple built above the Kallichoron, the "Well of the Beautiful Dances," also called Parthenion, the Virgin's Well.[†3] One representation of the well was as an entrance to the underworld. The well is also a symbol of the soul and of things feminine. A well uncovered by excavators in the sanctuary at Eleusis had a stone pavement around it, a patterned dance floor indicating the basic figure of the dance that was at one time performed by the initiates until about the 5th century B.C.E.[4]

*Some others were the Hesperides (Gibraltar), the Isles of the Blest, the Roman Fortunate Isles, Fairyland or Avalon of the British Isles, and Celtic Apple Island, which was ruled over by nine sisters. In the Book of the Dead, the goddess Amenta is shown welcoming the dead with open arms to the Egyptian western land of immortality, known as the Land of Women.

†Early versions of the Demeter/Kore story in Greece picture Persephone going into the underworld to minister to the deceased and prepare them for rebirth.

WELL OF THE BEAUTIFUL DANCES. ELEUSIS, GREECE. PHOTOGRAPH BY IRIS STEWART.

Circumambulation was an important part of funerary rites. In an ancient Akkadian poem, a ritual mourner declares, "Now DN who goes in a circle around the city, she, his professional mourner, goes in a circle around the city."[5] Another text says, "The daughter-in-law (of the king) will wash the feet (of the dead crown prince, her husband). Three times she shall walk in a circle around the bier."[6] Three is always an auspicious number of the Mother-Creator. These were powerful rites, and women's rites, even though the words used by modern interpretations of the priestess are "professional mourner" and "daughter-in-law of the king."

In ancient Greece, Athenians performed circular dances on the third day of the Anthesteria, a very ancient festival of the dead, similar to those held in India and elsewhere.[7] This correlates with the Gnostic theme of Jesus dancing forth from the grave on the third day, as well as Innana and other more ancient deities. All originate in the symbol of vegetation death, fall, and return, spring.

The funerary rituals in the burial of the pharaohs involved the whole community. The many sculptures and paintings of Egyptian funeral processions from before the first dynasty to the 20th dynasty (5th century B.C.E. to 12th century C.E.) show that the scenes of funeral ceremonials were always accompanied by women dancing and singing. Usually one woman holds a tambourine aloft and beats out a rhythm on it while others dance around her. In one tomb drawing, young girls wearing short kilts stand with their arms raised, one foot lifted above the ground in unison. Nearby, older women wearing long gowns sing and clap their hands, expressing sadness and hope. Tomb wall drawings of funeral processions also show acrobatic dances accompanied by clapping and the waving of palm branches. The dances for the *ka,* the soul of the deceased, were performed in a more solemn, ceremonial manner as the departed ones began their "night sea journey" to rebirth with the help of women as official mourners and musicians.

At Abydos, one of the three great religious centers of ancient Egypt, a special lamentation ceremony called the Silence of Mourning,* was practiced. Even though it was led by the *Qemat*, or singing priestess, no instruments were played and no singing was done to accompany the solemn dance movements.[8]

Historian Edward William Lane wrote about Egyptian funeral dancing in the mid-1800s:

*The Italian *cantilena,* from the Latin *Canta-Laena* or "Song of Mourning," is derived from this ancient slow dance movement.[9]

EGYPTIAN DANCING GIRLS, TOMB PAINTING, THEBES, C. 1950 B.C.E.

TOMB WALL PAINTING FROM MAGNA GRAECIA, ITALY, 450–400 B.C.E.

It is customary among the peasants of Upper Egypt for the female relations and friends of a person deceased to meet together by his house on each of the first three days after the funeral, and there to perform a lamentation and a strange kind of dance. They daub their faces and bosoms, and part of their dress, with mud; and tie a rope girdle, generally made of the coarse grass called "halfa," round the waist (as the ancient Egyptian women did in the same case). Each flourishes in her hand a palm-stick, or a *nebboot* (a long staff), or a spear, or a drawn sword; and dances with a slow movement and in an irregular manner; generally pacing about, and raising and depressing the body. This dance is continued for an hour or more, and is performed twice or three times in the course of the day. After the third day, the women visit the tomb and place upon it their rope-girdles; and usually a lamb or a goat is slain there as an expiatory sacrifice, and a feast made, on this occasion.[10]

Statues and images found on the many decorated walls in tombs at Tarquinia, north of Rome, tell us that dancing was very much entwined with the conception of the afterlife. A tomb wall painting from Magna Graecia, on the southern Italian peninsula (c. 450–400 B.C.E.), now housed at the Museo Nazionale in Naples, shows a line of women dressed in long robes and mantles called *himation,* with contrasting colored borders across their foreheads, and all wearing large circular earrings. The women dance toward their left, each with arms outstretched to hold the hands of the woman one person away, creating an interweaving arm pattern. The step looks measured and purposeful. There is a solidarity and solemnity about their dance. Similar dances are still found in the Balkans today, the women linking arms and dancing slowly in a circle without singing as they mourn their dead; the only sounds are made by the stamping of feet on the ground and the jingling of the women's jewelry. As part of a traditional funeral in Ireland, a group of hired women called keeners and mourners encircle the open casket, wailing for three days and three nights to keep the devil at bay while the soul journeys toward heaven, after which the burial rites and then the legendary Irish funeral party ensues. Encircling the bier to help the spirit on its way to its ancestors also helped in comforting the living. It was a dance for remembrance. Until 1840 in Bailleul in northern France, women danced in the nave of their church around the bier of the deceased. In Scotland, until the 19th century, it was accepted practice for a widow to leap in a lively strathspey (in 4/4 meter; *strath* means "valley") beside her husband's corpse, and it was a mark of small affection if she could not bring herself to do it with some enthusiasm.[11] Funeral *jotas* (fast dances) are still used in Valencia, Spain.

ETRUSCAN TOMB FRESCO, TARQUINIA, ITALY, 5TH CENTURY B.C.E. GABINETTO NAZIONALE DELLA STAMPE, ROME.

Biblical Clues

The Old Testament also indicates lamentation to be the role of women, as in 2 Samuel 1:24: "Ye Daughters of Israel weep over Saul"; Jeremiah 9:17: "Thus saith the Lord of hosts, Consider ye, and call for the mourning women, that they may come; and send for cunning women,* that they may come: And let them make haste, and take up a wailing for us, that our eyes may run down with tears, and our eyelids gush out with waters."

Mayer I. Gruber of Ben-Gurion University in Israel, looking for clues about the role of dance in Judaism, found that "it is probable that *sabab* (to participate in a circle dance or procession) refers to the circumambulation of the bier in Qoh 12,5 where we read . . . 'When a person goes to his eternal home, the mourners in the street

*Until the 13th century, the word cunning (from Latin cunnende, "knowing") carried the meaning of "learned." The root word for cunning may well be "cunt" or "kunte," indicating a connection to Cunti, the Oriental Great Goddess; Kunda, the Yoni of the Universe; the Old Norse Goddess Kunta; or Cunia, a Roman goddess who protected children in the cradle (cunabula). In ancient writings, cunt was synonymous with woman, though not in the insulting modern sense. As with so many words about women, this one suffers from transliteration guided by malevolent intent. Medieval clergymen labeled pagan shrines—typically holy caves, wells, or groves—as cunnus diaboli, "devilish cunt." The word cunning is now used to mean "wily" rather than "wise."

Andalusian danse funelre (jota) a'jizona (Province d'ahcante) 19th-century etching, Gustave Doré. Bibliotheque Nationale de France.

participate in the circumambulations.'"[12] This genre of dance is called *raqa* or *raqad* in Hebrew (from the Assyrian *rakadu*), which means "to step with stamping feet" in unison. The goal of this type of dance was to see the deceased out, and it consisted of circling the bier, the processional to the cemetery, and another circumambulation around the grave that included seven circles for each circumambulation. Gruber says, "Because the dance is frequently a feature of mourning rites it should not be surprising that in Syriac the root *r-q-d* came to have the two meanings 'dance' and 'mourn.' In the Hebrew Bible, however, *riqqûd* was understood to be a dance of joy. . . Hence Qoh 3,4 informs us, 'There is an appointed time to cry, and an appointed time to laugh, an appointed time to beat the breast, and an appointed time to dance.'"[13]

Funeral Dancing Today

William O. E. Oesterley's research into more modern funeral dance practices concurs with Gruber's biblical findings. "The strongest reason for believing that this custom was in vogue among the ancient Israelites is that it exists at the present day." Oesterley refers to the prescribed seven circumambulations of the bier, part of the funerary rites of the western Sephardim of Spain and Portugal.[14]

Ruth Eshel's documentation of a mourning ritual by Beta Israelis, immigrant Ethiopian Jews, in 1992 in Nazareth gives clear evidence of funeral dancing still in practice today:

> Consoling processions arrived from all over the country, led by "Kesses" (spiritual leaders) in black embroidered caps holding colored parasols and fly whisks. After all the processions

reached the courtyard a kind of hysteria started. A huge circle was formed. In the middle, women walked with seemingly no focus, weakened knees, banging their heads or folding their arms to the back and bending the torso fiercely forwards and backwards. Others stood bouncing quickly as if the ground beneath was burning. Several men arranged in couples encircled the dancing women. Segments of shouts filled the air. At noon, buses arrived to take the group to the cemetery for the typical Israeli Jewish burial ceremony, in which psalms are recited, the body wrapped in a shawl is lowered into the ground, and the mourners recite "The Kaddish," the prayer for the dead.[15]

The Kaddish, as we saw in chapter 2, is sometimes spoken or read in a dance-like manner, with the arms raised three times and the hands open as the supplicant rocks onto the toes.

Also in an Arab tradition that continues into this century, parties of women go up to the cemeteries a fortnight or a month after a funeral, stopping every few hundred yards along the road for a dance.[16] They make two circles by holding hands and dance what is called the Raksa dance. As they dance, they sing: "The Almighty, the Almighty gives and takes."[17]

In a funeral dance of the Abkia tribe in southern Sudan, the dancers, thirty women wearing robes of withered vines plastered with mud, move in a single file around a large mango tree. Although the music is rhythmic and lively, their grief is affirmed by the monotony of their repetitive shuffling step. The funeral dance goes on for seven days and nights as they mourn the departed soul, comforting and accompanying it on the first difficult stage of its journey.

In Roman Catholic services, the Lamentations are sung three times during Holy Week. In the 14th century, Lamento di Tristano was a dance, as was Kyrie Eleison.[18]

Now Let Us Dance

In this type of dance, you may choose your own focus. A Lamentation Dance doesn't necessarily have to be reserved for grieving physical death. Sometimes we need to grieve old losses, events from our childhood, an illness, or the end of a relationship. You may also dance through memories of trauma, assault, isolation, abandonment, anger, or failed relationships. Dancing the energy of grief and loss is a way of expressing and releasing the emotions through bodily movement instead of dwelling in thought.

This type of dance can be done either in community or alone, depending on what is appropriate for you. Because deep feelings may come up, you'll want to work in an environment that feels safe and supportive. For some this might be a mountaintop; for others it might be a large room at home (or at a close friend's home) set with candles, pillows, and so forth. Victims of severe trauma may need to work in conjunction with a professional therapist, should intense emotions surface.

Bring an incident to mind and notice your body's reaction. Is there a slight weakness in the solar plexus or

MARTHA GRAHAM IN *LAMENTATION*. NEW YORK PUBLIC LIBRARY FOR THE PERFORMING ARTS.

In the 1930s, Martha Graham developed an innovative solo masterpiece called *Lamentation*. In this dance she was enveloped in a tubular piece of fabric that functioned as a veil, shroud, or mourning cloth, depending on what your eye perceived it to be. In her unique way, she seemed to be struggling with the enveloping blackness of the shroud while simultaneously wrapping it about her body like a blanket for security and comforting. Focusing on the essence of suffering and grief, she distilled these emotions into a stark lone figure in a self-contained and solitary, yet universal struggle to deal with loss.

stomach area as you remember an error you made or a hurt you are having to endure, perhaps a transgression made against your body when you were a child. Pay attention to the feeling that accompanies whatever memory you are working through and amplify it with exaggerated movement. Use any arm movements, such as slinging or flailing; leg movements, such as kicking and leaping; or any whirling movements that suit. Also try contracting your abdomen, exhaling your breath, and holding. Then release and observe the physical effects and your emotional state, now seeing your "feeling" as a "sensation."

It is important to pay attention to your breath even as you move. Breathe in through the nose, with enthusiasm, then release through the mouth—just let it go. Allowing yourself the absolute freedom to express your feelings through your body and your voice will go a long way toward revealing and releasing the rage that often underlies grief, and the grief that often underlies rage. You may be surprised to find, as you continue with your breath work, that you're no longer holding on to the old emotions—you have breathed through them, and the charge is gone. When you reach that place you have reached your goal. Relax and rejoice!

A Traditional Lamentation Dance

A choreographic example of a communal dance you might emulate is described below by dance historian Curt Sachs. This dance is done on Easter Monday in Megara near Athens. You will notice that the dance matches the image earlier in this chapter from Magna Graecia, once a Greek colony so many centuries ago. Follow the rhythm of the reds, blues, and saffrons of the dancers' dresses and bordered mantles in this very sophisticated painting.

> In these *tratta* the women walk close together and take hold of each other crosswise: the first one grasps the hand of the third over the breast of the second; the second grasps the hand of the fourth over the breast of the third, and so on. And in this firmly linked chain they move, under the direction of a leader, slowly and sedately, without rocking to and fro and without distorting a feature. The left foot crosses the right, the right steps aside towards the right, and the left is brought up beside it. Then the right steps back obliquely to the right, the left crosses behind it, and the right again moves forwards obliquely to the right" to complete the pattern, which is repeated numerous times. The women sometimes form several chains, which meet and merge and separate again as they wind in serpentine patterns.[19]

11

Universal Rhythm: The Drum Dance

Music and rhythm find their way into the secret places of the soul.

Plato

I began taking dance class when I was in my thirties. I had never been very athletic and had never felt particularly coordinated; as much as I loved the music and could hear it in my head, it took me an entire year of attending classes before I got "on rhythm." I distinctly remember what it felt like when it happened. I just slid into place. For the first time in my life I felt connected, in sync. The whole class seemed to breathe a sigh of relief with me as I danced around the room. For the year leading up to that moment I had been trying to do the steps, but in Middle Eastern dance you do the rhythm, and the rhythm itself does the movements. In that moment the drumbeat became everything to me, lifting me instantaneously to a natural high. I wanted to know more about the power of the drum.

Music is made up of sound and rhythm. Like poetry, it penetrates the

Mud sculpture showing women playing drums and other instruments at an Egyptian Zar healing ritual. Photograph by Eva Cernik.

mysterious world of our emotions and dreams. It has long been the belief that music awakens the soul, recalling celestial harmonies heard before the soul was separated from God. When we understand rhythm and sound in their holistic nature and relationship, music becomes a source of healing and inspiration.

Women have always been music makers, and rhythmic patterns a vital link to women's spiritual expression. The matriarchal early planters invented the drum, underlining their ritual dance with a regular ostinato sound. Drums beat for the birth of a child, a coming of age, marriage, and a death in the community. It was said that the all-begetting Mother beat a drum to mark the rhythm of life.

The Latin root for *tempo*, being *tempus*, is akin to the word for sacred space; *temple* (Latin *templum*). Known to some as the key to another world, the drum has symbolic meaning, its round form suggesting celestial spheres and eternity. The drum is at once the altar and the mediator between humanity and divinity, heaven and earth. Drumming allows us to find the common rhythm, the movement emanating from a certain vitality or inner life force on the microcosmic/macrocosmic level. The common rhythm is the connecting force between two planes of reality, between the innermost recesses of absolute being and its outward manifestation in the world. Finding the common rhythm, the same

Drums beat out the rhythms of life. Photograph by Iris Stewart.

vital pulsation, can transform and interchange the two planes of self and other, inner and outer. It is the common rhythm discernible between the two that allows our perception of the movement of waves on the ocean to be analogous to that of a field of golden wheat rippling in the breeze or the change of the seasons to the life-death-rebirth cycle.

The common rhythm makes it possible for us to integrate the physical and instinctive with the spiritual, and to tap into psychic waves and the cosmic flow. The combined rhythmic/vibrational aspect of the voice, the instrument, the drum, and the movement of the dancer creates vertical and horizontal emotional bridges between us and the cosmos.

The search for the connection between self and the cosmos is the search of the mystic. In mysticism everything is vibration, and it is the unique quality of the vibration that determines the form of manifestation. Not only is the substance of the human being formed by vibrations; we as humans also live and move in vibrations—they surround us as the fish is surrounded by water, and we contain them within ourselves as the pond contains water. The human brain has four measurable rhythmic vibrations of its own: beta (talking, walking, and other daily activities); alpha (relaxed, meditative); theta (inspiration, creativity, and extrasensory perception); and delta (deep sleep.) Rhythm is energy, so it is not surprising that when we move to drum rhythms we feel as though we're being carried along by the beat—a feeling of effortlessness and safety that defines synchrony. Perhaps that is why rhythm seems to lift time out of the realm of the ordinary, as we know it, and transmutes it into timelessness. Rhythm is essential to transcendence; because of its power, the drum becomes a force in its own right, its mesmerizing beat affecting the soma and the psyche.

Drums are used for healing in all traditional cultures, certain rhythms being associated with specific spirits or saints. A dancer may identify or feel the need for communing with a particular spirit and will request that rhythm with which the spirit is connected. Healing rhythms are flexible, allowing for subtle variations in tempo and shifts in beat patterns. Healing rhythms are also multidimensional, like the pulse, and act on the heartbeat. Body rhythms change with the rhythms played. In his book *Drumming at the Edge of Magic*, Mickey Hart explores the impact of rhythm on physiology, claiming that the loud, sudden nature of percussive shifts trips the switches in the midbrain, the oldest aspect of the brain, which instantaneously reacts to stimuli with a flight-or-fight response. Flooded with adrenaline but with nothing to flee from or fight, the body wants to move, to dance, to entrain with the power of the rhythm. Says Hart:

> This seems to account for the physiological pleasure of percussion. But there is also a higher level, the level of the cerebral cortex, the part of our brain that handles symbolic levels of meaning. What the rest of the brain hears as rhythm and noise, the cortex conceives in a larger majesty.[1]

Multiple sound frequencies recurring at a steady rate appear to block the left-hemisphere aspect of the cerebral cortex. The left side of the brain (the methodical, intellectual side) cannot process polyrhythms, and at a certain point it begins to yield control. Vibrating through the vestibular fluid in the inner ear, acoustic rhythms affect equilibrium; body movements such as turning or swinging the head create a similar effect.[2] A range of resonances enters through many nerve pathways and coaches brainwaves into different patterns as it reverberates in the brain,

Female Drummer, temple carving, c. 11–13th century India. Asian Art Museum of San Francisco, Avery Brundage Collection.

producing deep images not available in everyday life.

Drum-inspired dance has the potential for restoring our sense of balance, for changing our focus, and for soothing the nervous system. Emotional states of joy and fear are energy-based and easily become rhythmically expressed; energy-depleted psychic processes, such as grief and depression, can shift with external rhythmic activation. As the right and left hemispheres of the brain are joined together in this way, a deeper integration takes place, one that expands consciousness.

By a variety of sizes and tonal qualities, drums interweave their individual sounds in complex ways to create a drum song. In traditional drum dance rituals, the content of the music depends on the community that performs it and the dancers who embody it—the dancers respond to the drummers and the drummers respond to the dancers. The talking drums may initiate a dance, or they may shift their rhythmic patterning to follow a dancer and then intensify it even further to urge her or him to yet more energetic self-expression.

No one can listen to all the rhythms simultaneously, not even the drummers. Therefore, even though there is a constant repetition of the same patterns, it is actually experienced as changing because the listener's focus shifts from one rhythmic line to another. At the same time the dancer needs to identify and maintain the integrating beat, called the metronome sense. The belly dancer may carry the drumbeat with vibrating hips while simultaneously carrying the harmony, sung melody, or theme with slow, snake-like arm and hand gestures, all the while moving smoothly forward. Chief Hawthorne Bey, performing and recording artist of traditional and contemporary African drumming, claims that, drumming and dancing, when viewed in their proper context, are synonymous with one another. After a while the dancer is literally dancing not upon the ground but on the music, the rhythm itself.

The Tuva, practitioners of the oldest shamanism in Mongolia, portray the drum as the horse that carries the spirit. Shamans in other cultures ride their drum up to the World Tree. In possession dances of Caribbean and West African cultures, ancestor spirits called orishas ride the rhythm of the drum down into the dancing bodies. Certain rhythms are identified with specific spirits or saints in the zar, voudoun, and other traditional dances.

A contemporary artist who fuses the forms of dance and drumming is Heidrun Hoffman. Her work, called Dance in Rhythm—Rhythm in Dance, is a blend of movement and drumming using the interaction of pulse, breath, voice, and clapping to awaken inherent rhythm through the body. Heidrun incorporates traditional styles of drumming on the Korean sam buk and tschanggo drums and the Japanese taiko drum with ethnic dance forms, such as the kathak and samba, modern movement, and the knowledge of the *TA KE TI NA* rhythm work.*

---

*The sam buk and tschanggo drums are used in Korean shamanism and folk music. *Taiko* is the word for "barrel drum" in Japanese. Traditional taiko drumming is a blend of martial art, dance, and music. *TA KE TI NA* is a path to consciousness through rhythm. See Reinhard Flatischer, *TA KE TI NA—The Forgotten Power of Rhythm*, in the bibliography.

Dance in Rhythm—Rhythm in Dance. Heidrun Hoffman, drummer and dancer.

Hoffman tells of her experience with rhythm:

> I have always liked to dance and express myself through my body, but with my drums I finally feel whole. Since I have discovered dancing and playing drums at the same time, worlds have been melting together, balancing my male and female sides, my aggression and my softness. Here I find quiet meditation, music, and direction for my movements. When I let rhythms of different cultures flow through me, I play them until they become my own. Each beat gives me a chance to grow and see myself and my life.
>
> The first steps of learning to play a dance drum are very crucial, and they were an unexpected challenge for me. I found the deepest satisfaction when I didn't push myself. Sometimes I felt moments of great joy, but also I often

La Behemiene (the Gypsy). She dances well the galliard, minuets, and passpieds; but one must always pay attention to her hands, rather than to her feet. Private collection: Debra and Madison Sowell.

experienced intense emotional waves. Ancient sadness and sudden anger came through, and I learned to channel them through my whole system. The anger transformed into an uplifting, positive energy, and the allowances for sadness became a truly purifying process. Both freed my soul. Now the drums are a powerful and joyful place to find freedom and peace. Drumming is flying but being deeply grounded at the same time. This is pure medicine for me."[3]

Working with the drums to create the dance. Photograph by David Garten.

All dance is timed and rhythmical. The rhythm may be intuitive or heard within; it may be free-flowing as in the Turkish taxim or built on phrases of breath as in yoga and chant. As an art form, it is metrical, mathematically organized, carefully counted. Pauses or nonmovement, just as essential as gestures and steps, all find their place in a rhythmic, numbered phrase.

Yet, while the whole spectrum of rhythmic beats and accents can be counted and practiced, the dance cannot truly be moved through the body until the counting is behind you and the pulsation is felt emotionally. As much as we have talked about rhythm, it is not the beat that brings transcendence. It is the pause, the suspended movement, the unexpected silence at the end of a phrase that hypnotizes. T. S. Eliot, in *Four Quartets*, said, "Except for the point, the still point, there would be no dance, and there is only the dance." Similarly, a Taoist text states that only when there is stillness in movement can the spiritual rhythm, which pervades heaven and earth, appear. The power of the interval is the message that lives there: You have time and space, and you have freedom from time and space. It is the interval—the space between the pulses, the heartbeat, the steps—that is the soul of rhythm.

Poets find meter for their verses in the rhythm of tapping feet. The heart beats our internal drum. The two-beat accent of jazz, descendant of African drums, brings us to unconscious reminiscence of the heartbeat of the womb. The beat goes on and on and on, and so it is throughout our lives.

Now Let Us Dance

The Drum Dance or Rhythm Dance may be done alone or with a group. To dance in rhythms you need to work with the drums, hearing them and feeling them. I recommend that you not start with a choreographed dance but instead dance raw, free form, working with the basics: basic rhythm, basic moves, basic instinct. You may move directly on the pulsation or downbeat, emphasize accents, or work in counter time to the beat. You'll get the most out of a Drum Dance if you just completely surrender to the rhythms you hear and feel, letting your body be carried into movement. Try dancing with your eyes closed; that way you won't be distracted or influenced by what someone else is doing.

Try using a rattle, jingling jewelry, or anything else that shakes and rattles as you move to further accent your dance. The effect of a Drum Dance is also greatly enhanced by vocalizing the rhythm, using nonsensical syllables. An example would be "Um-gugu-la-ho" or anything, as long as it fits the rhythm. Try walking around the room as you sound out the rhythms. Eventually you may get to the place where you can vocalize the rhythmic "off-beat" as you move to the downbeat, which can lead to some interesting possibilities.

Foot stamping as part of your dance is an excellent way to punctuate energy within a phrase and also to feel powerful. Because women have been expected to walk so tentatively and delicately on the earth in our pointed-toe high-heeled shoes, it may seem strange at first to see how hard and loudly you can stamp around. But stamping will literally ground you to the earth and connect you with your inner strength.

Start with your knees flexed and rib cage elevated, stamping from one foot to the other in a regular, easy rhythm. You can then stamp twice on each foot or change the pattern in other ways, as the drum rhythms inspire. You may want to add Indian bells to your ankles to accentuate your stamps even more. Next try to move sideways, forwards, backwards, or in a circle. Then try adding your voice. As you stamp, chant "Hu," "Ahh," or whatever holds appeal for you. Let it come from the belly, a full, satisfying sound. You can then develop this sound into a threefold beat: Left, Right, "Hu."

When dancing in a group, each person should start moving slowly to her own inner rhythm, but also observe how it feels within the group, working toward coming together in a common rhythm. Within our different ways of moving, different paces and carriages, different steps and directions, we are searching for something: a common pulse, a common beat in the sounds of our feet upon the ground. Once we have reached this nonverbal consensus, we build on the group spirit it expresses. When enough people move together in a common pulse with a common purpose, an amazing force, an ecstatic rhythm, eventually takes over. People stop moving as individuals and begin to move as if they were parts of a single body—not in a uniform motion but in deeply interrelated ways, tracing out the forms and patterns of a larger organism, being moved by a group spirit.

12

The Ecstatic and the Transcendental

Listen to the music with your soul. Now, while listening, do you not feel an inner self awakening deep within you—that it is by its strength that your head is lifted, that your arms are raised, that you are walking slowly toward the light?[1]

Isadora Duncan

Ecstasy is found in the world of dreamers and artists, those who show us the wholeness and holiness of life and spirit. Experienced through the senses, it is the opposite of the rational and the materialistic; it is the sensuous as distinct from the sensual. The word *ecstasy* comes from the Greek root *ex stasis*, meaning "to stand outside oneself." To be in a state of ecstasy is to be filled with a sense of joy too powerful for the body to contain or the rational mind to understand.

My first experience of ecstatic dance came during a performance I gave in an old church that had been converted into a community meeting room. With my red circular veil I began turning to the music of Maurice Ravel's *Bolero*,* which had always appealed to me. I especially liked the

---

*Ravel, who composed *Bolero* while working with the ballet dancer Ida Rubenstein, was not sure what he had created. It was not like anything else he had composed, nor did it fit into any established genre of music. He said about *Bolero*, "I have created a masterpiece, and it is not music." After hearing the piece played at its debut in Paris, a woman stood up in the audience and said, "Ravel is mad!" Upon hearing about the outburst, Ravel smiled and said, "Ah! She understands!" Perhaps *Bolero* really is magical.

Modern dancer Mary Wigman wedded form to ecstasy, the divine to the human, to produce her dance. Wigman was able to maintain a conscious presence and observe how her body moved even as she surrendered to the flow of the dance.

way dancing with the veil enabled me to interpret the subtle but complex rhythms as they began slowly flowing like a small lazy brook, gradually building up into the crescendo of a mighty river. Like an intricate arabesque, the *Bolero* theme weaves a repetitive pattern, though the pattern is never exactly the same. Each repetition ascends to another level of tonality, resonance, and emotion, creating a hypnotic, mesmerizing effect.

Almost immediately in that performance I sensed that something was different. Joining with the music, suddenly I was no longer aware of the audience or consciously following the choreography I had practiced so many times. With my arms outstretched but relaxed, I was conscious of the veil encircling me. As I turned, or rather was turned, the veil melted into a red cloud floating around me, lifting me. I became one with the music, moving without effort, floating upward toward the stained-glass domed ceiling. I can only describe the experience as a subtle but definite tuning in to a new wave pattern, a shifting of focus, a letting go of control. Totally engrossed in the wonder of the moment, I felt the purest joy!

The experience was one I will never forget. It proved to be a catalyst for my journey into exploring the possibilities of other planes of reality. Dancing to *Bolero* that day opened a door that led me to a life in which I have come to accept that I am safe no matter what happens. I have tapped into a similar wavelength many times since then. Through it, I have come to accept the Mystery.

Dance by its very nature is ecstatic. Almost every dancer who has written about dance makes reference to ecstasy, although she or he will often describe the experience in other terms. The experience of ecstasy is associated with a feeling of timelessness or eternity, adding another dimension to our familiar temporal existence. One may have a sensation of elevation or levitation, the feeling of a rising spring or a flowing stream. There may also be a sensation of heightened inner consciousness or awareness or an increased feeling of stillness and peace. Freedom from self, from guilt, from sorrow and desire accompanies ecstasy.

The receiver feels she has accessed knowledge of a totally new kind, identifying with the universe, with all living things, or with the deity. Ecstasy is a feeling of glory, joy, happiness, satisfaction. It is the state of mind that ensues, however briefly, from a religious experience, when everyday consciousness is stripped away, leaving only the essential self. Ecstasy creates both a catharsis and a creative inspiration, making the vessel of the body empty and fit for the divine to enter.

Ecstatic or transcendental dances have been known to almost every culture that has existed. The purpose of these dances was for general release or for communication with the Divine; some were for the purpose of curing a particular illness. Ecstatic dance relies on rhythms, clapping, breathing, and physical movement to achieve transcendence. Since entrance into the ecstatic state happens spontaneously, one is said to be seized or possessed by these powers, powers that are oftentimes regarded as an outside force. Whether it is a rhythmic release of energy or a deliberate religious act, ecstatic dance needs no onlooker nor witness. In that way, it is different from dance as a work of art, which is made conscious of itself and intended for observation. In Eastern dance, the dancer's complete absorption into the character or mood danced is called the Other Thought.

Ecstatic dance is an offering of one's own body to the Divine, negating the need for the dark side—scarifying and self-torture, sacrifice or the spilling of blood. (The original meaning of the word *sacrifice* was "sacred offering," not "sacred killing.") In dance we do not attempt to lose control but rather to change consciousness, to enter into the flow.

Ring seals and Cretan art from Isopata, near Knossos, give hints of transcendent practice. The scene's movements suggest a dance with the Great Mother, who is placed high and in the center, her head inclined toward a large snake. In her spiral descent, the Goddess's hair flies behind her, her skirt billowing. Two women undulate toward her, arms lifted high in front. A third dancer faces forward, arms aloft. Every aspect of the design is meant to convey a feeling of rapid whirling movement, a dance of ecstasy and incantation.

In *The Dancing Goddess*, Heide Gottner-Abendroth describes ecstasy as the simultaneous uniting of the powers of emotion, intellect, and action:

> When the interplay of those powers suddenly occurs, which is always improbable and rare, ecstatic moments are produced. They are moments of extreme lightness and freedom; they

'92

are chords of celestial energies played on the fragile instrument that is a human being. No one can hold on to those ecstatic moments, which is a good thing, because ecstasy cannot be endured for long.[2]

What is commonly called the ecstatic state is really a deepened state of relaxation. You are in control of your behavior; you are lucid, conscious, and able to concentrate, and can "awaken" at any time. Ecstasy is not easily or deliberately acquired, but if you watch for it, it may come to you more easily than you think. Expanded states of consciousness described as ecstatic, transcendent, and cosmic are accessible through meditation, yoga, breathwork, chanting, prayer, and movement. The secret is this: Ecstasy is not to be sought after; it is to be allowed to enter. However, once you identify certain portals for yourself, you can begin to tap into the ecstatic state more and more often; this happens to me now simply by hearing certain music or rhythms. Even with this level of accessibility, though, the transcendental or ecstatic state is not to be merely entered into on a whim. To do this can lead to habit, escapism, or druglike dependency. Rather, you must visit the realm of ecstatic consciousness with intention and then carry that visitation with you into daily life, bringing your ecstatic awareness into this plane and using it for mortal purposes.

Baile Flamenco is a dance of ecstasy and possession, *baile* referring to ceremonial. In Andalusian Gypsy dance, Olé or Polo refers to dance and song in which the dancer must wait and hope for her personal *duende*, or spirit, to enter and flood her with inspiration before achieving true artistry. Even in the modern form of flamenco, the rhythms, the movements of the dancer, the castanets, the guitar, and the singer all fuse to form an exalting sense of total, concentrated energy in a suspended crescendo that carries the spectator with it. Oblivious to the audience, the dancer is totally absorbed, swept along with the intensity of the music. Against this dramatic backdrop, the dancer's face, delicate hands and arms, and arched body tell us she is in full control of all the forces surging around her.

Perhaps the most widely recognized image of ecstatic dance is that of the whirling dervishes (Persian, *darwish*) of the Mevlevi Sufi order, founded by Mevlana Jalaluddin Rumi in the 13th century.* The word *darwish* translates as "the sill of the door," describing the dancer as standing at the door to enlightenment. Some Sufi orders, though not all, practice dance

*The Sufis are a small minority of the Muslim faith. They are not a sect, and there is no uniform body of doctrine constituting what is known as Sufism; strong evidence points to influences from Hellenistic culture, Perso-Indian ideas, and Buddhist traditions. Rumi integrated music, poetry, and dance into spiritual ceremonies and gatherings; he also honored women and equality. Although the history of Sufism includes a long roll of women, they are not easily found in Sufi writings and recorded history. Rabi'a al'-Adawiya, a saintly woman who was born in Basra and died in Jerusalem, is recorded as having been part of the development of the doctrine of trust in God (*tawakkul*) during Sufism's second century, replacing the rigorous asceticism previously rooted in religious observances (see Hastings, *Encyclopedia of Religion and Ethics*). Her many verses on the subject of divine love foreshadowed the ecstatic and enthusiastic mysticism characteristic of the succeeding age. Women participated in *sema* (sun) whirlings in the early periods of the order. Although Rumi was highly criticized by his contemporaries, Sufism survived in many places throughout the Middle East.

LEFT: ALLOWING ECSTASY TO ENTER. PHOTOGRAPH BY DAVID GARTEN.

MEVLEVI ORDER OF AMERICA, LED BY POSTNESHIN JELALUDDIN LORAS. PHOTOGRAPH BY MATIN MIZE.

movements prescribed to achieve spiritual ecstasy.

A whirling dance practice performed by women in ancient China may have been taken by the Mongols to Anatolia, setting the stage for the spinning routine of the Mevlevi dervishes.[3] In that dance, the women, acting as religious mediums, whirled with a flower in hand until they fell to the ground in a trance. Kitharas, shrill flutes, and drums accompanied the rite.

In this century Hazrat Murshid Suleyman Hayati Dede of Turkey was given the vision of full and equal participation of women once again in all aspects of Mevlana's works. In 1980 Postneshin Jelaluddin Loras was sent to North America by Sheikh Dede, his father, to carry the Mevlevi teaching and traditions to the West. Honoring his father's vision, Sheik Jelaluddin involves all members of the spiritual community in formal training and the music and traditional rituals of the Sema, Zikhr Allah (divine remembrance), and Sobjet (sacred discourse).

Dance historian Joost Merloo describes the Mevlevi Sufis' whirling dervish dance as a conscious and premeditated psychological technique aimed at achieving a state of spiritual exaltation and ecstasy.[4] The Mevlevis' dance, known as *tannoura* in Egypt, is an invocation and deep concentration upon the Divine name. Sufi al-Hujwiri, in the book *Kachf al-Mahdjub,* explains that what the Sufis do is not dance as we know it. He wrote:

> But when such agitation appears to be the result of heartfelt emotion, and the

head becomes absorbed by vibrations; and each moment becomes more powerful, more overwhelming, without ever being aware of custom or form—this kind of excitation is neither dance nor is it a game carried on with the feet nor carnal enjoyment—but rather the dissolution of the soul. How wrong are those who call this a "dance"; and how impossible it is for those who have not experienced divine will to claim that such a dance does not constitute union with divinity! To know divine inspiration and to have experienced such a state cannot be formulated in words. He who has not tasted of it cannot understand it.[5]

One can try to explain the effect as autohypnosis, but the Sufi would differ: the dervish knows exactly where she or he is at all times. She does not lose herself in ecstasy but becomes ecstasy. It is in fact a higher level of consciousness, a hyperawareness of self and surroundings. The dancer becomes a "sprinkler" of divine grace, spreading it over the aridity of our earthly existence as the state of sacred ecstasy is reached.

I am going to describe in general one Mevlevi Sufi order dance, the Sema, so we can get some sense of how it is practiced. The ceremony is preceded by a eulogy to the Prophet, a procession, and four salaam (salutes or movements), and several other symbolic rituals. Each semazen then slowly contemplates and acknowledges the godhead or divine in their neighbor by gazing at a spot between the eyes—one sees and recognizes, and turns.

Beginning with arms crossed over the breast, the dancer begins to whirl around counterclockwise while moving in a closed circle, clockwise group dance formation, slowly at first, then unfolding the arms as the speed increases, going from "withdrawal" *(gabd)* to "expansion" *(bast)*. Now the right palm is turned upward as a receptacle of Divine Grace, which passes through the heart of the dancer and is transmitted to earth through the downward-turned left palm. Sheik Kabir Helminski, the American representative of the Turkish Mevlevi Ensemble of the Mevlana Culture and Art Foundation, explained whirling to the audience in his introductory remarks for the Ensemble's 1997 Sema Tour of America:

> The individual semazen must be able to expand her/his awareness to include several dimensions at once: he or she must focus on his or her own physical axis, which in this case is the left leg and foot, revolving 360 degrees with each step, inwardly pronouncing the name of God, keeping an awareness of exactly where she/he is in space and the narrow margins of error in this tight choreography, feeling a connection through the shaikh of the ceremony to the whole lineage and also the founder of the order, Mevlana, and most of all turning with a deep love of God. The sheer impossibility of accomplishing these tasks through one's own will can push one toward another possibility: that of letting a deeper will take over. In this way, the sema becomes a lesson in surrender.

The whirling continues for quite some time; the dancer becomes a "sprinkler" of Divine Grace, spreading

Zar ritual for symbolic cleansing of environment. Harmonic Convergence, 1986. Horseshoe Hills, Sperryville, Virginia. Dancer: Anthea. Photograph by Rob Parker.

it over the aridity of our earthly existence as the state of sacred ecstasy (wajad, nirvana, samadhi) is reached. Toward the end, the powerful sound of drums evokes the day of the last judgment, and suddenly comes the invocation, embracing all the Names of God: Hu! The ceremony concludes with a reading from the Qur'an and a recitation of the Fatiha (poetry).

Another ancient form of ecstatic dance that has attracted the attention of historians, anthropologists, dance researchers, and etymologists as well as reformers and some government bureaucrats down through the centuries is the zar, a circle dance. The word *zar* ("circle") is thought to have been derived from the Arabic verb *zara,* or *zahar,* which means "becoming visible" or "perceptible." The word *munzara* is used to describe a participant.[6] While it is most widely known today as a woman's healing dance in Egypt, the zar has been practiced in Morocco, Yemen, Turkey, Tunisia, the Sudan, Saudi Arabia, and southern Iran, its practitioners ranging from relatively isolated traditional societies to Coptic Christians, Moslems, and Ethiopian Jews.

The zar rituals include dance, invocations or prayers, incense, and incantations; the ceremony may last from one to several days. As practiced in Sudan, the ceremony is a four-day event wherein the participants, on behalf of the one who has requested the ritual, seek contact with the Old Woman. Usually the one for whom the zar is convened asks for the ceremony because she feels she has developed a troubling malady caused by an evil spirit. (In today's psychological terms we would probably call her depressed.) The purpose of the ritual is to reconcile the one who is not well with the visiting or "possessing" spirit through supplication and placation.

The scheikha (priestess) leads the one to be healed in a dance, the repetition and the constant crescendo of both music and movements creating a hypnotic effect on both the dancer and the spectators. When the one being healed is able to identify the spirit (which is sometimes helped by the wearing of different costumes), the spirit is drawn into dialogue. Arches and contractions of the rib cage and/or abdomen are the signature movements of this ritual. The dancer's movements synchronize with the drumbeats, which steadily increase in intensity. As the dancer moves more intensely, or as a spectator indicates reaction to a song, the scheikha and her assistants stand directly over that woman, drumming and singing, encouraging maximum participation in the dance. This intensifying of the charged atmosphere assures the success of the zar. Eventually the dancer collapses in a trance and is later revived.

THE GUEDRA, PERFORMED BY TAURAEG WOMEN, MOROCCO'S "BLUE PEOPLE." PHOTOGRAPH COURTESY OF CAROLINA VARGA DINICU.

Ceremonies similar to the zar can be found in many other countries in Africa; the Gypsies (Romanies) have a similar ritual. The dance may share a common origin with the voodoo, candomble, and other African diaspora ceremonies found in Central America and the Caribbean. In Brazil, a comparable ceremony called the macumba is considered to be the "blood sister of the zar."

The Guedra (Ghedra), is a transcendental dance of the Berbers, the original inhabitants of Morocco, which is performed in the Spanish and French Sahara in southern Morocco and part of Algeria.[7] The Guedra is also known as the blessing dance, and it is considered to result in spiritual and emotional uplifting. Its name is derived from the drum used for the dance and for the cadence of the beat (the heartbeat rhythm, with emphasis on the second beat).

The Guedra of the Chleuh people is a solo dance performed by a woman as women and men arranged in a circle chant and sing, clapping their hands to the guedra rhythm. The dancer begins on her knees, completely covered with one or two black veils, from which she slowly and progressively emerges as she extends her arms forward. The main focus of the dance is the hypnotic hand and finger movements As the dancer's hands emerge from beneath the veil, she salutes the four directions (corners), North, South, East and West, followed by obeisances to the four elements: Fire, Earth, Wind and Water.[8] She touches her abdomen, heart, and head, quickly flicking her fingers toward all who are present to envelop them with good energy, peace, and spiritual love.

Although many of the ancient transcendental dances originated in cultures that lived closer to the earth than we do now, the ability to enter into ecstasy is first and foremost a matter of allowing that such a possibility exists and of permitting oneself to become so unbounded. Entering into ecstasy, however many times it happens, gives one an increasing sense of detachment from the mundane, even as we live in the everyday. We may not become "perfect" human beings through such experiences, but we gain a majestic quality that neutralizes the earth's glue. Visions, emotions, and dreams combine in wisdom, and we begin to see with the eyes of our heart. It shifts our center of manifestation from mind to heart, from exterior to interior, gently moving our focus away from the end result and onto the process. Through ecstatic identification with the All, a union takes place that causes awareness of self to recede before a growing sense of totality.

Now Let Us Dance

Transcendental dance transcends the conscious functioning of the brain or mind. Dancing from the inside out, it is not the mind that guides the dance movements or interprets the muscle function. Rather, it is through the built-up concentration of energy brought about by protracted spiritual and physical ritual movement that the mind is influenced, opening it to intuitive revelation.

In ecstatic group dance, energy moves through the participants in such a way as to suggest not only that we are all one, but also that there is more of us or more to us—that the whole is greater than the sum of its parts. There is contagion, a combined state of mind in which things seem unaccountably to unite and expand for a time. As in ancient times, group dancing provides the pleasure of collective participation. The persuasive rhythms of dance and chanting allow individuals in the group to form a union with one another, to momentarily drop the barriers of individualism—the ego's self-consciousness and the fear of separateness. With an open heart and trust within the circle, a higher vibration can be reached. When used with such positive intention, group energy has the potential to help restore balance and peace. People dancing together expand their individual boundaries and are moved by the larger force, the collective body. Becoming spiritually aware, you are able to focus and channel energy, by whatever name you choose to call it. This is the essence of the Mysteries.

Gabrielle Roth, self-proclaimed urban shaman, calls the ecstatic level of consciousness—an inner state of healing and purity—an egoless, timeless state of being in which we are completely electric, completely turned on. It is a state of being in which, in fact, we *are* divinity—divinity dancing. When asked in an interview what the Divine feels like when she dances, Roth replied, "Electrified emptiness. I feel full of emptiness."[9]

For your own solo dancing, you may want to study Gabrielle Roth's method of the Five Sacred Rhythms: *Flowing* starts with slow, heavy movements, rising and sinking, breathing deeply in and out, and leads into *Staccato*, a body jazz as you fuse with the beat, then *Chaos*, as you fall deeper and deeper into yourself, body gyrating and undulating. But "just when you think you're going to burst, or collapse, you land like a feather on the light side of yourself in *Lyrical* rhythm of violins sweeping you into a waltz. Then comes *Stillness* as tranquility enters."[10] Gabrielle Roth offers a video and music tape of her Five Sacred Rhythms (see Resources).

Roth has also said that "through her ecstatic prayer, the dancer herself moves closer to immortality." She loses herself: the ego that wants to be noticed dancing is gone. Feeling transported beyond the pull of gravity, the dancer enters the flow of grace, mapping the shortest distance from her soul to the Divine. The body leaves behind the expression of individuality and becomes the interface between the finite and the infinite.

Another form of Sufi movement that has recently come to the United States is called Zhikr (Turkish), Dhikr (Arabic), or Zekr (Persian), which translates as "remembrance," specifically remembrance of the Divine, and "being mindful."[11] The outward execution of this specifically Sufi form of invocation varies from one Sufi order to another but is of central importance in all of them. And just as in the case of the ritual prayer, the effect unfolds only gradually. An ancient precept says: "At first you pretend to do the zhikr; then you do the zhikr; finally the zhikr does you." Dr. Nahid Angha, cofounder of the International

Gabrielle Roth. Photograph by Robert Ansel.

Association of Sufism, author and translator of several books on Sufism, cautions, "To be effective and beneficial a *zekr* must be given to the *salek* [student] by a teacher; it cannot be read in any book, much less invented by the *salek*. *Zekrs* are given very confidentially only to those students who properly deserve them."[12]

Different zhikrs can be carried out alone or in groups, aloud or internally (zhikr of the heart), while sitting, standing, or turning around. The dance is a form of concentration that frees one from the limiting control of the senses and the intellect, an experience of ecstasy in which the personality is lost in love of the Divine. It is this act of concentration in the moment that opens the door to another kind of knowing. Zikhr is a combination of sound (external or internal), concentration, breathing, and movement, always undertaken under the guidance of a sheik/scheikha, or teacher. One begins the zhikr on the tongue, often corresponding with the breath, verbally repeating "La ilahe illallah," which can be interpreted as "there is nothing but Allah, or Divine Reality": 'Al' (all) 'lah' (nothingness). The head (sitting) or the whole body (standing) moves rhythmically from right to left. Other steps and arm movements may be added. The combination of sound and movement gives rise to specific breathing patterns, which may become consciously intensified. As concentration increases, the remembrance moves into the heart.

Eventually, as remembrance occurs on every level, the zikhr "La ilahe illallah" is realized throughout the being as the traveler is joined into unity with the Divine. One's being remembers through experience that there is nothing but the Divine, and separation dissolves "like a drop of water falling into the ocean."

Through ecstatic identification with the All, the Universal, or however we may try to define the experience, a union happens that causes awareness of self to recede before a growing sense of community or totality. Down through the ages this subtle but powerful knowledge has been available to those who have been able to recognize it.

The wisdom of the mystic leader is important because it is her or his responsibility to instruct and carefully watch over the pupil, lest the pupil be exposed to mental and psychic phenomena he or she is not prepared for. Therefore, I add a precaution that you be discriminating and thoroughly informed in choosing someone to study with.

For most of us at this point, our understanding of the traditional ways is very superficial. Most of us do not have the cultural experience or the trained leaders. Resist the temptation to "get high" through trance as just another way of going unconscious—we have enough ways of doing that already. Being in a high state of consciousness is our goal.

LEFT: THE MIND DOES NOT GUIDE THE DANCE MOVEMENTS IN TRANSCENDENTAL DANCE, RATHER THE MOVEMENTS INFLUENCE THE MIND. PHOTOGRAPH BY DAVID GARTEN.

13
DANCE OF THE ELEMENTS

For it is perfectly possible that the women initiates at Eleusis, with vessels on their heads, performed a dance in the course of which the fire—covered over with ashes—was fanned into flames. . . .The round of dancing women with lights on their heads and their reflection in the sea while the stars seemed to dance in accompaniment must have been an amazing spectacle.

Carl Kerenyi, Eleusis[1]

We as modern, urban-bound people have become unconscious in many ways to the effects of the elements. Why be concerned with fire? When the room gets chilly, we reach for the thermostat connected to a heater somewhere in the bowels of the building. Some of us experience the upheavals of rainstorms or hurricanes, or we read of the Midwestern farmer's concern about a possible drought, but for the most part, we simply turn on a faucet to an endless supply of hot and cold water. We seldom touch the earth, walking on cement sidewalks in fashionable leather soles, riding on plastic tires over blacktop roads.

Until recent times we have taken for granted an unlimited availability of natural resources. However, within the past few decades, it has become clear that we are unquestionably connected to and dependent on the environment, as the ecological system has come under threat to human mismanagement and misunderstanding of limits. While most of us may have lost forever our ancestors' ability to walk through a desert and sense the flow of an underground stream, find our way through a forest with the guidance of a star, or know how to journey to a place on a magnetic ley line for healing, we have come to realize that we must renew our reverence of the elements if we are to survive. By looking at the Grandmother's ways, we may redefine our own connections.

The four elements—Earth, Water, Fire and Air (Ether)—are the building blocks of all substances. The same elements form the foundation of life: the earth, the universe, and our own bodies. The red lotus was often a symbol of all four of the classical elements, indicating the primal condition before creation when all the elements were united in the cosmic womb. It is rooted in the mud of the Earth, supported by Water, and draws its red color from the Fire of the sun; its blossom partakes of the essence of Air, releasing its perfume into the breezes. Symbolism of the four elements is also found in the Tree of Life—the fig tree in some places and the pomegranate (apple) in others—which sends its roots deep into the earth to bring up the water that makes the red juice hidden within its fruit, while it reaches upward, transporting electromagnetism into the firmament and exchanging oxygen for carbon dioxide.

The Goddess was seen as the Mother Creator of the four elements. We find four-fold designs represented throughout the Goddess religion. These designs are often composed of a central circle with four circles or loops around it, suggesting concepts of the center as cosmic source and of the unification of opposites. Each of the four circles or loops encloses one of several symbols: cross, X, M, zig-zag, caterpillar, chick, butterfly, seed or double seed. Each is thus shown to contain the spark of life. There are also four repetitions in the rhythm construct of many ceremonies and dances.

Now Let Us Dance

In order to dance the four elements, you will need to become familiar with each element, physically, psychically, and metaphorically. I found that many traditions incorporate the four elements into their ceremonies in recognition of the subtle yet profound influences their different energies have on our lives. The history of these traditions will be discussed for each element in turn, along with descriptions of the style of dance recommended for that element.

In addition to these suggestions, you may want to include mantras for the elements in your elements dances, using the primal sound for each of the elements as the basis of your mantra. Created by Kali, India's pre-Vedic Great Mother, these primal sounds are "La," earth; "Va," water; "Ya," air; and "Ra," fire. It was Kali, whose Sanskrit name is Ma, meaning both "mother" and "intelligence," who mingled the four elements to create life, and symbols of the elements are found in each one of Kali's four hands.

Stamping and pounding help charge the energy of an Earth Dance. Photograph by David Garten.

Earth Dance

Without exception, deities for expression of the Earth have been feminine. Gaia (Terra) is our Mother, the provider and sustainer for every living thing, our beginning and our end. Represented by the cornucopia horn of plenty, an attribute of Ceres, Goddess of Agriculture and Abundance, the Earth element gives all and takes all back into itself. Kneeling and prostration of the body in religious prayer were once the means of closer contact with Mother Earth, as was the custom of going barefoot in sacred places. Dances to the Earth element imbue the dancer with a sense of being in tune with the basic life force, and through this connection a revitalization process begins.

When dancing to the Earth element, all movements are done close to the ground. Keep your knees bent, and experiment with leaning forward, dipping down, even squatting. Your hands and arms reach toward the earth, palms facing down as much as possible. Your feet should be flat on the ground. Stamping or pounding wakes up the energy of this dance, charging your body with the earth's electromagnetic energy.

You might also try rolling on the ground and making other movements that take you off your feet in order to connect other parts of your body to the earth. The Earth Dance is not intended for gracefulness but to connect our bodies to the natural world around us—to remind us that our flesh and bones were formed from the earth, that we are part of the earth, and that when we die we will return to the earth. In some cultures, a dance to the Earth is done on the knees.

Even though the focus of the movements is downward, the Earth Dance can have a wide open, freeing, and expansive feeling. Imagine yourself as a child playing on the stomach of its mother in order to open yourself up to the many movements possible in this dance.

Water Dance

Water has always played an important part in the mythology of ancient cultures. Eurynome, the most ancient goddess of the indigenous people of Greece, danced upon the waters of chaos; Aphrodite was born from the foam of the sea. Tiamat, the goddess of the ocean, had as her home the Red Sea. Brigantia (Brighid, Brigit), the powerful and still widely popular Celtic goddess, is not only the power of the new moon and of spring, but also of the flowing sea. The Promised Land of the Hebrews was said to be made of rivers of milk and honey.

Water is the element of renewal. Goddesses regularly dipped into the rivers for renewal. Bathing in the waters of the sacred Ganges River washed away the sins of humans. Baptism in the Jordan River assured eternal life. And let us not forget the elusive fountain of youth.

Water represents integrity, strength, forward motion, and determination. Yet, water is fluid. Water flows steadily onward, moving around obstacles in its way, changing shape and course as needed. But regardless of its path or destination, its essence remains intact. From water we learn how to stay our course, yet remain flexible and open to possibilities—how to maintain our

identity and personal integrity while coping with difficult people or problems.

Women have a special relationship with the Water element. The life-giving properties of water are sympathetic with the life-giving fluids of women's bodies: blood, milk, amniotic fluid. The comforting and cleansing properties of water are not unlike our tears, sweat, and even menstrual blood. Some women like to include a Water Dance as part of their menstrual rites.

A Water Dance can start as gently as a flowing spring and swell to a raging, swirling river. It can include changes in direction and speed just as a river can change its course. The symbols of water energy include swirls, spirals, ribbons, and long flowing patterns, all of which can be personified in dance movements. The undulation of the belly dance—the mother wave—often feels right during a Water Dance, the pulsations of the pelvis reflecting the water's ebb and flow. When you are the water, your energy is boundless as you rest upon the quiet wave just before it crescendos into a waterfall. You control the pace and the timing, choosing the dynamic and energy level that suits the body of water you are synchronizing with.

Try your dance in the rain and see how exhilarating that environment can be. Dance in the ocean, a river, or a swimming pool, letting the water engulf you and inspire different movements. You might even try dancing while lying down in a bathtub of water. Imagine yourself dancing with Persephone around the Well of the Beautiful Dancers.

Because water has its own sound effects, you may choose to dance to just this natural accompaniment. I have found, though, that the music of Debussy is particularly suited to Water Dances.

Air (Ether, Atmosphere) Dance

Air is the unseen cloak that enfolds us. It feeds life to our lungs and connects us to the cosmos through our skin. Air flows eternally. It is the endless firmament that houses the heavens. Air also represents the soul, memories, the life breath, and ghosts. In Egypt, birds, regarded as reincarnated souls, were symbols of the air. Similarly, it is winged Aurora who brings us the shining dawn.

Our word *atmosphere* comes from the Greeks and others who postulated a World Soul in the form of air to emphasize the importance of this unseen element. The word *atmos* comes from the Sanskrit *atmen,* meaning "breath." Since our breath affects our entire body's health, what better way to acknowledge this miracle than to practice deep breathing in this dance. In-breathing, or in-spiration (inspiration), is what the muses brought to seers and poets—the power of understanding and creativity.

A dance to the element of Air should be light and free flowing. Zig-zags and whorls inspire motions for this dance. Wear loose clothing that can "catch" the air as you move to accentuate your steps and to enable you to see and feel the air dancing with you. Similarly, dancing with veils, streamers, or ribbons will allow you to feel yourself floating or flying through the air.

Imagine yourself dancing with serene Eurynome, who set the wind in motion to begin her work of creation.

LEFT: THE STILLNESS OF THE WATER INSPIRES PREMA DASARA IN THIS WATER DANCE ON THE COAST OF HAWAII. PHOTOGRAPH BY DOYA NARDIN.

Take her hand as she whirls and whirls. Dance with Ophion, Eurynome's wind serpent, who was created from the north wind. Sail with the goddess Ishtar of ancient Mesopotamia, who sailed the skies in her beautiful, luminous moon boat through the Milky Way, Heavenly Milk of the goddess Hera. Feel the cosmic energy of the Indian goddess Shakti, the Shining One.

An Air Dance should ideally be done outdoors so the naturally occurring air currents can further inspire and amplify your movements. Dancing by the ocean or on a mountaintop, where wind currents are often strongest, can be truly exhilarating, but even light breezes in your own backyard can lead to a wonderful dance. Even when the air is totally still—either outdoors or when you dance indoors—you can still feel the air rushing by you as you leap, glide, spin, or run. Let your movements be directed upward, lifted, and light.

Fire Dance

The Fire element represents the sun and lightning. Its dynamic energy is one of continual testing and renewal. It also represents creativity, warmth, and passion. Fire is the element most often associated with ritual. The lighting of candles has long been seen as a symbol of sanctification and marks the beginning of many sacred rites.

Fire and light were the highest cosmic components for the ancients because they emanated from the sun and stars. For millennia, fire has been considered a potent symbol of transformation and generation. It was believed that women's blood was a form of fire, a manifestation of the moon's light.

Although scholars may not be able to pinpoint how and when we first mastered fire, most agree that it was women who mastered its use. Women first controlled fire in the tending of the hearth; the hearth in the home was the first altar. It was believed that if the hearth fire went out, the family itself would become extinct. Fire was literally a tool, a weapon, and a barrier of protection for a woman and her children. By creating hearths, kilns, and shrines, women changed the course of civilization.

Women's affinity with fire is also reflected in the many goddess associations with this symbol. The goddess Fuji of Japan; Egypt's Sekhmet (Lady of the Tongues of Flame), Nut, and Hathor; and Italy's Diana Lucifera (Light Bearer) are examples. The torch is especially connected with the Greek goddess Demeter. The Eleusinia (rites to Demeter) included a "torch day" when followers moved along the shore with lighted torches in order to purify the land and ward off pestilence. Torches were also used in the most solemn ceremonies at Eleusis, which took place at night. A sacred dance was performed in which fire was carried on the head in a covered vessel called *kerna*, or "small hearth."[2] In the Mystery Night procession, priestesses also performed a dance down to the sea in the course of which the fire, covered over with ashes, was fanned into flames.

The Katha-rouene (Catherine Wheel)* represented a ring of light that marked a circular solstice fire dance, a

*Later described as the instrument of St. Catherine's torture in her martyrdom.

Diana Lucifera, the light bearer.

Left: Air Dance. Jamie Parnum is able to "catch" the air with every fiber of her costume. Photograph by Kelly Richards/Val Vista Lakes Studio.

MAENADS CARRIED FLAMING THYRSI IN THEIR DANCES.

remnant of the old worship of Fortuna with the turning of her wheel of time (which also became the Wheel of Fortune).[3] Some of our current Christmas festivities are a remnant of this ancient solstice dance.

Maenads carried flaming thyrsi (torches) in their ritual dances. They would run to the ocean and dip them in, and when they withdrew them from the water, the torches would still be lit. In India, *deva-dasis* carried sacred lights in processions to sculptured deities ensconced in the temples. A remnant of this tradition exists in a ritual called *jata-karma samskara*, "birth impression" ritual, in which a sacred lamp is lit in the room of a delivering Hindu mother to attract guardian devas.

During the Jewish Feast of Tabernacles, there was a ceremony of which it was said in the Mishnah that whosoever had not seen it had never seen a real feast. It was the Torch Dance, which took place in the court of the women in the Temple on the second day of the feast and was attended by multitudes of women and men. The celebration also included the singing of psalms and processions of people.

Fire Dances are still found in many women's dances and ceremonies throughout the world. In Scandinavia, maidens slowly dance behind St. Lucia, the Queen of Light, who wears a crown of six candles in her hair during a procession on December 13th.* The candles are fixed in a coronet of living leaves dug from under the snow. In the Turkish wedding tradition, a women's henna ceremony is performed for the bride at night, including a large circle dance in which the participants hold lighted candles on plates. Both the henna decoration and the candles are considered to have a generally protective function. Similar kinds of dances are found in other countries such as Persia, North Africa, and Malaya, where it is called *menari hinei*. In Eastern Caucasian Armenia, a women's dance called the Mom Bar, meaning "candle dance," is traditionally the last dance done at wedding parties.

The dance of the candelabra (Sham'adin), which has been traced to the Turkish influence during the Ottoman reign, can be seen in modern-day Egypt in performances by belly dancers in nightclubs, at folkloric dances, and at weddings. Bearing the candelabra with perhaps a dozen candles on her head, the dancer sways from side to side, walks with hip shimmies, and twists her body with remarkable balance and fluidity. Dropping to her knees and finally lying on her side, head elevated to keep the flaming candles steady, she glides along the floor in serpentine movements.

Although you may not feel ready to dance with a ring of fire on your head, there are many ways you can incorporate fire into your dance: having your witnessing audience circle around you with lighted candles, creating a ring of candles on the ground so there is no need for anyone to hold the flames (especially if you plan not to have witnesses to your dance), or dancing around a central fire—a classic Fire Dance tradition. The way you use fire in your dance will have a great impact

*From the reality of the living light of lamps carried or worn in the ritual ring dance came the solidified form represented as the halo (or *uaello*, the wheel) in paintings and statues of later periods.

on the mood you create and the energy you connect with and release through your dance. A Fire Dance, like a Water Dance, can be either meditative and serene or dynamic and wild, just as fire can be a single flickering candle flame or a full blazing bonfire.

Because fire is associated with energy, heat, and passion, Fire Dances tend to be more energetic than the other elements' dances. Many dancers like to include the use of drums to keep the energy of the Fire Dance at its highest level. Flamenco-type music, or classical music such as the *Firebird Suite*, is another way to evoke the passion and energy of the Fire Element. Wearing red flowing clothing allows you to personify the fire's dancing flames with your own movements. Let yourself become the mythical firebird—the phoenix rising.

A dance to the Fire Element can make you feel extremely powerful—as powerful as the life-giving sun. The sun's penetrating rays, the blinding light from which you cannot hide, the all-consuming heat are all powerful images that can be kept in mind as you dance. You may choose to identify with Kali as the goddess of Fire, her flickering flames full of compassion, purifying and rejuvenating. Or think of the garland of flames that surround the Hawaiian volcano goddess Pele. No one can resist the wisdom fires emanating from Pele's body; they consume all delusions.

The Fire Dance is also a great dance to help you work out anger as you dance with force and sudden striking moves just like a bolt of lightning, or

CANDALABRA DANCE. EGYPTIAN FOLKLORIC TROUPE, MAHMOUD REDA, DIRECTOR. CAIRO, EGYPT. PHOTOGRAPH COURTESY OF *ARABESQUE* MAGAZINE.

with consuming and engulfing motions like a fire gone ablaze. Whether you dance to feel powerful or to release anger, the emotions and exuberance possible from dancing in the open air around a roaring central fire is an experience not to be missed.

Dance of the Four Elements

The following dance is adapted from a very old Celtic blessing of all the elements and from *Dances of Universal Peace: Europe II*, 1988, and can be danced with the audiotape listed in the Resources section.

Dancers form a circle and then turn to the right or left to face a partner. Shaking the partner's hand, the dancer steps past to take the hand of the next person, and onward in a basket-weave or grand right and left fashion while singing the following phrases:

1. Deep peace of the running wave to you,
2. Deep peace of the silent stars, [stars are the symbol for fire]
3. Deep peace of the flowing air to you,
4. Deep peace of the quiet earth.

At this point, all stop and stand in place; those who face counterclockwise raise their arms and bring their hands down in front of their partners in a blessing gesture, as they sing:

5. May peace, may peace, may peace fill your soul.

Next, those facing clockwise copy this gesture toward their partners, and sing:

6. Let peace, let peace, let peace
7. Make you whole.

LEFT: ORIENTAL DANCER EVA CERNIK SHOWS THE SERENE AND MEDITATIVE ASPECTS OF A FIRE DANCE. PHOTOGRAPH BY FRITZ RENNING.

14
Mirror Dance

There is a deep core in our being that is of the nature of a mirror that can never be tarnished by the impressions upon it.

Hazrat Inayat Khan, The Mysticism of Sound and Music[1]

Looking at dance as a way to rediscover some of women's symbols and rituals as they may once have been, I found the mirror. Imbued with a spiritual quality, and symbolic of the supernatural qualities of the sun, moon, and stars and their influence on the lives of humankind, the brilliance of the mirror reflected the intelligence of heaven. The mirror was often suspended from the ceiling of the temple during certain rites and ceremonies as a heavenly representation. The infinite number of reflections provided by mirrors facing each other reflected the infinity of time and the belief that each element of the universe contains within it all the other elements of the universe—a theory now verified in quantum physics. Metaphysically, the mirror provided the means by which fire was drawn from the sun and water from the moon. The roundness of the mirror symbolized the canopy of heaven. Small mirrors are integrated into dresses and costumes throughout the Middle and Far East and are always circular.

The mirror is often found in the burial sites of priestesses and important women in places throughout the world, including Egypt, Crete, Etrusca (Italy), Corinth, Mycenae, Japan, Olmec and Aztec regions of South America, Siberia, Mongolia, and China. Mirrors were placed in the

The Mirror Dance helps increase people's sensitivity to each other. Photograph by Matin Mize.

coffin or tomb, usually on the chest of the deceased, in the hope of bringing the deceased into ultimate harmony with the celestial world, with heaven, and with the ancestors into whose world she or he had traveled. At Catal Huyuk in Turkey, mirrors of obsidian were buried with the dead in shrines.[2] Celtic women were buried with their personal mirrors, which were supposed to be their soul-carriers.

The mirror was also the proverbial soul of a Japanese woman. It was given to a bride by her mother as part of the wedding ceremony. The mirror was filled with the ancestral spirits with whom she could commune, even though separated from her family. For her it was an intimate friend to whom she could reveal her innermost feelings and cleanse her soul.

In Far Eastern philosophy, the cosmic mirror symbolically provided the critical point where yin and yang could exist in perfect balance, thereby achieving peace and harmony in all things throughout the universe. In Chinese Confucian and Taoist practice, mirrors held cosmological symbolism and were miniature replicas of the ideal (not the geographic) world. A ritual mirror in China was made in a process whose roots date back at least to the Han dynasty (100 B.C.E.). Molten bronze was poured into a mold that created a picture in relief on the back of the mirror. Through a unique and complex process, the image, which may have been signs of the zodiac, and later the Buddha, was invisible until it was aimed at the sun and its reflection was cast on a wall.

The mirror was also associated with the Divine Goddess. The Egyptian goddess Hathor is often depicted as a woman wearing a headdress with cow's horns and a sun disk or round mirror between the horns. In India, the Great Goddess was called the Mirror of the Abyss, in which Shiva constantly reflects himself. Parvati holds a mirror that reflects the radiant light of the divine presence. The mirror *(Darpana),* as a symbol of wisdom and at the same time of the emptiness of all worldly matters, is one of the specific attributes of the Indian goddess Durga.

The practice of allowing the heart to act as a mirror is used in many Sufi schools and is called *mujahida*, the struggle to keep one's inner impressions clear. When a person can reflect the whole world in the mirror of his or her heart, this grace-filled moment is called *mushahida,* a state of being that provides a greater witnessing and experience of reality.[3] Some traditional circle dances were danced counterclockwise to illustrate that the other world is a mirror image of this reality, the twin of the ordinary secular one.

From some tropical countries come certain zodiac dances, for which a round pattern is supplied by a subtly contrived mirror a foot or so in diameter, usually made of a silver-bronze metal alloy. It bears an engraved pattern of an ancient circular design. The mirror is held so as to receive on the surface a single beam of moonlight or sunlight in a darkened room. This incident beam is then reflected onto a white marble floor, where it appears enlarged as a slightly ovoid form on which a girl dances according to the rhythmic pattern of the chant and music. One of these mirrors from 13th-century Arabia carried a triple design, the outer circle showing an Arabian zodiac, the next circle the days of the week, and the innermost circle the *rukh* bird.

The mirror is also associated with miracles. The term *miracle* is from the Latin *miraculum*, or mirror. Miracle plays, which included dance and "inter-ludis" (*ludis* indicating reflected light, a time for reflection), were offered as the "image" or reflection of a legend or teaching and were one of the most public forms of religious teaching.[4] In Tibet these are known as the *Tsam.*

As with so many symbols and rituals, folklore and superstitions developed around the mirror as a form of magic and fortune-telling, as in the mirror-mirror-on-the-wall in "Snow White" and the stories of Dionysus and Narcissus, whose souls were both caught in a mirror or water reflection. However, we can now recapture and again appreciate the mirror and its original intention. We begin by using the mirror as a vehicle for inward reflection. The mirror remains a powerful tool of introspection, a guiding metaphor for distinguishing between outward appearance and inner truth. It is a way of bringing into consciousness the content of the subconscious.

Every dancer can recognize her own

ambivalence about the mirror, even if she has never thought about it before. Studies show it can build self-esteem, but by the same token, it tells us the truth of our getting old, disclosing new wrinkles and bulges and showing us that we may never achieve the perfection the world demands of us.

For the dancer, the mirror is essential to the development of objectivity and further improvement in the dance form. Learning to use the mirror can be a little tricky, however. It can seem like the enemy, always shouting back your clumsiness. Or, like Narcissus, a dancer can become stuck to the mirror image and lose touch with the reality of the physical sensations within the body and with the purpose of the dance. The mirror can represent the encounter with the instinctual Dionysian earthiness of the body, which Western efforts to become civilized and rational have put in the shadow. Learning to face the mirror takes as much physical courage as psychological courage.

Used in a new way, the mirror can become our ally. With the mirror's aid, we may discover a new perception of images about ourselves and others unconsciously held in the mind. In the shining mirror we see that a beautiful object produces a beautiful reflection, and an ugly object an ugly one, yet the mirror makes no judgment. True wisdom is self-knowledge obtained through undistorted reflection or contemplation and receptivity. When the mind is tranquil, it becomes the mirror of the universe and reflection of all things.

Sacred dance is a mirror or a reenactment of the cosmic process, the macrocosmic order of the heavens. The dancer as microcosm and the universe or nature as macrocosm are two aspects of the same reality. Sacred dance represents our insights brought to consciousness and physical manifestation through reflection on, and participation in, our own creative process.

With the mirror as a guide, you as the dancer can become your own shaman. The energies explored, released, and redirected through your sacred dances become an instrument of creative and spiritual ends. In so doing, the body as *athletae Dei* (acrobat of God)* is the rainbow bridge, the *axis mundi,* that unites the cosmic and material worlds. As the priestess dancer you are the physical vessel that contains, reveals, and transforms divine images of the feminine. You are the medium through which archetypal images can be brought into reality, reflected, and made manifest.

Now Let Us Dance

You may be familiar with a mirror dance that is done in many settings, from dance movement therapy to relationship workshops. The dance helps to increase people's sensitivity to one another and develop trust. It is done in pairs, with partners facing each other.

In this dance, you take turns slowly leading the movements so that your partner can copy you exactly, mirroring

*In 1960, Martha Graham choreographed a dance entitled *Acrobats of God.* She took the title from early Christian ascetics who "subjected themselves to the discipline of the desert." The dance pointed to the trials, tribulations, discipline, denials as well as the glories and delights of the dancer's world.

your movements. There are no preestablished movements for a mirror dance. You may move in whatever way you choose, and for this reason music is very useful for inspiration. Use of your total body is suggested to avoid too much arm and hand movement, a common trap in this kind of mirror dancing. Eye contact is also very important. Keep your eyes fixed on your partner's, using your peripheral vision as much as possible to follow the movements being done. Partners can start at opposite sides of the room so they experience mirroring at a distance as well as close together.

Something to watch for: at some point in the dance, the leadership role will be assumed quite naturally by one or the other. A shift in leadership to the other person will also quite often happen without anyone prompting this shift. Partners may want to discuss this phenomenon and their feelings about it afterward.

15
Keys to Accessing Spirituality through Sacred Dance

An archetype is like an old watercourse along which the water of life has flowed for centuries, digging a deep channel for itself. The longer it has flowed in this channel the more likely it is that sooner or later the water will return to its old bed.

The Collected Works of C. G. Jung, Vol. X: Civilization in Transition

The purpose of ritual is the creation of a certain frame of mind in the participants. It is not a belief system, and it is not involved with supernatural manipulation or the belief that nature can be controlled by it; one is not worshipping idols or appeasing spirits. Ritual, by definition, belongs neither to this world nor to the divine form but plays the role of intermediary between the two for intrapersonal psychological centering and spiritual balancing. Rituals are about bonding and balancing, offering meaning from the familiar as well as the mysterious.

Dance as liturgy or ritual has always been a way to honor the sacred, the mystery, turning into the spiral of life and the universal, the ever-present flow of the Divine force. It has profound implications for healing, psychotherapy, spiritual growth, and the full unfolding of human potential. Sacred dance can be done by anyone and in any mode. It may be part of an ancient tradition or may emanate in the moment. It can range from simple walking steps in a circle to elaborately costumed processionals. When you can let go, the natural flow of energy dances you. It opens up the channels of the body to clear away old emotional blockages, belief systems that no longer serve, and memories the body has held onto long after their usefulness disappeared. We allow life to dance us again.

Bringing Sacred Dance Back to Life

The earth principle is a nutritive life force, which imbues an individual with a sense of being in tune with the basic universal rhythms the Grandmother knew so well. Group dancing is one way to tap into this life-sustaining source once again, giving the individual a sense of belonging. It is by the body, in the body, and through the body that Being manifests itself. Through language and movement, it signifies its presence.

In dance as ritual, our learning mode is reversed and the mind learns from the body. Dance is not only language, it is also "listening." Listen to the sounds of the waves within you. Consciousness uses the power of listening to come into the being. As the skill of listening grows, consciousness expands; searching for our essence, what is truly us, our true self, we begin realizing on deeper and deeper levels that we are all the same. Dance integrates meditation and action, dissolving the barrier between contemplation and everyday life, garnering the energies of *ruach*, the breath of God.

Because all dance is both a subjective and objective evocation of what is deepest within the psyche, it gives the dancer extraordinary control of spatial dimensions and a great sense of power, accomplishment, and freedom. This may be alien to the experience of the real world, where women's bodily movements are still limited to a surprising degree by social taboos. Whether you dance in your own room, in a class or group, or before supportive spectators, you will come to feel and emanate a sense of oneness with the group, the audience, the world, and with humanity. Now you become the creator of your own dance, your own movement, the energizer of your own body, your own world, and the molder of your own destiny.

We enter this process in order to explore our femaleness separately from the prevailing distorted concepts of femininity and our conventional female roles. Freeing ourselves to refocus inwardly and in community allows us to see who we are, and so this will be a complex but at the same time a simplified process of self-discovery. In the beginning we will find many voices within us that are unknown, repressed, afraid to speak, and unaccustomed to spontaneous and direct expression. We will literally be using dance as a bridge between consciousness and the psyche. Through dance we tap into the body's unconscious memories, layer by layer. Then the healing begins. As we continue our discipline of movement and image dialogues, poetic and private insights emerge through relaxed and spontaneous expression to show us the way.

Dance creates a sense of oneness with the group. Dances of Universal Peace, California, 1994. Photograph by Matin Mize.

The Role of the Audience in Sacred Dance

Dance as a performing art stresses an extroverted mode. The dancer moves for the teacher, fellow students, the audience. In sacred dance ritual, we don't have the division into performer and recipient where the artist performs the symbolic action and the audience contemplates it theoretically or judges its effect. Rather, the members of the assembled community all participate in some way, either actively or supportively. Thus, the ritual action is prevented from degenerating into mere effect, spectacle, or entertainment. In fact, the concentration of the witnesses focuses the energy of the movements and strengthens their transformative powers.

In the ancient community tradition of Flamenco Puro, for example, the atmosphere or milieu—*el ambiente*—is a highly important ingredient. The audiences are aficionados, initiated into the secrets of Flamenco. The singer/dancer receives strong support from the intense concentration of the audience, which stimulates and animates the artist with *palmas* (handclapping) and *el jaleo* (spontaneous, admiring, and encouraging shouts). Only in this *ambiente* can the Flamenco artist do complete justice to her effort and indeed surpass herself. It is crucial that the participating audience is knowledgeable and in tune; otherwise, the effect can be just the opposite.

Anna Halprin, founder of Tamalpa Institute near San Francisco, is one of the great pioneers of the transformative, healing, and therapeutic powers of dance. She focuses on a psychokinetic visualization process connecting image, movement, and feeling. Anna says, "in communities in which dance is a necessity, there is no difference between audience and performer. Everybody is there for one purpose—to make sure that the dance does its job." Audiences are not just spectators but are there to pray, to encourage, to help the performers achieve their task and to be totally and irrevocably present as witnesses. When I studied with Anna Halprin, I found I liked the idea of dance as a community ritual, a moving prayer from the collective spirit and vision of the people who create it, including the ones who act as witness. Witnessing by people who understand, encourage, and support its purpose, and thereby actively participate, makes the dance a powerful ceremony. In traditional societies where sacred dance is performed, intricate technical skills are highly valued, but technique is a tool, subservient to the emotion of the performer. The dancer's role is that of a channel bringing expressions from a higher realm to the audience. In order to dance in this tradition, the dancer needs to forget the ego, fame, or fortune and to perform only for the pure beauty and the possibility of a feeling of unity with the divine source. The one who dances is a lens that focuses that divine energy like the rays of the sun.

Creating Your Sacred Dance

The stage, the altar, the studio—whatever space you designate—is the sacred dancing ground, and the dancing time is time out of ordinary time. The dancers enter consciously, sensing the difference between the busy outside world and the dedicated dance space. This is the hallowed ground, dedicated to and ruled by forces that are not personal, not individualistic.

After one enters the sacred space there is, ideally, a period of quieting down. Physiologically, you might start with deep, slow breathing, bringing scattered thoughts to a still, introverted point of focus. You may find the supportive spectators joining in naturally, or you may plan to have them join in. The process may benefit from dialogue with or feedback from the witnessing audience, when appropriate. You may experiment with taking a few minutes after a dance to contemplate the work, speaking from the place of what each person experienced. This effect is entirely different from a performance, which aims to grab the audience's attention by a grand or loud entrance, and it is important for them to recognize and participate in this difference.

Here are some keys that will help your dance become more meaningful for you, which I derived in part from my work with the Dances of Universal Peace. Even one or two of these techniques will have quite a profound effect.

Let go of expectations and self-consciousness. Ability will come in time. Your dance is not an athletic competition or a formal presentation. It is a window through which we merge with the universal, satisfying the thirst that is in all our souls. It takes a while for the mind to yield control. Don't be surprised if the mind becomes rebellious, argumentative, or bored. Let it play itself out. This will give you time to develop a sensitivity to the environment and to the group energy, generating a transformative sensitivity to bodily communication while establishing communion with inner movements, inner dialogue.

Feel. The dances/rituals are designed to take us more and more into the universe of feeling. Resist the impulse to begin analyzing or judging; stay in the present, keep giving yourself permission to feel and allowing the dance to refine and purify your emotional life. Movement rituals can lead to states of calm peace or a joyous feeling. Simultaneously, while you enjoy the experience, practice keeping in your consciousness your connection to the earth plane, your earthly body, and the group body.

Breathe. Breath is life, movement, voice. A verse, a mantra, or a song can break habitual breath-holding and will train your breath for the extended exhalation that automatically causes a deep inhalation.

Listen to yourself and to others' voices recite the words or song, when vocalizing is included in your dance. Even if it is in another language and you do not fully understand the meaning of the words, listen to the sound. In Sanskrit, the sound itself has an impact. When you begin to listen, the voices automatically begin to harmonize. Find the center of the sound. Notice the energy rising.

Repeat. Ritual or liturgical dance is usually a simple formula repeated over and over again. This repetition takes you beyond the realms of everyday life through movement and mental attunement. Don't be afraid that everyone will get bored by the repetition. The external simplicity of the ritual, rite, or ceremony hides a complex transference of knowledge, a message from antiquity passed down through generations, reaching us not in material form but in spirit through the body. Concentration on a sacred phrase or symbol and on the movement of everyone together will ultimately touch your being in a deeper and deeper way.

Create a dance space. For some dances you may want a dance floor design. Patterns direct and contain energy and flow, giving direction to the purpose of the dance. The design can be permanent or temporary, indoors or outside. It may be composed of seashells and driftwood, of rocks and sticks formed into a pattern, or of a drawing in the sand. Make a circle, double spiral, or labyrinth design with ingress and egress.

Move together. Resist the temptation to do individualistic dance when dancing as a group. You will be amazed at how much stronger the dances will be when you concentrate on harmonizing with the others and your ego-sense of yourself starts to disappear. Small groups that meet, with consciousness, on a regular basis will be much more effective. Trust the dance. When you dance in a circle, the circle should be kept clearly a circle; it is good to place a special object or symbol or person, perhaps the drummer and the musicians, in the center from time to time. Begin with feeling your own body fully, then gradually become connected with the whole circle. Remember to make clear eye contact with others in the circle.

Music needs to be simple and rhythmic. The group movement is the focus; music accentuates the natural rhythm of the movement with the song, mantra, or sacred phrase. Drummers especially must bear this in mind, and avoid going off into self-expression.

Use a dancer's costume. Some dances or offerings are intensified by means of color, form, and materials. Costumes can lift a dancer out of her ordinary, everyday self, bringing her to a different state. For some, the ritual of donning a costume and the shedding thereof at the end of the ritual marks the boundary between the opposite realms of the personal and the archetypal, the divine and self. Dedicated clothes, a head covering, or a jewelry headpiece, together with the archaic practice of painting and decorating the body, bring us yet another trace of the dancing goddess or priestess. This is not to say that the costume always has to be ornate. Flowing gowns with kaftan sleeves, such as those worn by Isadora Duncan and Martha Graham in certain dances, are very powerful in their unpretentious simplicity.

Allow silence. After the sound, music, and movement stop, then enter into silence. In this silence one can absorb the qualities evoked during the dance. This is the most important part of the dance, so don't rush it. You are learning meditation through dancing, and learning the dance through meditation. Presence is heightened through silence, and there is a sense of the group's focused energy and the animation of the designated physical space, which becomes the temple, the sacred place.

Try again. It is highly probable that during some times when you are attending a workshop, dancing with your group, or practicing on your own, you will not feel connected. It is disappointing, I know, but you might be surprised, sometimes, to find that you feel the effects later. So, keep open for an "Ah-Ha!" wherever and whenever it happens.

Expect your life to change. The more you dance, the more you will find yourself in your natural pure presence as you move through the world. You will probably find, as I did, that you are able to prolong the calm and centered state of mind engendered through ritual dance in everything you do. At one point I discovered that just listening to particular rhythms or songs while driving along in my car could evoke that same sense of peace and attunement.

The dances I have suggested throughout this book affirm the dramatic principle that less is more. The simpler, the deeper. We don't want to be caught up in our uniqueness, our individuality. Save innovation and self-expression for another time. Move simply and slowly. Don't overact. Follow each move with your concentration, giving yourself and others an opportunity to meditate on your presence. At the physiological level, research in neurophysiology has shown that there is an information biofeedback process between your senses, muscles, and brain. Too much muscular effort overwhelms the brain's ability to make sensory distinctions and restricts the mind's ability to work on the body's behalf. Less muscular

One is never too young or too old to participate in sacred dance. Children at Delight in the Arts Camp, Camp Stoney, New Mexico, learn *Our God is an Awesome God*. Choreography by Keri Sutter, Surgite, A Sacred Dance Company, Albuquerque, New Mexico.

effort produces more sensory motor learning. Repetition and simplicity activate your brain's movement centers and generate a flow of valuable information between your mind and your muscles and body. This approach is seen in yoga, t'ai chi gong, and other meditative practices. Automatically, as if by magic, tension, strain, fatigue, and discomfort will disappear as your neuromuscular system reprograms itself for better health. You will notice that this effect stays with you in all the days that follow.

Some of the suggested dance rituals in this book are private rituals for use in self-discovery. Some of the dances are group rituals to join the participants in a united action, where all feel and act in concert. Rituals proceed from a form or theme, but the form gradually melts as repetition imprints the mind and all move as one. Remember, an authentic ritual not only satisfies a momentary need but can also radiate exponentially to influence world consciousness.

RESOURCES

The following is an overview of individuals and groups who are involved with sacred dance. Many approaches are included: churches, body-mind-spiritual work, dance therapy approaches, and others. Because organizations come and go and addresses change, for the most up-to-date resource listing, be sure to connect to my web page: www.SacredDancer.com (e-mail address: iris@SacredDancer.com).

With the Internet and modern communication, for the first time in history we can communicate, learn from, and share with others all over the world. Should you decide to join a group, look for the right intention of the person leading, and the people following, and make sure the basic ethical tenets of the group are in accord with your values and individual conscience. Since we are working at very subtle levels of energy, our level of consciousness or attitude can greatly affect the outcome of our dances.

Internet Resources

There is a vast community of dancers from all over the world networking on the Internet. My web page, as your first source, can be a way to keep updated on what is happening in other places, so you can connect. It will also have current listings of workshops, seminars, and dance meetings. Additionally, you can share your activities with others.

Groups

The Abode of the Message

5 Abode Rd.
New Lebanon, NY 12125
Telephone: (518) 794-8095
www.theabode.net

Catholic Women's Network in Santa Clara County

877 Spinosa Dr.
Sunnyvale, CA 94087
Telephone: (408) 245-8663
Fax: (408) 738-2767

Incorporates sacred dance in monthly rituals and annual women's gathering. Nonprofit educational organization fostering women's spirituality and personal growth. Complimentary copy of bimonthly publication available on request.

Christian Dance Fellowship of Australia

P.O. Box 210
Broadway, NSW 2007
Australia

Dance in Rhythm—Rhythm in Dance

Heidrun Hoffmann
P.O. Box 7224
Santa Cruz, CA 95061
Telephone/Fax: (831) 454-1445
www.dirrid.com

Retreats, workshops in rhythm and movement; Body Oracle cards.

Elinor Coleman Dance Ensemble

153 Mercer St.
New York, NY 10012
Telephone: (212) 226-5767

Shamanic movement, seasonal sisterhood ceremonies.

Eurythmy

School of Eurythmy
260 Hungry Hollow Rd.
Chestnut Ridge, NY 10977
Telephone: (914) 352-5020
www.eurythmy.org

Eurythmy School
Peredur Centre for the Arts
Dunnings Rd., East Grinstead
W. Sussex RH19 4NF
United Kingdom

Performing arts, therapeutic, curative, Waldorf School for children.

Findhorn Foundation

The Park, Forres
IV36 OT2, Scotland
Telephone: 44 (0) 1309 690311
www.findhorn.org

International Association of Sufism and Sufi Women's Organization

P.O. Box 2382
San Rafael, CA 94912
Telephone: (415) 472-6959
Fax: (415) 472-6221
www.ias.org

International Christian Dance Fellowship

11 Amaroo Crescent
Mosman, New South Wales 2088, Australia

International Liturgical Dance Association

3215 Bellacre Court
Cincinnati, OH 4528-5005
Telephone: (513) 451-6746

International Scientific Committee on Psycho-Corporal Therapy

831 Beacon St. #163
Newton, MA 02159
Telephone: (616) 630-9110
Fax: (617) 332-5856
E-mail: PPTI@aol.com

National and international conferences on body oriented psychotherapy.

Life/Art Process

Anna Halprin
15 Ravine Way
Kentfield, CA 94904
Telephone/fax: (415) 461-5362
E-mail: annahalprin@tamalpa.org

Marian Chace Foundation and American Dance Therapy Association

2000 Century Plaza, Suite 108
10632 Little Patuxet Parkway
Columbia, MD 21044
Telephone: (410) 997-4040
www.adta.org

Membership organization for dance/movement therapists. Conferences, publications.

The Moving Center

Gabrielle Roth
P. O. Box 271, Cooper Station
New York, NY 10276
Telephone: (212) 505-7928

Retreats, seminars, book: Maps to Ecstasy: Teachings of an Urban Shaman; *music tapes.*
Telephone: (800) 76-RAVEN
www.ravenrecording.com

Omega Liturgical Dance Company

The Cathedral of Saint John the Divine
1047 Amsterdam Avenue
New York, NY 10025
Telephone: (212) 316-7540
www.stjohndivine.org

PanEuRhythmy

Ardella Nathanael
5 Mt. Tioga Ct.
San Rafael, CA 94903
Telephone: (650) 366-2188

In Scotland:
The Scottish School of PanEuRythmy
9 Royal Terrace
Glasgow 93 7NT Scotland
Telephone: 011-44141-0141-332-39969

Sacred Circle Dance

Laura Shannon
82 Galba Court
Brentford, Middlesex
TW8 8QS, UK
www.dance.demon.co.uk

A Great Circle electronic magazine, with links to sacred circle dances in Europe.

Sacred Dance Guild

1909 E. 3380 South
Salt Lake City, UT 84106
www.sacreddanceguild.org

International, interfaith, interdenominational organization (with member chapters) of dancers, choreographers, clergy, and laypersons who minister and worship through movement. Resource directory, annual Sacred Dance festivals.

Tara Dhatu

Prema Dasara
809 N. Humphreys St.
Flagstaff AZ 86001
www.wpo.net/taradhatu

Workshops, retreats, pilgramages, performances, audio, videotapes.

Touchstone Farm and Yoga Center

132 West Street
Easthampton, MA 01027
Telephone: (413) 527-8723
www.sacredcircles.com

Dance camps, yoga, sacred circle longdance.

Veriditas Labyrinth Walk

Grace Episcopal Cathedral
1100 California Street
San Francisco, CA 94108
Telephone: (415) 749-6358
Fax: (415) 749-6357
www.gracecathedral.org/labyrinth

Retreats, workshops, labyrinth kits, books, tapes.

Other movement-related approaches to healing with practitioners worldwide: Authentic Movement Institute, Feldenkrais, Trager, hakomi, yoga, t'ai chi, Rubenfeld synergy, Alexander technique, Naropa, Somatics Society

Liturgical and Spiritual Dance Studies

California Institute of Integral Studies

1453 Mission
San Francisco, CA 94109
Telephone: (415) 575-6100
www.ciis.edu

Graduate Theological Union

Professor Doug Adams
2400 Ridge Road
Berkeley, CA 94709
Telephone: (800) 999-0528
www.gtu.edu

New College of California

50 Fell Street
San Francisco, CA 94102
Telephone: (888) 437-3460
www.newcollege.edu/womenspirituality

Wesley Institute for Ministry and the Arts

P. O. Box 497
Drummoyne 2047
NSW, Sydney, Australia
www.wima.edu.au

Publications

Ariadne Productions

Kathy Jones
56 Whiting Rd.
Glastonbury, Somerset, BA6HR
England
Telephone: 44(0)1458-831518
Fax: 44 (0) 1458-831324
www.islcofavalon.co.uk/local/h-pages/kathyj/k-ariadne.html

Self-created, in-the-round, audience-participation sacred theatre.

Armando

P. O. Box 24
Capitola, CA 95010
Telephone/fax: (408) 475-3591.

Videotapes, audiocassettes—traditional rhythmic modes for Arabic drum: dumbek, tabla, darbuka.

Caroline Records, Inc.

114 West 26th Street
New York, NY 10001

Circle of Song—Songs, Chants, and Dances for Ritual and Celebration

by Kate Marks
Full Circle Press
P. O. Box 428
Amherst, MA 01004

Continuum Press and Productions

Emilie Conrad
1629 18th Street, #7
Santa Monica, CA 90404
Telephone: (310) 453-4402
Fax: (310) 453-8775

Movement seminars, book publishing

The Dancing Church—Video Impressions of the Church in Africa and *Dancing Church of the South Pacific, Liturgy and Culture in Polynesia and Melanesia*

by Thomas A. Kane
Paulist Press
997 Macarthur Blvd.
Mahwah, NJ 07430
Telephone: (800) 218-1903
www.paulistpress.org

Delilah

Visionary Dance Productions
P. O. Box 30797
Seattle, WA 98103
Telephone: (206) 632-2353
www.jetcity.com/~visdance

Workshops, videotapes, including Dance to the Great Mother

Uzbek Dance and Culture Society

Laurel Victoria Gray
P. O. Box 65195
Washington, D.C. 20035
www.uzbekdance.org

Workshops, women's dances of the Silk Road cultures; music tapes, videotapes.

Dictionary of the Dance

by W. G. Raffee
A. S. Barnes & Co.
Cranbury, NJ 08512
ISBN 0-498-01643-9

Grapevine

92 Stamner Park Rd.
Brighton, East Sussex
England BNI 7JH
E-mail: mulreany@btinternet.com

The Music and Dance of the World's Religions: A Comprehensive, Annotated Bibliography of Materials in the English Language
by E. Gardner Rust
Greenwood Press
88 Post Road West
Westport, CT 06881
Telephone: (203) 226-3571
www.greenwood.com

Elizabeth Artemis Mourat

2945 Woodstock Ave.
Silver Spring, MD 20910
Telephone: (301) 565-5029

Workshops, photo archive, Turkish Romani music tapes, videotapes.

Oruj Guvenc and Tumata

Ocean of Remembrance
Worldwise Music, Interworld Music Association
RD 3, Box 395A
Brattleboro, VT 05301

Peaceworks International Network for the Dances of Universal Peace

444 NE Ravenna Blvd., Suite 202
Seattle, WA 98115
Telephone: (206) 522-4353
www.teleport.com/~indup

Realworld Records Ltd.

www.realworld.on.net/rwr

The Sharing Company

6226 Bernhard Ave.
Richmond, CA 94805

Catalog of books and articles.

Toma's Howie Drum Web

www.geocities.com/soho/9870/ethnic.htm

Pilgrimage/Study Tours

Ana Tours

Melissa Miller
1580 Tucker Rd.
Scotts Valley, CA 95066
Telephone: (408) 438-3031
www.anatours.com

Ariadne Institute for the Study of Myth and Ritual

Carol P. Christ, Director
Molivols, 81108
Lesbos, Greece
Telephone: (011) 302 5372 196

Jan Ruble, Tour Director
1306 Crestview Dr.
Blacksburg, VA 24060
Telephone: (540) 951-3070

"Dreaming About Egypt" and "Delightful Turkish Tours."

Eva Cernik
419 South Sherman St.
Denver, CO 80209-1701
Telephone: (303) 573-7610
http://home.earthlink.net/~evacernik

Includes dance classes by Eva and Egyptian/Turkish teachers.

Sacred Journeys for Women

P. O. Box 893
Occidental, CA 95465
Telephone: (888) 779-6696
www.sacredjourneys.com

NOTES

INTRODUCTION

1. Gerardus van der Lewiv, *Sacred and Profane Beauty–The Holy in Art* (London: Weidenfeld & Nicolsen, 1963).
2. Lillian B. Lawler, *The Dance of the Ancient Greek Theatre* (Iowa City: University of Iowa Press).
3. Agnes DeMille, *The Book of the Dance* (New York: Golden Press, 1963).
4. Walter Sorell, *Dance in Its Time* (Garden City, NY: Doubleday, 1981).
5. La Meri (Russell Meriwether Hughes), *Total Education in Ethnic Dance* (New York: Marcel Dekker, 1977).
6. Elisabeth Schussler Fiorenza, *Bread Not Stone: The Challenge of Feminist Biblical Interpretation* (Boston: Beacon Press, 1984).
7. Sorell, *The Dance through the Ages* (New York: Grossett & Dunlap, 1967).
8. G. Raffe, *Dictionary of the Dance* (New York: A.S. Barnes and Company, 1975).
9. Clarissa Pinkola Estes, *Women Who Run with the Wolves* (New York: Ballantine Books, 1992).
10. Ann Cain McGinnis, "Women and Music," Heresies, Vol. 10.
11. Anna Halprin, *Moving toward Life* (Hanover, NH: University Press of New England, 1995).

PART ONE

1. Steven Lonsdale, *Animals and the Origin of Dance* (New York: Thames & Hudson, 1981).

CHAPTER 1

1. Merlin Stone, *Ancient Mirrors of Womanhood, Our Goddess and Heroine Heritage*, Vol. 2 (New York: New Sibylline Books, 1979).
2. Carl Kerenyi, *Eleusis* (Princeton, NJ: Princeton University Press, 1967).
3. Ibid.
4. Ibid.
5. From *Peri Orcheseos*, quoted by W.O.E. Oesterley, *The Sacred Dance* (Cambridge: Cambridge University Press, 1923).
6. Ivor H. Evans, *Brewer's Dictionary of Phrase and Fable*, 14th ed., (New York: Harper & Row, 1989).
7. Patricia Monaghan, *The Book of Goddesses and Heroines* (St. Paul, MN: Llewellyn Publications, 1990).
8. Anne Baring and Jules Cashford, *The Myth of the Goddess, Evolution of an Image* (Middlesex, England: Penguin Books, Inc., 1993).
9. Dudly Young, *Origins of the Sacred, The Ecstasies of Love and War* (New York: St. Martin's Press, 1991).
10. Asia Shepsut, *Journey of the Priestess* (London: Aquarian Press; San Francisco: HarperCollins, 1993).
11. Charlene Spretnak, *Lost Goddesses of Early Greece* (Boston: Beacon Press, 1981).
12. Baring and Cashford. *The Myth of the Goddess.*
13. Monaghan, *The Book of Goddesses and Heroines.*
14. Wendy Buonaventura, *Belly Dancing* (London: Virago Press, 1983).
15. Walter Wiora, *The Four Ages of Music* (New York: W. W. Norton & Co., 1965).
16. Raffe, *Dictionary of the Dance.*
17. Henri Wild, "Les Danses Sacrees de l'Egypt Ancienne," Paris 1963. Quoted in *Arabesque*, Vol. 7, No. 1, May–June, 1981.
18. Wiora, *The Four Ages of Music.*
19. Raffe, *Dictionary of the Dance.*
20. Swami Prajnanananda, *Historical Development of Indian Music*, (Calcutta: Firma K. L. Mukhopadhyay, 1973).
21. Sophie Drinker, *The Origins of Music: Women's Goddess Worshiper; The Politics of Women's Spirituality* (New York: Anchor Books, 1982).
22. G. Jung, *The Collected Works*, Vol. 10, *Civilization in Transition.* (Princeton, NJ: Princeton University Press, 1970).

CHAPTER 2

1. Nor Hall, *The Moon and The Virgin: Reflections on the Archetypal Feminine* (New York: Harper & Row, 1980). From *The Bacchae*, by Euripides, translated by Gilbert Murray.
2. Robert Payne, *Lost Treasures of the Mediterranean World* (New York: Thomas Nelson & Sons, 1962).
3. Giovanni Becatti, *The Art of Ancient Greece and Rome: From the Rise of Greece to the Fall of Rome* (New York: H. N. Abrams, 1967).
4. Sarah B. Pomeroy, *Goddesses, Whores, Wives and Slaves* (New York: Schocken Books, 1974).
5. Marija Gimbutas, *Civilizations of the Goddess* (San Francisco: Harper & Row, 1991).
6. DeMille, *The Book of the Dance.*
7. Ananda K. Coomaraswamy, *History of Indian and Indonesian Art* (1927; reprint, New York: Dover Publications, 1985).
8. Maria-Gabrielle Woisen, *Sacred Dance: Encounter With the Gods* (New York: Avon Books, 1974).
9. Gimbutas, *Civilizations of the Goddess.*
10. Kerenyi, *Eleusis.*
11. Ruth Padel, "Women: Model For Possession By Greek Daemons," in Averil Cameron and Amelie Kuhrt, eds., *Images of Women in Antiquity* (Detroit: Wayne State University Press, 1983).
12. Raffe, *Dictionary of the Dance.*
13. Jacquetta Hawkes, *Dawn of the Gods* (London: Random House, 1968).
14. John Kieran, *The Story of the Olympic Games,* 1936 (New York: Lippincott, 1948).

15. Josephine Balmer, *Sappho: Poems and Fragments* (Secaucus, NJ: Meadowland Books, 1984).
16. Barbara G. Walker, *The Woman's Encyclopedia of Myths and Secrets* (San Francisco: HarperSan Francisco, 1983).
17. Lloyd Miller and Katherine St. John, *Radif-E Raqs: Collection of Dance Sequences of the Persian Tradition* (1987, not published).
18. Charles Seltman, *Women in Antiquity* (New York: Thames & Hudson, 1956).
19. William Blake Tyrrel, *Amazons: A Study in Athenian Mythmaking* (Baltimore: John Hopkins University Press, 1984).
20. Resit Ergener, *Anatolia: Land of Mother Goddess* (Ankara, Turkey: Hitit Publications, Inc., 1988).
21. Nancy Qualls-Corbett, *The Sacred Prostitute* (Toronto: Inner City Publishers, 1988).
22. Merlin Stone, *When God Was a Woman* (New York: Harcourt Brace Jovanovich, Inc., 1976).
23. Raffe, *The Dictionary of the Dance.*
24. Marina Warner, *Alone of All Her Sex: The Myth and the Cult of the Virgin Mary* (New York: Wallaby, Pocket Books, 1976).
25. Geoffrey Ashe, *The Virgin: Mary's Cult and the Re-emergence of the Goddess* (London: Arkana, 1988).
26. Tikva Frymer-Kensky, *In the Wake of the Goddesses* (New York: Fawcett Columbine, 1992).
27. Paul K. Meagher, Thomas C. O'Brien, and Sister Consuelo Maria Aherne, eds. *Encyclopedic Dictionary of Religion* (Washington DC: Corpus Publications, 1979).
28. *Encyclopedia Judaica* (Jerusalem: Peter Publishing House, Ltd. 1972).
29. Neil Douglas-Klotz, *Desert Wisdom: Sacred Middle Eastern Writings from the Goddess Through the Sufis* (San Francisco: HarperSan Francisco, 1995).
30. Gertrude Jobes, *Dictionary of Mythology, Folklore, and Symbols* (New York: The Scarecrow Press, Inc., 1962).
31. Gimbutas, *Civilizations of the Goddess.*
32. Curt Sachs, *World History of the Dance* (1937; reprint, New York: W. W. Norton & Company, 1965).
33. Elise Boulding, *The Underside of History* (Boulder, Co: Westview Press, 1976).
34. Mircea Eliade, *Rites and Symbols of Initiation* (Dallas, TX: Spring Publications, 1994), p.43.
35. Riane Eisler, *Sacred Pleasure* (San Francisco: HarperSan Francisco, 1995).
36. Rex Warner, ed., *Encyclopedia of World Mythology* (New York: Galahad Books, 1975).
37. Serenity Young, *An Anthology of Sacred Texts by and about Women* (New York: Crossroad Publishing Co., 1993).
38. Lawler, *The Dance of the Ancient Greek Theatre.*
39. Gimbutas, *The Civilizations of the Goddess.*
40. Steven Lonsdale, *Animals & the Origins of Dance* (London: Thames & Hudson, 1981).
41. Henry George Farmer, "The Music of Islam," *New Oxford History of Music* (London: Oxford University Press, 1957).
42. La Meri (Hughes), *Total Education in Ethnic Dance.*
43. Raffe, *Dictionary of the Dance.*
44. Barbara G. Walker, *Women's Rituals: A Sourcebook* (San Francisco: HarperSan Francisco, 1990).
45. *Arabesque,* Vol. 7, No. 4, November–December, 1982.
46. La Meri (Hughes), *Total Education in Ethnic Dance.*
47. Prema Dasara, "The Twenty-One Praises of Tara," *Pele 1992/TANTRA: The Magazine.*
48. *Ibid.*

CHAPTER 3

1. *In The Fiddler's House*, Public Broadcasting System, Producers: James Arntz, Sarah Lukinson, 1995.
2. Oesterley, *The Sacred Dance.*
3. Mayer I. Gruber, "Ten Dance-Derived Expressions in the Hebrew Bible," Chapter 4 of Doug Adams and Diane Apostolos-Cappadona, eds., *Dance as Religious Studies* (New York: Crossroads, 1993).

4. Douglas-Klotz, *Desert Wisdom,*
5. Raffe, *Dictionary of the Dance.*
6. Ibid.
7. Oesterley, *The Sacred Dance.*
8. John Stainer, *Music of the Bible* (New York: H. W. Gray Co., 1879).
9. *The Jewish Encyclopedia,* Vol. 4, p. 425a New York 1901.
10. Adams and Apostolos-Cappadona, *Dance as Religious Studies.*
11. *The Catholic Encyclopedia* (New York: Knights of Columbus, 1913).
12. Raphael Patai, *The Hebrew Goddess* (New York: Avon Books, 1978).
13. Douglas-Klotz, *Desert Wisdom.*
14. Oesterley, *The Sacred Dance.*
15. Elizabeth A. Johnson, *She Who Is: The Mystery of God in Feminist Theological Discourse* (New York: Crossroad Publishing, 1994).
16. Lynn Gottlieb, *She Who Dwells Within: A Feminist Vision of a Renewed Judaism* (San Francisco: HarperSan Francisco, 1995).
17. Arthur Weiser, *The Psalms; a Commentary* (Philadelphia: The Westminster Press, 1962).
18. Walker, *The Woman's Encyclopedia of Myths and Secrets.*
19. Alan Unterman, *Dictionary of Jewish Lore & Legend* (London: Thames & Hudson, 1991).
20. *New English Bible* (Oxford University Press and Cambridge University Press, 1961).
21. Margaret Kinney and Troy West, *The Dance, Its Place in Art and Life* (New York: Frederick A. Stokes Co., 1924).
22. Sorell, *Dance in Its Time.*
23. Elaine Pagels, *The Gnostic Gospels* (New York: Vintage Book, 1979).
24. Willi Apel, *Harvard Dictionary of Music* (Cambridge, MA: Harvard University Press, 1972).
25. Sorell, *Dance in Its Time.*
26. Peter Buckman, *Let's Dance* (Middlesex, England: Penguin Books, 1979).
27. Gloria Weyman and Lucien Deiss, "Movement and Dance as Prayer," *Liturgical Ministry,* Spring 1993.
28. Malcolm Godwin, *Angels, an Endangered Series* (New York: Simon and Schuster, 1990).
29. Menestrier, *Des Ballet Anciens et Modernes* (Paris, 1682), as cited in Margaret Fisk-Taylor, *A Time to Dance* (Berkeley, CA: The Sharing Company, 1967), p. 113.
30. Kinney and West, *The Dance, Its Place in Art and Life.*
31. Margaret Taylor, "A History of Symbolic Movement in Worship," in Adams and Apostolos-Cappadona, *Dance as Religious Studies.*
32. Sorell, *Dance in Its Time.*
33. Adams and Apostolos-Cappadona, *Dance as Religious Studies.*
34. DeMille, *The Book of the Dance.*
35. Lonsdale, *Animals and the Origins of Dance.*
36. Sachs, *World History of the Dance.*
37. Ibid.
38. Sorell, *Dance through the Ages.*
39. Louis Backman and E. Classen, trans., *Religious Dances in the Christian Church and in Popular Medicine* (London: Allen & Unwin, 1952).
40. Raffe, *Dictionary of the Dance.*
41. Ibid.
42. Ibid.
43. Taylor, "A History of Symbolic Movement in Worship."
44. Alan Bleakley, *Fruits of the Moon Tree* (Bath, England: Gateway Books, 1984).
45. Sorell, *Dance through the Ages.*
46. Raffe, *Dictionary of the Dance.*
47. William Ridgeway, *The Dramas and Dramatic Dance of Non-European Races* (Cambridge University Press, 1915).
48. Adams and Apostolos-Cappadona, *Dance as Religious Studies.*
49. Raffe, *Dictionary of the Dance.*
50. Ibid.
51. Ann Wagner, *Adversaries of Dance, From the Puritans to the Present* (Chicago: University of Illinois Press, 1997).
52. Jane Litman, "How to Get What We Want by the Year 2000," *Lilith,* no. 7, 1980.
53. *Dance,* December 1996.
54. Thomas A. Kane, Videotape: "The Dancing Church: Video Impressions of the Church in Africa," available from Paulist Press.

55. Carlynn Read, *And We Have Danced: A History of the Sacred Dance Guild 1958–1978* (Berkeley, CA: The Sharing Company, 1978).

CHAPTER 4

1. Walker, *The Woman's Dictionary of Symbols and Sacred Objects.*
2. Gay Morris, "Subversive Strategies," in *The Hard Nut* (Proceedings, Society of Dance History Scholars, 1994).
3. Rabbi Lynn Gottlieb, *She Who Dwells Within: A Feminist Vision of a Renewed Judaism* (San Francisco: HarperSan Francisco, 1995).
4. Armen Ohanian, *The Dancer of Shamahka*, trans. Rose Wilder Lane (New York: E. P. Dutton, 1923).
5. La Meri (Hughes), *Total Education in Ethnic Dance.*
6. Caroline Varga Dinicu, "Belly Dancing and Childbirth," *Sexology*, April 1965, and *Dance Pages*, Winter 1984.
7. Tama-Do ("The Way of the Soul") is the work of Fabien Maman, a French spiritual teacher, musician, and martial artist, as reported in *Gnosis*, Spring 1993, "Esoteric Sound and Color" by Jeff Chitouras.
8. Alfred A. Tomatis, *The Conscious Ear, My Life of Transformation through Listening* (Barrytown, NY: Station Hill Press, 1991).
9. Walker, *The Woman's Dictionary of Symbols and Sacred Objects.*
10. Tomatis, *The Conscious Ear.*
11. William Irwin Thompson, *The Time Falling Bodies Take to Light* (New York: St. Martin's Press, 1981).
12. Paul Madaule, *When Listening Comes Alive: A Guide to Effective Learning and Communication* (Norval, Ontario, Canada: Moulin Publishing, 1994).
13. Buonaventura, *Belly Dancing: The Serpent and the Sphinx.*
14. Karen Andes, *A Woman's Book of Power: Using Dance to Cultivate Energy and Health in Mind, Body and Spirit* (New York: Berkeley Publishing Group, 1998).
15. *Encyclopedia of Islam* 1960, as referenced by Magda Saleh, Ph.D., *Arabesque*, Vol. 19, No. 2, July/August 1993: "The Ghawazi of Egypt, A Preliminary Report."
16. Carolina Varga Dinicu, "Dance as Community Identity Among Selected Berber Nations of Morocco," Proceedings of the Society of Dance History Scholars Joint Conference with The Congress on Research in Dance, New York City, June 1993 p. 63.
17. Sachs, *World History of the Dance.*
18. Lonsdale, *Animals and the Origins of Dance.*
19. Sachs, *World History of the Dance.*
20. Jamila Salimpour, *From Cave to Cult to Cabaret* (self-published, 1978).
21. Jean Shinoda Bolen, M.D., *Crossing to Avalon* (San Francisco: HarperSan Francisco, 1994).

CHAPTER 5

1. Taj Inayat, *The Crystal Chalice: Spiritual Themes for Women* (Santa Fe, NM: Sufi Order Pub., 1981).
2. Leona Wood, "Danse Du Ventre: A Fresh Appraisal," *Arabesque*, Vol. 5, No. 6, March–April, 1980.
3. Edward William Lane, *An Account of the Manners and Customs of the Modern Egyptians* (1860; reprint, New York: Dover Publications, 1973).
4. Gimbutas, "Women and Culture in Goddess-Oriented Old Europe."
5. Gimbutas, *The Language of the Goddess.*
6. Ibid.
7. Nor Hall, *The Moon and the Virgin.*
8. Eliade, *The Forge and the Crucible* (New York: Harper & Row, 1971).
9. Monica Sjoo and Barbara Mor, *The Great Cosmic Mother: Rediscovering the Religion of the Earth* (San Francisco: Harper & Row, 1987).
10. Gimbutas, *The Language of the Goddess.*
11. Kerenyi, *Eleusis.*
12. Walker, *The Woman's Dictionary of Symbols and Sacred Objects.*

13. Mardi Rollow, "The Tunisian Experience," *Arabesque*, Vol. 5, No. 1, May 1979.
14. Jamila Salimpour, *From Cave to Cult to Cabaret* (San Francisco: n.p., 1979).
15. Ajit Mookerjee, *Kali: The Feminine Force* (Rochester, VT: Destiny Books, 1988).
16. L. Basham, *The Wonder That Was India* (New York: Grove Press, 1959).
17. Van Donzel, ed., *Encyclopaedia of Islam, II* (Kinderhook: Brill, 1996).
18. Jean-Paul Clebert, *The Gypsies* (London: Penguin Books, 1967).
19. Shahrukh Husain, *The Goddess* (New York: Little, Brown and Company, 1997).
20. Randy P. Conner, *Blossom of Bone* (San Francisco: HarperSan Francisco, 1993).
21. Mookerjee, *Kali.*
22. Robert Graves, *The Greek Myths*, Vols. 1 and 2 (Baltimore: Penguin Books, 1955).
23. Penelope Shuttle and Peter Redgrove, *The Wise Wound: Eve's Curse and Everywoman* (New York: Richard Marek, 1978).
24. Graves, *The Greek Myths.*
25. Raffe, *Dictionary of the Dance.*
26. Walker, *The Woman's Encyclopedia of Myths and Secrets.*
27. Shepsut, *Journey of the Priestess.*
28. Spretnak, *Lost Goddesses of Early Greece.*
29. Sabatino Moscati, *The Face of the Ancient Orient* (New York: Anchor Books, 1962).
30. E. Cirlot, *A Dictionary of Symbols* (New York: Philosophical Library, 1971).
31. Raffe, *Dictionary of the Dance.*
32. Walker, *The Woman's Dictionary of Symbols and Sacred Objects.*
33. Walker, *The Woman's Encyclopedia of Myths and Secrets.*
34. James Hall, *Dictionary of Subjects and Symbols in Art* (New York: Harper & Row, 1974).
35. Stone, *Ancient Mirrors of Womanhood*, Vol. 1 (New York: New Sibylline Books, 1979).
36. Ernst A. Heiniger and Jean Heiniger, *The Great Book of Jewels* (Lausanne, Switzerland: Edita S.A., 1974).
37. Walker, *The Woman's Encyclopedia of Myths and Secrets.*
38. Ibid.
39. Freiburg Herder, *The Herder Dictionary of Symbols* (Wilmette, IL: Chiron Publications, 1986).
40. Buffie Johnson, *Lady of the Beasts* (San Francisco: Harper & Row, 1981).
41. Ibid.
42. Walker, *The Woman's Encyclopedia of Myths and Secrets.*
43. Monaghan, *The Book of Goddesses and Heroines.*
44. Robert Payne, *Lost Treasures of the Mediterranean World* (New York: Thomas Nelson & Sons, 1962).
45. 600–1000 C.E. Pre-Columbian Art Reproductions, Cosmos International, Ft. Lauderdale, FL.
46. Gimbutas, *The Language of the Goddess.*
47. Ibid.
48. Herder, *The Herder Dictionary of Symbols.*
49. Walker, *The Woman's Encyclopedia of Myths and Secrets.*
50. *Hinduism Today*, August 1990.

CHAPTER 6

1. William Hamilton, "The Best Body for Ballet," *Dance Magazine*, October 1982.
2. Sorell, *Dance in Its Time.*
3. Katherine Dunham, *Island Possessed* (New York: Doubleday, 1969).
4. Selma Jeanne Choen, *Doris Humphrey: An Artist First* (Middletown, CT: Wesleyan University Press, 1972).
5. Martha Graham, *The Notebooks of Martha Graham* (New York: Harcourt, Brace, Jovanovich, 1973).
6. Graham, *Blood Memory* (New York: Washington Square Press, 1991).
7. Ibid.
8. Murshida Rabia Ana Perez-Chisti, "Autobiography—They Are by My Side," *Sufi Women: The Journey Towards the Beloved* (San Rafael, CA:

International Association of Sufism, 1998).
9. Ericka Ostrovsky, *Eye of Dawn* (New York: Macmillan, 1978).
10. Tristram Potter Coffin, *The Female Hero in Folklore and Legend* (New York: Seabury Press, 1975).
11. Ruth St. Denis, *An Unfinished Life* (New York: Harper and Brothers, 1939).
12. La Meri (Hughes), *Total Education in Ethnic Dance.*
13. Joan L. Erdman, "Dance Discourses: Rethinking the History of the 'Oriental Dance,'" Proceedings, Society of Dance History Scholars, 1994.
14. Kamae A. Miller, ed., *Wisdom Comes Dancing: Selected Writings of Ruth St. Denis on Dance, Spirituality and the Body* (Seattle, WA: PeaceWorks, International Network for the Dances of Universal Peace, 1997).
15. Perez-Chisti, "Autobiography: They Are by My Side."
16. St. Denis, *The Divine Dance*, ed. Neil Douglas-Klotz (San Francisco: PeaceWorks Press, 1989).
17. St. Denis, *The Divine Dance.*
18. Suzanne Shelton, *Divine Dancer* (New York: Doubleday 1981).
19. Carlynn Reed, *And We Have Danced: A History of the Sacred Dance Guild 1958–1978* (Richmond, CA: The Sharing Company, 1978).
20. Doug Adams and Diane Apostolos-Cappadona, *Dance As Religious Studies* (New York: Crossroad, 1990).
21. Joan Dexter Blackmer, *Acrobats of the Gods: Dance and Transformation* (Toronto: Inner City Books, 1989).
22. Carla DeSola, *The Spirit Moves: A Handbook of Dance and Prayer* (Berkeley, CA: The Sharing Company, 1986).
23. Laura Shannon, "Living Ritual Dance for Women: Journey out of Ancient Times," American Dance Therapy Association 27th Annual Conference Proceedings, Columbia, Maryland, October 1992.
24. Shannon, "Living Ritual Dance: Dreaming the Past, Dancing the Future," American Dance Therapy Association 28th Annual Conference Proceedings, Atlanta, Georgia, October 1993.
25. Isadora Duncan, *The Art of the Dance* (New York: Theatre Arts Books, 1928).

CHAPTER 7

1. Donna Wilshire, *Virgin, Mother, Crone: Myths and Mysteries of the Triple Goddess* (Rochester, VT: Inner Traditions, 1994).
2. Kerenyi, *Eleusis.*
3. Ibid.
4. W. M. Broner, *Naomi Nimrod, The Women's Haggadah* (San Francisco: HarperSan Francisco, 1994).
5. Lucy Goodison, *Death, Women and the Sun* (London: University of London, 1989).

CHAPTER 8

1. Gimbutas, *The Language of the Goddess.*
2. Starhawk, "Witchcraft and Women's Culture," *Womanspirit Rising*, ed. Carol P. Christ and Judith Plaskow (San Francisco: HarperSan Francisco, 1992).
3. Gimbutas, *The Language of the Goddess.*
4. Lauren Artress, *Walking a Sacred Path: Rediscovering the Labyrinth As a Spiritual Tool* (New York: Riverhead Books, 1995).

CHAPTER 9

1. Joost A. M. Meerloo, M. D., *The Dance, From Ritual to Rock and Roll—Ballet to Ballroom* (Philadelphia: Chilton Co., 1960).
2. Raffe, *The Dictionary of the Dance.*
3. H. E. L. Mellersh, *Minoan Crete* (New York: G. P. Putnam, 1965).
4. *Dawn of the Gods.*
5. Raffe, *Dictionary of the Dance.*
6. Walker, *The Woman's Encyclopedia of Myths and Secrets.*
7. Sachs, *World History of the Dance.*
8. Raffe, *Dictionary of the Dance.*
9. Sjoo and Barbara Mor, *The Great Cosmic Mother.*
10. Gimbutus, *Language of the Goddess.*

11. Anna Ilieva and Anna Shturbanova, "Some Zoomorphic Images in Bulgarian Women's Ritual Dancs in the Context of Old European Symbolism," in Joan Marler, ed., *From the Realms of the Ancestors: An Anthology in Honor of Marija Gimbutas* (Manchester, CT: Knowledge, Ideas & Trends, Inc., 1997).

CHAPTER 10

1. Graham, *Blood Memory.*
2. DeMille, *The Book of the Dance.*
3. Kerenyi, *Eleusis.*
4. Ibid.
5. Gruber, "Ten Dance-Derived Expressions in the Hebrew Bible."
6. Ibid.
7. William Ridgeway, *The Dramas and Dramatic Dances of Non-European Races* (London: Cambridge Press, 1915).
8. Raffee, *Dictionary of the Dance.*
9. Ibid.
10. Lane, *An Account of the Manners and Customs of the Modern Egyptians.*
11. DeMille, *The Book of the Dance.*
12. Gruber, "Ten Dance-Derived Expressions in the Hebrew Bible."
13. Ibid.
14. Oesterley, *The Sacred Dance.*
15. Ruth Eshel, "Dance of the Ethiopian Jews," Proceedings of the Society of Dance History Scholars Joint Conference with the Congress on Research in Dance, New York City, June 1993.
16. *Encyclopedia of Religion and Ethics.*
17. Oesterley, *The Sacred Dance.*
18. Apel, *Harvard Dictionary of Music.*
19. Sachs, *World History of the Dance.*

CHAPTER 11

1. Mickey Hart, *Drumming at the Edge of Magic* (San Francisco: Acid Test Productions, 1998).
2. Tomatis, *The Conscious Ear.*
3. Heidrun Hoffman, workshop in Santa Cruz, California, 1994.

CHAPTER 12

1. Isadora Duncan, *The Art of the Dance.*
2. Heide Gottner-Abendroth, *The Dancing Goddess: Principles of a Matriarchal Aesthetic* (Boston: Beacon Press, 1992).
3. "Mystic Orders of the Middle East," *Habibi*, Vol. 7, No. 8, 1983.
4. Meerloo, *The Dance: From Ritual to Rock and Roll.*
5. Bettina L. Knapp, "Islam and the Dance," *Arabesque*, Vol. 7, No. 3, 1977.
6. Fatma El Masri, "The Zar: A Psychological Anthropological Study," *Arabesque*, Vol. 5, No. 2, 1975.
7. Raffe, *Dictionary of the Dance.*
8. Carolina Varga Dinicu, "Dance as Community Identity Among Selected Berber Nations of Morocco: From the Ethereal and Sublime to the Erotic and Sexual." Presented at a joint conference of the Congress on Research in Dance and the Society of Dance History Scholars, New York City, June 11, 1993.
9. Lisa Alpine, "Dancing the Divine,"*Yoga Journal*, November/December 1990.
10. Gabrielle Roth, *Maps to Ecstasy: Teaching of an Urban Shaman* (Novato, CA: Nataraj Publishing, 1989).
11. Nahid Angha, Ph.D., cofounder of the International Association of Sufism and founder of the Sufi Women's Organization. Dr. Angha is one of the major Sufi writers and translators of Sufi literature of the present time. She was the first woman appointed to teach and hold gatherings in the Uwaiysi Tarighat.
12. Nahid Angha, *Principles of Sufism* (Freemont: CA: Asian Humanities Press, 1991).

CHAPTER 13

1. Kerenyi, *Eleusis.*
2. Kerenyi, *Eleusis.*
3. Raffe, *Dictionary of the Dance.*

CHAPTER 14

1. Hazrat Inayat Khan, *The Mysticism of Sound and Music* (Rockport, MA: Element, 1991).
2. Peg Streep, *Sanctuaries of the Goddess* (Boston: Little, Brown & Co., 1994).
3. Douglas-Klotz, *Desert Wisdom.*
4. Raffe, *Dictionary of the Dance.*

Bibliography

Adams, Doug, and Diane Apostolos-Cappadona. *Dance as Religious Studies.* New York: Crossroad Publishing Co., 1993.

Alpine, Lisa. "Dancing The Divine." *Yoga Journal*, November/December 1990.

Andes, Karen. *A Woman's Book of Power: Using Dance to Cultivate Energy and Health in Mind, Body and Spirit.* New York: Berkeley Publishing Group, 1998.

Angha, Nahid. *Principles of Sufism.* Fremont, CA: Asian Humanities Press, 1991.

Apel, Willi. *Harvard Dictionary of Music.* Cambridge, MA: Harvard University Press, 1972.

Arntz, James, and Sarah Lukinson, producers. "In The Fiddler's House." Public Broadcasting System, 1995.

Artamonov, M. I. *The Splendor of Scythian Art.* New York: Frederick A. Praeger, 1969.

Ashe, Geoffrey. *The Virgin: Mary's Cult and the Re-Emergence of the Goddess.* London: Arkana, 1988.

Backman, E. Louis. *Religious Dances in the Christian Church and in Popular Medicine*, translated by E. Classen. London: George Allen & Unwin Ltd., 1952.

Balmer, Josephine. *Sappho: Poems and Fragments.* Secaucus, NJ: Meadowland Books, 1984.

Baring, Anne, and Jules Cashford. *The Myth of the Goddess: Evolution of an Image.* Middlesex, England: Penguin, 1993.

Basham, A.L. *The Wonder That Was India.* New York: Grove Press, 1959.

Becatti, Giovanni. *The Art of Ancient Greece and Rome, From the Rise of Greece to the Fall of Rome*. New York: H. N. Abrams, 1967.

Blackmer, Joan Dexter. *Acrobats of the Gods, Dance and Transformation*. Toronto: Inner City Books, 1989.

Blakeslee, Sandra. "Behind the Veil of Thought." *New York Times*, March 21, 1995.

Bleakley, Alan. *Fruits of the Moon Tree*. Bath, England: Gateway Books, 1984.

Bolen, Jean Shinoda. *Crossing to Avalon*. San Francisco: HarperSanFrancisco, 1994.

Boulding, Elise. *The Underside of History*. Boulder, CO: Westview Press, 1976.

Broner, W. M., and Naomi Nimrod. *The Women's Haggadah*. San Francisco: HarperSanFrancisco, 1994.

Brow, Karen McCarthy. "Women's Leadership in Haitian Voudon." In *Weaving the Visions: New Patterns in Feminist Spirituality*, edited by Judith Plaskow and Carol P. Christ. San Francisco: HarperCollins, 1989.

Buckman, Peter. *Let's Dance*. Middlesex, England: Penguin, 1979.

Budge, E. A. Wallis. *The Egyptian Book of the Dead (The Papyrus of Ani), Egyptian Text Transliteration and Translation*. 1895. Reprint, New York: Dover Publications, 1967.

Buonaventura, Wendy. *Belly Dancing: The Serpent and the Sphinx*. London: Virago Press Ltd., 1983.

Campbell, Joseph. *The Inner Reaches of Outer Space: Metaphor as Myth and as Religion*. New York: Alfred Van Der March Editions, 1986.

Capra, Fritjof. *The Tao of Physics*. Boulder, CO: Shambhala, 1975.

Casserly, Gordon. "The White City of Algiers." *National Geographic*, February 1928, quoted in *Arabesque*, Vol. 3, No. 2, July–August 1977.

The Catholic Encyclopedia. New York: Knights of Columbus, 1913.

Choen, Selma Jeanne. *Doris Humphrey: An Artist First*. Middletown, CT: Wesleyan University Press, 1972.

Chopra, Deepak. "Bliss and the Quantum Mechanical Human Body." *Mind/Body Connection*, Summer 1993.

———. *Perfect Health: The Complete Mind/Body Guide*. New York: Harmony Books, 1991.

Cirlot, J. E. *A Dictionary of Symbols*. New York: Philosophical Library, 1971.

Clause, Bonnie T., ed. *Hula Historical Perspectives*. Honolulu: Department of Anthropology, Bernice Pauahi Bishop Museum, 1980.

Clebert, Jean-Paul. *The Gypsies*. London: Penguin Books, 1967.

Coffin, Tristram Potter. *The Female Hero in Folklore and Legend*. New York: Seabury Press, 1975.

Conner, Randy P. *Blossom of Bone*. San Francisco: Harper, 1993.

Coomaraswamy, Ananda K. *History of Indian and Indonesian Art*. 1927. Reprint, New York: Dover Publications, 1985.

Corley, Kathleen E. *Private Women, Public Meals: Social Conflict in the Synopic Tradition*. Peabody, MA: Hendrickson Publishers, Ltd., 1993.

de Lubac, Henri. *The Eternal Feminine*. San Francisco: Harper & Row, 1968.

DeMille, Agnes. *The Book of the Dance*. New York: Golden Press, 1963.

Desmonde, William H. *Money, Myth and Magic*. New York: Freepress of Glencoe, 1962.

DeSola, Carla. *The Spirit Moves: A Handbook of Dance and Prayer*. Berkeley, CA: The Sharing Company, 1986.

Dinicu, Carolina Varga. "Belly Dancing and Childbirth," *Sexology Magazine*, April 1965, and *Dance Pages Magazine*, Winter 1984.

———. "Dance as Community Identity among Selected Berber Nations of Morocco." Proceedings, Society of Dance History Scholars Joint Conference with The Congress on Research in Dance, New York City, June 1993.

Donzel, E. Van, ed. *Encyclopaedia of Islam, II*. Kinderhook: Brill Academic Pub., Inc., 1996.

Douglas-Klotz, Neil. *Desert Wisdom: Sacred Middle Eastern Writings from the Goddess through the Sufis*. San Francisco: HarperSanFrancisco, 1995.

Dunham, Katherine. *Island Possessed.* New York: Doubleday, 1969.

Einzig, Paul. *Primitive Money*. London: Eyre Spattirwode, 1963.

El Guindy, Howaida, and Claire Schmais. "The Zar: An Ancient Dance of Healing." *American Journal of Dance Therapy*, Vol. 16, No. 2, Fall/Winter 1994.

Eliade, Mircea. *The Forge and the Crucible.* New York: Harper & Row, 1971.

———. *A History of Religious Ideas*, Vol. 1. Chicago: University of Chicago Press, 1978.

———. *Rites and Symbols of Initiation.* Dallas, TX: Spring Publications, 1994.

El Masri, Fatma. "The Zar, A Psychological Anthropological Study." *Arabesque*, November 1975.

Encyclopedia of Islam, 1960, as referenced by Magda Saleh. *Arabesque*, Vol. 19, No. 2, July/August 1993. "The Ghawazi of Egypt, A Preliminary Report."

Erdman, Joan L. "Dance Discourses: Rethinking the History of the 'Oriental Dance.'" Proceedings, Society of Dance History Scholars, 1994.

Ergener, Resit. *Anatolia: Land of Mother Goddess*. Ankara: Hitit Publications, Inc., 1988.

Eshel, Ruth. "Dance of the Ethiopian Jews." Proceedings, Society of Dance History Scholars Joint Conference with the Congress on Research in Dance, New York, June 1993.

Estes, Clarissa Pinkola. *Women Who Run with the Wolves,* New York: Ballantine Books, 1992.

Evans, Ivor H. *Brewer's Dictionary of Phrase and Fable*, 14th ed., New York: Harper & Row, 1989.

Fairservis, Walter A., Jr., *The Origins of Oriental Civilization*. New York: New American Library, 1959.

Farmer, Henry George. *The Music of Islam*, New Oxford History of Music. London: Oxford University Press, 1957.

Farrah, Ibrahim. "Dance Encyclopedia—The Guedra." *Arabesque*, July/August 1978.

Fiorenza, Elisabeth Schussler. *Bread Not Stone: The Challenge of Feminist Biblical Interpretation*. Boston: Beacon Press, 1984.

Flatischer, Reinhard. *TA KE TI NA: The Forgotten Power of Rhythm*. Berlin: LifeRhythm, 1992.

Frazer, Sir James. *The New Golden Bough*, edited by Theodor H. Gaster. New York: Criterion Books, 1959.

Friedlander, Ira. *The Whirling Dervishes.* New York: Collier Books, 1975.

Frymer-Kensky, Tikva. *In the Wake of the Goddesses*. New York: Fawcett Columbine, 1992.

Ganesh, Indumathy. *Hinduism Today*. August 1990.

Gaster, Theodor H. *Myth, Legend and Custom in the Old Testament*. New York: Harper & Row, 1969.

Gimbutas, Marija. *Civilization of the Goddess*. San Francisco: HarperSan Francisco, 1991.

———. *The Language of the Goddess*. San Francisco: Harper and Row, 1989.

———. "Women and Culture in Goddess-Oriented Old Europe." In *The Politics of Women's Spirituality,* edited by Charlene Spretnak. New York: Anchor Books, 1982.

Gleick, James. *Chaos: The Making of a New Science*. New York: Penguin, 1987.

Godwin, Malcolm. *Angels: An Endangered Species*. New York: Simon and Schuster, 1990.

Goldbert, Benjamin. *The Mirror and Man*. Charlottesville, VA: University Press of Virginia, 1985.

Goodison, Lucy. *Death, Women and the Sun*. London: University of London, 1989.

Gottlieb, Lynn. *She Who Dwells Within: A Feminist Vision of a Renewed Judaism*. San Francisco: HarperSanFrancisco, 1995.

Gottner-Abendroth, Heide. *The Dancing Goddess: Principles of a Matriarchal Aesthetic*. Boston: Beacon Press, 1992.

Graham, Martha. *Blood Memory.* New York: Doubleday, 1991.

———. *The Notebooks of Martha Graham*. New York: Harcourt, Brace, Jovanovich, 1973.

Graves, Robert. *Greek Myths*. London: Penguin Books, 1981.

———. *The Greek Myths,* Vols. 1 and 2. Baltimore: Penguin Books, 1955.

———. *The White Goddess*. New York: Farrar, Straus and Giroux, 1992.

Gray, Laurel. *Habibi*, Vol. 7, No. 9, 1994.

Hall, James. *Dictionary of Subjects and Symbols in Art*. New York: Harper & Row, 1974.

Hall, Nor. *The Moon and the Virgin: Reflections on the Archetypal Feminine*. New York: Harper & Row, 1980.

Halprin, Anna. *Moving Toward Life*. Hanover, NH: University Press of New England, 1995.

Harding, Karol Henderson. "The World's Oldest Dance: The Origins of Oriental Dance." *Society for Creative Anachronism*, No. 70, November 1993.

Hart, Mickey. *Drumming at the Edge of Magic*. San Francisco: Acid Test Productions, 1998.

——— and Fredrick Lieberman. *Planet Drum: A Celebration of Percussion and Rhythm*. San Francisco: HarperSan Francisco, 1991.

Hastings, James, ed. *Encyclopaedia of Religion and Ethics*, Vol. 6. New York: Charles Scribner's Sons, 1926.

Hawkes, Jacquetta. *Dawn of the Gods: Minoan and Mycenean Origins of Greece*. New York: Random House, 1968.

Heiniger, Ernst A., and Jean Heiniger. *The Great Book of Jewels*. Lausanne, Switzerland: Edita S.A., 1974.

Herder, Freiburg. *The Herder Dictionary of Symbols*. Wilmette, IL: Chiron Publications, 1978.

Hirsch, E. G. "Dancing: Biblical Data." In *The Jewish Encyclopedia*, Vol. 4. New York, 1901, p. 425a.

Hitouras, Jeff. "Esoteric Sound and Color." *Gnosis*, Spring 1993.

Humes, Edward. "Expert Finds Genes Carry a Tune." *Sacramento Bee*, January 8, 1988.

Husain, Shahrukh. *The Goddess*. New York: Little, Brown and Company, 1997.

Ilieva, Anna, and Anna Shturbanova. "Zoomorphic Images in Bulgarian Women's Ritual Dances in the Context of Old European Symbolism," In *From the Realms of the Ancestors: An Anthology in Honor of Marija Gimbutas*, edited by Joan Marler. Manchester, CT: Knowledge, Ideas & Trends, Inc., 1997.

Jaffrey, Madhur. "A Total Theatre Filled with Dance, Music and Myth." *Smithsonian Magazine*, June 1979.

Jobes, Gertrude. *Dictionary of Mythology, Folklore, and Symbols*. New York: The Scarecrow Press, Inc., 1962.

Johnson, Buffie. *Lady of the Beasts: The Goddess and Her Animals*. Rochester, VT: Inner Traditions International, 1994.

Johnson, Elizabeth A. *She Who Is: The Mystery of God in Feminist Theological Discourse*. New York: Crossroad Publishing, 1994.

Juvenal. *Satire, Juvenal and Persius*. New York: Putnam, 1924.

Kane, Thomas A. "The Dancing Church: Video Impressions of the Church in Africa." Videotape. Mahwah, NJ: Paulist Press.

Khan, Hazrat Inayat. *The Music of Life*. New Lebanon, NY: Omega Publications, Inc., 1988.

———. *The Mysticism of Sound*. Geneva: International Sufi Movement, 1979.

———. *The Mysticism of Sound and Music*. Rockport, MA: Element, 1991.

Kerenyi, Carl. *Eleusis*. Princeton, NJ: Princeton University Press, 1967.

Kieran, John. *The Story of the Olympic Games, 1936*. New York: Lippincott, 1948.

Kinney, Margaret, and Troy West. *The Dance: Its Place in Art and Life*. New York: Frederick A. Stokes Co., 1924.

Kirk, Martha Ann. "Biblical Women and Feminist Exegesis: Woman Dancing Men's Ideas of Women Dancing Women." In *Dance as Religious Studies*, edited by Doug Adams and Diane Apostolos-Cappadona. New York: Crossroad, 1993.

———. "Mystic Orders of the Middle East." *Habibi*, Vol. 7, No. 8, 1983.

Knapp, Betinna L., "The Classical Dance of Iran." *Arabesque*, November/December 1978.

———. "Islam and the Dance." *Arabesque*, Vol. 7, No. 3, 1982.

La Meri (Russell Meriwether Hughes). "Learning the Danse du Ventre." *Dance Perspectives Magazine*, Spring 1961.

———. *Total Education in Ethnic Dance*. New York: Marcel Dekker, Inc., 1977.

Lane, Edward William. *An Account of the Manners and Customs of the Modern Egyptian.* 1836. Reprint, New York: Dover Publications, 1973.

La Plante, John D. *Asian Art.* Dubuque, IA: Wm. C. Brown Company, 1968.

Lawler, Lillian B. *The Dance of the Ancient Greek Theatre.* Iowa City: University of Iowa Press, 1964.

Lederer, Wolfgang. *The Fear of Women.* New York: Harcourt Brace Jovanovich, 1968.

Lewis, I. M. *Ecstatic Religion.* London: Routledge, 1989.

Litman, Jane. "How to Get What We Want by the Year 2000." *Lilith*, Vol. 7, 1980.

Lonsdale, Steven. *Animals and the Origin of Dance.* New York: Thames & Hudson, 1981.

Madaule, Paul. *When Listening Comes Alive: A Guide to Effective Learning and Communication.* Norval, Ontario: Moulin Publishing, 1994.

Malm, William P. *Japanese Music and Musical Instruments.* Tokyo: Charles E. Tuttle Co., 1959.

Martial, *Epigrams.* Cambridge, MA: Harvard University Press, 1947.

Martins, John. *Book of the Dance.* New York: Tudor Publishing Company, 1963.

McGinnis, Ann Cain. "Women and Music." *Heresies Magazine*, Vol. 10, 1984.

Meerloo, Joost A. M. *The Dance: From Ritual to Rock and Roll, Ballet to Ballroom.* Philadelphia: Chilton, 1960.

Mellersh, H. E. L. *Minoan Crete.* New York: G. P. Putnam, 1965.

Menestrier. *Des Ballet Anciens et Modernes* (Paris, 1682). In Margaret Fisk-Taylor, *A Time to Dance.* Berkeley, CA: The Sharing Company, 1967.

The Merriam-Webster New Book of Word Histories. Springfield, MA. Merriam-Webster, 1991.

Miller, Kamae A. *Wisdom Comes Dancing: Selected Writings of Ruth St. Denis on Dance, Spirituality and the Body.* Seattle: PeaceWorks, International Network for the Dances of Universal Peace, 1997.

Mills, Jane. *Womanwords: A Dictionary of Words About Women.* New York: Free Press, 1992.

Monaghan, Patricia. *The Book of Goddesses and Heroines.* St. Paul, MN: Llewellyn Publications, 1990.

Mookerjee, Ajit. *Kali: The Feminine Force.* Rochester, VT: Destiny Books, 1988.

Moscati, Sabatino. *The Face of the Ancient Orient.* New York: Anchor Books, 1962.

Murphy, Joseph M. *Working the Spirit: Ceremonies of the African Diaspora.* Boston: Beacon Press, 1994.

Nadeau, R. *News & Views.* Cerritos, CA: Nadeau Test & Treatment Center, April 1993.

New English Bible. London: Oxford University Press and Cambridge University Press, 1961.

Nicholson, Renold A. *A Literary History of the Arabs.* London: Cambridge University Press, 1956.

Nieuwkerk, Karin van. *A Trade Like Any Other: Female Singers and Dancers in Egypt.* Austin, TX: University of Texas Press, 1995.

Oesterley, W. O. E. *The Sacred Dance: A Study in Comparative Folklore.* New York: Macmillan, 1923. Reprinted 1960, *Dance Horizons*, Brooklyn, NY.

Ohanian, Armen. *The Dancer of Shamahka*, translated from the French by Rose Wilder Lane. New York: E. P. Dutton & Co., 1923.

Ostrovsky, Ericka. *Eye of Dawn.* New York: Macmillan, 1978.

Ozelsel, Michaela. *Forty Days: The Diary of a Traditional Solitary Sufi Retreat.* Brattleboro, VT: Threshold Books, 1994.

Padel, Ruth. "Women: Model for Possession by Greek Daemons." *Images of Women in Antiquity,* edited by Averil Cameron and Amelie Kuhrt, Detroit: Wayne State University Press, 1983.

Pagels, Elaine. *The Gnostic Gospels.* New York: Vintage Books, 1979.

Patai, Raphael. *The Hebrew Goddess.* New York: Avon Books, 1967.

Payne, Robert. *Lost Treasures of the Mediterranean World.* New York: Thomas Nelson & Sons, 1962.

Perez-Chisti, Murshida Rabia Ana. "Autobiography: They Are by My Side." *In Sufi Women: The Journey Towards the Beloved.* San Rafael, CA: International Association of Sufism, 1998.

Plaskow, Judith, and Carol P. Christ. *Weaving the Visions: New Patterns in Feminist Spirituality.* San Francisco: Harper Collins, 1989.

Pomeroy, Sarah B. *Goddesses, Whores, Wives and Slaves*. New York: Schocken Books, 1974.

Prajnanananda, Swami. *Historical Development of Indian Music*. Calcutta: Firma K.L. Mukhopadhyay, 1973.

Qualls-Corbett, Nancy. *The Sacred Prostitute*. Toronto: Inner City Publishers, 1988.

Raffe, W. G. *Dictionary of the Dance*. New York: A. S. Barnes and Company, 1975.

Ranke-Heinemann, Uta. *Putting Away Childish Things*. San Francisco: Harper-SanFrancisco, 1994.

Rawson, A. L. *The Comprehensive Pronouncing Bible Dictionary*. Philadelphia: A. J. Holman & Co., 1872.

Redmond, Layne. *When The Drummers Were Women: A Spiritual History of Rhythm*. New York: Three Rivers Press, 1997.

Reed, Carlynn. *And We Have Danced: A History of the Sacred Dance Guild 1958–1978*. Richmond, CA: The Sharing Company, 1978.

Ridgeway, William. *The Dramas and Dramatic Dance of Non European Races*. New York: Benjamin Blom, Inc., 1964.

Roth, Gabrielle. *Maps to Ecstasy: Teachings of an Urban Shaman*. Novato, CA: Nataraj Publishing, 1989.

Sachs, Curt. *World History of the Dance*. New York: W. W. Norton & Co., 1937 and 1965.

St. Denis, Ruth. *The Divine Dance*, ed. Neil Douglas-Klotz. San Francisco: PeaceWorks Press, 1989.

———. *An Unfinished Life*. New York: Harper and Brothers, 1939.

Saleh, Magda Ahmed Abdel. *A Documentation of the Ethnic Dance Traditions of the Arab Republic of Egypt*. Ann Arbor, MI: University Microfilms International, 1980.

———. "Egypt Dances." Doctoral thesis film, New York: Library for the Performing Arts, 1979.

Salimpour, Jamila. *From Cave to Cult to Cabaret*. San Francisco: self-published, 1979.

Sandel, S., S. Chaiklin, and A. Lohn. *Foundations of Dance/Movement Therapy: The Life and Work of Marian Chace*. Columbia, MD: The Chace Foundation, 1993.

Schwartz, Charles. *Money Symbolism: The Psychological Standards of Value That Back Money*. Unpublished thesis, Zurich: C. G. Jung Institute, 1978.

Seltman, Charles. *Women in Antiquity.* New York: Thames & Hudson, 1956.

Shelton, Suzanne. *Divine Dancer*. New York: Doubleday, 1981.

Shepsut, Asia. *Journey of the Priestess*. San Francisco: HarperCollins, 1993.

Shuttle, Penelope, and Peter Redgrove. *The Wise Wound: Eve's Curse and Everywoman*. New York: Richard Marek, 1978.

Sjoo, Monica, and Barbara Mor. *The Great Cosmic Mother: Rediscovering the Religion of the Earth*. San Francisco: Harper & Row, 1987.

Smith, Donna Lea. "Morocco and its Dances." *Arabesque*, December 1982.

Sorell, Walter. *Dance in Its Time*. Garden City, NY: Anchor Press, Doubleday, 1981.

———. *Dance through the Ages*. New York: Grosset and Dunlap, 1967.

Spretnak, Charlene. *Lost Goddesses of Early Greece*. Boston, MA: Beacon Press, 1981.

Stainer, John. *Music of the Bible*. New York: H. W. Gray Co., 1879.

Starhawk. *The Spiral Dance*. San Francisco: Harper & Row, 1979.

Stone, Merlin. *Ancient Mirrors of Womanhood,* Vol. I. New York: New Sibylline Books, 1979.

———. *Ancient Mirrors of Womanhood,* Vol. II: *Our Goddess and Heroine Heritage*. New York: New Sibylline Books, 1979.

———. *When God Was a Woman*. New York: Harcourt Brace Jovanovich, 1976.

Streep, Peg. Sanctuaries of the Goddess. Boston: Little, Brown & Co., 1994.

Taggart, James. *Enchanted Maidens: Gender Relations in Spanish Folktales of Courtship and Marriage*. Princeton, NJ: Princeton University Press, 1990.

Taj, Inayat. *The Crystal Chalice: Spiritual Themes for Women*. Santa Fe, NM: Sufi Order, 1981.

Tannahill, Rea. *Sex in History*. Lanham, MD: Scarborough House, 1992.
Taylor, Margaret. "A History of Symbolic Movement in Worship." *Dance as Religious Studies*, edited by Doug Adams and Diane Apostolos-Cappadona. New York: Crossroad, 1993.
Teubal, Savina J. *Sarah the Priestess: The First Matriarch of Genesis*. Athens, OH: Ohio University Press, 1984.
Thiel-Cramér, Barbara. *Flamenco: The Art of Flamenco: Its History and Development Until Our Days*. Remark, Sweden: Lidingö, 1991.
Thompson, William Irwin. *The Time Falling Bodies Take to Light*. New York: St. Martin's Press, 1981.
Thorsten, Geraldine. *The Goddess in Your Stars: The Original Feminine Meanings of the Sun Signs*. New York: Simon and Schuster, 1989.
Tomatis, Alfred A. *The Conscious Ear: My Life of Transformation through Listening*. Tarrytown, NY: Station Hill Press, 1991.
Tyrrel, William Blake. *Amazons: A Study in Athenian Mythmaking*. Baltimore: Johns Hopkins University Press, 1984.
Unterman, Alan. *Dictionary of Jewish Lore and Legend*. London: Thames & Hudson, 1991.
van der Lewiv, Gerardus. *Sacred and Profane Beauty: The Holy in Art*. London: Weidenfeld & Nicolsen, 1963.
Wagner, Ann. *Adversaries of Dance: From the Puritans to the Present*. Chicago: University of Illinois Press, 1997.
Walker, Barbara G. *The Woman's Dictionary of Symbols and Sacred Objects*. San Francisco: HarperSanFrancisco, 1988.
———. *The Woman's Encyclopedia of Myths and Secrets*. San Fransisco: HarperSanFrancisco, 1983.
Warner, Marina. *Alone of All Her Sex: The Myth and the Cult of the Virgin Mary*. New York: Wallaby, Pocket Books, 1976.
Warner, Rex, ed., *Encyclopedia of World Mythology*. New York: Galahad Books, 1975.
Waters, Frank. *Book of the Hopi*. New York: Penguin Books, 1972.
Weiser, Artur. *The Psalms: A Commentary*. Philadelphia: Westminister Press, 1962.
Weyman, Gloria, and Lucien Deiss. "Movement and Dance as Prayer." *Liturgical Ministry*, Vol. 2, Spring 1993.
Wild, Henri. "Les Danses Sacrees de l'Egypt Ancienne." Paris, 1963. Quoted in *Arabesque*, Vol. 7, No. 1, May/June 1981.
Wilshire, Donna. *Virgin, Mother, Crone: Myths and Mysteries of the Triple Goddess*. Rochester, VT: Inner Traditions International, 1994.
Wiora, Walter. *The Four Ages of Music*. New York: W. W. Norton & Co., 1965.
Woisen, Marie-Gabriele. "The Divine Mother Dances." *Arabesque*, Vol. 9, No. 4, January/February 1984.
———. *Sacred Dance: Encounter with the Gods*. London: Thames & Hudson, 1974.
Wood, Leona. "Danse du Ventre: A Fresh Appraisal." *Arabesque*, Vol. 5, No. 6, March/April, 1980.
Yagan, Murray. "Sufism and the Source." *Gnosis*, Winter 1994.
Young, Serenity. *An Anthology of Sacred Texts by and About Women*. New York: Crossroad, 1993.
Zolla, Elemire. *The Androgyne: Reconciliation of Male and Female*. New York: Crossroad, 1981.
Zukav, Gary. *The Dancing Wu Li Masters: An Overview of the New Physics*. New York: Bantam, 1979.

INDEX

An "i" following the page number denotes an illustration. An "n" indicates information found in a footnote.